❧ THE HOUSE IN THE MOON ❧

"I am ready," Elik whispered.

"Good. Unbind your braids. You must have no knots, anywhere."

Elik pulled the lacing from her hair.

"I will give you the gift of a word. With this word you will rise on the air and travel to the house in the moon. The word is old, from the time when animals could talk. Listen."

Elik listened, and nodded.

"There will be a gut window in the wall of the house in the moon. Through it you will see a bench, where the souls of the dead sit. You may look, but do not go in; and above all, do not speak to the dead. Now close your eyes."

Elik closed her eyes.

"Now say the word. Now go."

She said it, over and over . . .

By Elyse Guttenberg

Summer Light
Daughter of the Shaman

Published by HarperPrism

DAUGHTER
~ OF THE ~
SHAMAN

ELYSE
GUTTENBERG

HarperPrism
A Division of HarperCollinsPublishers

■■ **HarperPrism**
A Division of HarperCollins*Publishers*
10 East 53rd Street, New York, N.Y. 10022-5299

This is a work of fiction. The characters, incidents, and
dialogues are products of the author's imagination and are not to
be construed as real. Any resemblance to actual events or
persons, living or dead, is entirely coincidental.

ISBN 0-06-105474-7

Cover photo © Westlight

First printing: July 1997

Printed in the United States of America

Visit HarperPrism on the World Wide Web at
http://www.harpercollins.com

❖ 10 9 8 7 6 5 4 3 2 1

ඥ

To Luke, and Selena, and Grier,
with love.

And then in the midst of such a fit
Of mysterious and overwhelming delight,
I became a shaman,
Not knowing myself how it came about.
But I was a shaman.
I could see and hear in a totally different way.
I had gained my *qaumaneq*. Enlightenment.
The shaman light of brain and body
And this in such manner that
It was not only I who could see
Through the darkness of life,
But the same light also shone out from me,
Imperceptible to human beings, but visible
To all the spirits of earth and sky and sea,
And these now came to me and became my helping spirits.

—As told to Knud Rasmussen by the Iglulik Shaman Aua
Report of the Fifth Thule Expedition

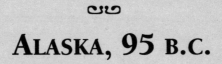

ALASKA, 95 B.C.

1

One good way to hunt a bear is this—in early winter, when frost as light as smoke marks the place a bear is hiding, dreaming in its den beneath the snow, then two men with long-handled spears can find that bear. They can rouse it from its grass-lined bed. If they can reach it with their spears, nudge it, then it might come out and let them kill it.

There are rules a man must follow if he wants that bear to come. Never to speak its name out loud. Only to call it *Carayak,* that Fearsome Thing or that Dark Thing. And he has to whisper, and never brag, because that bear can hear his thoughts. It understands the speech of all animals, including people. It would think the man had no respect.

But if he does remember, if he's careful instead of proud, if he listened to the words the elders spoke all those nights sitting, sharing stories, then it's said the bear will pretend it doesn't know two hunters are out there. The bear will put up a fight but afterward, it will make a gift of its skin so their families will be warm. It will tell others of its kind that there are good people there, people worthy of their flesh.

This is important. A person's thoughts must be

awake to the animal's needs, even more so when it's dead. Otherwise that bear's spirit could find a way back. It could scratch around long enough, angry enough, it opens a path from the Land of the Dead and walks back into the village, just like that. Hungry for revenge.

Allanaq had found the den earlier that season, during the cool Moon When Young Geese Fly and the sound of wings beating grew so loud even the wind sat to listen. Allanaq had been inland, a full day's walk behind the Long Coast village, following caribou tracks above the cutbank of a narrow creek.

He didn't see the bear, only signs that it was near, foraging for blueberries and spawning salmon. The water had been low, the way it sometimes was at the end of a dry summer. And the ground was scratched up and moss and grass were dragged about, and he found a few piles of shit that still were soft with berries the bear had eaten. Allanaq marked the place, the creek bed, and which way the hills stretched east and west. Then he went back to tracking caribou and waited for a colder season when the bear would be asleep inside its den.

It's best for a hunter that way, safer, because the bear, a black bear especially, isn't thinking about a fight. It won't come charging the way a brown bear might, or the way it would in summer if you happen between a sow and her cubs. And the work won't be so hard, the way it can be if you kill it inside the den and have to find a way to drag the entire huge weight of the animal up, out on the ground again.

By the time Allanaq returned with Drummer, his hunting partner, deep drifts of crusted snow lay over

the frozen creek. Frost from the bear's mouth surrounded the hole it had built for a door.

Allanaq knelt to the entry. The tufts of snow were so
light, when he touched them they blew from his hand.
Like a puff of smoke: a man tries to touch it and suddenly it's gone. Like air. Like nothing there at all.

With his parka sleeve, he swept a wider circle of the
loose, top layer of snow. No markings showed, no sign
of any animal foolish enough to sniff so near the hole.

Along the creek there'd been a scurry of tracks, one
trail where a lynx had been racing down a hare. A scattering of tiny bones and a ball of fur, the droppings of
an owl. And wolves definitely, but they'd run off. Not
as if they hadn't found the den—more like they'd
smelled it and then turned back.

As if they hadn't dared come near.

Allanaq leaned back on his heels while Drummer
eased their longest spear down inside the hole. The
point was made from the bone of a bear's foreleg.
The driftwood shaft was heavy and well smoothed. He
angled it down, reaching and poking against the frozen
inside walls, searching for the feel of something soft.

He couldn't find it. Drummer glanced over his
shoulder and shrugged. Without speaking, he handed
Allanaq the spear. They traded places. This time
Allanaq tried.

He was a taller man than Drummer, with longer
arms that made him better at reaching. His fingers were
longer too. And that was something people said about
him, that the reason the flint blades he shaped held
their edges longer than other men's was because his
hands were different than most of the Real People. The
way he was different, adopted from another place.

Because he was Seal People, he'd told them. Because he came from the Place Where the Land Points Into the Sea, though few people asked him about it anymore. Not about his hands or his taller height, or the way his nose was straighter or his face decorated with more tattoos.

He tried not to think about it. Why should he when, after four winters living among Real People, no one whispered anymore about his open-worked ivory carvings or the way he set his bifaced flakes into a knife handle.

Allanaq felt a hint of resistance, not hard as if he'd struck frozen dirt, but firm and soft at the same time. He glanced to Drummer, signaled with a nod.

Drummer was one of the few men he'd trusted from the start. A soft-spoken man, never the kind to point to a stranger whenever he needed someone else to blame his troubles on.

It had been a wise choice, the two of them becoming hunting partners. Elik, his wife, had suggested it. Women were good that way and Elik was among the best, knowing which boys would grow into what kind of hunter. Whether they would be careful or too loud, stingy or willing to share. And whether that sharing extended to a tall, sharp-nosed man whose skin-covered boat had appeared one day, out of a fog.

And in that boat, one frightened young man barely alive while his dead father sat leaning up against him. It had been enough to scare most people away.

Until finally another winter had passed, then another. Allanaq had brought no bad luck to their catch of walrus or seal, caribou or fish. No spirits had followed out of his land into theirs.

And now here were Allanaq and Drummer, both near the same age. Not relatives—hunting partners needed to be chosen from other families. And Drummer could throw farther, but Allanaq ran faster. And both had wives, though Drummer's already had a child, a daughter who laughed as she straightened her chubby, short legs and tried to walk.

Elik was home, pregnant with theirs. He smiled to think about the way she went about lately: walking quickly between houses so the child, when it pushed its way out, would also come quickly. Wearing her long hair loose, without bindings, so the birth would also be loose, without pain.

Elik was carrying the child low—he'd heard the women say so. And she was heavier than Drummer's wife had been, though it wasn't her time yet. If it had been, he would have been reminded—more than once—not to make this trip. Hunting, especially bear hunting, wasn't safe for a man whose wife had just given birth. A bear's spirit is too strong. And birth, like death, is a time when too many paths are open between the Land of the Dead and this one. It's too easy for trouble to sneak its way inside.

Allanaq held the spear still. He opened his hand to let it slip along his mittened palm. Drummer squatted beside him and they held quiet, listening, watching, until the spear shifted. It lifted, then settled back.

Drummer knelt and rested his ear nearly on the snow. The side of his face was chilled when he rose again, his eyelashes frosted, but he'd heard it, the slow steady inhale of air, the sound of its sleep. They both had heard.

This would be the first bear they'd tried for alone, and

it was a good sign, having it come and show itself. With no women about—that was important too. Women didn't like to be near when bears were hunted. And bears, everyone knew, didn't like to have them either.

There were stories told about the First Times, when it was said a woman had been the mother of the first bear, and so no woman ever since then wanted to eat bear's meat, not even to see it killed. It was too much like eating her own flesh. Not something that joyously happened.

Allanaq carried their heaviest spear to a level spot of ground a short distance from the entry. While Drummer unwrapped his bow from its sealskin case and fanned his flint arrows out beside it on the snow, Allanaq braced the long spear between his feet. He checked his footing, made sure he wouldn't slip.

With a second spear and a longer ice pick added to the butt end, Drummer returned to the entry. His gaze was all on Allanaq, waiting for his nod. When it came, Drummer started poking the spear in the hole. Jabbing hard, angling this way and that.

Allanaq aimed the spear so the point would pierce the bear's chest. Exactly there: it would rise to its hind legs, and then lunge.

He whispered a song, not a shaman's song such as his father would have owned, but a hunter's song, respectful yet strong:

> *Come You Dark Thing.*
> *Come wake and see the sky.*
> *Winter is not so cold*
> *And I am only a small man.*

A moment later and he heard it, a thick muffled sound, almost beneath Drummer's feet. The plug of grass moved from inside and quickly, Drummer switched to his bow, a strong one shaped with a wrap of sinew into a double curve. It was the kind of bow that was made to please a bear, to draw it to the weapon, let it proudly die. By the time Drummer fixed his aim, the bear's dark muzzle was poking out the hole.

Allanaq tensed as the bear's eyes, thick neck, then shoulders followed. Once outside, the bear seemed less confused about being woken, and more angry. It shook itself; then, with a heavy, lolling motion, it swung its head sideways, sniffed the air, and lifted its snout.

And then it found him. It rose to its hind legs, arms steady. It waited, but only one moment. And then it dropped to all fours.

Allanaq braced and the bear ran, one smooth step, and then another. A lunge that was part flight, lifting and then falling toward him. Down!

The spear shook between Allanaq's hands. The point disappeared near the bear's collarbone. Its hind legs kicked above the ground and Allanaq's knees bent forward. His arms felt as if they'd split from their sockets, but he clenched tight. Held and clenched his fists and the shaft and the animal roared while Drummer's arrow flew for its heart.

The bear flailed at Allanaq but his claws couldn't reach. The thick ring of hide midway along the shaft kept its weight from sliding closer. By the time the bear understood, it was on the ground and dying already, impaled with the spear through its chest. One arrow leaned into the thick muscle above its shoulder, two more swayed between its ribs.

Drummer fitted another arrow to his bow cord, but he didn't use it. They waited until the end of the spear shaft quit moving. Then, keeping a cautious distance, Allanaq walked up behind the bear's right shoulder.

He tried being careful not to look directly in its small eyes. And to be mindful of his thoughts. It took a bear four days from the time it died until its spirit finally left. Four days, and until that time the soul hovered near its body, stayed close to the smell of its blood on their weapons.

There was a patch of lighter color drawn from the bear's jaw to its neck and then around, almost as if a blanket of different fur had been thrown over its shoulders, the way an old woman threw on a second fur to keep out the cold. Allanaq glanced lower then winced, surprised to see it was a female.

Somehow he'd been certain this one was male. It had been so large, so heavy. He thought of Elik shuffling along a path at home. The way he'd turned back to watch her before he left, trying not to smile, not to tease the way she reached her hands below her belly to lift the child's weight.

He stopped and made a gesture to chase the thought away. It wasn't good, holding thoughts of both his wife and the bear at the same time. It wasn't lucky. At least this wasn't the season for bear cubs. It wouldn't be until near spring that a sow emerged with her hungry children scampering behind.

Drummer came and stood beside the bear's feet. He'd brought their skinning knives and a scrap of hide to work on. They hadn't yet talked about which way they'd butcher the meat, and there was the skull to take care of.

Allanaq's own people would treat the bear with the greatest respect. The men would cut the head away first, then leave the meat until midwinter, till they were certain the life had gone out. They would offer it small knives and arrow points to hunt with, anything that might be useful in the next world. And they would cover its eyes, ears, and nostrils with plugs, the same as they would for a human. In case it was angry, no one wanted a bear knowing who they were.

Drummer would take some care, but Allanaq wasn't sure what he'd prefer. Whether he'd say the skull should be tied up in the brush, or burned. Whether it mattered exactly how many days they waited, or if they ate a little meat now.

All this time living among Real People, and he still wasn't certain what they'd choose.

He stepped back, waiting while Drummer bent to his arrows, gripped hard to wrench them from the chest.

The wind had picked up and Allanaq turned to follow its direction. The view was nearly open; there was little brush, and the willows reached only as high as a man's legs. Along the creek bed, through the snow's glare, something moved. He caught a flicker, a dark color disappearing around a curve. It was the size of a dog, but different. Not a wolf; its legs were too short, too close to the ground. "What is that?" he whispered. He felt edgy suddenly, his voice too loud and thin.

"Where?" Drummer looked up.

Allanaq pointed, and a moment later a fox ran out from the tangle of brush. A red fox. White-edged tail streaking behind, black-tipped ears.

Drummer looked curiously back at Allanaq. "It's just a fox," he shrugged. "That's all."

Allanaq nodded but his arms had started shaking, he didn't know why. He pulled his hands inside his sleeves to warm them.

There, along the open path of the creek, the fox was back. Drummer wasn't watching. The fox lifted its tail. Pointed its ears high.

Why wasn't it afraid? It should have smelled the bear and then run off; it might have come back if it was curious enough. But to run toward a man with a bear's death on his hands? That didn't make sense unless the fox was starving. Or something else was wrong.

A shudder moved along Allanaq's spine. A memory he didn't like to follow.

It was of Red Fox, the man who killed his father. The shaman who had stolen into their house—not here, but in his own home, the Seal People's Place. After all those months of lies, stealing his father's secrets, shaman-songs he had tricked his father into sharing. Red Fox had broken into their house with his four cousins, men who once had been Allanaq's friends. They had spoiled his father's amulets, bound his hands, and Allanaq's next. And then cast them out in the boat. Abandoned them to a fog so thick, Red Fox must surely have hoped they would drown, that his father's ghost would never find its way back. That Allanaq would never be able to take revenge.

Anguta, his father, had not survived the journey. Allanaq had been found.

Allanaq reached for a fist-sized rock, knocked it loose from the frozen ground. All in a motion he stood and heaved it, threw it in a hard, straight line toward the fox. He missed. The rock fell quietly into snow. The fox lit off around the curve, how far he couldn't say. He didn't want to see.

He looked back at the bear, and then looked again. Something was different.

He stepped closer, nearer the head. A slick of blood had dripped from its mouth, darkening its fur, shining in a trail down to the snow, red snow. It wasn't the blood though . . . something else.

The eyes—the bear's eyes were open. Both of them. Dark circles followed where he moved. *It wasn't dead.* . . . It was watching him. He tried to call but his throat knotted. No sound came out.

Drummer leveraged his foot against the bear's ribs, tugged the spear until it came free.

Allanaq motioned for him to wait.

"What is it?" Drummer asked.

"I thought there was—" Allanaq stopped. The bear's eyes were closed again. He waited, but no movement followed, and now he wasn't certain anything had moved. "Here," he said, hiding his thoughts. "Let me start."

He took the knife Drummer had tucked in his belt; it was one Allanaq had made himself. With its chipped-flint side blade and its wood handle carved to show the face, teeth, and ribs of a seal, it was the kind of knife Elik's uncle used to beg him to hide from Drummer's brothers.

He started the long cut, slicing through the thick hide first, a sawing motion from the pit of its crotch to its throat. He tugged the fur back, laying it open like a blanket on the snow.

Then again he started cutting, through muscle, exposing the organs. The inner fat was a brownish color, thick and soft, its smell a deep warmth against the wind. He angled the knife to cut again, but his hand stopped, hovered without moving. The bear was a mother. Inside, beneath her heart, two bear-children lay asleep.

Drummer knelt beside him. There was a long silence, then: "It doesn't mean anything," he tried to sound assured.

Allanaq grimaced. The dead cubs curled together under a membrane thin as ice. Their eyes were lidded and shut tight. Hairless. "With a caribou," he whispered, "it doesn't mean anything. Or with a seal. We often take mothers in the calving time."

He moved so Drummer wouldn't see his face. Drummer's child was well, old enough to be strong. These two cubs were more like his own child might be, small and hairless, and while it was true that both humans and animals had souls, once born they would be different.

The human child Elik would give birth to in another few months was already larger than these. Grown, it would be smaller.

How could a hunter such as he, a man who studied wind and weather, not spirits, like his shaman father, or his wife or Malluar her teacher—how could he know what was best? He looked to Drummer. "What should we do?"

"Burn the head. Offer songs of apology."

"Is that all?"

"What else did we do last time, when my brother was with us?"

Allanaq didn't answer. When he was a boy he used to watch the way the men treated the bear's head, with more respect than other animals, even the bearded seal, even the whale. They were always careful to leave it carvings, tiny slate points if it was a male, a sewing needle for a female.

Drummer's people did what was needed, and no more. But what if there was more? Something he'd forgotten?

Perhaps he would bring a small section home for Malluar. At her age, it was safe for a woman to touch a bear. And as a shaman, maybe she would be able to learn if he'd done something wrong. Some taboo he'd forgotten?

"We could hang the skull for a marker in a tree?" Drummer offered.

"No."

"But then people would see it and they wouldn't come near. It's a small thing, but it's safe."

"No," Allanaq said, but the word came out so loud, it startled him. He took a breath, tried to sound reasonable. "With a Dark Thing like this, with cubs, we need to do more, not less. We need to do everything we can."

He leaned back. What if this were a test of some kind? What if the bear was trying to learn whether they were respectful?

Allanaq passed the knife back to Drummer. He walked a short distance, trying to find if there was a path between the fox tracks and the bear's den, something along the creek, or maybe on the snow-covered flats behind the brush?

Something was wrong. He could feel it. Something in the smell of the air, not clear the way it usually felt in winter, but with a scent. What was it?

He stared at the curve of Drummer's back, not at the snow where the dark pile of heart, kidneys, and lungs were already separated out.

So many times over the last few winters he'd wondered if they looked alike, he and Drummer. Allanaq wore his black hair short now, the way Drummer wore his. Both had eyes that turned down at the corners. And both had skin colored brown as a silt-running stream. And on both their chins, in the corners below the lips, there were holes for labrets. Allanaq had cut his during his second winter here, so he would look more the same as these people. Though how could he really, while his face was covered in lines and swirling tattoos that showed the proud markings of the Seal People, and Drummer wore none?

He turned, hoping Drummer hadn't caught his scowl. "Make sure you leave a bit of grease near its head, so its spirit has food."

Drummer's hand slowed. "Are you thinking we should leave?" he offered.

"No." Allanaq shook his head. Leaving would be cowardly, and worse. "We'll mourn for it and pray its spirit only wants to learn what kind of people we are. That's all. And we'll show it. We'll do everything." He spoke quickly, nervously, listing whatever he knew: "We'll walk around the head—the same direction as the universe moves. And we'll remember not to hammer, so we don't frighten its soul. And we'll comb its fur. And we'll change into our oldest clothes and throw these away when we're done. When we're sure it's fully dead."

It was morning when the baby started kicking to come out, night when the waves of tight-fisted pain finally moved and grabbed lower, harder, deep enough inside Elik's bones, she dared hope that now, finally, something more would happen.

She caught her breath, clung tighter to the thongs that hung from the roof of the caribou-hide birth hut. The pain rolled through her, heavier than before.

"Soon," Malluar whispered. "Soon."

Too soon. Too early for the baby to come. Elik clenched her teeth, tried forcing the pain aside.

Her husband should have been home. If not inside the *qasgi* where the men gathered and slept, at least near the village. Allanaq should have been untying knots wherever he could find them. Should have been careful not to hammer, not to shout, not to do anything that could make the birth difficult. Instead, he was out with Drummer, hunting, when he should have been home.

Except he couldn't have known. How could he? That the baby would come too early. Why so soon?

The contraction faded. Elik opened her eyes and looked to Malluar. The older woman held her gaze low, locked on the moss padding beneath Elik's legs. The hand she held against Elik's thigh felt cold and warm at the same time, slippery with blood and fluid.

Elik let go the thong, slowly eased herself to the floor.

And why hadn't Malluar seen this coming? She was the village's oldest woman, a shaman. If she hadn't known, how could a man?

For that matter, why hadn't Elik seen it herself? In a dream? Some kind of sign? She also was a shaman. Malluar should have allowed her to trance, no matter that she was pregnant. She might have heard the voices of her spirit helpers. They might have warned.

It was earlier in the season than Malluar had told her to expect the birth, far earlier. And early wasn't a good sign. She had been sitting with the women in her aunt Nua's house—yesterday? today?—she didn't know anymore. There'd been a wet, warm feeling and she'd risen from the sleeping bench and stared in fear at the dark stain soaking into the hides where she'd sat.

Sewing during labor—that wasn't good either. Pricking the skin of an animal that had once been alive? What if its spirit took that needle and turned it around to stitch the baby tight inside of her?

Nua had tried to be helpful, hushing the other women as they counted off the seasons on their hands. They'd drawn their lips tight, lowered their glances not to show their thoughts.

Early meant small and small meant weak. No one had to speak the words to make them true.

And didn't they all know Elik had already lost one child—dead before there was anything there to hold. A clot of blood. The pain of empty cramps. A death before she'd realized there was life. She didn't want this baby to die. She wanted it in her arms, at her breast, wet and kicking and strong.

She swallowed. Her lips were cracked, her throat

parched. The only heat inside the tiny hut came from the single seal oil lamp. It was all that was allowed. One lamp and one woman to help. Malluar, with her shaman drum and her songs. And outside, surrounding the hut, one ring of dog turds Nua had shoveled into place, desperate to hide the human scent from spirits.

Please, she prayed. *Don't see me here. Don't come near . . .*

Elik rose to squat on her knees again: another tightening had begun. A tightening—but that was all. Shouldn't there be more? She didn't know. Her other baby had never grown this large. Was this the way her sister's children came? Was it the same for other woman? Every time?

Malluar moved closer, in between her knees. "It's coming," she said calmly and she pressed down firmly against Elik's stomach, pressed again to find the baby's head, its knees, its shoulders.

Elik choked her cries. She bore down. Held. Then held again. Something was changing. Happening. Finally. It would end . . .

She looked down, but all she could see was the mound of her stomach ripple and change, as if it was a foreign thing, not part of her body at all. She saw Malluar's hands moving in. She sucked in her breath, squeezed her eyelids shut as Malluar began a birth-charm song. *"This is blood from the little sparrow's mother. Dry it up!"* she sang. *"This is blood that flowed from a piece of wood. Dry it up."*

The next time Elik opened her eyes, there was a baby in Malluar's hands. She could see only parts: a skinny leg with a wrinkled knee folded up. A large head. Whitish film like a hood. A strong, bitter smell. And quiet.

Too much quiet.

"Spit in its mouth." She hurried Malluar. "Make it strong."

Malluar didn't answer. The baby's head barely filled her hand. Its feet reached not even so far as the crook of her elbow. Elik strained to watch as Malluar wiped a finger around the nostrils, opened its mouth and leaned closer, breathed her living air inside.

Elik caught sight of the dark sac of testicles. So large? But her sister had had boys. She remembered Naiya warning her not to be surprised. "It's a boy?" she asked.

Malluar nodded. She reached for the mussel shell she had brought to cut the navel string.

Elik heard no crying. Nothing. Weakness crept along her legs and arms. She slipped lower onto the moss. There was a ringing in her ears so high-pitched and thin, it drowned out every other sound. Was that the baby? No. No baby.

Malluar said something but this time, Elik didn't want to hear. She didn't want to know.

The next thing she felt was Malluar's hand on her stomach, pushing down, harder than before. "Push." Malluar said. "Push and the afterbirth will come. Easier than the child—I promise."

She wasn't sure she could. It was too much the same. Too much like birth, which was like death.

And now there was another sound: a scrap of hide being folded. And behind that the persistent notes of Malluar's shaman's song coaxing the blood to stop.

Better to sing, Elik thought. Better than to admit what neither wanted to say: that Elik would always be like Malluar, a woman who grew babies inside her womb, not once but many times. Babies who never lived.

Then, just when she prayed it was all finished, a sudden pain returned, as if someone tied a cord around her waist and tightened. Elik grabbed for the thongs, grit her teeth, opened her eyes.

Malluar was kneeling, hunched between her knees. Elik looked below the older woman's silvered hair to the empty scrap of hide she'd set out, waiting to catch the afterbirth.

A moment later and Malluar called, a single cry, tight and scared. "What is it?" Elik craned to see.

Malluar scooped something into the skin, then turned, her shoulder blocking Elik's view. "You don't need to know," she said.

"The afterbirth? Will you bury it?"

"Hush. No. It's more than that."

More than the afterbirth? What could that be? Heavily, Elik lay back on the floor. The birthing hut roof seemed too close and tight, menacing, not a shelter. "Tell me," she said, and she turned her face to the wall.

There was a long quiet, then finally, Malluar's whisper: "It's another baby. Dead."

Elik stared as her breath turned to frost on the dark, overlapped skins.

When had it happened? What had she done that allowed her body to deceive her so fully? She had been so certain this one would live.

She had dreamt of a boy, more than once. She'd

heard his eager laugh. Imagined his plump arms lifting to her face.

She didn't understand. She would have had three children by now. Three, and her husband would have had no trouble providing. He was a good man. The animals had always given themselves when he hunted.

Where was he? It wasn't safe for him to be gone, not knowing about this death. Deaths. She bit down on her lip, forced herself to watch.

Malluar was unwrapping the suit of clothes Elik had sewn for the child to wear. Leggings and jacket stitched from bird skins the way she'd been taught: waterfowl if a child was born in summer, whitest ptarmigan for winter.

"May I watch?" Elik asked. Her voice was surprisingly strong.

Malluar glanced first to the skyhole, then to the small arm of light reaching beneath the door flap. "We have to be careful," she said. "There's no way of knowing what spirits are near."

"Did it, did either of them, breathe?"

"They never lived." Malluar raised the feathered jacket above the first child's head. She held the sleeves like wings, poised above the arms. But then she stopped, undecided. Two children. One suit of clothes. She set the jacket down, brought over the leggings.

Quietly, Elik tugged a corner of the hide Malluar had thrown over the second infant. She slid it nearer, but Malluar turned at the sound, set her hand atop the bundle. "Please," Elik said. "I want to dress them."

Malluar sighed. "How could it be safe? What if some evil jumped inside, follow you back to the village?"

"This birth—Malluar, it wasn't my fault. I did nothing wrong. You've watched, every day. I ate no food from another man's catch—only my husband's. And no meat that was forbidden. I drank from my own bowl, carefully, never outside."

"Then perhaps not you," Malluar said, "but someone did. Death comes as punishment for our wrongs."

"Malluar—please. What if I never have another?"

"Hush!" Malluar warned. But then she softened, remembering the other voice inside her, not just the shaman's, but the one that never forgot how it felt to be a young mother, burying her children, with nothing left to hold. She shook her head, but she pulled open the flap, revealing the child inside.

Elik held her breath. The child's skin seemed even thinner than the other, translucent as the gut on Malluar's drum. It was a second boy, smaller but otherwise the same. Eyes closed, no hair. He was covered in a pale grey membrane, blood already caked to brown. Was it her blood? Or the child's?

He was so small, how could he ever have blood inside? How could he have crawled or walked, or even had the strength to cry?

She didn't speak as she lifted the hand on the first one, slipped it in the jacket sleeve. The leggings she put on the second son. They were so long, they covered almost to his neck. Only the head peered out above the whitest feathers. Perhaps with such clothes as these they could fly away? Light as a bird, they could rise and their spirits would travel wherever they wished?

Her hands started shaking, her thoughts all brittle with fear. What if the fault *was* hers? There were so many rules a woman needed to follow, prohibitions, instructions. What if there was something she had forgotten to do? Or, what if it was the shaman-light that burned inside her, the same as inside Malluar? The heat so strong it would always scorch an infant's weaker soul?

Behind her, Malluar picked up her flat, walrus-gut drum and began a droning reminder: "For two months you must cook your food in your own private pot. You must keep your own food dish. The clothes you wore today must be burned and an older set put on. You must not eat of any bird, and not its eggs. Not heart, head, or tongue of any land or sea animal. And you must have no relations with your husband until the sun is once again in the place in the sky where it now sits. There are rules you must follow, as all Real People must, otherwise you will bring illness, more death, into the village."

It was the full dark of night when Allanaq returned. A brisk wind sent the clouds rushing out of the inland mountains down toward the houses and the frozen sea. In the sky, the moon had opened a hole and its light shone bright enough off the snow that he and Drummer had pushed themselves, walking through the early winter dusk, hurrying their way back home.

Inside the dug-out, sod-covered house Elik stiffened, glanced to Malluar, then to the square of gut covering the skyhole overhead. There were sounds on the mounded roof: snow crunching, footsteps she'd been waiting to hear, the short, high bark of dogs tethered outside near the meat-drying racks. The footsteps faded, then grew loud again, this time near the house's entry tunnel.

The moss wick Elik had been twisting slipped into the pool of melted seal fat. The lamp dimmed but Elik ignored it. She and Malluar had been sitting on the planked wood floor beside the fire pit, waiting. It seemed that was all she was allowed to do anymore. The one thing Malluar, with her watchful eyes, considered safe. "Will he know?" Elik asked.

Malluar listened toward the entry-well in the center of the floor. "Perhaps. If he stopped first to share his catch in your aunt's house, Nua would tell. Or if he goes to the *qasgi*, your uncle Grey Owl might. He would say it was better to learn from relatives than gossip."

Elik glanced nervously about the house. The drying rack above the fire pit held a few rolled caribou skins. She grabbed for the nearest, wrapped it over her naked shoulders, breasts, and stomach.

Eight days earlier Allanaq had walked with Drummer out of the Long Coast village, northward on their hunting trip. Eight days ago, and her stomach had been low and round, with a thin line tracing its way from her navel to the dark hair between her legs.

Six days ago and Elik had given birth to sons. Five days and she had buried them. For the next four days, while she waited for their spirits to make their way to the Land of the Dead, she had sat in this house and mourned them.

One day more, and now the hump of her stomach was loose again, empty. As were the blankets that should have held a child on the sleeping bench behind her. One child asleep and one beneath her parka, at her breast.

Elik pulled the blanket closer and made sure it covered her stomach as Allanaq climbed up through the tunnel entrance into the floor of the house. His hood was already lowered, his shoulders straight, not stooped beneath a load of meat. And his hands—they were also empty.

Thankful, she allowed a smile. She had prayed that the animals had walked away from him and hidden, just this once, while death was all around. Their small household wasn't hungry. Their food cache was full of frozen caribou meat, seal oil, and dried fish.

She rose while Allanaq wiped the frost from his eyelashes. There was a bulge under the belt of his parka, a packet of some kind, but certainly too small for a caribou haunch. He carried no other pouches. And his weapons were already put away somewhere. In the *qasgi*, with the other men's? Leaning against the house outside, in the snow?

Allanaq hadn't spoken yet.

For all he could tell, the house was no different from when he'd left. Malluar bent to the fire, lighting a bundle of wild celery the way she always did when he returned from hunting. Cleansing the air to chase away any unseen spirits that might have followed him home.

And Elik had smiled, almost as soon as she saw him. Her round, full face was flushed and there was a sweet air of shyness about her. Soon, he would hold her beneath their blankets. On their sides with him behind her: the rounder this child made his wife grow, the more they both liked it that way.

He handed his parka to Elik to beat the snow from the fur. She moved slowly, not so much clumsy as heavy with her pregnancy, he thought. *Not much longer*, he wanted to whisper. *Only a little while more.*

The knot that had tightened inside his stomach as he and Drummer separated outside their houses began to loosen. He squatted beside the fire pit, waited for Elik to bring the warm broth she always greeted him with.

"The dogs barked loudly," he said. "They seem glad to have me home."

Elik glanced at Malluar. "Grey Owl cared for them while you were gone. Did he tell you?"

"I didn't see him. In the morning, I'll go and thank him."

"You didn't look for him in the *qasgi*?"

"Not yet, no. I hurried to come home."

"And Drummer also, he's home?"

"Home, and probably sleeping already. He's a good man," Allanaq touched the firestones to see if any heat remained. It didn't. But then, Elik could cook a meal as easily over the seal oil lamp. He chuckled. "Drummer's a good man to hunt with. Patient with my foolish ways."

"Perhaps your husband is hungry?" Malluar coaxed Elik along.

Allanaq looked up just as the two women glanced away from each other. He had been so worried about the bear; poor Drummer had spent nearly every night reminding him of the time his brother Kahkik had caught an old, grey-muzzled bear just behind the village. And the one Singmiut killed—that one had been pregnant also, and nothing had gone wrong. And now here he was, warm and safely home, and all was as it should be.

With a sigh of relief he pulled out the small parcel of bear meat and passed it to Malluar. Had she been a shaman but any younger, he would not have risked giving it to her. But a woman who no longer bled was the same as a man: neither her spirit nor the bear's would be offended if she ate.

Besides, who else could he ask? Not Elik, a pregnant women followed too many prohibitions. And if she wasn't pregnant, that would have meant she bled. There were a few men in the village good at forecasting weather, but none so strong as Malluar. No one else who could send their soul out of their body in a trance and speak with spirit helpers, ask if something was wrong.

He had wanted to talk more with Drummer about this, but Drummer was like most of the Real People that way, the kind of man who listened more to the sound of the wind—what direction it came from and whether it brought ice or thaw, storm or game—and less to the world that could not be seen.

"Why waste words," Drummer had asked, "when a man's breath is needed for hunting? Why ask what a man can never know?"

But Allanaq needed to talk. No matter how long he lived among Real People, they still said and did things he didn't understand. It was lucky for him he felt comfortable living with a shaman—not every man would.

Perhaps it was because Malluar reminded him of his father, the way neither of them ever forgot a story they once had heard. The way they were so full of their shaman-secrets, their endless warnings, their trances, and their songs.

And as to his wife . . . he stole a glance at Elik. Her face was in profile, her long braids falling nearly to the fish she was slicing now, laying out in his wooden dish.

He would always be thankful that he'd found her. That she had wanted him, a stranger who would have been dead but for the kindness her uncle showed, adopting him as a son.

Malluar took a bite of the meat. With her knife cutting cleanly between her fingers and her tattooed chin, she sliced free a chunk. "What is this?" she asked. "The fat's thick. It doesn't taste like caribou."

"Its coat was dark," he said, being careful not to name the bear directly. *Let her see, inside the meat . . .*

"It's nothing small." Malluar kept on chewing.

Allanaq watched. *A shaman would know, if anyone would.*

She sucked loudly on the meat, searching, not for the taste anymore, but for something deeper. She licked at it, worked it around her mouth. "What is this?"

Allanaq turned away from her narrowed eyes. "It was down there, sleeping, you see."

"Down there?" Malluar stopped her chewing. For one moment she held the meat between her teeth, her lips open. Then suddenly she spit it, half-chewed, into the fire pit.

Wet. Shapeless. Grey. It didn't matter—she knew

what it was. "You mean in a den? You brought *Carayak* meat into this house? At such a time?"

"What time? It's for you," Allanaq said. "Only for you. We've spoken of this before . . . "

Elik stood, stepped away from them both. "You hunted that animal? While your wife was in labor?"

"What labor?" Allanaq's face twisted. He turned, searched the sleeping platform where an infant would have nestled. Nothing was there. Not in Elik's place, where the furs were rolled against the driftwood wall. Nor in Malluar's place. He would have found the smell of milk, sweet against the smells of oil and fish and urine pots. There was no child here.

With her foot, Malluar pushed the rest of the meat farther, away from her reach.

Allanaq crossed the floor; two steps and he stood in front of his wife. His hand went out, whipped the robe from her shoulders.

Elik tensed, but she didn't move.

He stared at her stomach. Flat. At her veined breasts and the dark circles surrounding her nipples. Swollen, larger than before he'd left. His heart began to race.

Elik shuddered as he spun toward Malluar. "Where is the child?"

"Gone."

"Gone?"

"Something happened." Elik's voice was small and cautious. "It wasn't my fault. Malluar agrees. I did nothing wrong."

"When?" His gaze darted around the house, from the storage baskets to the drying rack to the sleeping bench, anywhere but at Elik, he couldn't look at Elik.

"It was too soon. Too early," Malluar said. "If I'd known her time was near . . ."

Allanaq stepped back and his foot grazed the open packet of meat. His hands remembered the weight of his knife—not the killing lance buried in the bear's chest, but the moment when his stone blade sliced through the muscle, opened its dark flesh as if it were a door revealing a room inside.

"I would never have gone," he said.

"Sometimes one child will grow, but not the other," Malluar said. "With these—"

"These?" Allanaq's face darkened. "How many were there?"

"Two," Malluar said, and behind her Elik whispered, "Sons."

Allanaq didn't move.

Quietly now, more gently, Malluar asked, "Tell me, could you have done something? Anything that might matter?"

"No. I don't remember. It's possible."

"What did you do with the claws?" Elik asked. "With the teeth?"

Malluar turned so Elik could see her one clear eye without a cataract, warning her to hold still. "If there is blame here," she said, "we will find it."

"I gave the claws to Drummer."

"Did you eat any meat from the head?"

Allanaq shook his head no.

"What of the brain? Did you touch that?"

"No. We buried it."

Elik looked to Malluar. "Was that wrong?"

"No. Burned would perhaps have been better. As long as it isn't brought back to the village. But there's something else here. I feel it. I don't know what."

Allanaq sank to the floor. He lifted his knees, pulled his heels tightly in. "Are they buried?"

Malluar nodded. "All proper. All rituals for the dead were followed."

Allanaq winced. More talk about these Real People's burials. His father was buried here. Twice, though not even Malluar knew about the second time. The first had been the very day Grey Owl towed his umiak into the village. While Allanaq was too weak, too lost inside his heart to protest. They had buried his father with their few paltry songs. No gifts. No ivory eyes to replace the lost vision of the dead. A pile of stacked rocks to keep away dogs. That was what they knew.

The second time his father had been buried was during the dark of night. He and Elik had secretly moved the bones, to protect them. That had been during Allanaq's second winter, when too much hunger had turned the men sick with fear. He had grown nearly sick himself, ill with worrying about Drummer's oldest brother and his ranting threats to dig up the skeleton, burn his father's bones as if he was an enemy, not a great shaman, worthy of respect.

Even now, there was a fear that haunted him, so often he didn't like to admit how strong it sometimes grew, the way it kept him from sleep. It was the fear that without his Seal People's proper rituals, his father's spirit would remain forever beside those bones. Earthbound, tethered like a dog on a line. Unable to find the path to the Land of the Dead.

A ghost could starve, the same as a living man who wasn't able to hunt. And though he brought gifts, harpoon heads and knives, how could a ghost hunt in a land he never knew?

How could his father's soul be born again, when no one in this place knew the name of Anguta, to give it life inside a newborn child? Except for him. A man whose wife bore only death. He glanced to Elik, turned away, but not before she caught the look.

A shudder of loneliness passed through him.

Malluar added a slice of blubber to the hook above the seal oil lamp, fixing it to melt and feed the wick, brighten the house. "Tell me again," she said when the light was steady. "Where you went with Drummer. Tell me everything, how you found the den, what you saw."

Allanaq stared at his hands. "It was the season when caribou shed their velvet. A good time, I thought, for bulls with full antlers and a heavy layer of fat."

"Did you find any?"

"Later, yes. But that day all I did was to follow a creek bed. Elik knows, I told her—I came across clumps of dark fur and signs of scratched-up grass. I left to come back in a colder time, when I hoped it would be sleeping."

Elik shook her head. "You said you were going caribou hunting. Nothing more."

"A man doesn't name that animal to his wife. I was being careful." Abruptly, he lifted his gaze. "Were you?"

"If I didn't know what you hunted, how could I know to be careful?"

"Hush," Malluar told them both. "Now, tell me, was the bear sleeping?"

"Yes."

"You saw nothing more?"

Allanaq hesitated. "About the bear?"

"If it was a bear," Elik added. "But what if it was another animal, something that changed its shape to trick you? Its teeth—were they proper? Its eyes?"

"Hush," Malluar warned her again.

"All was proper. I thought." Allanaq rubbed his face in exhaustion. "In the den, we found nothing. On the snow surrounding the entry—nothing. When it was dead, we placed gifts atop the skin. Needles and a woman's knife, because it was female. And we didn't eat the meat; we cached it. Malluar, this wasn't my first bear. Not Drummer's either."

"And yet," Malluar said, "something is different. You say it was female? Was it pregnant?"

Allanaq lowered his gaze.

"So," Malluar said. "That in itself means nothing. What of the cub?"

"Cubs." Allanaq forced himself to tell. "There were two. Both males."

Elik's eyes widened.

"Something has happened," Malluar whispered. "Some part you've forgotten, or never found. The young die. And the old. Hunters die and mothers. But always there is a reason. Someone caused that bear's soul to grow angry, make it come here, hungry for revenge."

"The bear killed the two boys? It wasn't me?"

Malluar didn't answer.

Elik looked to the shaman as her eyelids begin to flutter. Malluar stared at the skyhole. When she looked back, a change had come over her face, tightening on one side, slackening on the other. "You're going to trance?" Elik asked.

Again Malluar didn't answer, but she didn't have to. Elik could already see the change coming over the shaman, the way she narrowed her attention, shutting out the house, the people around her, everything but her own inner vision.

Elik sat herself opposite Malluar. She arranged her legs and watched so closely that her shoulders and arms, hands and feet took on the same position, the same angle as the older shaman's.

But suddenly, before she could pull back the words, or wait to think about their wisdom: "Let me trance," she said. "Please? Let me try?"

Malluar opened her eyes in surprise. "What?" she said. "What are you asking?"

Elik hesitated. There was anger in Malluar's voice, but not enough to make her apologize, take back the words. "It seems . . ." Elik searched for the words to explain. "If it was the bear that killed my sons, then its spirit already knows my voice? Perhaps it would speak to me?"

"And when it did?" Malluar asked.

"When it did, I would ask why it was angry. If someone has done wrong—"

"What wrong? Whose anger?" Malluar cut her short. "Haven't I taught you—it takes years before a new shaman has the strength and wisdom to control a spirit. Any spirit. And all that time the spirit is strong, the young shaman is weak. There is no way of saying what could happen. What it could do to you, to this house.

"For now," Malluar continued, "you will sit, and I will search. You—" She motioned Allanaq to the hearth. "Take up a handful of ashes. Go on. Rub it on your face. If by chance the bear enters, it won't see you."

She turned back to Elik. "You remember the time a man named Pikak died? In the Fish River village?"

No. Elik shook her head. She did not remember.

"He had killed a caribou near a pond where a giant worm lived. The worm climbed inside the dead caribou's mouth. Pikak carried that worm on his back, not even knowing. When his wife cooked the meat and fed it to their children, they died, every one of them. No one ever went inside that house anymore, because how could they know if the worm was still hungry?"

Malluar reached for the packet of bear meat. In the warmth of the house, the meat had already started to thaw. A puddle of blood darkened the wrapping.

"We will see what the bear's spirit has to say." She motioned to Elik. "Bring my drum. If you want to learn you must listen. And you also—" She shot a glance at Allanaq. "Sit here but don't talk. Cover your face. Do not try to see."

Pushing aside her disappointment, Elik did as she was told. She took the large, flat drum from the wall, set it beside Malluar. "Will you tie your hands?" she asked.

"No," Malluar said. "Not this time. I feel too tired, too strained for that kind of ordeal. I will drum and sing, and if any spirits are near, perhaps they'll choose to speak."

Elik buried the lamp wick in oil, snuffing out the light. Then, even before she found her seat, Malluar's drumming filled the house. *"A jai. Haja jaja. A ja. A jai. Haja jaja. A ja. A jai."*

The drumming went on. The singing. The layers of dark and smoke and sound. Elik lowered her head to her knees and listened. Waited. Until finally, after a long, long while, there was a smell, a warm smell almost like boiled meat, but different. The drumming slacked and then ceased. Elik crawled over to light the lamp.

She returned and the three of them sat in a circle around the meat. Malluar leaned forward and spit on it, nudged it, rolled it on its side. The meat caught the lamplight, shone with its own grease.

Then, as suddenly as if she'd burned her hand, Malluar pulled back. "That bear," she said, and she looked up in surprise. "It wasn't dreaming of a man, not of a woman either. Only its cubs, and the fat salmon it would teach them to catch in the spring."

"What then?" Elik asked.

Malluar spit again on the meat. She glanced to Elik, pointed. "What do you see?"

Elik took a turn. She leaned on her wrists, stared till the tapered form of a front, and then a rear end took shape. "I see a fox."

"Where?" Allanaq looked closer. "I don't see."

"There," Malluar pointed to the part nearest her knee. "Now, what else?"

"Eyes," Elik said. "Two dark spots, in the face. I see them."

"As do I," Malluar said. "Now sit back. Those are the eyes of a shaman watching through the fox."

"But the bear—?" Allanaq asked.

"This is not about the bear," Malluar said. "The two children inside your wife were already dead before you killed that bear. Why didn't you tell me you had seen a fox?"

Elik sucked in her breath. "You saw Red Fox?"

"I didn't know."

"Tell me again," Malluar said. "I'm old and the mind forgets. Who is this?"

"The shaman who forced me and my father from our home."

"So. There it is. We have it." Malluar stretched her shoulders.

"Red Fox came here?" Elik asked.

"It must be. He sent his spirit looking out through the eyes of that fox. The fox saw the bear. The bear saw Allanaq. And behind him, you—" she looked to Elik, "sitting at home."

"But I've done nothing improper."

"Nor I," Allanaq protested. "Are you sure it was Red Fox?"

"So it seems."

"Does he know I'm here?"

"I can't say." Malluar leaned wearily against the wall. "But tell me. Would he care? Was he your enemy, or your father's?"

"My father's, and mine through him."

"Does he know your father's dead?"

"I don't know."

"But if he did know? If he found out somehow, would he then decide to come looking for you, knowing you would want revenge? Or would he wait for you to come after him?"

"Is he that strong?" Elik asked. "Would he think you blamed him for your father's death?"

"I do."

"So, there. We know he's strong enough to send spirit helpers to kill his enemy's grandchildren before they grew up to kill him."

Elik shook her head, confused. "But you said the two were already dead, inside of me."

"I was wrong," Malluar said. "I've heard of this before. Shamans killing infants, stealing parts of their bodies for the power it brings. Sometimes they take the eyes. Sometimes a hand."

"I didn't bring this on," Allanaq said again.

"No. But here you are. This shaman is very cunning. He killed your children as a warning. Do you need another? Or can you stay away from him?"

Elik glanced to Allanaq. A sadness clouded his face. He didn't look at her, didn't smile. "Is it true for both of us?" she asked Malluar. "We're not to blame?"

"Blame or not," Malluar said, "you must yet be careful."

"What do you mean *yet*?"

"It means," Malluar said, "that this Red Fox isn't finished with his hunt."

Allanaq looked up. There was no sadness in his face, but an anger now, so deep, Elik pulled back in surprise.

"I'll tell you what *yet* means," he said. "*Yet* means *still*. And *still* means that a shaman powerful enough to open a path and find us, is powerful enough to use that path again.

"It means that I can no longer wait. That I have already waited and hidden like a coward, too long. It means that Red Fox searched for my father, and he found you, my wife, because your shaman-power guided him. And he will always find you, and my children will never be allowed to live, nor my father to rest.

"I had thought the time for revenge would come, someday. But how can someday come when I am not there to bring it?" Allanaq's glance turned inward. "We will go back. A son's duty to revenge his father's death is sacred. There's no time left for waiting."

2

It was late in the spring moon, already past the Time When Seals Are Born, well into the season when the skies are crowded and noisy with returning birds.

The pack ice that had held against the shore was gone now, broken off and sunken with the changing tides. Only a few small boulders of ice still floated near the shore. They bumped and grated and melted into flattened pans, no use to anything but the gulls and shore birds looking for a perch.

Elik lowered the clam she'd dug into the water, rubbed it to help the breaking waves clean the sand from its grey stippled back, the closed line of its mouth. She flicked away a strand of seaweed, then tossed it to her sealskin sack, that clam and then another.

She kept on with her work, digging then rinsing, walking then digging again. She needed to try harder not to think so much, not to worry about the journey she and Allanaq would soon begin.

She'd purposefully wandered farther along the shore, past the scattered spots where her aunt and the other women were digging.

Nua's outline in the glaring sun was narrow as a

blade of grass, bent at the waist, feet and arms pointing to the gravel beach. Kimik, working at Nua's
shoulder, was nearly hidden behind her own full sack
of clams. And there was Two Ravens with her
youngest girl poking her head above the rim of her
hood.

And more women farther back, beside the line of
new spring tents. Meqo and her daughter Squirrel balanced in front of the tall drying racks, scraping hair
from a caribou skin. At another frame, Little Pot
worked at splitting a walrus hide that would become
one of the skins for covering an umiak. Not Allanaq's
boat, someone else's.

The women had already stitched together the skins
that covered their boat, a hand's count plus three more
bearded seal, they'd lined them end to end.

On the same day the men carried the wooden part
of the boat out from the *qasgi* and started lashing the
ribs together, the women took out their bundles of
sinew and twisted the strands into thread, pieces so
long they had to wrap them around a bobbin to keep
them from tangling.

They worked the boatskins two women to a seam.
Elik had sat beside her aunt Nua, Kimik beside her
mother, starting in the center and stitching toward the
end. A double-lapped seam, with each stitch biting only halfway through the hide so that no hole
could leak, so the sinew would swell and grow
waterproof and the boat would swim, as safely as a
seal.

It had been hard work and their fingers turned red
and raw. But it was good work also, with laughter and
gossip and the spring sun shining in their eyes. Elik

had not complained, not then, when the time for leaving still seemed far away.

Closer to the water, but well above the tide line, a few of the men were standing about an upturned umiak. Someone had lit a fire on the beach, using the boat to shield it from the wind.

She picked out Allanaq first. With his chin near the height of most men's eyes, her husband was easiest to find. Then Drummer, leaning on his pronged fishing spear, his older boy perched atop his shoulders. Her uncle Grey Owl stood closest to the sea, watching into the wind as if already, though his legs were still strong, he was practicing to be an elder, hungry for a sign of when his children would return.

The women kept digging, searching for the dimpled holes that marked the clam trails. Each time they found one they leaped with their sticks, laughing as sand and spray rained on their hair and faces. Elik smiled, but she wasn't ready to join them.

They seemed so bright, so filled with laughter while she—she felt like a stranger walking through an empty house. With the umiak finally finished and their gear nearly packed, she wondered if this was the way Allanaq had felt when Grey Owl first found him. An outsider watching others watching him. Never quite sure what to do with his hands, his feet, his eyes.

Kimik waved for her to join them but Elik shook her head. "Not yet." She pointed east along the shore as if to say she'd dig in that direction. Then quickly, before her friend decided to join her, she turned and hurried away.

The shoreline curved and Elik kept walking, far

enough, she hoped, so no one would follow. She wedged the sack with its heavy load of clams behind the shelter of a rock, then found a path on the uphill side of a gully where the water-soaked ground was dryer, easier to walk.

It was not going to be a simple thing, leaving the Long Coast shore. Not that she didn't want to leave. She did. At least, most days she did.

Most days, she welcomed the idea of a boat journey. She wasn't afraid of the sea. She was strong. Her stomach was flat again, her legs and back and breasts still young. And she liked to travel though, like most women, she'd never been farther than the nearest Real People villages, the Bent Point village, the Fish River village. And most often, those trips were made in winter, walking on snowshoes. Summers, women were too busy with fish camp to take the time to visit.

But there were other days also, these last ones especially, when she was filled with premonitions. Something was going to happen. She didn't feel safe.

Then again, she asked herself, when had she ever felt safe, truly safe?

Safety was for children carried inside their mother's parkas. Something that lasted for the span of a day, changeable as the wind, the ice. Safety was not something for women who were shaman, who dreamt strange dreams. Someone who had always been different from the women she had just left along the shore.

And she was different. It was something she had long since given up trying to understand.

Not in every way, of course. Girls, wives, grandmothers—all needed to marry and prepare food and scrape furs.

She still cooked with the other women. Fished with them. Trapped for small birds and ground squirrels. Except that Nua's thoughts, or Kimik's, or any of the other women's thoughts stayed where they put them, while her thoughts danced and leapt and reached for something more, a yearning that came over her, like no other woman she knew.

And she waited. That was the other thing she did: waited for Malluar to keep the promises she made, not once but many times. She had promised to teach her how to summon the spirits who spoke to her— and they did. They called her, whispered in her ears as she walked by the sea, sang as she picked berries on the tundra. She heard them, the voices of the spirits, she always had.

Elik sighed. The wind had settled, all but the constant breeze off the sea.

She followed above the wetland bog, tracking the gully to a level rocky outcrop. Beyond, she could see the flat expanse of meltwater ponds, so many they seemed to touch, rim to rim, like an immense abandoned village with no remains but for their tent rings.

Loons were swimming there; she could hear them when she stood still. Their call was filled with laughter, the high-pitched wild sounds they often made in spring. She listened as she squinted against the bright sky, peered back in the direction of the village. No one had followed.

She thought about going farther, then decided against it. The sun was warm here, the large shelf free of melting snow and runoff. The view was open. East and west of the ponds the muskeg was waterlogged and farther inland the snow continued as far

as she could see. The ground would be spongy, difficult to walk on, and there'd be few new shoots to
eat.

She could steal the moment, she decided as she
stretched out on a slab of lichen-covered rock. Quiet.
That was what she needed, a chance to settle her
thoughts. She lay down, straightened her parka.

It was the right thing she would do, leaving with
Allanaq on this journey.

They had talked about it and all agreed. If she
stayed, she would become a burden to her uncle. Or
she could move her things into Drummer's household
and stay there as second wife behind Two Ravens. But
Two Ravens already had children, an older boy from a
first husband, and this new one, still too young to sleep
through the night. Two Ravens was a good woman but
she was young herself, not the kind of wife who'd easily want to share.

Nor was living alone possible. She could do it. She
wasn't afraid to try. The problem would come from
other men. She wouldn't be safe. She'd be stolen, quick
as that.

With Allanaq she was needed. Wives often traveled
with their husbands, not on hunting trips perhaps, but
certainly on longer journeys such as this. A man
needed the skills a woman could provide, the same as a
woman needed a man. To hunt. To trap. To cook and
sew and carry. There was always more than one person
alone could manage.

And besides, this was their journey, not just his. It
didn't matter that she'd never known his father.
Allanaq's life and hers had been linked from the day
she first saw him in the *qasgi*, his body painted red

and black, his arms lifted, hammering as he danced the story of how Red Fox tied their hands and set them adrift in a boat with no paddles, no food, no weapons.

If her husband could have no peace until he returned to his own Seal People and dealt with this man Red Fox, then that was where she belonged. With him. Helping against his enemy. There really wasn't any question.

Far above, the bowl of the sky hung down. Layered white clouds moved quickly, thin ones below, rippled patterns following as if in a dance.

If this had been winter and the night clear, she would be able to look up through the star-holes. She wondered if, as Malluar said, the Land Above the Sky was the same as this world, except that the seasons were opposite. She wondered if the seal and walrus people in the Land Below the Sea looked up and wondered the same thing about her as she wondered about the sky.

She didn't know. She would have to ask Malluar. And when she was home again, she would remember to leave off a bit of food for her own mother and father and grandmother, so their souls would have something to eat.

And in a few days more, when she and Allanaq were finally in the umiak, they would paddle all day and at night the ache of exhaustion would fill her and she would be able to sleep, really sleep. There were so many nights when she didn't. Nights when dreams teased and frightened and woke her with their changing shapes. Sometimes it was all she could do to wait for morning, when the walls would stop their trembling, and the spirits who came in her dreams would lie down, quiet.

Quiet. That was what she needed. Sleep. And after she slept, her thoughts would clear. She would find words that were the right ones Allanaq wanted to hear. And she would say them and he would smile again, the way he used to. And someday, when Malluar said it was safe, they would start another baby. She would like that. They both would.

Drowsily, she pillowed her head in her arms, listened to a loon's laughter as it called its mate. A new sky of billowing clouds swam into view. There were patterns like breaking waves and faces in the waves, heaped and toppling one atop the other. There were eyes opening and closing and peering, all of them peering down to earth.

Who wore eyes like those, she wondered? Clear and strong, with outlines so distinct. There were mouth shapes and curved lines like flippers. Seals and walrus, beluga—sea mammals? Such odd clouds. The way they massed and swam and formed again. As if they were looking for something. Swimming and searching.

Her eyelids closed.

Sleep.

The word sounded close, as if someone had whispered in her ear.

Sleep.

Another time she would wonder who had spoken. Not now. Now she wanted only to rest, to sleep.

Turn over. We want to see the light inside of you. . . .

She yawned and stretched and rolled her back toward the sun. Breasts and belly nestled on softer moss. Her thoughts grew thick.

We want to call you. We are thirsty. . . .

Something warm licked her fingers, moved around near her armpit, rooting about, following the smell.

We long to return home. We are thirsty. . . .

The wind? Was that the wind she felt?

Her eyelids fluttered. Soft moss brushed her face. A mosquito landed on her neck. And something else . . .

Elik roused herself up from sleep.

Her hood was twisted, her arm reached beyond her head. Her fingers . . . Something wet was tickling her fingers.

She turned; close up in front of her eyes stretched a field of brown and green moss. And a grey shadow, rising from the ground.

Dark ears. Long body. A mouse? No.

She whipped in her hand, abruptly sat, and found herself looking down at the black-tipped nose of a ground squirrel that had been sunning itself. Round ears, the grey fur of a male, small feet. A squirrel.

But—no. The animal scooted back, turned and looked again. Now it was larger than she'd thought, the snout longer, the ears pointed. The squirrel seemed to change, transform itself even as she watched.

Not a squirrel at all.

She'd been too close to see: the animal dropped to all fours, growing, changing as it darted away. Now it had a tail, long and thick, where before it had been only a squirrel, now it seemed a fox.

If only it would stay still, she could see what it was. Small to large. Fox to wolverine?

What was it? It darted around a hummock. When it came out it looked like a squirrel again. Why couldn't she see what it was?

Elik looked down at herself. She was sitting on her knees, her hand hooked over the top of her leggings, inside below her belt.

What was she doing, lying like that on the tundra? Someone would think she was no better than a child, playing with herself beneath the open sky.

She climbed to her feet, started to back away. But now as she turned she caught sight of something moving: far in the distance a speck of brown against a smooth slope of snow. One speck, and then a second smaller one sliding downhill behind the other. It was a bear, a sow with its new spring cub.

Had it seen her? How stupid could she be! One girl out alone, when she knew well enough that bears were waking now, foraging and hungry and cranky from their sleep.

The sow stopped. It was too far for Elik to be sure, but it looked as if the bear had lifted her muzzle. As if she was sniffing the air. Searching.

Caw-oww. Now one of the loons called and Elik's skin prickled. She spun about, found the fox–ground squirrel thing up on its haunches, watching her again. Its skinny arms were doing something with its face. She didn't know what until she realized it had opened its mouth.

Whatever it was, spirit or demon—it was trying to speak. She knew what was happening. It would lift back its head and reveal its true face hidden in the soft fur of its chest, the *inua*, the spirit soul inside its body.

It was going to send her a vision. Speak to her the way a spirit helper would. It would tell her things she needed to know. Like the Wolverine who once had become her helping spirit. Like the spirits that spoke to Malluar. This squirrel . . . or fox . . . whatever it was— it might teach her a song of power. Tell her . . .

No! Shaking now, frightened, Elik backed away.

Nothing. That's what it would tell her. Nothing, because she wouldn't let it speak. She mustn't. This was what Malluar had warned. That a demon would come to her if she wasn't careful, try to make her be its wife. Some dead and angry spirit—what if she had yawned? It could have climbed inside her mouth . . .

She choked back her fear, turned, and started running.

Hadn't she been warned a hundred times, a hundred times a hundred, never to sleep beneath the open sky? Not to stand under northern lights or lie on the ground where something could snatch her, touch her, sing its words inside her ears.

She kept running, racing and tripping over the spongy ground, falling then picking herself up again. Back along the gully, then above the incoming tide, retracing her steps. She found her clams, then kept on rushing until she realized the women were gone. The shore was deserted. Slower now, she held her steps. If she ran, it would only draw attention. If she shouted, the wrong ears would hear.

Up the rise and toward the houses. Which way? Not to her uncle's house. Allanaq might be there and she would never be able to catch her breath, hide her fear before he saw it and questioned her.

She found Malluar seated outside her wet-weather tent, a braid of sinew looped between her hands as she played at shaping figures. Behind her, the door flap stood open, weighted with a rock. Elik dropped her sack and peered nervously to see if Allanaq was inside, but no. The tent was empty. Elik fumbled with her belt, knotted it more properly around her waist.

Malluar lifted her string figure for Elik to see: between the thumb and first finger, a woman with breasts and two legs. She dropped a section of the loop and the two legs turned into four. She lifted one side and a different figure appeared. A walrus. She glanced at Elik, then away. The string figure showed the walrus rising. One loop for a tusk, another for a flipper. The walrus dove into the sea.

"On the tundra—" Elik tried to calm her voice. "I fell asleep. . . ."

Malluar looped the cord to start again.

"Something was there. I don't know what."

"A vision?" Malluar let her string wait.

"It was a ground squirrel. At least, I thought it was. After the wind. Then I sat up. It changed itself into a fox."

"A fox? What wind? Child, what are you saying?"

"It was an animal spirit. Maybe something dead that lived in the ground? I don't know. It stood in front me. And it changed. It asked for fresh water. It was thirsty."

"That's not so. Seals thirst for water, not squirrels. What do you have in that sack?"

Elik looked blankly at the bulging sack. "The clams? I dug them on the beach."

"Did you rinse them?"

It took a moment to remember. "Yes."

"The grit?"

"Yes."

"It looks heavy. Is there enough for one meal, or to save?"

Elik took a deep breath, tried to make herself think about the food. "Enough to put most away."

She opened the braided handle, pulled out the first clam she touched. By then the fears that had followed her back to the village had fled. In their place, a familiar disappointment began to grow.

"Perhaps we could boil them? With seal oil, that would be good."

Elik nodded.

"Did you touch it, with your hands? Or were you asleep?"

"Touch what? The clams?"

"This vision," Malluar said. "What else are we talking about?"

Elik held still. She would run if Malluar told her to run. Or sit, all through a day and a night. She would walk alone onto the sea ice, or wait, or drum, or face any wind, sing any shaman-song Malluar told her to sing. If only Malluar would speak, help her learn, finish her initiation. Instead, she confused her, told her to wait. Told her it was the spirits who would do the choosing, and she the one who must be patient. Always patient.

"I saw a squirrel," she answered quietly.

"Come sit." Malluar tapped the ground. "You've been running."

Elik flattened a scrap of caribou hide on the damp ground.

"So," Malluar said. "You think that perhaps you were seen by a spirit? A red fox?"

Elik's eyes widened at the name. She hadn't made the connection. "It wasn't him," she protested. "It was . . ."

"What?" Malluar stopped her. "Why are you flushed? Were there mice bones nearby? Scraps of rabbit fur or ptarmigan feathers? Signs of anything a living fox likes to eat?"

"Nothing. I—I don't know."

"You didn't look. You don't know. Which means it may have been the same Red Fox. You have gone out on the tundra, alone. And fallen asleep, alone. And you were found—exactly as I warned. Elik, that man is a powerful shaman. He could have killed you. You're like a child beside him."

"The child you keep me?"

"What did you say?"

More politely, Elik lowered her gaze. "I asked if you would teach me more? Allow me to learn?"

Wearily, Malluar leaned back against the tent supports, closed her eyes. "I have been teaching," she said. "All along. And you are learning, but your mind is still waking, like a child's. There is *alerquun* and there is *inerquun*, instructions and laws—you know that. But there are so many, for any woman it takes a lifetime to learn them all. For a shaman, even longer."

Malluar looked down on the girl's smoothly braided hair and a hint of annoyance flared. Her own hips ached and the ankle on her left leg made her want to shout every time she leaned on it. Yet here was Elik, running and flushed and always asking for something she herself had spent a lifetime fighting to learn.

And yet . . . She shook her head, sighed. Surely, she had been as willful herself once. Had hidden and eavesdropped and stolen amulets where she hadn't been allowed.

Perhaps the problem was only that the more Elik

reminded her of herself, the more she turned into her own uncle, Kashek, who gave away his amulets and songs only as he lay near death. Jealous, that man had been. Suspicious, even of his own relatives. And for all his promises, in the end, he never transferred his powers into her.

She wouldn't be that way, Malluar decided. She would help, but she wouldn't rush. Elik was young still, and the young always hurried. She softened her tone. "You will be gone with your husband," she said. "Perhaps a long time. Surely through the summer season. When you return we won't be hurrying to fish camp, or trade fairs. Winter will settle in and I'll teach you more. Is that good?"

Elik nodded, tried to smile.

"In the meantime, there is still much you may do. You may practice head-lifting divination, to learn why a person is sick. Or attempt to change the weather. Or search with your eyes closed for things that are lost—women are always loosing needles. Men lose their favorite knives. And now that I think about it, that may not be a bad idea. People would respect you, and among strangers, respect is safer than being feared. Think what would happen if you tried, as the most powerful shaman do, to send your spirit to the moon and ask the souls of the animals there to return to earth? Think how you would be feared; whether you failed or succeeded, you would always anger someone."

Malluar stopped. She felt out of breath from so much talking. Still, the girl held her mouth so tight, it was easy to see she was holding back her words. "It is difficult, I know," she said. "There are many needs, voices, pushing at a person. Perhaps I'll give you something?" Malluar turned over the hem of her parka, felt along the patterned black and white caribou skins Elik had stitched for her.

She brought out a pouch, opened it, and pulled out a dark, feathered skin. "This is from a loon's head. I want you to take it."

The amulet was brittle as an old drum head. As Elik held it, sprigs of downy feathers came loose in her hand.

"It's old," Malluar said, "but it's worked for me."

"What does it do?"

"What all amulets do. The flesh remembers. It turns back into the animal it was. And while the fox is smart, the loon is wiser. It can fly and dive and swim and its song is power. The loon is the most important spirit helper a shaman can gain because it alone has vision to see below the sea and above the sky. If Red Fox tries to come again, the loon will catch his attention and trick him into diving into the sea. The fox would drown and you would be safe."

"Will it be my helping spirit?"

"No." Malluar stopped her. "This is an amulet only."

"Is there a song for it? Will you teach me a song?"

"What?" Malluar opened her mouth in surprise. Did Elik think she would give up her greatest songs? Songs that had the power to break an enemy's bowstring, or call an animal back to its tracks. "Perhaps when I am dead," she said, and there was a warning in her voice. "When I have no use for them myself, you may find a way to learn them. But till then, put the loon away with your others. It would only speak to you if you called it from a shaman's trance. And that—you must not risk."

Elik swallowed her disappointment. She had heard

all this before. She would hear it another day. "I understand," she said. "Red Fox could find me."

"And he will, if you let him. He searches for Allanaq's father, but he would take the daughter-in-law just as well." Malluar stretched her legs, rose heavily to her feet.

She looked to the shore and Elik followed her gaze to where a row of narrow-decked kayaks and larger umiaks stretched above the breaking waves.

Allanaq was there, bent over their boat. But what was he doing walking around the umiak that way? Checking the women's stitches to see if the hides were taut? Or greasing the seams with caribou tallow, checking again that they wouldn't leak?

No. He was holding something in his hands: a small pot, she wasn't sure what kind until she saw the red paint, from alder wood, shining on the prow. He was painting ownership marks, a fish shape with open jaws so the boat would move through the water as safely as a fish moved. Whole, not dead.

"Please," she looked up. "Don't tell my husband what I saw."

Malluar gave her an odd look. "Doesn't a man have a right to know something that touches him so close?"

Elik didn't answer. She looked back to Allanaq, but she felt Malluar's eyes on her, watching from the side.

"When you return from this journey," Malluar said, "and are no longer unclean from the dead-birth, then I will teach you songs. Powerful Songs. Will that be good?"

"Yes," Elik said. "That will be good. Thank you."

The umiak seemed smaller today than yesterday. Certainly with all the gear they needed to load, there was less room inside than when the men had carried the newly finished boat closer to the shore.

She lifted the heavy roll of tent skins into the boat, checked that their weight balanced on each side, then tucked them tight against the ribs.

A few paces above her on the gravel beach, Grey Owl stood with Allanaq. They were discussing the route, pointing west to where the shore turned and land faded into sea. Allanaq looked beyond the waves to where the rocky hump of Ayak Island rose, just visible in the haze.

She waited before lifting another load, trying to hear. Grey Owl scratched a picture in the dirt, pointed again. Allanaq pulled worriedly on his chin.

And if Allanaq was worried, how was she supposed to feel?

No one in the Long Coast village had heard the story more often than she, of how the boat that carried Allanaq and his father away from their home had been swallowed in a fog. How the fog held tight, day after day, while the father died and Allanaq was too lost to find his way home.

If her husband, sitting in that boat, had seen no shoreline all that distance, and if Grey Owl had never been farther north than Ayak—than how were they supposed to know now which shore to follow?

Elik strained to hear their talk: Kalulik, a place with rocks on the beach that Grey Owl had heard of but never seen. And another island, larger than Ayak. Then two more, called Imaqliq, that were even farther across the open water. "If you follow the shore instead," Grey

Owl said, "you'll come to a range of cliffs where murres nested."

Allanaq handed something to Grey Owl. A knife? She caught the flare of light on stone—obsidian? And something Allanaq said about payment for work still left behind.

Elik stepped to the rear of the boat. What was left behind? She wondered, but then someone touched her arm and Elik startled.

Her aunt Nua laughed lightheartedly. "It's only poke-fish," she said. "Too dead to bite. Set it upright, so it doesn't spill."

Elik flushed then turned to hide her embarrassment. Together, she and Nua lifted the heavy seal poke, set it in beside another.

She needed to stop worrying, if not for her own sake, then certainly for Nua's. She caught her aunt's profile just as she started for another load. Wide cheekbones, three straight tattoo lines drawn beneath her chin: Elik pressed her aunt's face into memory.

Nua had shed no tears for this trip, though Elik remembered other times when her aunt had cried. Wailed and mourned so loud, people grew afraid she might die. That had been the winter her son died, drowned in the same place that, a year later, Allanaq was found.

And Elik's own brother Iluperaq—he too had been lost—how long ago now? Three winters? With Iluperaq it had been a hunting accident. And only her father knew the truth of that story, and he was gone also. Dead by the end of the following winter, along with her mother, her grandmother.

There were days when Elik still prayed that the sea

hadn't swallowed Iluperaq but instead had carried him, spat him out on a distant shore. That somewhere a man had adopted him the way Allanaq had been adopted here.

Would her brother try to come home as soon as it was possible, she wondered? Or would he find himself a pretty wife to stitch his parka, then slowly forget the way he came?

For that matter, would Allanaq have been content to stay here, patiently living out the years, if it weren't for his father's sake?

She didn't know. She didn't think she ever would. There were too many things her husband kept to himself. But then, no wife ever heard all a man's thoughts.

Elik returned to her packing. Trade goods were put away first, in the bottom layers. The load was huge, since they didn't know how long they'd be traveling, or what they needed for themselves, what they would need to give away.

There were beaver and land otter pelts that had been traded from Forest People. Pelts for parka trims, white fox and wolverine, and her best caribou hides taken in late summer when fewer insects bored their holes— those she packed carefully away from salt water.

Into one basket she packed bundles of sinew she had sorted by length and thickness. Into another she tucked sewing kits with bird-bone needles and ivory needle cases. Skin scrapers and women's curved butchering knives, the kind Allanaq made so well that any woman, anywhere, would envy.

Waterproof boot soles she'd worked on whenever the season allowed. Two extra pairs she had already chewed into shape, crimping the heel and toe. Sealskin leggings and caribou leggings, boots with the hair left on and mittens with the hair removed to make them waterproof.

And for as long as she had worked on their skins, Allanaq had worked on the boat itself.

It was no small task building an umiak in a land where wood was so precious. Sometimes a man had to wait a full season longer than he'd planned, waiting for another year's ice to go out and new summer storms to blew the driftwood in.

Sometimes it was only the hardest bargaining— Allanaq's best ivory harpoon heads for a length of wood he spotted near another man's house—just right to fit the curve of a bow piece, a deck beam. A straight length for the gunwale.

The wood for the boat was brought inside the *qasgi*, since that was the largest place in the village. Then, while Grey Owl and Drummer, Drummer's brothers, and the other men passed the long, dark evenings mending their fishnets, carving new antler, Allanaq split and steamed and bent the lengths of ribs.

He drove in wedges to split each water-smoothed log, rough-shaping them first, then planing them with his stone-bladed adze. He carved pegs and pounded them into a curve, then steamed the wood until it softened, then pegged it again to fit each curve.

He shaped the bottom flat, the length longer than three men lying down. And measured by the distance between his elbow and the joint of his smallest finger for the bow piece; the elbow and the knuckle of his long finger for the deck beam. The stern and the bow pieces were dovetailed and tapered. And there were flat floor timbers, and slender ribs with notched edges that fit into the gunwales, and the gunwales were pegged and lashed together till they ran smoothly from stem to bow.

And now, along with her own baskets, Elik loaded Allanaq's that were filled with hunter's weapons: flaked knife points struck from a core. Shaft-smoothers and awls and pointed burins.

There were smaller pouches filled with beaver-toothed woodworking tools. Antler harpoon heads, some of the barbed type, some of the toggling kind that twisted beneath a seal's inner muscle.

Some, she knew without looking, were quickly chipped, in her Real People's style, of basalt and slates. More were made in her husband's Seal People's style, harpoon heads with holes drilled through to knot a retrieving line. Flaked blades shaped with wavelike patterns.

And all of them covered with the spirit markings he insisted on engraving—lifelines, eye-dots, skeleton markings to please the animals they hoped to catch.

Elik finished loading Allanaq's gear near the stern. Later he would sort his things himself, decide what he needed to kill Red Fox. All she wanted was for it to be done, and over. That, and to come back home again. She and her husband both still alive.

She rearranged the weight of a walrus stomach filled with oil, then turned to see Malluar approaching from the houses. She walked crookedly, one shoulder lifting toward her ear, the other bent under the awkward load of a sack.

For all the shaman's finery Malluar had dressed her-self in, for all her amulets and warnings, she seemed to have grown more frail this last winter. So slight, her bones looked more like a bird's than a woman's. And distracted, that was the part Elik didn't like. The way she sat for long stretches, staring toward the sea, chewing with the few flat teeth she had left.

Again, Elik tried to stop her thoughts. She had to stop thinking so much, stop worrying. The world held enough fears without adding to them. She was leaving. She would come home.

Malluar held a covered bundle out toward Elik. "You must take this," she said.

Elik stood and brushed the gravel off her leggings. She unwrapped the hide, looked down at a small oval bowl. She flipped it over; in its scooped-out base, a male and female caribou that Allanaq had painted danced backward toward each other. "My woman's bowl?" she asked in surprise. "I thought the mourning time was done."

"Not on such a journey," Malluar firmly said. "I heard this in my sleep. You must mind all the earlier restrictions again. To eat from your cooking pot and no food from anything that flies, not its eggs or heart or head. Nothing fresh."

Nua stepped in to join them, then backed off as she heard the older woman's tone. She turned instead toward the cluster of laughing boys and girls and naked toddlers tumbling toward the boat. They lifted their hands toward her sack, laughing for the treats that came when a new boat was launched.

"Here in the village, it might have been safe," Malluar continued. "But on a journey, you must be even more careful."

"Yes, grandmother." Elik clenched her hands at her sides. *A few more months. It was only a little more of the same.*

"Our eyes see but a small part of what is visible," Malluar said. "The animals see more. They see the death-air that should have been birth, and they are frightened. You must remember, most of all, not to have relations with your husband, for one full year. And you mustn't . . ."

Mustn't trance, Elik finished the words herself.

Malluar went on, her voice turning to a drone, but Elik no longer listened. It was almost too difficult, trying to understand. To be a Real Person was to accept those things which could not be changed. And yet to be a shaman was to try, through amulets and songs, to do just that.

Not eat fresh-killed meat? She had done that before.

Not eat from someone else's bowl? That too, she could do.

Not lie with her husband? Would it matter, when she still felt as barren as the moment she learned her sons were dead.

And yet she remembered, so clearly, the last time Allanaq had held her. He had sneaked up behind and tugged her down on the sleeping bench. He'd stretched out beside her—Malluar hadn't been in the house, and so they had stolen the privacy—twining their legs together, laughing.

Allanaq had played with her hair ties, loosening her braids, nuzzling his mouth against her neck. *Soon,* they had promised each other. *Soon the mourning time will be finished and it will be safe for them to love each other. Without fear of jealous spirits.* Allanaq's eyes had been mischievous and wide—but he and Elik had waited. Obediently, they had waited.

Elik looked up. Nua had set another sack in front of

Malluar. "Give her these before we chase her luck away with talking," she said.

Malluar nodded. She let her voice grow lighter. "New amulets to speed you home," she announced. "A seal's nose, to guide you through the water. A ptarmigan head, so you will be a strong runner. A bee, to give you a strong head. A gull's foot, to make you a good fisher."

Elik took the amulets by their stitched-on ties, looped them along with others she already wore on her belt, but she was saved from having to speak by Grey Owl's voice, calling over the wind.

It was time. Grey Owl and Drummer came and stood on one side of the boat, Allanaq took the stern. While they waited for the tide to help lift the weight, Elik looked to her husband. She fixed a smile on her face to show him she was glad, but he kept missing her look. His gaze was firmly on the sea.

The bottom scraped, then rose on the next wave. Nua tossed the line and Elik splashed a step, then leaped inside. Allanaq climbed in, then quickly braced his paddle against the soft bottom. Elik took up her smaller paddle, searched for balance.

Then, last of all, Nua handed her a bowl filled with cut-up meat. Elik tossed the choice bits of food and fat to the children racing into the water to reach them. Skinny girls and pushing, laughing boys, they ran into the shallows, caught what bits of food they could, then darted out again, till a moment later and the meat was gone. The children disappeared.

The bow lifted, then slapped down into a trough. Elik slid into place against the gunwale. She glanced behind to where Allanaq sat in the stern. His arms and paddle were already searching for the water's pace. She dipped her paddle in, matched her stroke to his, wide then pulling in, lift then wide again.

The umiak pulled away, straight out first, then turning to follow the shore. Elik glanced back as Grey Owl walked along in the water, not even caring how the waves splashed over his boot tops. Nua walked along with them on the land, then started running. And behind them, Malluar, her drum held quiet at her side.

Elik turned back around to paddle. In only a few more days they would be gone, everyone in the village except the oldest would have moved on to their summer fish camps, to the mouths of rivers and creeks where the salmon liked to come. Some of the younger men would go muskrat hunting; it was a good time for pelts. A few others would turn inland for caribou; some for sheep in the mountains.

With luck she and Allanaq would find his village quickly and be done with this business. The trip home would be easier; they would at least know which way to turn. Perhaps they would make it back before freeze-up. Later than that, and winter would settle in. The sea would hide itself beneath the ice. She didn't want to think about being gone so long.

She turned to smile at Allanaq but his attention was more on the distant rollers. She watched a moment— there was a stiffness about his shoulders, almost as if he was uncomfortable with the paddle. But no, it couldn't be that.

His face? He wasn't wearing labrets, she realized. That was odd. Grey Owl had been wearing his, a fine jade pair, she'd noticed as they pulled away. And wasn't a boat launching exactly the time a man wanted to look his best—not to frighten the sea animals with the sight of hungry, human teeth?

She paddled a few strokes more, glanced over her shoulder again. This time it did seem as if Allanaq turned away, purposefully bending into his stroke, but only at the moment when she'd turned.

Her stomach knotted. They had had so little time to talk these last long days. She tried to think of a harmless question, something small that surely he would answer. Then, no—she changed her mind.

Perhaps Malluar had warned him, the same way she'd warned her, to stay away from Elik's blankets? What husband wanted to travel with a wife he wasn't allowed to touch?

And didn't Allanaq already have more than one man's share of worries? Not only the boat and the need to hunt on shores he didn't know, but how to find his village. And what to do about Red Fox when he did.

Better to say nothing. Her fluttering stomach already made her ashamed of her girlish thoughts. She settled into the crook of the boat-ribs, fixed her grip on her paddle.

The morning turned to afternoon. The clouds opened and a white sun peered through. The waves were a series of gentle rollers and Elik and Allanaq held their double-ended paddles to a constant rhythm, following beyond sight of the Long Coast shore, but still in known territory and always with the land in sight.

They passed channels and creeks that looked as if they'd be good for netting salmon. And a low swampy place, and another beach with scattered rocks that stood out in a heavy orange color that she pushed into her memory in case they came home this way. It would be good for paint-making and dyes.

Birds hovered and swam around them. Bright-beaked eiders and puffins. Long-necked cormorants. Gulls argued about fish, and eagles circled and veered as they hunted for their nestlings. Elik watched for seals, but if there were any, they kept their heads hidden beneath the waves.

As did the giant worms Nua had reminded her to watch for. There was a story she'd told about a place called Hunting Bag Strap, where a giant worm hid deep inside a pit, tricking people to come inside so it could eat them.

There were two men Nua used to know, Kilitik and Sidaru. They had set up a hunting camp, then disappeared until years later when another man found a leg bone where they were thought to have gone. Surely, Nua had said, it was one of the men. They had been eaten by the worm, and all that was left was the bone it spit out.

She pointed the hill out for Allanaq but he only shrugged and said it wasn't worms that worried him so much as people.

But they didn't see people, not all through that first long day, and no matter how far they paddled. Often though, Allanaq slowed to study a line of driftwood that stood out in a shape, almost like a food rack. Or grasses that looked to be the bent-willow frame of a tent, but in the end were only grass and nothing more. And once, as they came around a point, Allanaq whispered to her to keep on paddling while he reached for his bow case and fixed his bentwood hat against the glare. He pulled back the bow cord, and aimed, but the boat floated all the way to the other side of the point, and nothing ever moved. Not the rocks. Not the grasses. Only the slightest push of wind.

By the time Allanaq steered them in toward a freshwater stream, the sun had made a circle around the roof of the sky. Ayak Island remained a haze, grey-shadowed and ahead of them still in the west. Elik jumped out first, dragging the bow line, and Allanaq beached the umiak on soft sand.

They tied the boat to a buried driftwood log above the high tide mark. Then, while Allanaq checked the hull to see how well the skins had survived their first day, Elik picked through the tangled row of driftwood.

The wood was good, not rotted, with branches that snapped cleanly under her weight. She thought about the meal she would cook, how fine a broth would taste. They had both eaten only dried salmon, but now she could start a stew of the ptarmigan she'd brought for Allanaq. Perhaps after she gathered wood, she could hunt up a few spring shoots of sourdock. Allanaq liked it when she mixed saltwater with fresh sourdock to flavor the meat.

Except that as she emptied her arms of the first load of wood, Allanaq finished with the boat and started walking away. She straightened in surprise, and watched him leave. He carried his fishing spear in one hand, bow across his back. But he'd said nothing. How long would he be gone?

Elik's stomach twisted in a sudden knot. She cupped her hands. "You'll come back?" she called.

Abruptly, Allanaq stopped. He sent her a look that, even across the distance, was all too easy to read. Then he turned and started walking. That was all. Not a word.

Embarrassed, Elik picked out a few stones for a fire break. She shouldn't have shouted like that, calling attention to their boat. What if there were enemies near?

Even if there weren't, a man didn't like having a wife hover over him. Shouting for anything to hear which way he planned to hunt. It was stupid, worse than a useless thing to do.

Elik built a fire, poured water into two pots, one for Allanaq, a separate one for herself.

By the time he returned Elik had stretched a small shelter on the beach above the boat. She had smoothed a floor, and added grasses, then skins on top of that. And she had just finished hauling rocks to hold the tent corners down when she caught sight of him walking along the ridge line of the beach.

If he'd gone hunting, she couldn't tell: his load seemed empty. Definitely, he carried no game. *No foolish questions,* she promised herself. *No talk about a woman's constant fears.*

He took a seat on the ground beside the fire's warmth. And though she held quiet, he said less. Only that the warmth felt good. That the wind was strong enough to keep the insects down, but hardly more.

Shyly, Elik brought his bowl. For three full winters they had lived together, and never had he been so quiet around her. She felt like a new wife offering food to a new husband while her parents watched.

He sipped the broth, then put the bowl aside. He took out a bit of antler he'd been carving, but not once did he hold the work up for her to admire, the way he usually did, explaining the shape he planned, telling her again how his father had taught that in order for a weapon to be strong, it must first be beautiful, or the animals would never come.

She squatted on her heels beside the fire, waited till his bowl was empty, then asked if he wanted more.

Allanaq shook his head no.

She cleaned the bowl with sand, then came and sat behind his shoulder. "So?" she searched for something to say, "did you see anything along the beach?"

He shrugged. "We're nowhere yet."

Elik tried again. "Which way did Grey Owl think we should try?"

Allanaq snorted. "Grey Owl knows where there are cliffs, but only cliffs he's seen. A few rivers. A large bay. The same two islands any man should know. But that's all. A lifetime among Real People, and that's all." Allanaq pushed the antler from his lap, then stood, stared out to the sea.

The sky was changing and farther out the waves seemed higher, steady but not seriously rough. There would be no sunset—the season was too full of light for that. And there were layered strands of thin clouds with hints of blue behind, a thicker cloud cover in the distant west.

"I almost remember," he said, more to himself than aloud. "The coast moving around a point, and rocky cliffs. But maybe not. In the fog, I never knew. I never saw clouds, or birds, to help me guess. Should we keep to shore, or should we wait? We might meet traders who know the routes. If we search, it could all be wrong."

Elik listened with relief. It was the route that

troubled him, that was all. What man wouldn't be concerned, traveling through unknown territory? "Most places we've seen have been low and sandy. If we follow the coast—" she started, but Allanaq interrupted.

"Look at that boat," he said. "I'm worried that Grey Owl had me build it too wide. Maybe it was good along your coast, but for Seal People?" He shook his head. "What we used to do, when we had enough hides, is add sealskin flaps along the sides. When I was a boy and my father took me paddling, if a rough wind came up, I'd help him lift the flaps and he would lash them over the deck, covering it like a kayak." He stopped, looked at Elik. "Do you know what worries me?" he asked.

Elik smiled, glad to be asked. "That you won't find a safe route home?"

"No. That I will. That at any fish camp, at any point of land, we could sail into Red Fox's camp, and he would kill me first, before I killed him. Or if not him, his relatives. Bird's Mouth and Samik, Mink and No Bird. They could be sitting on their roofs, watching toward the sea. The ice stays longer there, did I tell you that? All their harpoons would be sharpened for hunting and they'll see us long before I figure out who they are. They'll kill me dead, and then take you."

Allanaq turned and peed into the sand. He checked the boat knots one more time, then walked back to the tent Elik had made and climbed inside.

Elik pushed Allanaq's chewed-up bones into the fire, then tossed on sand. She set their bowls upside down beside the coals, then waited outside the tent till she heard no more moving. And then she crawled in, to the empty space inside.

Allanaq lay with his hands behind his neck, his gaze on the dark roof overhead. A narrow space remained alongside. But for her short inner trousers, she removed all her clothes, leggings and boots. She took his boots and pulled out the grass padding, to let the soles dry. By the time she stretched out, Allanaq had turned to face the angled wall of the tent skins. She pulled in her knees, stared at his back.

He was solid, nothing boyish about him. His shoulders were wide, but stiff and bunched looking from the long day paddling. And he had a smell about him, familiar as the scent of his sweat, his hair. A safe smell, like the smell of a cook fire. The smell of thick fat, ready to eat.

She reached across the small space between them. With her thumbs and fingertips she touched his shoulder, the base of his neck—gently. Only for a moment, but he jumped.

"What are you doing?" he snapped.

"Nothing—?"

Allanaq turned and glared at her; even in the shadowed tent his mouth's tight line was visible. "How can anything you do be nothing?"

"I only meant to ease your back."

"My back? Or something else? It's prohibited. You know that. Unless you want to bring bad luck?"

"No. Of course not. Please." Elik shrank away.

A thick silence filled the tent, and then a sound Elik hadn't expected. Allanaq sighed. His eyes had softened. He lifted his hand, touched her dark braids. "Of course you don't," he said. "But you must remember. You are one of my Seal People now. Not Real People. And among the Seal People the laws the elders teach are as old as the First Times. They are not to be forgotten whenever the need fits."

Allanaq moved his hands to his own face. "I should never have cut these," he said, and he felt along the labret hole that had been cut beneath his chin. "They'll think I'm a stranger. No one will know me. They'll kill first, and look at the rest of me later." Without glancing at Elik, he pushed free of the caribou robes, then stepped naked, over her legs.

Elik covered her mouth with her hands, not to cry. She listened to the drag of his parka as he slid it over his head, his naked foot stomping out a place to lie down. The boat ground on rocks as he leaned against it and she edged away from the tent flap, not to hear more.

It was since he killed the bear, that was when this started. He had taken to sleeping in the *qasgi* more than with her. Telling stories she'd never heard, of his father, and cousins, and Red Fox. And he looked at her differently now, when other women walked by with their children in their parkas, as if wondering why none of hers ever wanted to be born.

He'd grown cold toward her. It was true, but it was only because he was so distracted, she told herself. Single-minded. And wasn't that the way a hunter needed to be? The way he was taught from the time he was a boy? To be directed, without thoughts of women to slow his hand and waste his vision?

She could understand that, any woman could. And perhaps he was right, and it was easier to sleep alone than to hold back your hands, worry how they could feel so empty.

Early the next morning with only the most necessary, simplest talk between them, Allanaq finished his meal from the night before and Elik ate from their stores of dried fish. Then, while he wrapped his hunting bola around his forehead and walked off to hunt birds, Elik repacked their gear and waited for the incoming tide to lift the boat.

Little had been unloaded, but she worked to shift the weight more evenly, and moved what little fresh meat they'd brought into the cooler bottom where it wouldn't spoil. She refilled the one water bladder they'd emptied with fresh water, and rolled up the sleeping furs.

Allanaq had already refastened his long harpoons to the spear guards near the gunwale. If they saw a seal he would try for it, he said. They needed fresh meat, and these weren't waters he knew.

She pulled a coil of rope out from where it had gotten buried; then moved his box of harpoon points nearer to the stern; if he needed them, he wouldn't want to have to ask where they were.

It was when she tucked the box against the rolled-up sleeping furs that she found the pouch. It was a small one, made of a soft, light-colored skin, with a drawstring fitted through a hollow ivory closure. She easily recognized the closure as Allanaq's work: an animal figure, part whale and part wolf. No other carver she knew spent the effort working to show how a killer whale turned into a wolf, a woman into a walrus.

She tugged open the cord. She wasn't sure where he'd want it. Among his clothes? If it held points it should go with his harpoon. Most of all, she didn't want to anger him. She'd slept so little, her thoughts and eyes felt muddy, as if she were staring through water.

The pouch was oddly beautiful; Nua's work possibly, but she didn't remember her aunt making this one. It was small, too small for Elik's hand to fit inside. Something clinked, not sharply, the way flints would sound.

Elik peered over the tangled row of driftwood. Allanaq was nowhere in sight. He'd told her nothing about his plans again, how long he'd be gone, or where. She squatted on the sand, emptied the pouch into her cupped hand. Tiny stones came pouring out, a few twigs of wood. Some grey, most white.

Except . . . no. They weren't stones, and not twigs either. They weighed hardly a thing. She scratched her fingernail down the length of a longer one. Too hard for wood, she decided.

With growing curiosity, she lifted her cupped hand to her mouth. Bone would have one kind of taste, old bones especially had a way of catching, holding to the tongue. Stone slipped away. Whichever these were, she was already certain they were amulets. What surprised her was that she hadn't seen them before.

Allanaq wore one of his small ivory carvings around his neck, a walrus, as finely worked as the loon he'd given her when they first met. Other amulets he kept sewn to his parka, the same as anyone else. But these . . . ? Something here was different.

The twig-shaped one stuck: bone, she decided. And the surface was pitted with holes smaller than stars. It was an animal bone, perhaps. Or perhaps a man's?

She had heard of people digging tools up out of the ground, tiny blades made from flint and obsidian that people said were made to be small because they were used by dwarf-people who once lived on these shores.

What if these were their bones? The long ones could be their legs or arms. She didn't see any heads.

A hair of curled moss stuck to one. And there was a smell, almost like spring when the dead layers of leaves rise from under melting snow, but this was stronger. A smell of rot and too much moisture.

The next bone scratched more easily, she lay it down beside the first. And then another, but by then it didn't matter. She had already figured out what these were: the long thin bones of a full-sized hand. A human hand. The fingers were larger than hers—a man's.

Without skin, they no longer showed the tattoo marks Allanaq had once described for her, how his father's hands were proudly decorated with the secret signs that shamans wore. Life lines. Animal signs. The tracks his spirit helpers had taught him to make.

But why had he taken his father's bones? It was bad enough to steal a burial gift from the dead, but those things could be given back. Meat. Fat. Hunting tools. How could an entire hand be returned?

Elik straightened, watched along the beach. There was no sign of Allanaq yet, but she didn't want to be caught. Her hands started to shake. A few of the bones, the smallest, rolled to the ground. Quickly, she picked them out from the clump of beach grass. She had to blow off the sand, then quickly slide them back in the pouch.

All but one. She would keep one, she decided. Not the longest, that would be too easily missed, one of the others. She didn't know why. Perhaps because she felt lonely. Perhaps because she was a little annoyed. She only knew that the bone stuck fast to her hand and didn't want to jump back in the pouch along with the others, and surely that meant something. She let it drop instead into her own small amulet pouch that she kept inside her parka.

She pushed Allanaq's pouch back against the roll of furs. She didn't want him knowing what she'd found. Or what she had just done. She didn't know herself why she did it.

Then, in case she had been watched, she bit off a mouthful of dried fish and spit it into the grass, an offering for those who might have died there. "Eat. Go not in hunger," she said, and then, in a whisper, she added another plea: "Don't see me here. Don't tell."

By the time Allanaq returned, he had a sling of eider ducks over his shoulder, black feathers already plucked, the cavities of their stomachs gutted and washed. Elik felt them and praised them and told him how fat they were and sweet. He smiled a little, and she decided that was enough. They didn't need to talk. She covered the birds in oil, then packed them in an empty seal poke.

The morning fog had lifted and they waited only for the next wave to help them with an easy launch, then out they sailed, slicing the tide, then angling with it.

All that day they paddled in sight of land—close enough so they would see a camp fire if there was one, or a fish-drying rack, a village they might want to visit; far enough so they could hide from anyone they didn't want to meet.

Elik grew used to the rhythm of her paddle again, the lift and rise of the bow, the wind whistling its song.

It was still morning when they passed Ayak Island.

The closer they came to the craggy shoulders, the more Allanaq grew excited, nervous, craning about and searching.

Not for people—no one but walrus lived on the island—but for the place. Elik could almost hear his thoughts, searching for where his father died. It would be nearby, somewhere. She knew the tale.

Allanaq held his paddle above the water. He turned, distracted and too quick. Water spilled over the gunwale and she leaned hard, balancing to the other side. She plunged her paddle in, straight down an arm's length from the boat, held it rooted in the wave. Allanaq never noticed.

"It was somewhere near here," he said. "My father's breath went out of him not far from here."

Elik steadied the boat, letting let him talk as much as he needed. By the time they started again, the wind had changed. It blew out of the north now, lifting heavier waves but nothing the boat couldn't handle. They kept on that way till midday, when Allanaq lowered his paddle again. Elik felt the umiak slow and she turned around. This time Allanaq pointed his chin for her to see into the dark water, just off the side of the stern.

A movement caught her eye: the sleek black head of a seal, pointed nose lifted, watching to see who'd come.

The seal dove, then emerged again, this time closer, on their other side.

Allanaq set his paddle aside, then reached for his harpoon and grooved throwing stick. He checked once to make sure the dart head was fitted to the shaft, the towline into the head. While Elik let the boat glide nearer, he fit the harpoon shaft to the groove of the throwing stick, lifted then leveled the stick above the water.

He locked his knees. The waves were higher here, cupping the boat, rocking it. The lower part of the seal's body was a blur beneath the surface but it watched him curiously, steadily.

Allanaq raised the shaft higher, then heaved it, hard and straight as the boat lurched behind his movement.

The seal dove, head first, flippers splashing behind. Safe.

He'd missed by an arm's length. Elik politely lowered her gaze as he reeled the harpoon back by its line, recoiled it, fixed it in front of his feet. Then again he set the harpoon to the groove in the throwing stick, adjusted his hand.

Elik twisted around to see. He was holding his shoulders tight—not a good way to aim. He looked to both sides, back toward Ayak, and then skyward, checking the wind.

"Perhaps if I call it with a hunter's song?" he said, then without expecting an answer, he began:

> *Drive animals toward me—*
> *Thou Man who lives inside the Moon*
> *Above the sky*
> *Send me gifts.*
> *Let me be unseen*
> *Between the earth*
> *The sky and the sea.*

The seal poked its head up again and Elik smiled to show she was pleased. Allanaq nodded and almost returned the smile until he caught himself and looked away. The boat lifted on a wave and he resettled his arm, but even with the song he seemed nervous. By the time he flung the harpoon, he was already too late.

The seal did not reappear. Elik held quiet, not wanting to shame him further by noticing. She waited till she heard him exchange the harpoon for the paddle. Then she took up hers.

They had gone only a few strokes when Allanaq said something. She turned to find his paddle lifted again, water dripping from the blade to his hands.

"What if it was here he died?" he whispered. "And that's why the song didn't work? It wouldn't be strong enough."

With a sigh, Elik lowered her eyes. He was worrying about his father again—no wonder the seal had fled. *If your father had died on land,* she wanted to ask him, *would you hesitate to walk? If he choked on food, would you no longer eat?*

"What if my father's spirit knew we were here?" Allanaq squinted heavily at the thought, then, louder suddenly: "Watch how you sit," he snapped. "Don't touch the water. The seal will know where we are."

Elik lifted her hands in surprise. She laid her paddle across the bow to show him she would do nothing knowingly to jeopardize his aim. They needed the seal; they carried only a little fresh food. They both had planned on catching more.

"You may as well tell the seal you're here," he said again. "A hunter needs to show respect to the animals. But so does his wife, even more so—" Allanaq stopped and Elik reddened under his stare.

"My Sealing People are so much more careful than

yours," he said. "You don't even know, do you, what it's going to be like when you come among them? They'll say you're ugly with only those three small tattoos on your chin. The way your uncle said the women would find me ugly, and he forced me to cut these—" Allanaq pointed toward the empty holes in his chin. "And the women will listen to the way you speak your own mind and they'll look up between your legs and try to poke their fingers inside you to see if you are a woman or a dog. The same as your women pulled me to see if I'd grow hard like a man, or a dog dressed up as a man."

"You are so sad," Elik whispered. "The seal must look at this boat and see nothing but tears. No seal will come—"

"Then you call a seal. Try. You're a shaman, no?" Allanaq's voice was so tight, so filled with anger, the words floated back around and he heard them, heard the way he sounded.

His mouth hung open in surprise. He closed it, quieted his breathing. Finally: "Forgive me," he said. "That was a useless thing to say. I should not blame you for being a shaman."

"If you say so," she whispered, "I will go home. From here, I can easily find my way along the shore."

If Allanaq heard her, he didn't answer. He broke off a small bite of the salmon he'd chewed on earlier, dropped it over the side of the boat. Then he took up his paddle and Elik turned to hers.

Behind them Ayak Island receded into the distance; a bulky, grey-headed figure with shoulders dipping beneath the sea. By midday they were paddling into a steady rain. The shoreline had turned north and they continued following it, with the winds slowing them all the way.

Most of what they saw looked to be lowlands and the same moist tundra they'd left behind. Willow. Dwarf birch. Alder, but not much. Two times during the day the sky cleared and they caught sight of foothills and of inland mountains, they couldn't tell how far.

They passed a series of bluffs with exposed, grey rocks and birds nesting on the ridges, waterfowl flying everywhere. They passed a hunting camp, but only a circle of rocks was left to show where someone had raised a tent. And once a place with a tall silhouette of a man built out of piled stones; the cairn might have marked a caribou-crossing, or a burial. They didn't talk about it and they didn't try to find out which.

But more and more often, Allanaq took to standing in the boat while Elik steadied its rocking. He searched the shore, the sea, as far as the clouds allowed. He wasn't looking for his father now, but only in the hopes that he could be more certain which route his boat had taken when it found the Long Coast shore, which way he needed to steer now in order to find the way back.

With no darkness, and not even a twilight to end their day, there was no need to stop paddling for any reason but their own hunger and tired shoulders and caring for the boat. They waited till they found a likely looking strip of a sandy beach, then pulled in to rest.

They hauled the boat in to what turned out to be a small protected bay with a rocky point to the north and south. The beach itself was shallow, with a sharper incline above. And there was a place where a stand of

willows grew luxuriously tall, enough so they were surprised there was no village here, since it seemed a place
that even caribou might come. There were berries
which she could eat, and not far away they had seen
cliffs where there might be eggs for Allanaq, not her.
And fresh water and plenty of animal signs.

They relieved themselves and straightened their legs
and Elik gathered dry cotton grass for their next day's
fire, not to use up the supply she'd brought. Allanaq
ate one of the eider ducks he'd caught, while Elik ate
her fish, and then they went to sleep beside the boat,
quietly and quickly.

The next day they woke to a fog so thick, it sent
Allanaq back to the comfort of his sleeping furs and
Elik to gathering firewood, but only close by.

To break the waiting, she cooked his second duck,
though she worried a little about the amount of fresh
food he had already eaten. She dug up a little rhubarb
that she found on the beach ridge and thought about
walking back for the *masu* root she thought she'd seen
growing, but she didn't want to risk wandering or getting lost.

When finally he did wake, Allanaq stretched out of
sleep. His hair was tousled, but he was smiling, more
than she had seen since they set out. He ate and
dressed and offered a morning prayer to the sky. When
he sat to take the bowl she offered, he pulled out a
stone knife and a piece of driftwood he must have
picked up along the shore.

He studied the length of it a moment, then turning it around so the wide end pointed south and the
narrower tapered end north, and started carving it
into a map. "I think," he said, as he dragged the

knife along the wood, "I think we may be going the right way."

Elik looked up in surprise, then came and watched behind his shoulder.

"There were a few landmarks. I fell asleep thinking about them last night. I don't know how many days out of my Seal People's village it was, but I had finally freed my hands and brought us in to search for drinking water. We found some, but we didn't stay. We floated on. There was one day after that without fog. One single day. I remember rocky cliffs, different than the ones near my home. It could have been those we passed yesterday. I heard birds this morning, did you?"

"Maybe. Yes. I might have."

"That was autumn though, not early summer. They could have been the last of the birds, making for their winter home. I saw another place." He pointed his knife point toward a crimp in his driftwood map. "A large slough comes off a river, then empties into the sea. I think I would know it by the color of the water, where the two come together. It's possible. I can't say more. But it's possible."

The day passed slowly. Elik set up a small lean-to for a shelter and Allanaq checked to make sure the boatskins would properly dry. He mended one place on the bottom where gravel had rubbed the skins, not hard—the spot was only thin, not cut through—but with time to pass it was better to do the work now than save it for another time.

The fog held. Beyond the shore, there was little to see. Little to do. They moved around each other with a sullen care, but none of the full anger Elik had heard yesterday. When they were ready to sleep Allanaq climbed first into the tent, then edged as far from Elik's side as the small space allowed.

The following day it was Elik who woke first. She glanced once to see if Allanaq was asleep, then climbed quietly out. Over the sea, the fog had lifted with the rain. Condensation rose, then burned itself away. She lifted her hands, surprised to see how far in the sky the sun had circled.

Elik slipped on her boots, then picked her way between the larger rocks and the water's ragged edge. There were starfish caught in a small backwater, bright in their coats of purple, reds, and pinks.

Black, finger-sized mussels clung to seaweed and rocks she hadn't known were there. The mussels were large and plentiful enough, and she returned for a digging stick and a sack, then worked at prying them loose. Her bag was nearly full when an orange-backed crab scuttled from a rock, then disappeared into a long, rolling wave.

Farther out in the open sea a movement caught her eye. She watched the water; one time and then again, she caught sight of the straight outline of something long and white.

She held her breath. A whale was out there. Not Arveq, the great bowhead that two people alone could never hope to catch, but *cetuaq*, the white whale, swimming to the shallow, warmer waves to feed on herring.

Startled, she raced along the beach, thinking to follow, to see if the beluga stayed. But then she stopped. It wasn't one whale out there, but two. Long bodies, sleek and proud. They came up for a drink of air and then went down.

A third appeared, rising to swim alongside the other. Then a fourth. After that she lost count. She started to shout, then stopped herself. Belugas were quiet creatures; like human women, they carried no weapons when they swam. These would be part of a second season run. The first would have come earlier, with the walrus, when the ice went out.

She turned and sprinted for the tent.

Within moments Allanaq was dressed in his boots and parka and out in the glaring light. He shielded his eyes, picked the whales out from the waves. They both stood quietly, watching, but only long enough to agree the whales were too far to be harpooned from the shore. There was no choice but to risk the time taking the boat out and hope the whales stayed near.

Quickly, they set a few of the larger sacks on the ground. Then, with Elik lifting the bow and Allanaq the rear, they walked it, awkward and heavy as it was, down the beach and into the water.

They paddled hard and fast, straight from the line of breakers, then angling their path. They switched places as they neared the whales, Elik climbing to the stern to steer, Allanaq readying his harpoons. He had already fixed the socket pieces and foreshafts. Now he added a flint blade into the largest of the toggling heads he'd brought. He checked the heavy towline, making sure it was well tied through the hole in the foreshaft, then he readied a second harpoon and again checked the point, the head, the foreshaft and socket, the lines.

Neither one of them spoke, but Allanaq motioned and Elik paddled the umiak to exactly where he pointed. There were no rocks to trap the whale in low tide, no shallows, and the whales were fast swimmers. Once struck, they could easily escape.

There, to the right and in front of the umiak, the whales surfaced and breathed. Curved white bodies glided, rolled beneath the waves, then returned. The nearer they came the more they slowed, until gradually, somehow, they realized they were being followed. Two shy ones doubled back—one the flinty color of a younger whale. A third one passed under the boat. Ivory white, it was long and cautious. It was the one Allanaq wanted.

Elik followed with long smooth strokes while Allanaq aimed for the high point of the whale's back. Tensely, he shifted his harpoon, watching along the spine. He had already lost the seal. He didn't want to watch the whale swim away.

He moved once to check his balance and then he heaved the harpoon, hard and strong. In a burst of speed, Elik pulled through the water, cutting across waves while Allanaq grabbed his next harpoon, aimed and hurled it after.

Too far. Both harpoons missed.

Elik didn't dare look at Allanaq. Neither uttered a sound as he reeled in the lines, readied the harpoons again. Elik held her paddle quiet, waiting, hoping her noise hadn't driven it away. She stilled her thoughts, willing away any anger, any thoughts or fear the whale might hear and hide from.

Until finally, the water calmed and they found them again, two whales, and then a third. Streaks of colors beneath the waves. More were farther out, but they tracked these, the closer ones, following their wake as it rose and changed, different from the surrounding water.

Allanaq gestured, and quickly Elik started throwing pebbles she'd brought from the beach, loudly scattering handfuls of pebbles that confused the whales, herded them toward the shallower water where they could not dive so deep or swim so fast.

Allanaq picked out a whale, the same long one he'd seen before. He lifted his harpoon, fixed his hold in the finger rest, and watched as it rolled forward and submerged.

On the whale's second roll, just as it filled its lungs with air, Allanaq struck. This time the harpoon pierced the skin and held, separated from the shaft exactly as he'd hoped. He flung the second, a barbed point, and again it held. Blood trailed through the water. The whale sounded, then dove.

Tensely, they waited. A struck whale could easily sink. Or it could double back and they would lose it. Even hit, it could swim away to die. Harpooning it— that had been the easy part. Tracking it into deeper waters, bringing it home, that would be harder.

Allanaq freed his heavy killing lance, set it near at hand. Moments passed, lengthened. Two whales appeared, farther out than before. They sounded, dove, then made their way toward deeper waters. Allanaq looked back over his shoulder and silently stared at Elik.

Her hands were inside the boat, not the water. She had done nothing wrong. Neither of them had.

"Call it," he said.

Elik looked up in surprise. "You want me to sing?"

"Do it. Make it rise."

"I don't know any whale songs," she said, and her thoughts reeled with Malluar's prohibitions.

"Then a hunting song," Allanaq said, more urgently.
"I'm not asking you for a shaman's trance. Only a hunting song. Anyone uses those." Allanaq turned back to
search for the whale.

Elik's brows knit. It was true, what he said. She'd
nearly forgotten. Even Malluar mentioned the smaller
things any person might try—divination, weather
changing. Only not a trance. Later, she would think
more about this. For now, the red cloud marking the
whale's blood was fading. There wasn't time to wait.

She spit in her hand and dipped her fingers in the
water, this time wanting the whale to know who she
was, wanting a path that would lead it toward the boat.
She remembered a song Malluar had once traded to a
man, someone who was going to hunt in a strange
land. It was a humble song, well fit to their day. *"I am
ashamed,"* she began . . .

> *I am ashamed,*
> *I feel afraid and perplexed.*
> *My grandmother sent me out,*
> *Sent me out to search.*
> *I am on an errand*
> *After the dear game,*
> *After the dear sea mammals.*
> *But alack! I am in fear and perplexed.*
> *My great-grandmother and grandmother*
> *Sent me out to search.*
> *But I am ashamed.*

Almost before the song was done, Allanaq caught
sight of the whale rising in shallower water not far from
the boat. It moved slowly, the way a man might if he

was listening. With a look on his face that was almost a smile, Allanaq turned to Elik and pointed.

A shudder of awe passed through her as she finished the song. It had come. For a song she had sung, the whale had come.

Quickly then, remembering to be thankful, not proud, she took up the paddle. Working in tandem, they quickly reached its side. The whale seemed in no hurry to leave, as if it was glad they had arrived. Two gashes dragged from the height of its back; Allanaq's long harpoon lines trailed in the water.

Allanaq braced himself and, with thanks to the whale, he drove his repeating lance into the animal's ivory skin. The barbed point disappeared. Allanaq yanked the shaft free, repeated the strike with another point, and then another.

Now even the water seemed to calm around them, helping them to haul the whale in with the retrieving lines.

It was dead, its head and tail drooping at both ends, and they had to lift and cut a hole in one flipper to secure the whale alongside. From a drinking bladder filled with fresh water, Elik spilled a few drops over the whale's mouth, giving it the taste it had thirsted for.

They rode the tide in after that, beaching boat and whale on the steep stretch of beach below their tent.

Elik climbed out with the bow line in hand, and Allanaq smiled to show his relief. "It's a good sign," he said. "Perhaps I shouldn't fear this homecoming so much. Perhaps, the seal knew the whale was waiting. If the seal had come to us, we might have camped elsewhere and missed the whale."

Elik smiled, then turned to hide her own relief.

Allanaq was right. The seal and the whale must have spoken with each other; the whale would not have given itself if it found them disrespectful. And now they wouldn't have to worry about food. There would be extra, and they could make plans for caching the meat until they returned.

They tied the whale off securely with a line that went around a heavy, buried log, then looped it through a gash they cut in its lip, and back again cinched with an antler line closure.

The first cut they made was a slice from the tail fluke. Allanaq ate it quickly, giving thanks to the whale—and a share for the ravens watching from higher up the beach.

Elik stepped back as Allanaq ate the outer skin. The whale was sea-mammal, not fish, and until it was no longer fresh she would not taste it. But she watched him and tried not to think about how delicious the outer skin must be, raw and chewy with the thick layer of fat.

After that, she and Allanaq butchered only a small section, a single long chunk of meat cut from one side of the whale's back. They were more tired than they had realized, and the day had quickly passed. A wind was rising and the tide with it.

Elik took out enough gear to build a larger camp then their last, using two more tent skins and weighing the ends with rocks against the ground. Other beaches had offered longer, loose sections of driftwood, but there were enough smaller ends here that she could snap them off and build a fire tomorrow, not tonight.

By the time the shelter was ready, the wind was stronger. Elik turned to watch Allanaq standing at the water's edge, just clear of the blowing spray. He was watching the weather, waiting to see which way the wind might move, what it would do to the sea.

It was blowing from the north now, a cold wind, bringing colder air. And in the sky, a layer of clouds stretched also out of the north, thinner than during the day. Watching it, he seemed to grow more quiet, thoughtful and tight again, and though he smiled as he climbed inside the tent, he had few words to say.

Elik finished securing the few slabs of meat they had cut to a stand of driftwood she had lashed into a tripod. Then, quietly, she followed inside the tent.

Allanaq was already undressed, his parka stored above the damp ground to dry. His eyes held a tired look she didn't like to see, dark rimmed and pensive. She pulled off her outer clothes, left on her woman's inside trousers, and stretched out, bending her knees to fit the space he left between.

There was quiet for a while. Elik lay with her eyes open, the patterns on the tent skin enlarged in front of her face.

"I have been thinking," Allanaq said. "How this is the right thing I've done, returning to the place I was born. This whale today, it's a sign my father's soul is helping. He wants to return home. He wants his soul to be born again, in a child given his name."

Elik thought about the pouch of bones she had discovered. "What will you do," she asked. "When you find Red Fox? Do you have a plan?"

"Not yet. But I will," he said, then he rolled over, widening the gap between them.

Elik lay awake. Tired as she was, there was little hope for sleep. The winds were loud, and a rain had begun. It pelted the roof skins, puddling then dripping near her ear. There was no rhythm to help lull her into sleep, only a plinking sound, a high-pitched voice inside her ear.

Allanaq's arms lay outside the sleeping furs. Arms. Wrists. Hands. She looked at him with an ache she was glad he didn't see.

He confused her, the way he changed from one day to the next. From the one seal he missed to the whale they caught.

He was asleep already, his loud breathing fallen to a rhythm. There was too much sadness in him, too much weight for one man to hold.

3

Elik woke to the sound of sea birds calling from outside, swans whistling, and gulls, always gulls, arguing
over food. The walls of the skin tent were too thin to
block the noise and she lay with her face burrowed in
the crook of her arm, too tired to do anything but
crawl back inside the bedding and sleep.

Sleep. She had been dreaming. She remembered
now. A storm had risen out of the north. Like the spirit
of an angered wolf it howled and whined and turned
the sky to darkest grey.

There was more to the dream. She remembered a
heavy wind that shook Allanaq out of his sleep. He had
stood—no matter that the tent roof was only tall
enough for him to sit—he *had* been standing. His
mouth was open, eyes wide in fear and anger, at her as
much as at the wind.

The walls of the tent had started flapping, and
she had crawled after him to find that a storm had
risen. Winds shook the waves to a white-tipped
frenzy and the gravel beach had all but disappeared.
The sand, the tent, the world all around—even her
boots—were soaked. Her leggings clung heavily to
her skin.

Someone had been calling her name, shouting through the wind.

A line appeared for her to cling to, as if she had fallen from a boat and would drown if she didn't catch it, grab tight, and hold on.

Except that was wrong, because she was the one on land and the line stretched into the sea.

It was a strong line, cut from a thick hide, and it could have held her except that the lengths were clasped together with ivory cord fasteners, and the faces carved on them frightened her.

They were seal faces with downturned mouths, thirsty mouths, with a smell like skins that weren't cleaned of the blood-smell. She wouldn't touch the line. She wouldn't follow it into the sea. She kept her arms at her sides and backed away.

That was all. If there was more to the dream, she didn't remember.

She rolled over. Another bird's call interrupted from outside, a raven's throaty laugh this time. A moment later and a second raven answered. A third from the opposite direction, closer toward the sea.

Ravens? Hunting near the shore? She and Allanaq had seen other birds—auklets fishing around their umiak, petrels and cormorants in crowded rookeries, murres skimming the water. Eagles and gulls, but few ravens, not since they'd left the Long Coast.

Elik reached over, expecting to waken Allanaq. Instead, her hand fell on empty bed skins. Abruptly, she sat up, Allanaq was gone. His clothes, boots, the blankets, all empty.

She made a quick cutting motion in the air, slicing the dream away. She felt beneath the skins on his side of the tent. They were cold as the ground; she couldn't guess how long he'd been gone.

Was he angry again? She'd hoped he might wake up feeling better, that the whale and sleep might have brightened his fears.

Unless she'd cried aloud, he couldn't have known she was dreaming. Another shaman might have power like that, to see inside a person's dream, but Allanaq was not the kind of man to go looking into dreams. He shunned such things.

She lifted the draped end of the flap. Outside, the summer sun was high over the sea and the tide was in, much closer than she and Allanaq had guessed last night. Waves rolled, then broke just short of the curving tangle of weeds, broken shells, and tiny rocks.

A raven strutted into view and she turned to follow, expecting to see Allanaq standing over the whale, peeling back layers of black-skinned fat. Ravens and gulls would be lining up behind him, impatient for a share.

A motion caught her eye—a fourth raven, then another, a full hand's count. One of the ravens sat quietly on the boat, another stood atop the tripod she'd erected. But she didn't see Allanaq. Anxiously, she jumped to her feet, then stood a moment, confused.

There was no Allanaq and no sign of the beluga.

Where the whale had been tied, the only thing remaining was the one slab of meat she'd hung to dry.

The world had shifted. There was still the sea, the salt wind, the hungry birds. But not the beach.

What had been a long, inclined slope the night

before had transformed itself to a strip of grey land.
There'd been tide pools moving back to lagoons to
the west and east. They were flooded now. Gone.
All but their boat and the buried limb where they'd
tied the whale. That was there. But no whale. No
whale and no sign that the fault was anything but
theirs.

Not theirs—hers. Her fault. She was the one who
called herself a shaman, and she hadn't even guessed
the wind might steal the whale. Allanaq would blame
her, whether he said so or not. The relief, the joy they
both had shared when they hauled the beluga to
shore, it was gone now, worse than if it had never
been.

Her throat tightened. She searched the beach for a
hint of birds scavenging for meat, or the slender curve
of white—it should have been there still, tethered in a
stiff line to the log.

She squinted past the breaking waves. Allanaq
would have chased the whale if it was possible. If
the knots had loosened, he'd have raced into the
water. He'd have hauled the whale back. Unless their
lines had snapped and there was nothing left to
grab.

Carefully, she retraced the short distance from the
tent to the buried log. She circled till she found a
shadow, a slight depression marking Allanaq's footprints. She let out her breath. He was alive. The whale
was gone but their boat was still here. He couldn't be
angry enough to desert her, could he?

He'd crossed in front of the umiak. And there—heel
marks wherever there was sand between the rocks to
show a print. He'd gone walking. No—the stride was

too long for a walk. He'd gone running after the beluga. It had to be.

Which meant her dream had been no dream at all. A storm must have risen during the night. Allanaq would have woken, shouted for her to come. The waves must have lifted the beluga. There was no other way it could have escaped, unless it had turned itself into a wolf and run off. There were stories of how white whales did that, changed into wolves so they could hunt awhile on land.

A wind rose off the sea and chilled her arms. Her leggings, parka, and boots were inside the tent, and without the boots she wouldn't go far. But which way should she go? Or should she wait?

The tide was still going out; these newest waves no longer reached so near the boat. The sky looked as if waiting to rain.

She should at least roll their bedding so the furs wouldn't soak up groundwater. Then gather driftwood for a smudge fire to dry the whale meat. If there was any left to dry.

Elik pulled out her leggings and started to dress outside, where it was easier to stand.

It was then, when her back was turned and she stopped to wipe the sand from her feet, that she felt it. A change. Two of the ravens flew off. The sea gulls squawked louder than before.

She turned, expecting to find Allanaq, but no one was there. She clutched her sealskin boots against her breasts, stared along the shore.

She was making herself nervous and she knew it, jumpy and afraid. Find some work, she told herself. That would be better. She needed to feel something more solid in her hands then this feather-light waiting. This hollowness inside.

She finished dressing, then retied her braids. She started for the boat again to check whether the stitch holes needed greasing. Maybe the bottom had dragged on barnacles? Maybe there was a weak point she could patch?

She stepped around a hummock of grass and saw it—a shadow gliding to the side, nearly behind her. Something dark more than quick.

She turned, but nothing was there.

Could it be caribou? Was there a herd that ranged out here? They hadn't traveled so far north that all the world had changed. And it wasn't Allanaq. He'd have followed the sea, not turned inland. She stood quietly.

There was one spot along the height of the beach ridge—she'd seen it earlier—where the grass seemed flattened. A path trampled from the other side.

As she watched, a man rose up from behind the ridge where no one had been before. He stood with his hands at his sides, watching her. He wasn't even trying to hide.

Elik lifted her hand to her throat, then just as quickly lowered it, trying not to panic.

How long had he been watching? From when she crawled naked out of the tent? Before that—in her sleep?

Her thoughts raced: there was a harpoon inside the boat—unless Allanaq had taken it. But the man could reach her first. He didn't look so old he couldn't catch her.

Her woman's knife—where was that?

All her life she'd heard stories of women being stolen. Sometimes kept, sometimes murdered. And there were other stories too—of men killed in hunting accidents, and sometimes their starving bones came back to life. They turned into demons, *tunraqs,* they were called. They hid on beaches. Waited for human prey. What if this man was one of those?

Elik swallowed, forced herself to act calmly. Did he think she was alone? A woman without a man?

He started toward her, not rushing, but not slowly either. A little stiffly, as if he'd hidden something in his sleeve. A knife? Or a bow, maybe, slung lengthwise behind his head? Last night, she had thought the beach was picked too clean of driftwood. Why hadn't she shown Allanaq?

She started walking—back to the tent. It was better to have her hands busy, reach a knife in case she had to run. . . . She rolled aside a corner rock that weighed the tent skin, started pulling it down.

If she ran and he caught her, she would fight back. She would. She'd killed a man before. Killed him and burned his bones so he'd be dead forever. He had been one of the Forest People, one of a group who had come after Allanaq. Except, Allanaq reached them first. Their one guard who had fallen asleep—Allanaq killed him with an arrow. The second man, wrestling with knives. It was when the third one sneaked up on Allanaq's back that she'd killed him, with a lance that time.

Where was Allanaq's lance? In the umiak?

"*Waqaa.*"

Elik clasped her hands to stop the shaking. What had he said? *Waqaa?* Was that a word?

She turned to face him—but slowly, stealing a glance first to his hands. They were empty, as was his belt, his boot tops where a sharp flint could be hidden.

"*Waqaa.*" He said it again, this time bobbing his head. He wasn't Real People, she saw that at once. But not Forest People either. Not like that man she'd killed. What he was, was some kind of fool, walking up on a stranger's camp without first learning who they were. Without waiting in the distance till he was welcomed.

The man's face was boxlike, with a chin that disappeared into the straight lines of his jaw. His skin was tallow colored, like a blade of last year's dried grass, darker than hers. Darker than Allanaq's too, though the corner fold of his eyes might be the same. She couldn't guess his age—younger than Grey Owl, older than Allanaq? And his face—it was covered everywhere in tattoos.

Cheek lines and nose lines, lines moving up from each corner of his mouth. Not the straight lines the women of the Real People wore below their chins, but more like Allanaq than any other man she knew. And yet . . . not exactly the same.

And no labrets. But that in itself said little about the kind of man he was. She had to remember—Allanaq had worn none when her uncle first found him.

She looked to his hands—they were as cut and worn and callused as anyone's but a child's would be. One finger was missing, the stump long since healed.

With a large, obvious motion, Elik glanced along the beach, wanting him to understand she wasn't alone. There was a husband. A man would be returning soon.

The next time she turned, he was standing at their

umiak, bent over at the waist, leaning wide to study the bow piece. He ran his hand over the ownership marks Allanaq had painted on the hull, pausing, tracing the design. Then he walked along the frame, staring, as if his eyes could see inside their packs.

Moving slowly, Elik pulled out one of Allanaq's bent-wood boxes. Maybe the man wanted to trade. She would give him one of Allanaq's harpoon points, and maybe he would go away.

She opened the lidded box and held it out. The man fingered through them, then picked out a well-made socket piece with teeth that Allanaq had carved to look like a polar bear. He slipped it away somewhere inside his parka. He pointed to her cooking pot.

The man was hungry, that was all. Hunger would take the most respectful of men and change them into something so impolite, they walked up on a woman alone, asked for food before it was offered. She motioned at her mouth.

The man smiled.

"I'm sorry there isn't more," she said. She wanted her apology to sound sincere, not afraid. She didn't want to show fear. And now that she thought about it, there was a sense to it.

If a man wasn't looking for a fight, wasn't it safer to wait for a husband to leave? It might not be polite, but if it was only food he wanted . . . ?

"My husband went hunting," Elik said loudly. "He will be back soon." She took down the strip of back meat they'd cut last night, a good piece with fat attached. She lay it down on a scrap of sealskin, cut it into chunks. She scooped the chunks into an empty bowl—not Allanaq's and not hers, of course. She set the bowl on the ground before him, as if he were an honored guest.

The man squatted on his haunches, picked out a bite, and pushed it into his mouth. His stomach was noisy, talking to the food before he swallowed it. Politely, she turned aside while he ate, but she could feel his eyes, glancing over the bowl's rim to the boat again. The meat they'd left to dry. The tent. The shore.

He emptied the bowl, wiped the grease from his mouth, not like a demon but the same as any man would do. He rose, offered a tick of a smile, then helped himself to looking through the boat again.

Now, *this* she did not understand. A trader would never be so forward as to go pawing through someone else's belongings. What was he doing, counting out the numbers of seal pokes inside? How much oil they'd brought? How much food? The bearded sealskins that covered the boat were white and new. She wished they were older, patched and thin so this man wouldn't think she was rich.

His own clothes looked poor—the leggings cut from a brown and white skin—dog, perhaps. She couldn't be certain. The parka was belted at the waist and straight-hemmed—the same as any man. But even the patches were worn. Which meant that this stranger, whoever he was, lived without benefit of a woman's hands. No wife or her relations, no mother, sister or daughter to care for his clothes.

A man alone, living or traveling without a woman— that wasn't someone she could trust.

"My husband is hunting," she said.

The man didn't answer.

"We found a whale. *Cetuaq*—white whale." She pointed at the meat, repeated the word in case he hadn't understood. He watched her lips move. "My husband brought it in," she said more loudly. "Last night."

The man motioned to the boat, the tent, the sea. "Has a name?" he asked.

"Name?" Elik nodded her relief. The word sounded like something Allanaq might have said. "Allanaq. My husband tied it off, the whale," she pointed. "But the wind rose. While we slept. From the sea, it blew in from the north. A male north wind. It . . ."

"Allanaq?" the man looked to the markings on the boat, then shook his head as if she had said something wrong. "What did you do?" he asked.

"Do?"

"To disrespect the whale, cause it to run away."

Elik pulled back in surprise. "Nothing—I did nothing wrong. It was my song that helped to calm it!"

The man wrinkled his nose in disapproval. "You are a proud woman to speak so loud."

Elik lowered her gaze, tried settling her thoughts. She'd spoken carelessly; the man was right. He'd done nothing so wrong that she should forget her manners.

Above them, the sun peered from behind a trailing cloud. It glimmered off the water's surface and caught Elik's eye. She turned, scanned the length of the sloping beach.

This time she saw something: a slight line of a man, distant still, but definitely following back along the darker tide line. It was too far to discern Allanaq's expression, but the sun outlined his head and shoulders, his arms lifted behind. Elik leapt forward.

The whale! He was towing the whale, playing the line so it slacked, then tightened in time with the tide, floating rather than dragging its weight home.

Elik raised her arm in greeting but the stranger was already ahead of her, stumbling on rocky gravel, splashing through water high as his boot tops. By the time Elik reached them, the two men were working together, maneuvering the long carcass in toward the beach.

She jumped in below Allanaq, grabbing hold of the line nearest the whale and pulling and tugging along with them. The first moment there was a chance, she leaned back toward Allanaq. "I don't know who he is," she whispered.

Allanaq worked to keep his footing. He bowed his weight into the line as if he hadn't heard. It wasn't till a large wave broke over their knees, loud enough to hide his voice, that he spoke. "You be quiet," he warned. He threw a glance toward the man holding fast to the line above them. "Remember where you are, away from home."

Elik lowered her gaze but Allanaq was right. It was better to keep quiet, wait till they understood who this man was, what he wanted.

Hand over hand, the three of them hauled on the towline, first in the water, then edging their way up to higher land. They played out the weight, waiting on each wave to help lift the bulk of the whale's head, its body and tail. And then finally, as Elik raced to kick the sharpest rocks away from its path, they heaved the full length of the beluga up and out of the sea.

By the time the whale was beached and safely tied, Allanaq knew who the stranger was.

They stood with the whale between them now. Allanaq's gaze raced from the man's heavily tattooed face to the patches on his clothing, to the beach ridge where other hunters might be waiting up behind. Finally, his mouth turned up in a smile. "Skinner," he said.

Elik looked at her husband in surprise.

The man squinted harder at Allanaq. "Who are you?"

"You don't know?"

"I knew a man who looked like you. But he had no holes in his chin. And besides, he is dead."

Allanaq grit his teeth, and Elik glanced from the stranger back to her husband. Allanaq had spoken, she had just seen his lips move the same as they always did, but his voice sounded different. Or perhaps it wasn't his voice, but the words, the way he spoke them, faster, more like this other man's, less like his own.

"He's not dead. I lived."

"Where is your father?"

Allanaq looked again to the ridge line where a row of tall beach grass leaned sideways into the wind. Were other people there? Was that a weapon someone lifted too high? Forgot to hide?

He waited till he was sure it was only the wind, the grass and nothing more. He turned back to Skinner. "My father is dead."

Skinner eyed Allanaq more closely. Anyone could see the one tent they had erected was only large enough for two people. And in the boat, there were only two paddles, a double-ended spare was lashed far-ther down, out of reach. "How do I know you are alive?" he asked, "And not a demon who stole Anguta's food and now wants more?"

"Would a demon work so hard for whale meat? Would a demon travel in a skin-covered boat or . . ." Allanaq followed Skinner's gaze as it moved from the seal pokes filled with oil to Elik, to her clean, shining hair, the wealth of stitchwork on her parka. He smiled. "Would a woman share a tent with a demon?"

"Women crawl into places a man would never think. Besides," Skinner's gaze slid along Elik's waist to the outline of her hips. "What would I know of women?"

"Where is your own wife, Little-Creek?"

Surprised, the man lifted one brow. "You know her name?"

"She drew my first tattoos, when I was a boy. That would have been the years when you were . . . where? On the river near the Paatitaaq village?"

"Is he Seal People?" Elik asked, but neither man answered.

"No—I remember, after that she went up to the Rabbit Hills to live with relatives. It must have been the Kuugzuaag village?"

"My wife," Skinner said, and he watched Allanaq carefully, "is married now with another man. Tell me something I don't know. Who is this?" he nodded toward Elik.

"This is my wife."

"But I watched her last night, when you brought in the whale. Anguta would never have allowed Qajak to keep a woman who paid so little respect to a whale. A woman who brags," he added.

Qajak? Elik leaned forward, still trying to follow the quick turn of words. She knew Allanaq's father's name. Anguta. She was certain of that. But who was Qajak? And what had this man—Skinner, that was his name—what had he just said? "You were watching since last night?" she asked. "You hid while we were working?"

Allanaq hushed her and Elik looked, caught his frown. Whatever else was true, the man's quick words already troubled him. "But she gave the whale fresh water," Allanaq said. "She did do that."

Skinner cocked his head and watched the younger man as if he was the one who wasn't certain of the words. "What is she?" he asked. "She talks like a child, hard to understand."

Allanaq shuffled uncomfortably. "She's Real People."

"Seal People are also real." Skinner said, and he chuckled at his own joke, then: "How do you know she's human?" he asked, and he watched for Allanaq's reaction. "How do you know she's not some animal in a woman's form?"

"They took me in," Allanaq tried to explain. "Her uncle saved my life."

"Ah, so Qajak took on obligations to feed a poor man's niece?"

Elik bristled; those words she understood. She waited for Allanaq to tell the proud story of how they had waited more than a winter to live as husband and wife. Until after Malluar allowed her first attempts as a shaman. After Allanaq brought home a whale, and killed the Forest People, and tried to find her brother.

Except he didn't say those things. He didn't say anything she wanted to hear. Instead, he slumped down against the umiak, gathered his knees against his chest. His eyes, hands, everything about him looked like a young boy, dejected, unable to find his bearings on the endless, rolling sea.

And the name—Qajak—she remembered now. That was Allanaq's name from his first home. Among her Real People he would have been Kayak, the same word as the boat, except that her uncle had decided to name him for his own son who had died.

This man with the hungry mouth, Skinner? Was he some kind of relative?

"It is possible," Skinner said, and his voice grew bolder the more he saw how Allanaq's shrank. "I'm not a shaman to understand these things, but that dead whale—" again he watched Allanaq's reaction. "That whale could have brought the wind. It could have grown angry at a woman's boldness, decided it wanted to leave."

Allanaq lifted his hands, dropped them. "There are so many things I've forgotten, and failed to do. What else could we have done?"

The man considered the question. Even with the whale and the storm, the small camp showed the care of a woman's hand. "Was she cutting anything when you hunted?" he suggested. "Or sewing? The whale feels the pricks of a woman's needle as surely as it feels a hunter's harpoon. It would swim away."

"No. She was with me in the boat."

"In the boat?" Skinner raised his voice. "You allowed a woman in the boat while you hunted? A wife belongs in the house, as quiet as the whale's soul sits inside its body. The wife should move slowly and sing for the whale to come."

"She did that. She sang." Allanaq looked hopefully toward Elik. "She could do more. She is not afraid."

"More?" Skinner looked to the whale. Its outer skin was battered from being dragged and scraped over rocks. Pale strands of flesh hung rudely from the wound. He pulled thoughtfully on his chin, then shook his head in a large gesture showing his dismay.

"We gave it fresh water, for its thirst," Allanaq said.

"Water you give to a seal. To a whale you give more."

"Is it too late?"

"Not yet," Skinner said. "You must take the hunters' ritual meal first. Did you do that?"

"A little?"

"You and I must kneel by the whale. You, as the successful hunter, on the right. It was not my harpoon that took it, so I belong here, on the side."

Allanaq raised his knife, but Skinner nudged his hand closer to where the liver would be. "Not there, you need to make it smaller."

Allanaq nodded, moved his blade. He marked out two cuts in the outer skin, bit deeper with his stone knife, then cut the lines again. He peeled back the layer, then pulled out the liver and stretched it, blubber and all, along a flat length of driftwood Elik found. He lifted his knife to cut, but Skinner stopped him again.

"The wound." Skinner pointed toward the largest gash.

"Did I forget something?"

"You need to care for the wound first. Close it with a plug, not to waste the blood."

Elik coughed behind her hand. Politely, she waited

till Allanaq looked her way. "Isn't it late to worry about wasting blood?"

"Late?" Skinner looked only at Allanaq as he spoke. "How can it be late to respect the dead? Have you no fear of shaming the whale, risking its anger?"

"If the whale was angry," Elik reasoned, "then it would have been angry yesterday. Not today when the blood's already thick and we can easily—"

"Not easily," Skinner rested his hand on Allanaq's knee and spoke gently, as if to a child. "You have been gone a long time. You have forgotten—nothing is easy where a whale's spirit is concerned. If you hope for another to come to you, ever again, the only important thing is to be careful. Now, have you plugs to close the wound?" Allanaq nodded. "What kind? Ivory, or antler?"

"Both."

"Good. The whale would want your best. But first, tell your wife to wait over there." He waved toward the tent.

Allanaq turned to Elik, but she had already risen, already heard enough to know she didn't trust this man. Seal People or not, his words were too sweet, his voice too high and deceptive. Like the tattoos circling his cheeks and eyes, so many she couldn't figure which way his thoughts were flowing.

Skinner flipped through the ivory and antler pieces Allanaq spread before him, not only wound plugs but polished animal figures carved into tools, handles, figures of all kinds. There were seal and walrus faces on drag handles, polar bears on harpoon sockets, female figures with scratch lines to show their genitals inside their bodies, male figures with their penises out.

Skinner selected one, the figure of a walrus with the spine and ribs showing, circles on the hips to show where the soul moved in and out. He turned the piece about, admiring its smoothness, the steady work in its engraved lines, but he didn't keep it; he set it carefully back beside the others. "So," he said. "You are telling the truth. No one but Qajak carved so well. These are the eye-dots your father taught you to carve. The joint-marks only a man of the Seal People would take the care to make. It must be the spirits have brought us together, and you see how lucky you are to be found by a relative, that I wasn't someone else."

Allanaq picked up the walrus, looked at it in his hand.

"I can only guess your thoughts," Skinner said, "the joy you must feel being with a relative again?"

Allanaq didn't answer. He returned the walrus to its box, took up his knife, and sliced the thick slab of liver into two equal strips. From that he cut squares, two large ritual pieces. "Share with me this meat," he started, but Skinner lifted his hand in protest.

"No, no. Too much. The hunter's meal belongs to the first harpooner," he said. "I was not in the boat. . . ."

"You didn't have to be. The whale would be gone if you had not been here to help. Not only with your hands, but your kind words."

"Well, perhaps. That is true. . . ."

"No, not perhaps," Allanaq said sincerely. "I am honored to share with a man, a relative. It's a good day when I have found this beach." He finished slicing the rest into small thankful pieces, asking the whale to forgive him, a poor hunter who would starve but for its gift of meat. He pushed the chunks toward Skinner.

Skinner plucked one, then leaned back, savoring the raw taste. Allanaq also chewed. When he was done, he neatly cleaned his knife with sand. Skinner rose and paced off the length of the whale's carcass. "It's a good size," he called. "Longer than two large men."

Allanaq beamed with gratitude.

"I could start the butchering here, perhaps. By the flipper?" Skinner pulled a knife from inside his sleeve. He held it, waiting for Allanaq's permission to help.

Elik leaned forward. She'd known the man had a knife, she'd guessed from the start, the way he rubbed his arm when he first walked up on her, hinting at the threat.

Skinner turned but not quickly; he was no agile young man. The sun caught the edge of the flint: it was a bifaced blade in a good antler handle. But when she saw the point she had to cover her mouth not to laugh. It was nicked, misshapen. And if the blade was as dull as it was chipped, it was no wonder he'd kept it hidden.

Curious, she walked nearer, but Allanaq's hand was suddenly on her shoulder. "Stand back," he said sharply. "Do you want something else to go wrong? And mind you, be quiet."

"But his knife . . ."

"What? Is there something wrong with a man using his knife? The man is a relative. Do you want to shame me now? Was I ever anything but polite among your people?"

Elik lowered her eyes. Allanaq was right. Skinner had done nothing wrong. He had not threatened or stolen. He had not tried to grab her before Allanaq returned. And here he was now, doing nothing more harmful than swatting mosquitoes and brushing flies away from the meat. She hoped he had not heard her unkind words.

While Allanaq started a slit from the chest down to the whale's anus, she watched, only enough to satisfy her curiosity that the cut Allanaq made with Skinner was no different than her father or uncle would have done.

She hauled up water from the shallows, rinsed out the bloodied cavity after the intestines and organs were removed and set aside. In the end, of course, they hadn't bothered with the wound plugs—Skinner had only wanted to examine Allanaq's carvings more closely. They turned the whale on its belly, reaching for the underside, then laying out slabs of meat marked off by the size of Allanaq's forearms.

After that they divided the work, the men first cutting and dragging away the heaviest sections, upper quarters first on the height of the back, down toward the tail. Each time they were done with a slab, Elik used her curved woman's knife to cut it into smaller chunks. The white skin she kept attached to the pink meat, so it would hang from the makeshift rack and dry in the wind. The yellow, fatty blubber she trimmed, then set aside so that later it would be rendered into oil.

They cut the flippers after the back, Allanaq repeating the names of each share after Skinner, as carefully as if he were learning the verses to a sacred song. *Taliguq*, he said. The flippers. *Qimigluich*, the back and sides.

Elik threw more water over the sections that had picked up sand, then piled them, first in a mound out of the sun's way, then moving the piles to the water's edge to wash.

She freed the stomach and set it aside to empty; later she would make it into a watertight container. And the intestines also, she would clean them and dry them, and later cut them into strips for a waterproof parka, for a window piece, a drum head. Most of the organs the men would eat raw, after she scraped them and cleaned the insides. The tongue. The brain. The heart. Both the fore flippers would also be eaten raw, and the hind flippers. The tough, white skin would later be made into boot soles, and lines.

The butchering went on for the better part of the day, and through all but the heaviest work, Skinner kept up a constant chatter. He named the names of people Elik had never heard of, but Allanaq certainly listened as if he had.

Hunters and wives, elders and their stories, Skinner entranced Allanaq with news of which boy had caught his first seal, whose little girl had become a woman and celebrated the first berries of the season, her first parka, her first stitched pair of boots. Skinner laughed and talked, and as much as he talked, that was how much Allanaq lapped up his words.

Elik kept politely quiet, listening whenever her own work brought her near the men. And the more she heard, the more she grew used to the words. The rushing sounds slowed and grew clear. Most she understood, and those she couldn't, she guessed from the pattern of talk.

Something in the man's darting gaze reminded her of her own father Chevak, the way he used to enter a house counting first: weapons, women, pelts, and food. Only when his stomach was full did he remember to be polite. Surely, this man with his broken knife could be no worse. Besides, Elik reminded herself, she wasn't her mother, having to worry over the poor luck of her husband's catch, when here they had a rack of meat and rich yellow fat to fill their boat.

Finally, most of the butchering was done. Skinner stretched his neck and shoulders and pointed inland, the way he'd come. He murmured something about returning to his camp for a better knife, and then he disappeared over the beach ridge.

Elik waited only till she was sure the wind wouldn't carry her voice in case he had stopped, hid or listened. She turned to Allanaq. "Who is he?"

"A cousin." He sounded annoyed, as if she should have known.

"But what kind? Mother's brother's son?"

"No. More distant."

"How much more?"

"Mostly, when I was young, he lived in another village." Allanaq shrugged, to show it made no difference. "But he is Seal People, I promise that. . . . And more important, he's closer to my relatives than to Red Fox's."

"What does his name mean?"

"Only what it sounds like. I don't remember where it started, from an aunt, or somewhere. He has other names too, but this one is his oldest. We're lucky we found him. He wants to help. It was more dangerous for him to have found me than the other way around. Maybe it was good that the beluga swam away. Maybe, the same way we thought the seal had given us the whale, this was the whale's way of summoning Skinner. Else we might have left without finding him."

"I think this man is hungry," Elik said, "and that's all. Look at his clothes, how old they are. And there's no people here. No one but him."

Allanaq wasn't sure he agreed. "What are you saying?"

"I don't know." Elik grew uncertain. "Just—what do you know of this man, truly?"

Allanaq looked to the trampled grass where Skinner had disappeared. He seemed to weigh the question, more so than Elik expected. Finally: "We didn't hunt together," he admitted. "But everyone knew his wife. She was a good woman."

"Was?"

"Is. Skinner says she's married now, with another man."

"Do we need him?"

"We need his eyes. His arm that can hold a knife."

"He wanted you to let him help. That way he could say he earned a share. That was all he was after. He needs our food. He's starving."

"We need his help and we can feed him, there's enough for all."

"This time, but what about next? What will he ask for?"

"He's a relative. You don't barter with relatives. You share." Allanaq said, then more firmly: "Have you forgotten—how dead I would be if Grey Owl had spoken the way you do, rather than offering kindness. I would be dead, and you would be married to an old man, whatever man your father would have given you to." Allanaq started to leave.

"I would have run away. You know that."

Allanaq reeled about. His face reddened with anger. "This man is the son of my mother's cousin. He was married with my father's brother's niece since before they were grown. We'll finish cutting the whale shares, the same as Drummer and I would have done. You will serve food, the same as if Skinner had always been my hunting partner. Now go, start a hole for an ice cellar for the meat. Do something more useful than complain."

In a dark mood, Elik picked up the caribou shoulder blade they had brought in the boat for a shovel. She starting along the beach ridge, searching above the sand. Here and there, she turned over a rock, a clump of moss, but she had no heart for digging and she gave it up the instant she realized Skinner had returned.

Quietly, she threaded her way back, coming up behind the boat. She picked up the whale back sinew she had separated out, brought it closer, and sat down with her women's knife to scrape it clean. The men were speaking in hushed voices. She didn't want to miss their words.

If Skinner had meant to bring back a better knife, Elik couldn't see it. What she did notice were his boots: he'd tied a scrap of sealskin around the soles, fastening it with a knot. A few fresh strands of grass padding pushed through a hole in the stitches.

She lowered her gaze, not wanting his poverty to embarrass him. These looked like an old pair of winter boots, not a waterproof pair for spring. His feet must have gotten wet earlier in the day, but he'd had no second pair to change into. Surely, no woman provided with skins would allow her husband to go about with damp, cold feet.

If there was a woman at this camp of his? If there even was a camp? He was a poor man with hunger dripping from his tongue. She wondered why Allanaq didn't see that.

The two of them were resting now, sitting cross-legged below the boat, their parkas hanging on a stick below them. As Elik watched, Allanaq offered Skinner portions of the raw *muktuk*, the rich outer skin with a layer of yellow fat.

An anger rose in the back of her throat, not because she didn't want to share, but because of the way Skinner talked, as if he was weaving a magic over her husband. But why, if it worked so well on Allanaq, did it leave her untouched?

Unless it wasn't magic at all, only the words Allanaq had wanted so badly to hear.

The next moment, as if her thoughts betrayed her, Allanaq glanced her way. She lowered her head, concentrated on the sinew before she cut it all to pieces. But she'd seen his face; it was guarded, a little unsure. Skinner was saying things about her. She was certain.

She set the sinew in water to soak; then with small, quiet steps she walked over, pulled Allanaq's parka from the driftwood pole where he'd left it, his parka and Skinner's also. She found her sewing kit and sat to work, close enough so she could hear the men, and with luck, be forgotten.

Skinner's parka had a long hole along the seam on one side. She found that hole, then a tear along the back. Like his boots, the skins were aging. The hairs were brittle, snapping off even as she held the garment in her lap.

How long had he worn the same clothes, she wondered? Two winters? Brittle skins would do him little good much longer. She sewed Allanaq a new parka each year. A heavy, doubled-layered suit of caribou-skin clothes for winter, lighter skins that he wore with the fur turned out for summer.

She threaded her bone needle with a length of sinew, started a stitch.

"You haven't fared poorly," she heard Skinner say. "You are strong enough to survive the sea. Lucky enough to have a wife. And the boat. Trade goods. And now, plenty of whale meat."

Allanaq glowed with the compliment. "Tell me," he asked. "How did you know I wasn't an enemy?"

Skinner smiled. "It was your boat, the way it's built wide, not like a Seal People's umiak. Except there were your markings, they made me wonder."

"The ownership marks," Allanaq smiled. "No one knew I painted them part Seal, part Real People. That way, I hoped, whoever I found would recognize something."

"Which was the reason I waited. Exactly the reason," Skinner said. "Till morning. A strange boat lands upon my beach, and I didn't want you to think I was stealing your meat. I didn't like to fight a man I didn't know. So I held back."

Elik watched as Skinner chewed on the thick *muktuk*. The instant his mouth stopped moving, Allanaq passed him another, larger than the first, and then fresh water after that.

She didn't like the look of his mouth, the way it

seemed tight without labrets. Too thin, too open. And reckless, as if he didn't know enough to care what watchful spirits might think. She lowered her gaze again, preferring to listen, not to look.

"It's good to see that Anguta's son hasn't come back a child," Skinner said. "I've heard of that—men who are lost on the ice and they come home, they don't remember who their relatives are. They have to be taught to do things all over again. Not you . . ." Skinner hesitated, " . . . but maybe your wife?"

"What do you mean?"

"I'm sure it's because she's a stranger. Not Seal People. It's too bad she doesn't know how to watch her manners more. But then, at least she's fat. She looks healthy. Except," Skinner paused again, this time pointing to his face with a circling motion. "I was wondering. Is she ugly, or is that the way—?"

"She is only different."

Elik stole a glance to Allanaq. He sat with his hands in his lap, his eyes staring apologetically toward the ground.

"Her face is naked with so few tattoos," Skinner said. "What is she? A child?"

Allanaq moistened his lips, looked to the sea.

"What kind of people make only three lines on a woman's chin? What is that?" Skinner tapped Allanaq's arm to get his attention.

"That is how they do that."

"They?"

"Her people. Her family. When I came," Allanaq stumbled, "I looked just as different to them. People said my clothing was dog-clothing. They dried fish-skins, wore them for clothes in the summer. They

called me dog. But they were the ones wearing fish-
skins."

"Fish?" Skinner wrinkled his nose. "Still, you sleep
with her?"

"We are married."

"But, I mean—does she lie down for you? You have
children?"

"No. No children." Allanaq's voice sounded flat and
tired.

"Is she barren?"

"She is under restrictions. We have no relations."

"Ah . . ." Skinner twisted around to have a look; Elik
yanked at her stitch. "She did something wrong?"

"No. It wasn't that. Someone was watching her, too
close."

"Someone tried to kill her?"

No, Allanaq shook his head. Then, thankfully, just
as Elik thought she could bear no more, he picked
himself up from the gravel beach, turned from
Skinner's prying.

"I should find a place to bury a few of the whale
bones," he said, and he glanced along the height of the
beach. "There is a quiet place somewhere? Where dogs
wouldn't go? I should say my thanks, and give this
whale its peace."

Elik woke early the next day, ahead of both men. With
the bone shovel in hand, she walked along the beach
ridge, searching for the stand of rye grass where yesterday she had found a likely place to dig. They would
need an underground pit-cache that stayed frozen,
something that wouldn't fill up with rain or runoff.

Large enough so whatever whale meat they left behind would stay cold and safe from dogs and wolves until they returned.

She walked with her hood up, her eyes tearing in the wind. She and Allanaq would be staying on this beach four days more, not for the work, but out of respect—the same as if a person had died. Four days if the death belonged to a man, five for a woman. The whale's soul would be treated no differently than a human's.

And for four days, there was still much work to do: chipping a pit in frozen ground, lining it with grass. Rearranging their gear so their seal pokes could be filled with the whale fat.

Elik found a spot, well hidden in the grass. She marked it by lining it up with a hill and a rocky outcropping, farther inland. She started the digging, this first time going only as far as the ice allowed. The sun and air would help it thaw, and later she would come back and build a fire inside, then dig out the muck, then dig again.

The men were still asleep when she returned to the camp. She gathered up a load of driftwood and built a small fire using chunks of blubber to help the damp wood catch.

Finally they woke, and climbed from their separate sleeping places almost at the same time. Together, they walked to the shore to piss. They lifted their hands to greet the day.

By the time they were seated at her fire, they were laughing and talking as if they were the closest of brothers.

" . . . And they hunt seals," Allanaq was saying, "but

they like to catch them with nets as if they were fish. And few of the men know enough to check the currents with a bit of ice floating in an open crack."

"And the seals come that way? They catch enough to eat?"

Allanaq nodded. "Now, tell me again," he asked. "What else has changed since I've been gone?"

"I can't think of everything at once," Skinner laughed. "Ask me a small question, so I know where to start."

"The houses? Is anyone living in my house?"

"The women still cook," Skinner laughed. "The men still sleep in the *qasgi*."

Elik felt the man's gaze on the back of her head, but she refused to turn, to let him enjoy her discomfort. She pierced the whale's wrinkled skin with a knife, set it in a bowl in front of Skinner first. And though she was careful not to lift her eyes, and to sit back a distance while she ate her own meal of dried fish, she was more than aware of that other hunger in his mouth, the way he stared markedly at her hips and legs as she squatted. As she moved. As she worked.

He reminded her of her sister's old warning: not to look too busy or a man would think you were flirting. Not to offer food, or he would think you were offering yourself.

But she was already married. How could he think she would be so forward, with her husband sitting beside them?

If Allanaq was aware of the way Skinner watched her, she couldn't tell. She moved to the far side of the hearth and took out her sewing and she listened, as much as she was able.

It was on the fourth day that Skinner tried to touch her, not lewdly, only on her hand, but it made her jump. She had served him from a dipper carved of musk-ox horn. The dipper had drawn his attention, or so she thought, until his hand slowed and his fingers stroked their way over hers.

She pulled back, but the touch was unmistakable. The water spilled. Allanaq glowered, and awkwardly she offered a second drink. This time Skinner merely smiled as he took the spoon. He wiped his mouth and admired the smooth handle before passing it back.

"It's good to travel with a woman," he said, watching as Elik slid purposefully closer to Allanaq. "It's the woman who lifts her bowl to the sky, asking for a good year. And when the Man Who Lives in the Moon looks down deciding what to send, it's the woman he sees first."

"She keeps her own bowl," Allanaq said, but he had missed Skinner's intent. "And she cooks her food in her own pot. If she wants any children to live, she has to eat separately."

"That's only polite," Skinner said. "But you didn't tell me she was wealthy. Is that musk-ox?"

Gently, Allanaq touched her sleeve. "She eats no fresh meat," he said to Skinner, "because of the children who died."

"Children?"

"Twins. Both born dead."

"Ahh." Skinner nodded to show he understood.

"It was last winter," Allanaq said, and his discomfort was obvious. "It doesn't matter now. Now, I need to think to the next winter. I need to make plans."

Skinner plucked another bite of whale meat from the bowl. "Tell me again how it was when you left."

"It was late summer."

"That was when your trouble started?"

"My trouble started long before—the time of Red Fox's whale vision. That was the year of the hard famine. Two children died. And Sheshalik's wife. One Pot's only son disappeared on the ice. It was a year of bad luck that only broke when Red Fox tranced and found the bowhead. My father found none."

"Maybe," Skinner suggested, "maybe it's better if you don't go back just now."

"No!" Allanaq spoke loudly. "There is no choice."

Skinner pursed his lips. "This is no small deed. All Red Fox has to do is convince people you are a ghost."

Elik whispered into Allanaq's ear: "Ask him how he came to be here?"

"What does she say?" Skinner spoke out first, then laughed when Allanaq repeated the question. "I am here," Skinner said, "because your husband's father was not the only man Red Fox didn't like to have about."

Elik was surprised. "He tried to kill you too?"

"He might have, but I gave him no chance. I left first because I wanted to stay alive. Do you see my wife anywhere?" He held up the hem of his parka, as if to show how sorry he had become. "Do you think a man would choose to live alone? Without benefit of a wife's help?" He glanced to Elik. "Even a wife who is a nuisance?"

"But why did he try to kill you?"

"He was jealous. All shaman are jealous, just as—"

Allanaq wasn't interested in Skinner's banter. "Who

else would side with me over Red Fox? Who else is gone?"

"No one. But even among our own cousins, not everyone would agree to Red Fox's death. Some might help, if only by keeping their doors closed. But others would warn him. They all fear him." Skinner glanced at Allanaq out of the corner of his eye. "Of all the people he tried to kill, only you survived."

"Not you."

Skinner made a noise in the back of his throat. "I am not Anguta's son. You are. People would listen to you."

Quietly, Elik asked, "Enough people want Red Fox dead?"

"I want to go home," Skinner said.

"As do I," Allanaq said. "But I need help. A man needs relatives and hunting partners to stand with him. If Red Fox has wronged enough people—"

"Hunting partners, did you say?"

Elik turned at the sudden lift in Skinner's voice. She looked to Allanaq, but he was too caught up in his own thoughts to notice. "I can continue up the coast, as a trader," he said.

"You think Red Fox is searching for you?"

"For my father, I think. Not me. We don't know if he is aware of the death of my sons."

"Two sons," Skinner said kindly. "Brothers who died because of Red Fox. As we too are brothers."

"Brothers, yes." Allanaq repeated.

"You see that, don't you. We have become brothers more than cousins. We have no one else. Brothers," Skinner said, then added, "or perhaps hunting partners?"

Elik wrinkled her nose in disgust. The man was not clean. His head showed flecks of white shit from the lice that no one troubled to pick from his hair. He had no weapons of value, none that he had shown. And yet, here was Allanaq, smiling.

"Yes," Allanaq agreed. "We should pledge ourselves as hunting partners. In my house, you would have the favored seat."

Skinner bowed his head. "My catch would be your catch."

"We would be two men who depend on each other."

"When we visited, your house would be open for me. Your food. Your weapons. My wife Little-Creek would be your wife. If you needed her when you traveled, for help or while you hunted. And in turn your wife," Skinner said, "would be mine."

Allanaq started to answer, but Elik had risen. Angrily, she took his sleeve. She would not demean herself by speaking in front of this man. She would not allow him to see her anger. But she would make Allanaq listen. She pulled at him, refusing to speak until they were far enough away that the wind wouldn't carry her words back for Skinner to hear.

"He wants me in his blankets," Elik said. "That's all he wants. Not to help. Not to share."

"He hasn't asked for you yet," Allanaq tried to reason. "He could have, any of these nights. But I explained the prohibition on you. And he respects it. He sees how you eat, how careful you are. I don't understand what you fear."

"I fear how much you believe him, while the truth is that everything he does is for a reason. He doesn't ask your permission to sleep with me, because he will take me as soon as you aren't looking. He has your food. He wants your woman."

"What he wants is to go home. Can't you see that? You are thinking only of yourself. You are thinking of your own home, and Grey Owl and Nua, and the relatives you miss. As does he. How is it you don't understand?"

"How is it you cannot see?"

"See?" Allanaq said. "I will tell you what I see: Red Fox, everywhere I look. Red Fox who brought my father gifts and kind words, and listened to an aging man's stories. And then stole everything my father would freely have given. And now I see Skinner, a man who will help give my father peace. Why is that bad?"

"He's not so kind as you make him seem."

"Nor so angry as you make him."

"A wife is not something a man should merely take."

"But we are speaking of a hunting partnership. Not a theft. Skinner and I will be exchange partners to each other. No different than with Drummer. Would you embarrass me? This is not something a wife should turn away from. And you must think ahead—I cannot fight Red Fox alone. All will be well."

Elik opened, then closed her mouth. She shivered, deep inside her bones, then turned away as she tried to collect herself. She felt old and tired and lonely, all at the same time. And yet perhaps, she told herself, so did Allanaq. She didn't know. His glances, his words—so much of what he said was different now. "This Skinner—do you truly think he will help? This is what you want?"

"He is family. He will help. And yes, this is what I need."

"I will not complain."

"There. You are a good woman," Allanaq lifted her

chin toward him. "This is not easy for you, I see that now. You are farther from your home than you have ever been. Without your aunt, your cousins. I know. But if a man notices you softening your husband's boots with your teeth so the skins aren't ruined, if he sees you sewing and he eats your food, he is only saying how worthwhile you are. Be glad. But go on now. Perhaps you should try to sleep."

Elik agreed. An exhaustion came over her, from the work, the travel, the strain of trying to understand this husband who once had seemed as much a part of her as her hand.

She climbed into the tent, glad that at least she wouldn't have to be so careful how she sat, how she arranged her legs. She stretched out with her head to the wall skins, then changed her mind, turning to the door flap instead, listening.

Skinner was talking. "Did you tell her it was better this way?"

"She is my first wife, as you have yours. Even if you need her work, and we exchange, she is still my wife. If I took another, she is still first."

"Do her people understand that a man may throw away a wife if she doesn't properly share food, if she hides the best for herself?"

Allanaq glanced toward the tent and quickly, Elik slid back into the shadows. "Elik doesn't do that," he said.

"They all do, if they're hungry."

"My wife is a shaman," Allanaq said firmly.

Elik lifted a corner of the flap, peered out to see Skinner shrug. "Are you afraid Red Fox will trouble her children, if she has any?"

It took Allanaq a moment to answer. "You understand, don't you, there is a prohibition on her?"

"For now," Skinner played with the cuffs of his parka. "But not always. Besides, it takes more than one time beneath the blankets to start a child growing. If she ever had any, in the future, I mean—they would be our half-and-half children. Yours and mine. They would grow up calling me the same word for father as they called you. Red Fox would no longer care. I would have made your children safe."

Allanaq didn't seem certain. "He would kill one child as quickly as another. If he thought any part of my father's soul was alive again, inside a child."

"You think too hard," Skinner said. "Red Fox will be dead and our sons will all be brothers." Elik lifted the flap higher. Skinner's smile was as proud as if these children he mentioned were already born and clamoring to help him home with a seal. Till a moment later, and his mouth changed. "She isn't going to refuse, is she?"

"Refuse?" Allanaq repeated, and Elik darted back inside. She hugged her arms around her chest, tightly pulled in her knees. It didn't help. Skinner's voice pushed through the tent skins, inside her ears.

"Complain. Where she comes from, are the women quiet? Do they argue?"

"They are good people," she heard Allanaq say. "A little careless, but good. But enough. I don't need to talk about them. I want to talk about which route I need to take. The coast, out to the sea? Which way?"

"The coast," Skinner said. "With that long boat, you could trade all the way. You could come home rich. But you shouldn't hurry, it might not be safe. You should first move up along the villages. Speak to people before you arrive. If you're clever, Red Fox could be the last to know."

Elik relaxed a little. They seemed to be done with their talk about wives and exchanges. She no longer heard her name, only the route.

"After the point, there is a low swampy place you'll come to in a day," Skinner was saying. "It's good for seal hunting, and you'll probably find people there. There was a trade fair, but it could be finished. If no one's left, it means they went on to Agiapuk, for summer fishing. Follow the coast again, and the highest place is a rocky headland. That's called Kinigin, high bluff. It's steep, and black, but it's a good lookout. You can stand there and see everywhere. The way the land moves north into lagoons and low-lying islands. The way the mountains are, inland."

"I saw that, I think." Allanaq sounded excited. "There were narrow beaches, long lagoons behind, separating the land. And mountains—it would be difficult on foot, inland. It's good we'll both have boats."

"Boats, yes," Skinner agreed. "Of course, we might have to wait on the winds."

Elik listened only a little more. The two men had risen. She heard the scratch of sticks on gravel: drawing maps. Naming people she didn't know.

She fell asleep with a bad taste in her mouth, fears she prayed she wouldn't dream about. She pulled her sleeping furs over her face, closed out what little sound reached inside.

The next time she knew anything, she was alone in the tent, but the wind had come inside. The wind, and also light. She sat up, surprised. Her view to the boat

outside had changed, replaced itself with an upright
driftwood log. She could still hear Skinner and
Allanaq's voices, but farther away. How long had she
slept?

She rubbed her face to wake up, pulled on her boots
and trousers, then peered outside. A thin fog sat over
the water and the tide was in. The umiak sat upright,
rocking in the shallow waves. Above the boat, on the
beach, Skinner and Allanaq huddled over a pile of baskets, rolled-up skins, food containers.

Why was the boat in the water, she wondered as she
climbed out of the tent and walked toward them.

Allanaq stiffened when he saw her, but neither man
stopped what he was doing—sorting, moving gear.
"Take more of the whale meat," Allanaq said.

For a moment, Elik thought he was speaking to her.
But no—that didn't make sense. There were two separate piles of meat. The packets nearer Allanaq were
taller until he rearranged them, pushed more than half
toward Skinner.

"Not for myself," Skinner smiled his protest, "but for
our wife."

"There's enough, you see?" Allanaq said, "even if our
plans go wrong."

"What plans?" Elik asked. "What are you doing?"

"I wouldn't complain of a harpoon," Skinner said.
"Mine broke just a few days ago. That's what I was
doing when I found you, searching for driftwood for a
shaft."

"But you see, I have more than I need. Take this one, I
brought it to trade. It fits the groove in the short paddle—
here, take that also for Elik, in your boat—they fit
together, like this."

"What boat?" Elik asked.

Allanaq waded into the water, high as his boot tops. He leaned inside the umiak, brought out a toggle-headed harpoon already fitted with a stone point and sealskin lines. He passed it back to Skinner. And then the paddle. And then another weapon, a pronged fishing spear that would be good not only in streams but for ice fishing in the winter.

Skinner's eyes widened in appreciation. He added it to his pile.

A sour, helpless taste rose in Elik's mouth. Had they planned and talked all night, and left her alone to sleep? What was happening here? She crossed to the water's edge, directly in front of Allanaq. This time he couldn't ignore her.

"I'm going ahead in the boat," he said tightly. "You'll come next."

"You're coming back for me?"

Skinner called from the beach: "We decided it was safer that way. One man traveling without a woman, he'll move quicker. He needs to speak secretly, visit around. We'll be the ones who let out the word, but carefully. We'll be safer because we can hide."

"We?" Elik turned back to Skinner. She didn't understand.

"This is the plan. We'll take the same route, behind him, of course."

Allanaq slogged past her out of the water. He added two more stomach containers of oil to Skinner's pile. Skinner looked down in delight. "Oh, no," he said. "You take it. You'll need it to trade, to buy back loyalty."

"I've more than enough," Allanaq said, and he

waded back to the boat, this time climbing all the way inside. Even with his weight added, the boat rode higher, emptier.

Elik looked from Allanaq, to Skinner, to the pile. "I can't carry that."

"He has a boat," Allanaq said.

Elik shook her head. "I'm to travel with him? That's what you're saying?

"It's simple," Skinner said. "We follow while he poses as a trader. What he's really doing is finding relatives to help against Red Fox."

Elik splashed into the water. She clung to the gunwale, balancing against the waves. "But how do I find you?"

"I'll leave messages," Allanaq said. "In the houses along the way."

Elik's voice rose in fear. "What if there are no houses?"

"I'll build cairns out of rocks to mark the way. You'll catch up. I told Skinner you wouldn't like it, but he's right. I need the greater time, to plan with people and reach the Seal village before freeze-up."

"Pray for an easy south wind," Skinner called. "And make sure you take all your things from the boat."

Elik spun about. "My things?"

"Women's things. That horn dipper. Sewing kit. Check that you have them. You don't want to be poor."

"But I'm leaving also!"

"Of course. Of course. But we will be two people, and he is only one."

Elik's jaw clenched in disbelief. Hand over hand, she pulled her weight along the gunwale, trying to turn the boat, hold it back.

Allanaq lifted his paddle on the opposite side. "Take

it. Take it all. If two men are partners, everything that belongs to one, belongs to the other."

He leaned his paddle into the gravel, started to push off.

Frantically, Elik snatched for the handle, tried grabbing it from his hands. "Where will we meet?"

Allanaq held tight, but his voice was softer. "Somewhere before the Seal Point village. I'll leave messages." He slid his hand over hers. "I'll be safe. Nothing will happen."

"How long? I don't want to—"

"It's safer this way," Allanaq looked past her to Skinner. The two men exchanged a glance.

"What if we get separated?"

"We won't," he said. "My father died in a boat of his own making. I do not mean to die in this." He took back his hands, angled his weight onto the paddle, while Skinner hurried to prod the stern. The boat rattled on the incoming breakers, then rose, and smoothly slipped away.

"I'll come for you," Allanaq called. "If you don't find me, I'll come back. The whale meat will be here if we need it."

Elik splashed into deeper water. "What if I want to find you first?"

Allanaq lifted his voice against the wind. "Look for Ice Stick or Sheshalik among the men. Higjik among the women. Skinner knows the way."

Elik stood where she was, the water lapping high as her thighs, spray wetting her face. "That man? That man is already lost," she said, and she looked back to see Skinner dragging the baskets and rolled skins farther up the beach.

"These will be four skins," she heard him counting,

"enough to trade for a parka. These green, early skins are worth less than the scraped. The soft ones I could trade for oil."

She covered her eyes, but the glare of the sun made the boat seem thinner, as if already the fog were eating it. As if it were a ghost boat, guided by a ghost, seeking a ghost's revenge.

4

Elik rearranged the carrying strap across her forehead, then angled the load behind her back till it no longer felt awkward. She balanced the weight of the extra seal oil Skinner had insisted they bring with another sack bulging with gear on her shoulder. Then she turned and looked to see if Skinner was ready.

He wasn't. He squatted on the gravel where, earlier that day, Elik had watched Allanaq's umiak disappear into the greens, greys, and moving blue of the sea.

The tide was in again, skimming the gravel just below where their tent had stood. Skinner's patched boot soles were nearly getting soaked, but he didn't seem to care. With a noisy satisfaction, he examined the fishing spear Allanaq had given him, admiring the sharp, barbed prongs and smooth, straight handle.

Elik watched as he cinched the lines, fit the spear against his bow-case so his load would move as one. He added another roll of skins to his back, then filled his hands with the wolverine-skin tool kit Allanaq had given him for a gift.

Allanaq's points, knife handles, his jade whetstone and bolas. If the load was heavy, Skinner didn't seem to mind. He glanced to where the dot of Allanaq's boat had turned north to follow the coast. "Is that every-thing?" he asked.

"Except drinking water," Elik nodded toward one last water bladder lying in the depression where the boat had sat. "I have no place . . . ?"

"Leave it," he said. "There's a stream we'll reach. If we wait to drink later, we can carry more now." He looked about the empty camp. "What about the whale meat?"

"I brought."

Skinner looked to Elik's back, to the size of her load. "Enough? Can't you carry more?"

"I thought we would fish?" Elik nodded toward the spear, then quickly wished she hadn't spoken.

Skinner's eyes flared in annoyance. "What's this? I trade my safety, my camp, for a stranger-woman—not even a Seal woman—and now she won't help carry? My cousin bragged how strong you were and I believed him. If you want the water, go ahead. But what's the use of water without meat? Unless you know better than I do what we'll find?"

He lifted his chin, squinting as if he searched for game. "Maybe. But perhaps we'd better take more. Go back to the pit. Take as much as you can carry."

He turned to walk, then turned again. "And catch up. I don't want to double back searching for you, sav-ing you from your own feet."

Skinner started inland, not following Allanaq along the shore, but over the crest of the beach, to where his camp and boat must be, the direction she had first seen him appear.

Elik watched only long enough to make sure of the way. Then she turned, retraced the path to where the food pit was carefully hidden with a large, grey rock to mark the spot.

She knelt beside the rock, cleared the grass and moss aside. The hole was wide and deep, with a hollow wind that made her shiver when she reached inside. She stretched her fingers, felt below the top layer of grass to the meat and blubber below. She pulled out first one stitched-together packet, then another.

In the icy ground, the yellowish meat had frozen already, safe and without any smell to attract hungry thieves. For a moment, she considered staying. There'd be plenty of meat, and the skinniest strips were already dry. She would be allowed to eat those, since they were no longer fresh. Even without it, she'd seen enough fish and small game along these shores for one woman for the remaining summer.

If Skinner came looking, she'd already scouted out a few places she could hide. She knew he was lazy; sooner or later he'd give up. And Allanaq would come looking for her and . . .

No.

She had to remember, no matter his promises, the seas turned. Weather changed. Allanaq might not be able to return before winter. And even if he did, she wasn't at all certain anymore that he wanted her. As unwilling as he'd been to talk with her when they started this journey, that's how quickly he'd jumped to make this partnership with Skinner. To share her, and make his plans at night, while she wasn't there to object.

What if he wouldn't forgive her for running away from a man, a relative, who'd given up his own plans

to help Allanaq? A man he'd entered into a formal partnership with?

He'd be ashamed. And she would become the butt
of too many jokes.

Elik wrapped the meat in grass to keep it cool, then
loaded as much as she could carry in the bottom of her
sack. She closed the entry carefully, so no sun reached
in to warm the meat and spoil it before they returned.

If Allanaq did come back. If he lived.

By the time she found Skinner he was beyond the
soft beach path, walking inland where the wind no
longer carried the force of the sea.

He took a turn she hadn't tried in the few days
they'd been here, and it wasn't long after that she saw
the upright poles of a food-drying rack. A string of
shriveled herring circled one of the corner stands.
The remains of some other meat that was small—
maybe muskrat, maybe fox—and then a short row of
salmon draped across the top. The salmon was old,
pecked and shredded by gulls, but Skinner walked
familiarly up to it. He dropped his packs, started tugging down the fish, stuffing the better pieces into his
bag.

Baffled, Elik searched for a sign of more. "This is
your camp?" she asked.

"Not anymore," he said, and his mouth and tattooed
cheeks crinkled with his smile.

"But you said your camp was inland, too far to
walk?"

"Did I?"

"Where is your umiak? In a stream? I don't see a—?"

"Boat?" Skinner finished. "No boat?" His voice
sounded shrill on the wind, confusing.

Elik glanced about. The only other structure in sight was a rough skin tent on a frame of willow poles, worn hides tied off for a door flap.

Skinner bit off a mouthful of the red fish, chewed and talked at the same time. "The sea gets rough this time of year."

"Do you have a dog? To help pack?"

"Do you see a dog? Do you see food for a dog? I was lucky to eat. Luckier still that when I made this camp, hoping to be near a trade fair, I wasn't killed. I came down that path," he pointed north, the way Allanaq had gone. "I didn't see anyone. I thought the men must have gone walrus hunting. I called when I found their food racks. I did call. But some old ragged woman saw me and got scared. How was I to know the season was too early for trading? We'll be going the other way. Inland."

Elik felt weak suddenly, too small to stand under a sky so large. She let her packs slip from her shoulder. "How do I know you don't mean to trade me?"

Skinner took a long, measuring glance at her hair, her parka. "I thought about it," he admitted. "But to who? The trade fair is over by now. The Sinramiut people and the Kauweramiut are all gone. No one stays longer, else they'd miss their own caribou season."

"Then how do I know you'll take me to the Seal People's village?"

"You don't." Skinner smiled at her discomfort, but a moment later he softened. "Listen, I'm not a terrible man. Your Allanaq is my best hope for going home, that's why. And home is the only place where I can eat without always having to worry whether I catch anything or fail."

Elik felt for her pack, sat down.

"Get up. What's the matter with you? What's one route to another? We take a boat, or follow a trail. Didn't I just tell you, I want to go home? You have legs under those fine stitched furs, don't you? Or are you telling me your hands are too small to carry your new husband's food?"

"You are not my husband."

"Aren't I?" Skinner pressed his wide chin to his chest. "A man who can provide will often take two wives. Even more."

"A wife can run away from a husband. I've done it before. I—"

"Ha! Where would you run?" Skinner lifted his arms wide. "And even if you found Allanaq, why would a man take back a woman who shamed him? My cousin and I agreed to become hunting partners. Every catch, we share. Our house, our boat, and you. We will each call you *nuliuyuk*, the wife who two men share. Now pick up your load. We start eastward."

"Already?" Elik asked. "Aren't you taking more from your camp?"

"There's nothing here," Skinner said. Then with a chuckle, he started behind the tent and along a mossy tract, not even troubling to check whether she followed behind.

It was no use staying. Elik felt a heaviness inside, as if something foul had moved into her stomach. She took up her packs, waited till he was far enough ahead she didn't have to listen to his talk.

This man wasn't going to live long, she told herself, with his bragging and his lies. He would turn out to be no different than any man who let himself grow slow, and foolish, and dead.

And somehow she would be brave, she swore it. She would remember how much harder it must have been for Allanaq, arriving as a stranger on her Real People's shores. As if he'd fallen, not through fog but through sky, losing his first world, falling into new.

At least she had the advantage of seeing the land she crossed, a chance to memorize the way back home. She would sing a prayer, also. Allanaq had reminded her she could still do that, so long as it wasn't a shaman's prayer, but something anyone might sing when their load was heavy. And if it happened that a spirit heard her words, then perhaps, someday, when Malluar's restrictions were no longer needed, that same spirit would speak to her again. It would remember that her feet had stepped lightly. It would help her find the way home. *"I will walk,"* she started to sing, *"with sinews strong as the little calf . . . "*

> *With leg muscles strong as the sinew*
> *On the shin of a little caribou calf.*
> *I will walk with leg muscles strong as the sinew*
> *Of a little hare.*
> *I will take care not to walk toward the dark.*
> *I will walk toward day.*

For the rest of the day, Skinner kept to a trail. It moved, at first, away from the sea, and she thought they might be going directly inland. Except that before long she realized they had only been crossing a narrow strip of land leading out to the point where, she supposed, if Skinner hadn't been lying, a trade fair might very well have occurred.

The path was a southern route around a large bay.

Skinner chose his steps with more care than she would have guessed, sometimes through tall grass, sometimes on gravel. Toward the north, as far as Elik could see, there were mountains, the highest with snow smoothing the rounded peaks. On the opposite shore of the bay, flat land gave way to a string of hills. In some ways, it was much the same as the lands they'd already crossed, with beaches and sparse shrubs. A land of moss and muskeg, willow and brush, nothing different than what she had always known.

The few times she did walk alongside Skinner, she traded her dislike of his constant talk for whatever details he was willing to share. He had not lived in that camp long, only the one season, but he described what he knew, telling where on the flats or up in the hills he'd hunted, whatever he'd learned from the few other people he'd met.

They passed two smaller sand spits separating that first large bay from a smaller, eastern one. And then a channel he said was named Tuksuk, which was at the end of another that he called Little Channel.

He talked for a while about the route they would follow, how most likely they never would have met if the season had been different. How this was a good place to start an inland route, following the rivers, because south, in the interior, the mountains were too difficult to cross.

They would keep to the known trails, he said, and follow a river called the Kuzitrin, to another one called the Noxapaga to another called the Inmachuk, which would let them into the sea again.

He bragged a lot as they walked, pointing out where he'd fished a halibut longer than he was tall. How he'd slugged it over the head with a pole till it died at his feet. And where another time in a high pass in the mountains he had killed a sheep with one arrow, then fallen with the entire carcass over his shoulders as he tried finding a path along a gully. Tumbling—he showed her how the sheep's horns had wrapped around his neck and saved his life as they fell over loose silt and gravel.

Elik listened, but she was never sure how much to believe. And if the mix of brown, black, and white dog-fur leggings he wore was any sign of the real truth, she wondered how he dared to brag.

She'd never heard of anyone wearing dog, not when caribou was warmer and sealskin more waterproof. She remembered how Allanaq had covered his mouth in surprise the first time he saw her people wearing fish-skin clothing in summer. His people would have laughed, he'd told her later. Called them poor, or foolish, or addled in the head.

And she had tried to teach him that among her people—where he now lived—fish were said to be light and good for summer. They shed water. They filled the rivers in endless numbers. And the stitching—even the youngest girl could properly dry and prepare the skins and stitch the layers without her fingers having to bleed from open sores.

But dog?

The only men she'd ever known to wear dog skins were greedy men, the kind who bragged about their hunting, then dressed in rags because their wives had too few skins to do anything but patch old clothes. Men who complained while better hunters slipped into their boats at the first sign of daylight.

Another thought troubled her. It still was the summer season and there was no night. But the season would turn, and with all these rivers he named, the route sounded long. If winter came, and she still was traveling with this man, how could there be any hope for the two of them to survive?

Without warm clothing, a man could not easily hunt. If he could not hunt, there could be but little food in his house. Without food, he would not have the strength to bring home skins for a starving wife to stitch into warm clothing. Without warm clothing, he could not hunt. . . .

They stopped often that first day, also on the second, and the third. Anytime Skinner said he was thirsty. Anytime a ptarmigan or ground squirrel or hare reminded him of food. Skinner sat himself down first, then called for meat and also for the water he had told her not to bring.

Elik slid her packs to the ground, and carried the water to where Skinner leaned against a rock. He sat with his legs stretched out, head tilted back. Her shadow crossed his face and he opened his eyes, took the water, and drank.

"Do you hear that?" he asked, and he cupped his hand to his ear.

Elik listened. There was wind and a chattering squirrel, and overhead, the sound of a loon flying toward a tundra lake.

"That's Jumps Across," Skinner said, and he nudged her leg with his foot. "You have to be careful. Watch where you wander. There's a story." He made his voice slow and ominous.

"Someone died in a house there. It was flooded. Have you ever seen that? A house where the water comes in while you're sleeping, and you don't know what's happening, and you're breathing, but it's water?"

Elik stared at the ground. She took back the water, but instead of drinking from the spout as he had, she poured some into her own dipper and drank from that.

Skinner watched as she drank, his eyes taking in the curve of her neck, the way she pushed her braid away from her face. "They died in that house," he went on. "That sound behind the wind? You hear it?" he turned and pointed, as if he knew exactly the spot where the sod house stood.

"There was a *tunraq* who heard them screaming to get out. He was a demon with a skull but no skin, skeleton hands. Their voices were like a drum, leading him closer. Closer to their house. Listen!" He hissed. "Do you hear it?"

"No," Elik put away the dipper, refusing to let him scare her.

"But you do know people who died? Yes? Family? A father maybe, a mother?" Elik didn't answer. "Aren't you afraid of their ghosts?" he nudged her boot again. "Of what the dead can do?"

Elik stepped back, out of his reach. She squatted beside her pack. She didn't want to listen to this. If he was trying to scare her, he had already succeeded, but not the way he hoped. She pulled out one of the stitched-together packets of whale meat.

He took it almost before she offered, sliced it open with a sweep of his knife, then buried his face in the meat. "Which way did your people live?" he asked when he was done.

Elik pointed, south then east along the coast.

"Did you have another husband first, before Qajak? Maybe someone who died?"

Elik felt his heavy glance on her face. At home, a girl would get a pinch or a scolding for causing a man to look at her that way, wasting his vision when he was supposed to save it for a hunt.

She wondered why he asked. There had been another man, a shaman, the summer after she first became a woman. Though she had spent more time hiding from him than sleeping in his bed. She had never lived in his house. Still, they had called it a trial marriage. "My first husband was Seal Talker, shaman of the Real People." She watched him out of the corner of her eye. "Do you know the name?"

"A shaman?" Skinner looked to her belt, scowled at the amulets hanging there and on her sleeves. "And this shaman, this Seal Singer—?"

"Talker. His name was Seal Talker." Elik hid a smile. Perhaps being the almost-wife of a shaman was not such a useless story to tell.

"You're not afraid to speak his name?" Skinner asked. "Is he alive?"

"Some say he is dead. I never saw him buried."

Skinner hesitated, and this time Elik rushed to ask her own question. "How much longer till we reach your Seal People's village?"

"A few days, maybe. The weather will decide."

Elik tapped her leg. Was he lying? Did he even know? "Will we meet other people first? Allanaq mentioned Ice Stick and someone—Higjik?"

"Those people?" Skinner grunted. "Those people help no one. And you—you should stay away from shamans more. Take your husbands from among hunters, like me. Qajak—your Allanaq—he isn't a bad man though. He was still young when Red Fox and his father began to fight. It isn't always the best thing for a boy, being the son of a shaman. But at least he was protected. People watched themselves when he was around, perhaps too much. He never learned how to tell when someone was lying. He never asked enough questions. Like the route he took. He was so worried. All he ever had to do was follow the coast. He would have been home."

Elik flinched, then tried to hide it.

"And anyway, we won't meet Seal People here."

"How do you know?"

"Few Seal People come this far south. I did, for the trading. But everyone else will be hunting inland for caribou, far north, and east of here."

"But you told Allanaq he'd find relatives along the coast? People he could persuade against Red Fox?"

"Farther north, he might," Skinner said, then he laughed. "Didn't I just tell you, Qajak never knows a lie? He was so happy to believe me, I couldn't let him down. But there'll be a few people, it's possible. Let him search. In the end, he'll find his way back to the Seal People's village just the same." Skinner finished the last bite of whale meat, licked his fingers.

"We should go," Elik said dryly. "Before night."

"In summer?" Skinner asked, and he laughed again at the thought of Allanaq never knowing to follow the coast; but then he stood up just the same, hefted his pack.

Elik started walking again, not angrily—she didn't want him to think she was angry—and not afraid. What was more important was that she spend her time memorizing the channel, the wetlands, the hills. Everything she needed to remember in case she needed to walk this way alone.

It was warm now, but she had to also think ahead toward winter. Traveling would be easier on snowshoes then in bog. But she would have to worry more about food. As long as she could trap a hare or fish, she wouldn't starve. And she would think nothing of stealing from Skinner. Or if she found a boat. At least he had told her that she need only stay to the coast. South. She could always go home.

The next time Skinner stopped was near an outcropping of green and black lichen-covered rocks. The sun had circled overhead; it was a white ball cutting through clouds. There was wind, enough to hold down the mosquitoes, but not so much that it burned her ears.

"We'll stop here," Skinner called. "I remember this place. You see these rocks? I camped here before."

Elik tugged the carry strap from her forehead, eased her packs to the ground.

"There's a caribou-crossing," he said, but Elik didn't turn to see.

She was growing used to his talk, the way he pried and said little that mattered. Questioned, then teased.

"I've seen brown bear . . ." He tried to make his voice sound menacing as he pointed toward a finger-shaped pond with more of the lichen-covered rocks alongside.

Even with her back turned, Elik could feel his eyes constantly watching her. "A woman has to be careful of bear," he said. "They smell her stronger smell."

He waited, then grew annoyed when she didn't answer. "Are you in your bleeding time?" he asked.

Elik tightened her mouth. She didn't want to answer. Men often asked women that—menstruating mattered if a man was planning to hunt. It mattered to the animals who were frightened by the blood. It mattered to the hunter's success. Still—she didn't like the way he asked, the way he watched her. She kicked a rock loose from the moss. "Will we camp here?" she asked. "There's stones I could use to weigh a roof skin."

Skinner wouldn't be swayed. "Among my people," he said, "it's a woman's duty to warn men when they're in their bleeding time. They wear their parkas with the hoods lifted, and they keep their eyes lowered. And they're careful—more careful than you—not to touch a man's weapon, lest it's spoiled and the animals run from the human scent."

"I'm careful," Elik said. "You see the way I keep my own cooking pot. You see I don't eat with you. Nothing fresh. No birds. No eggs."

"So does that mean you're not bleeding? Or you are?"

"I'm not." Elik held her breath, waiting for his next question. It didn't come. Instead, she heard a sound and looked up to find Skinner shuffling through Allanaq's baskets. His packs, she forced herself to remember. Not Allanaq's any longer. Not mine.

He was looking through a box of blades, a chipped biface, another of basalt. He ran his finger over the cutting edge, then checked to see if the skin was broken. "What is this?" He held out the blade.

"An end blade."

"But it's dull," he showed her his finger. It hardly cuts. Why would he make it this way?"

"You lash it to a shaft," she answered, "for a knife or an arrow. Whatever you need—"

"No," Skinner cut her off. "Don't answer with your woman's foolishness. I know what a blade is. Why isn't this one better flaked?"

Elik sighed. She had heard this before: Grey Owl used to lie awake and whisper about Allanaq. Allanaq, in turn, whispered about the way the men netted seals as if they were fish, and spent their days piling up sinker rocks.

Seal People cut diagonal flakes, moving across the stone in bands so complicated, the men among her people only laughed at the long mornings Allanaq required for his work. Laughed—when they weren't afraid—of the way his blades kept a sharper, better edge.

"Our men chip them quickly," she tried to explain. "There's so many stones."

"Quickly?" Skinner wrinkled his nose. "The animals don't come for *quickly*. They come for the beauty a man puts in their work. They come because they enjoy a weapon well made. I'll go see if this new *quickly* point is any use scaring something up from the land."

Skinner took a few moments lashing the point to a shaft. He left his own bow on the ground but took Allanaq's bird dart and then, the rest of the basket. He started away.

The quiet suited Elik; it was becoming more difficult every day, listening to Skinner's pointed questions about her blood, his teasing about her husbands.

She separated the tent skins into two piles for two tents. For hers she used an upright harpoon shaft as a center support. For his, she paced off a distance—not so far the space would call attention to itself—but enough so he wouldn't lie in his tent and listen to her breathing.

By the time she was done, a light drizzle had begun to fall. Elik lifted her hood so the rain wouldn't catch in its pocket, then untied the knots on the fishing spear Allanaq had given Skinner. She was tired, but the pond was nearby and she wanted to be somewhere that Skinner wasn't. Not his voice. Not his things. Not his questions. Not his smell.

The pond, when she reached it, seemed to shake under the pattering rain. The far end was fed by the creek, and it seemed well used, if the crisscrossing of tracks on the soft ground was any sign. She saw her first fish almost as soon as she stepped to the slippery edge. It was a trout, with a silver and green flash of color along its side. She lifted the spear, then just as quickly let it down. The fish was already gone, not even interested in her spear.

She tested her footing, then stepped farther in, beyond the ankle-deep edge. The bottom of the pond held firm and she stepped again, deeper than her boot soles, high as her calves.

And whose fishing spear was it? She wanted someone to explain. Skinner's Seal People, who seemed to care only for caribou and seal, not fishing? Two beaver-claw hooks were all he had in his belongings.

No spear. No nets. No weighted sinker rocks. Why was it so much better to have his fancy points to hunt, when he didn't have a fish spear till Allanaq gave him one?

She stepped along the edge of the pond, feeling for secure footing. The water squeezed her boots against her legs. She saw another fish, long as the first one but fatter, the fin on the height of its back trailing gracefully behind. The fish darted, rushed. Another trout veered within reach and she stabbed for it, thrust the shaft into the water. She missed and lifted it, and quickly hit for the shadow again.

And why did he ask all those questions about her bleeding? He wouldn't come near her, would he? Allanaq had clearly explained Malluar's prohibitions. She heard him herself.

She didn't trust Skinner, didn't know what he was thinking. Not for all his talk about rules that must be honored, taboos respected. But surely a man who talked so much about rules wouldn't touch a woman, someone with death still inside?

Allanaq *had* told about the dead-birth, hadn't he?

Maybe, when she was done here, she should go find cranberries and rub them on her thighs in case Skinner asked again. She had heard of a story like that, a woman who saved herself from being stolen by pretending there was blood.

She stepped through the pond to the narrow end where it met the creek, then waited for the water to clear. It did, but the fish moved away. She lifted the pronged fish spear, and with a hard abrupt swing, stabbed into the water. The splash rose up, soaked her face, but the hit was useless, wide and wasted.

Elik snorted in disgust. She looked for another fish. "Why shouldn't you swim away?" she said aloud. "When all there is to hear is anger in my voice, not power."

She waded along the edge through a row of grasses that bent into the creek. No fish. No sign of their shadows. No flip of a tail. Not even an insect to lure them to the surface.

And whose fault was it but her own?

No fish would come while so much anger lurked in her thoughts. Not a fish, and not a caribou. The animals would hear her anger and hide.

Elik stepped out of the water and set down the spear. She stood quiet, closed her eyes. She let the touch of the wind cool her face. She felt the summer sun on the top of her hair.

"My mind is not weak," she whispered. "Not weak, and not proud. Dear fish. I will not disrespect your skin. Your gift. I call you, with this song. You want to come."

More gently now, Elik stepped into the creek, between a slick of mud and a branch. She slowly waded in until she found a place where the current was less strong. She held still, looked to her right, into the depth: there were two fish, two shadows nosing against the grasses.

She lifted the spear, found its balance, then aimed exactly to the fish's side. There! A single sharp jab.

Instantly, the fish was out of the water, wiggling in the air, stuck through two of the barbs. It was a fat-bodied whitefish, large-scaled and prickly. She waded out and pried the fish off with her foot. Then she was down in the water again. The second fish had waited;

it must have liked her song. She found its shadow, raised the spear, struck, and it came right to her. This one was larger; its silver body thrashed to escape the barbs. Its mouth gulped down air. With a quick blow from a stone, Elik cracked its head, thanked it for its life.

She hooked a finger through the gills on each fish, then carried them both in one hand, the spear in the other. She tried not to feel proud as she started back. The fish had come not because of any skill, but because of the song.

And yet, wasn't any catch a good sign—a small sign, but good? She remembered the way she felt when she and Allanaq first brought in the beluga, its weight on the towline pulling through her hands.

She smiled as she cut a length of green willow from a stand beside the creek. At home she would have had a clay pot to cook the fish in, or a stitched birchbark pot to fill with water. Traveling, though, it was much easier to roast the fish whole, the way her grandmother used to do at summer fish camp. She pierced the fish one on top of the other without gutting them, then angled the wider end of the willow into the ground. And she built a fire, slow and green, so the fish wouldn't burn, and she turned them often, cooking first one side then the other.

The willow burned to coals, and the long day's walking eased its grip. The loneliness eased its grip.

She wasn't certain which way Skinner had gone, but it would be good if he too caught something. She was permitted to eat fish fresh, but Skinner wasn't going to like it when the last of his whale meat disappeared.

With the smell of whitefish sizzling on the stick,

Malluar's prohibitions seemed more reasonable. Give up fresh meat, and her children would live. Finally. Someday. Not like the first miscarriage, two winters before. Not like this more recent one, with two sons dead.

She still remembered the way she had held her hand on her stomach, feeling them kick inside. She had been so sure they were going to live. She had dreamt of them inside, beneath her heart, a small fluttering, like the motion of a bird's wing . . .

She stopped, shook the thought away. It wasn't good, dwelling on the dead. Such thoughts had a way of inviting spirits in, calling them back to life.

And now, here was the fire, cooling itself to a bed of coals; she had hardly noticed. The fish were done. Finally, she heard Skinner call, his voice scaring the tundra birds into the sky.

Elik leaned the fish away from the fire.

She smiled to show she was glad he'd returned. She glanced to his back to see what he'd caught, but for all she could tell, his pack was as empty as when he walked away.

And yet, he seemed content. His ears had reddened in the wind and he rubbed his face. He breathed in the fire's scent, nodded at the sight of the tent, the fish, the trailing smoke. He squatted across the fire from her, lifted his hands toward the sweet breath of heat.

Elik offered the fish and he took it, licked his fingertips wet, then picked at the gold-baked skin to see if it was hot.

"I was thinking," he said in a reasonable voice, "how hungry a man can get. How lucky a man might be. This place here, I don't know it, you see. I never was here much. But any hunter who stays in a place long enough learns its stories. There are signs of caribou-crossings and small game. There's always ptarmigan when there's nothing else to find. You wouldn't go hungry living here." Skinner looked up at her to see how she answered, but she didn't know what to say.

She poked the fire, hid behind its smoke. What did he want now, with all his talk of game but nothing to show in his hands?

"Your parka," he said. "It's very beautiful. Did you do that work yourself?"

Elik held politely quiet. This man made no sense to her. His talk jumped in circles she didn't understand.

"I have some sewing, I thought you could fix?"

Was that all he wanted? Anyone needed only to look to his parka to know the fur was going bald. She had skins. She could make him another, but not while they were walking. "Maybe I could fix your boots," she offered.

Skinner's smile broadened. He leaned back to enjoy the fish. As soon as he was done he started talking again. "My first wife always said a man should have three new pairs of boots each year, and a house should have extra crimped soles ready." He sighed at some memory, stared at the few fish bones he had not eaten.

"Did you bring a fishnet?" he asked.

Elik shook her head no.

"But you could make one? There's willow enough to be stripped and braided. Your husband said Real People spend most of their summer fishing. He said in the season when we hunt caribou, your women set nets?"

"We fish."

"I can almost taste it, caribou and whitefish boiled over a fire. Blueberries mixed with yellow fat."

Elik turned so she could look at him without having to stare. His mustache was slight, his beard wispy with a few center strands tinged in grey. His nose was flat across the bridge, more like her own father's than Allanaq's prominent nose. But from there its ridge line was sharp, pointing spearlike toward the square of his chin.

"It's too early for blueberries." It was the only thing she could think of to say.

"Maybe now it's early," he said, and suddenly there was a hint of something else in his voice. "But later . . . you'll see. They'll fill the bushes, round as eyes. And you could set a seining net? Something that's good for that creek over there. And bring in more whitefish, burbot, and salmon."

"Why would we want a net here, when we need to keep going?"

This time it was Skinner who didn't answer. He rose, crossed to the lean-to Elik had set up, the one with her packs, not his that she'd leaned into a pile. And then, without a thought to asking permission, he grabbed hold of the drawstring closure on one of her smaller sacks. He tugged it open. "How much of his carvings did you bring?"

"None." Elik rose and stared in disbelief as he stole through her bowls, dippers, scraping tools. Everything that had been in the sack he scattered on the ground.

"Do you have more of Qajak's points?"

"No. I told you."

"Any walrus ivory I could trade?"

"No."

Disgusted, Skinner flung aside the empty sack. He crossed back to the fire, kicked the willow pole into the coals, fish and bones and clinging skin and all.

"What use are you?" he demanded. "What use if you hardly talk and you mope all day. What use to anyone?" Smoke from the fire blew in his eyes, he fanned his hands in front of his face, then turned. "What did you say?" he asked.

Nothing. Elik squatted by her pack and baskets, hurrying to gather them up.

"Yes you did. I heard you." He stepped around the fire. "You called me lazy, didn't you? Me, lazy? While you slept late, and lost that whale? Me?"

He loomed over Elik till she rose, then he backed her toward the lean-to. "As if you were the one who caught the whale when it was lost? Did you do that?"

"No," Elik felt behind her for the tent. "You did that. Not me."

"You are a fool. No—worse than a fool. You're the kind of woman who brings disaster on a man. And for you, I offered my wife to Qajak?"

With a sudden motion, he lifted his hand and struck her face. Hard and sharp, the sting of his knuckles whipped her cheek.

Elik fell to the ground in surprise. She felt her mouth: there was blood on her hand. Blood on her fingers and trailing from her mouth.

Skinner looked at his own knuckles, glaring in surprise. Then, not to show weakness, he lifted the lean-to's door flap. "Get in," he said.

Elik stared at the dark opening.

"Get in." He swooped down, grabbed her wrist.

She shielded her face from another slap. When it didn't come, she tried reasoning: "Didn't my husband tell you . . . ?"

"Tell me what? " Skinner forced her closer.

"That I'm watched. There are spirits, following me . . ."

Skinner dragged her on her knees, pushed her head-first into the low tent, then followed her inside, talking all the while. "You are foreign, do you know that? Do you think that I, a simple man, can know what is true for your people, right for mine?" He pulled his parka off, over his head.

"There are rules . . ."

"For a woman who is an exchange wife, yes. Sit up. Don't cower. Your husband promised you would not complain. What did you think I wanted you for? Catching fish? Take off your leggings."

In the small, dark space, there was no choice but to do as he ordered.

"He warned me you were headstrong. But what was his, is mine."

"But he told you—I heard him tell you—I am the mother of dead sons. If you had seen them, you would know . . ."

"Don't try to scare me with your woman's tales."

"But my husband—your own shaman's son—he never touched me, since the death began."

Skinner hesitated. "You're lying?" he asked, but then he chuckled. He knelt alongside her, his face nearly in hers. "It doesn't matter, whatever you say. If it isn't your woman's time, then there is no blood. And if there is no blood, then it cannot be used to hurt me."

He lifted his fist and Elik raised her hands for a shield, but the blow didn't come. He pushed her back, then down. She shut tight her eyes, refusing to help as he took his penis in his own hands. He wet his lips and stared at her as he held himself, urged his *usuk* to grow hard. He sprawled over her, his loose stomach grazing hers. He had to force her legs apart himself, still holding on to himself as he held her to the ground.

Elik made a sound as he kept pushing at her, but he stopped her, heavily. With his hand jammed over her mouth, he started her lip to bleeding again. He whispered in her ear, "If you scream I'll hit you, then not even a husband would want you back. And don't you bite, understand? I don't want your teeth marks on my skin."

She was dreaming.

There was a wind and it was flowing over the sea, over a shallow lagoon where the waves were brown and green. And swimming in the very center was a beluga, a long white beluga with its black eyes showing, tail cutting below the sea. And there, on the height of its back, sat a loon. Just like that. Black and white feathers like a necklace of bones and shell beads. Calm eyes looking ahead. And the whale was swimming in large circles and slow paths, and the loon was singing.

That was the important part about the dream, that he was singing his spirit song. High like a woman, then low like a man. And then sometimes, both a man and a woman together at the same time. *"Aiee Aiee, Aee, Aya Ya Eiay."* That was all, just the singing. And it didn't matter that she didn't know what it meant. The whale did, and the loon did, and she was only glad that as long as she could hear it in the dream, she felt safe.

Until the singing faded, and Elik heard instead the sound of rain pattering, dripping overhead, near her ear. Her eyes opened. She stared at the hairless patch on the tent skin near her face. She felt the pressure of someone's leg lying over hers.

Daylight forced its way in. She turned; Skinner was there, asleep on his back. His mouth hung open and he made small, bubbling sounds, then rubbed his face, slept on. Carefully, Elik slid her foot out from his.

There were dry, crusted patches where he'd rolled himself heavily off of her last night. On her legs, the bedding, almost everywhere but where it belonged. She would have belittled him if it would have made a difference, earned her anything but his fist across her face.

Besides, it wasn't his short-lived attempts that troubled her now. It was the smells on the fur, in the tent: his spray of semen, their sweat, and strongest of all—her own woman's smell, signaling. Calling as clear as if it were a trail of smoke rising from a fire.

If she was watched, if Malluar was right, then her smell would be found. The scent would catch Red Fox's attention. And if not his, then surely a demon *tunraq*'s. Something would find her. She wouldn't be able to hide, or control the spirit. Or anything.

Elik shivered at the thought but then quickly, before Skinner woke and dragged her back under him, she crept from his side. She glanced back once, almost wishing there was blood on him. Her woman's blood so the demons would find him, so the animals he hunted would know what kind of man he was, that it wasn't her fault.

She reached for her parka, but her hand grazed Skinner's pile of clothing first. She felt something sharp, needlelike. There were blades of grass, last year's dry grass clinging to his parka, stuck among the furs.

As soon as she saw it, she knew what it was. Dry grasses, not from the tent floor but from outside. Skinner had never gone hunting yesterday. Never done anything but take himself off, just far enough to be out of sight. He hadn't troubled to lie to her. He never said he had hunted. She was the one who'd assumed it. When all he'd done was to lay himself down on his back and sleep. Sleep, while she fished and worried, and tried to find food and he did nothing at all.

He was a lazy man, that was why he was alone. That was why he hid from people at that trade fair he talked about. Because he had stolen. Because he was a man with a weak mind who no one wanted. And that story he'd told about how Red Fox was jealous of him, and so put him out of their village, the same way he'd put Anguta out—it wasn't true. The only thing that was probably true was that Red Fox grew tired of his laziness. He could never hunt for a family. And maybe somewhere there was a first wife, but more likely, she guessed, there was no girl's mother who ever wanted Skinner for a son.

Elik crawled the rest of the way outside the tent, then stood and lifted her face to the rain, let it drip down her forehead, her neck. The cooling water stung the cut where Skinner had slapped her, and she scraped the trail of caked blood that clung to the corner of her mouth and chin.

She stood there, simply stood, staring toward the

southern hills behind them and the river valleys they had yet to cross.

The mountains had never seemed so huge while she was in the boat with Allanaq. She had thought they were hills. She had never worried about the mass of snow whitening the peaks. The months, she realized now, the seasons it might take either to go through them, or back along the coast, or ahead.

She wanted Allanaq.

If he didn't want her, she could accept that. She would go home. A man wasn't like a woman, but Allanaq wasn't like other men. He was driven, ruled by one need, and everything he did for the sake of that need, he believed right. But had he even thought beyond the day Red Fox would die? She wondered.

Skinner was right in one thing: Allanaq had been quick to believe his simple lies. Did he want her anymore? She didn't know.

And yet, as she thought about it, one possibility came to mind. Something she might try, before Skinner woke and found her. Now, while the anger burning inside her stomach was strong enough to make her brave. She would find a way to bring Allanaq back.

She would use her amulets and call him. No matter the warnings, the prohibitions Malluar had laid on her. She would do it. Skinner hadn't cared when he broke them. Nothing evil had happened during the night.Perhaps she was far enough from the place her sons were buried?

She felt along the inside seam of her parka to where she kept her amulet pouch, tied through a loop. She would take his father's bone and put herself in a trance. The bone was part of the father. Like the soul that clung to the bear's skin after death, the bone would remember its shaman-power. Anguta would want to find his son. The bone would see into the distance for her, farther than her human sight was able. It was possible—the power was in them. Now. Before Allanaq journeyed too far.

She glanced back inside the tent. Skinner's hair lay like strings across his arm. The sound of his sleep was heavy, thick and slow as his lazy hunting.

She turned, hurried along the path to the pond where she'd caught the fish, then to the far side of the pond where a low stand of willow brush outlined the stream bed.

A calm certainty filled her. She found a place to sit, took out the pouch, and tipped it open. Two amulets fell into her cupped hand. The first was the loon's head Malluar had given her. But—that was odd, hadn't she dreamt about a loon just before waking? She'd nearly forgotten. The loon had been singing, calmly swimming and singing.

She smoothed a feather at the back of its head; the wispy down came loose each time she touched it. Better to put it aside for safety. It wouldn't matter anyway. She had no idea what she would use it for.

The second amulet was the straight, skinny bone. She set it on a patch of bare ground beside her. Then, with a thought, she pulled her other amulets off her belt: the seal's nose, the ptarmigan head. A gull's foot. A bee. A wooden raven. And one more—from around her neck, she pulled off the thong with the ivory loon Allanaq had long ago given her for a present. It seemed the right thing to do, to have nothing, no stray powers, no other spirits to interfere.

She lay them all on the ground, then picked up the bone. Only the bone.

She closed her fingers over it, closed her eyes. The wind lifted her hair, dried her mouth. It moved over the pond and sang to the small, rolling waves. Within moments the snug warmth of her hand flooded into the bone.

Being of Allanaq's father, wouldn't it know the son? Wouldn't that which had been living seek its own?

She tried imagining the bone clothed in flesh. The way that, once, it would have held harpoon and paddle, dipper and bowl. She pictured, and imagined. Turned the bone and felt along its flank.

But that was all. Nothing happened.

She opened her eyes, glanced toward the tent. No sign of Skinner, but certainly, no man could sleep much longer. She needed to try again.

What was it Malluar used to say? That all charms must be spoken softly, with lowered voice and every word repeated.

Perhaps the bone had been dead too long and it needed something stronger to help.

She didn't have a shaman drum. Though Malluar never began a trance without one, Elik had never been allowed to make her own. And besides—she couldn't risk it with Skinner so near.

Then perhaps with a song, not a hunter's song as Allanaq had suggested, but a shaman's song? Nothing had gone wrong when she sang for the fish. And even with the beluga, the only bad luck her singing had brought was Skinner.

Which, though? The best songs were hoarded, like property. And as with most shaman things, Malluar kept her strongest ones to herself. Later, Malluar always promised. They will all be yours. But later had never come.

There was only one time Malluar had allowed her to go out and try to gain a song on her own. All the other times Elik had asked, she had been either pregnant or mourning, and Malluar had a hundred reasons why she mustn't trance.

Except that one time, the first time. Elik remembered; she had gone into the wilderness on a vision quest, alone for five days. Without food. Without rest. In the cold solitude of winter. She had searched for silence, and fallen into a trance, until finally a Wolverine-spirit had come and given her his song. It was a good song, a powerful song, but as with everything, Malluar warned her against using it.

Never speak those words aloud, Malluar had said. Don't remember the way you felt when the Wolverine came. Don't remember the promises he made when he pulled back his hood and a man stepped out and the song he gave you lifted your spirit-eyes, carried you over beaches, higher than the clouds, over the village, the shore, and the sea.

And Elik hadn't, not once since she learned she was pregnant. She had never allowed that feeling of power to come into her. Never risked calling on spirit helpers she might not be able to control.

Elik took her breath and the next moment started to sing, her voice so sudden and clear it nearly startled her. *"You animal you,"* she started, the first verse of the song the Wolverine had taught her.

She waited, looked around. Nothing seemed to change. Nothing happened.

"You animal you, you are coming to me. Ya, ya yu, ya axa yu . . . " She sang another part.

A cool breeze shivered along her neck. There was a scratching sound. Something from behind her? She turned, glanced both ways.

No. Nothing was there. Nowhere she could see.

Her stomach jumped, and a little less calmly, she sang the rest of the words, the way they'd been given. *"Animal, Strong Animal, you are coming to my Song. You come nearer to the entry of my house."*

The scratching grew louder. Nothing so large as a caribou. Not a bird. It was too different from that.

Elik turned. She blinked against the glare of sunlight splintering on water. It wasn't until her eyes cleared that she saw it: a solitary wolverine, standing along the rim of the pond.

White Stripes, she'd heard the men call a wolverine. It stood still, if it was possible for an animal like that not to move. Dark furred, with an ivory stripe like parka trim from behind its shoulder, running to its tail. It was beautiful. Large as a wolverine could be. She held her breath. She didn't dare move.

Was this the same one she'd once met? She couldn't tell. That one had come as a man, its wolverine fur worn like a jacket to show the living soul inside. This one wasn't changing. Not yet.

She sang again: *"Ya, ya yu, ya axa, yu. You are coming to me, beautiful and strong. My Song brings you."*

Was that right, she wondered? Was that all she was supposed to do?

No. She still needed more. But the wolverine was moving now. It pulled back its teeth in a wild grimace.

Long, white, and angry. The stiff white guard hairs on its back stood upright in a warning.

It came nearer, slinking. Its claws clacked against gravel. It must have come down from the hills. Or been sleeping on the ground nearby, like a caribou.

"Ya, ya yu, ya axa, yu." She sang to calm the wolverine. Then sang again, quicker. Louder.

It was supposed to turn gentle, not stay wild the way it did when it hunted beaver in the creek, or stole from a wolf kill.

The wolverine lifted its chin, forming a stiff line from its nose to the height of its back. A deep, throaty growl rolled from its mouth.

Nervously, Elik rose to her feet. The wolverine snarled as it edged around one side, circled in an arc, closer.

Elik stepped backward. She had no weapon. No way to stop it.

The wolverine lunged and she jumped away. It darted at her heel, nipped, then darted for the other.

Elik stumbled back. *"Ya, ya yu? Ya axa, yu?"* Malluar was right. How had she dared assume she could control a spirit? She must have said something wrong. She must have—

She wheeled about, started to run—too late to hear the footstep, the man following up behind.

With a scowling anger, Skinner raised his arm to strike.

Elik screamed, not at the man, but at the wolverine behind him. Skinner's hand knotted to a fist, just as the wolverine leapt, its claws like knives, long teeth bared.

And all in a moment, Skinner's fist crashed against Elik's neck and she fell, back and down, just as the wolverine swiped. She twisted to a ball, knees to her chest, arms covering her neck, her face. She tried to move but Skinner kicked her with his foot, he kicked against her shoulder, beneath her ribs.

He was shouting and kicking, but she didn't understand. She felt the blood on her hands, wet and thick on her face, her cheeks.

Skinner stopped.

She dared a look, past Skinner to the wolverine. It had backed off but it was there still, its snout lifted, sniffing the air. In disgust it caught the man's human smell, his crotch, his odor. It wrinkled its nose and pulled back. Then as she watched, it hissed and turned, and then fled.

"Get up." Skinner said.

Elik held her face. "All right. It's leaving."

Skinner rolled his eyes in disgust. "What are you saying this time? What's leaving?"

"The wolverine. It's gone now."

"What? *Qapvik?* There's no wolverine. Get up. You have too many stories. What did you think—you could run away?"

With a slow effort, Elik lifted herself. Her side ached where Skinner had kicked her, but it was the blood she wiped from her face that frightened her more. Streaks of blood, not like anything Skinner could have done, but like claw marks.

Her fingertips glistened. She lifted them to her face, sniffed, then lowered her hand and stared at the shining catch of blood.

Skinner looked at her and grimaced. "The rocks must have scraped your face. I didn't hit that hard. Go clean yourself."

Gladly, Elik did as he said. She knelt at the pond's

edge, splashed and rubbed the cold water into the cuts. It wasn't till she turned to wipe her hand on the ground that she saw her amulets—they'd been kicked, scattered about the ground. She found the loon skull first. Then the seal's nose, black against a tiny purple flower. The ptarmigan head next.

She moved slowly, gathering them up, her thoughts reaching in a hundred directions. Till out of nowhere, Skinner kicked at her hand. "No you don't . . ." he yelled, and the amulets spilled and tumbled from her hands. Into the moss. Thrown near the willow brush.

"What were you doing?" Skinner demanded. "Trying to steal?" He bent to the ground, snatching at the tiny feathered loon, the bone, the tiny pouch with the bee.

"What are these?" he asked. "Food? No. Amulets— that's what they are, aren't they? Were you hiding them?"

"They are women's things mostly, " Elik lied. She wanted them back, but the best way to get something from Skinner was to show they didn't matter. "They're good for childbirth," she added as she tore a square of moss from the ground, pressed it to her face to stop the bleeding.

Skinner pursed his lips. "And that's all? They're not worth something?"

"They are, but only to me. My grandmother passed on the ptarmigan. The fishskins are from when I was born, to make my sewing fine as their scales."

Skinner grunted. "What were you doing then?"

Elik ignored him as she lifted the moss and gently explored her cheek.

"Never mind," Skinner said, and he lowered his gaze as he took the pouch from Elik, pushed the amulets back inside. "But don't think you can use these against me. I didn't hit you that hard. By the time your husband sees you again, your face will be healed. Don't you tell him that I hit you, and I won't tell him you tried to run away. Now let's go. I don't like this place.

"And besides," Skinner continued as they started walking. "Your husband should have told the truth. You don't give pleasure. You lie there and you don't move. You don't sound glad. You don't do anything to help. Not anything at all."

Elik took down the tent skins, tied the roll with a length of straps. Skinner tossed the amulet pouch into the top of her carry-sack, then kept out of her way as she worked, and she kept out of his.

She had been hit before, not since living with Allanaq as his wife, but often as a girl. She had been clumsier than her sister Naiya and far more often underfoot. Their father thought nothing of smacking her shoulder, her head. Pinching her legs—but that he did only when there was no other man nearby to see; it would have shamed him, having his temper seen. Losing face over a girl.

It was her mother who taught her not to complain. Not to show pain. Or speak first, before her father. Or louder than her elders. Her mother taught what she herself learned as a girl: how to chip ice and haul water in winter, how to cook and how to start a fire, and most of all how to prepare skins, and how to sew.

She had been taught that the skills a daughter learned when she was young proved the value of her worth when she was married. And married she was. To Skinner now, the same as she was married to Allanaq.

And no matter how much she felt a prisoner to his small words, no matter how much he spoke to her as to a child, then made her lie down as his wife, she would not lower herself to shout or whine or allow this man to see her cry.

She didn't know what had happened with her song, or why the wolverine had come at all. Her best guess was that Malluar had been right all along, warning that she was too new a shaman to control the spirits. And the stories she had always heard, about death and the demons who would devour her flesh if they caught her—they were true. All true. If she wanted to live, she would have to obey.

Only when she fixed the wide strap across her chest and forehead and settled the weight of her sacks behind her, did she allow herself a touch of food. She felt no hunger, but starving would gain her nothing. She pulled off a few strips of the driest whale meat, tucked it in her belt for later. Surely, it was safe by now, the life gone out of the wind-dried pieces.

Skinner came up behind her as they started walking. As if in apology, he shifted the pack behind her, cinching the strap for a better hold. When she turned, he winced at the sight of her face. "It'll heal," he said. "Women always do."

Elik fell in behind him, eyes pointing toward the ground.

They walked all that day and the next, and then more after that. Each day was much the same as the one before. They walked in rain, and they walked in wind, from the narrow channel where they had long since left Allanaq, skirting the southern shore of a huge basin of salt water. East and north again after that, then east.

They followed the rivers, which followed the passes, which was the easiest way to travel without a boat. There were occasional shrubs of willow and sometimes taller aspen, a skinny stand of birch. And everywhere there were tundra ponds and gullies and the earliest blueberries and cranberries were beginning to ripen. There were muskrats and beaver in the rivers, everywhere. And fish and hare and small game and birds, always birds.

What bothered her most was that Skinner had come this way before, and yet said nothing about how long the journey would take. It didn't matter that he knew where the passes were open, or where the flats were wide. The route, so long as they followed the rivers, was easy, but long, terribly long.

Each day they walked from morning when they woke and broke camp till the sun circled wide enough and Skinner dropped his pack as suddenly as a dog drops his tail. Elik set up their tent and Skinner took the fish spear and bola and walked away, saying he would hunt.

And sometimes he did; sometimes he brought back a sleek wet muskrat or a hare, a mallard. Once a porcupine, which brightened his spirits when she pulled the quills to save. Most days, though, he found a way to return just at the moment when the smoke of Elik's fire drifted neatly to the sky.

At night, as the first sign of evening began to reappear, he would check the wind for the next day's weather. And then make himself yawn, and then climb first inside their lean-to.

And each night, always the same, Elik put him off as long as she was able. While she buried the bones of whatever meal he'd eaten, and finished what sewing she could find. Until he called from inside the lean-to, complaining of his thirst, or that his boots were stuck, or damp and she needed to dry them before tomorrow.

He came back out if she tried to sleep elsewhere, and stood over her, threatening a beating. He grabbed her wrists and pushed her inside, then pushed again to force her in beneath his sleeping robes. Then underneath his too-soft weight, his flailing attempts, impatient as a man can be.

She clenched her jaw and refused to make a sound, not the slightest noise, while he rubbed his mouth on her neck, rubbed his penis on her stomach, her thighs, talking to it, urging it first to hurry, then to wait.

Each night the same, his hungry rubbing, his roving across her body. Till his lips turned dry and his penis sprayed and then went soft and she found some place to send her thoughts where the clumped strands of his black hair didn't hang across her face. Where the smell of his sweat and scalp and skin didn't fill her nostrils.

It was the middle of a clear day, the first easy day after two of steady rain. They came around the mound of a domed, rocky hill and Skinner suddenly stopped her. He motioned, urging her back, away, behind him.

Elik hesitated till she saw his face, tightened in fear.

"Get down," he tugged her parka. "Someone's there. I don't know who."

He crouched and Elik hurried to follow, balancing her loads, rushing to hide behind an outcropping of rocks. She peered over his shoulder. "What is it?" she asked.

"A man. Someone alone." The rocks were tall enough to safely hide, and Skinner leaned far out, trying to see.

He pulled back in, wiggled free of his pack, then climbed a few steps higher to a ledge just above. Elik also dropped her pack, then waited until the pebbles stopped scattering from his feet. She climbed up and stood behind him, the two peering out from the cover of a craggy grey rock.

Away in the distance, in a draw below their hill, beside a slow waterway, a single black-skinned tent rose over a frame of bent willow. Elik made out a circle of stones: a hearth on the tundra. And beside that a raised platform for food. A dark spot that looked to be a dog—if it moved she would be more certain. A cluster of poles, maybe weapons, she didn't know what kind.

Skinner pointed. On the bank beside the water, a rope of smoke rose and circled higher, white against the greens and browns of the tundra, fading against the white of the sky.

"Who are they?" Elik asked. "Seal People?"

"It shouldn't be." Skinner sounded perplexed. "This isn't any direction we come for caribou. Bird's Mouth and his brothers and Ice Stick—they all planned on hunting with Red Fox. But that was west and north of here. Far closer to the Seal Point Place."

"Which way are we?"

"South, and inland. I told you, we'll get there." He turned, glanced in annoyance at her. "It was lucky for you, I saved you. Don't forget that. You'd be dead if you'd gone with Qajak. Either people are going to be afraid because he's Anguta's son, or they'll be afraid because he's Red Fox's enemy."

"What do we do? What if you know them?"

Skinner leaned out for another look. "I don't trust this," he said. "It's the caribou time. We always follow Red Fox, wherever his spirit helpers show him where to hunt."

"The entire village?"

"Most. Maybe not the eldest. A few women too close to childbirth. They stay behind."

"And if this isn't Seal People?"

Skinner chewed on his lip. He looked from the open valley north, then back the way they'd come, and then higher. There were rocks, enough to hide them if they kept to the inside and made no noise that the wind might carry. They could skirt this valley, it was possible. Pick up their trail on the other side.

Elik followed his gaze, then stopped him before he spoke. "Let's find out first who it is," she said. "I'm in no hurry to climb up there."

Skinner chuckled. "Go, then, if you're so brave."

Elik's nostrils flared. "All right . . ." She found a handhold, leaned out to study the camp. Till suddenly, Skinner grabbed her parka, tugged her back.

"Do you want us both dead?" he hissed. "Do you know what you look like?"

"I'll tell them what a strong husband I have, not afraid to beat his wife." Elik pulled from his grip. She leaned out again, careful of the loose gravel. There was a man down there, she saw him now. One man, standing beside the large tent.

Skinner caught the change in her expression and rose to peer down. His shoulders tightened and he leaned anxiously forward, squinting toward the man, his tent, the cache.

"Can you see?"

"It's Kaviaq," Skinner whispered. "But he was hunting. He should have been hunting with the others. Why would he be here?"

"Kaviaq?" Elik tried the name. "What does it mean?"

"It means you stay back," he said, "and hide, and you do nothing, nothing at all. You understand?"

"But who—?" Elik called, but Skinner was already gone, clambering down rocks, hurrying across the flats, not even trying to hide. She watched, baffled, as he stopped abruptly in front of the tent.

The man stood taller than Skinner, and from the way they talked—Skinner with his arms moving excitedly, the stranger more calm—they definitely seemed to know each other.

Elik found a better ledge, lower down, with a seat between two rocks to cradle her and the view more open. If this man was one of Skinner's people, then maybe they wouldn't fight? Maybe he was another of Red Fox's cast-offs, like Allanaq and Skinner. And if this Red Fox had grown so frightened that he cast out every man he didn't like, then how strong could he truly be?

Finally, when the waiting seemed almost unbearable, Skinner stepped away from the man. He turned and peered up at the rocks, circled with his arms, signaling her to come down, bring their things. And he sent a smaller sign also, though she could see the taller man caught it, standing behind Skinner the way he was. Come quietly, Skinner signaled. And behave.

She took up her own sacks, then looked to where Skinner had left his. She had no interest in carrying them down. Let him come back, share this load he insisted on carrying. She wedged it, along with the heaviest tent skins, into a protected corner between two rocks.

She didn't hurry. It had been so long since she'd seen or talked to anyone but Skinner. There was a knot in her stomach, larger than she liked to admit, but there was nothing she could do about it except to start slowly down with a warning to her feet not to trip. Not to run. Not to do anything but wait, hope that by morning, she would still be alive.

She hadn't yet reached the stranger's camp when Skinner ran partway back to meet her. His breathing was ragged and too quick, and only part of what he said made sense. He had promised the man that his wife would cook whale meat. "Large as a feast," he said, but then he stopped. His eyes widened with a thought. He poked her chest.

"You tell nothing, you understand? There's more to the story of Red Fox and Anguta than your husband ever told. If you want to be alive, say nothing unless you hear me say it first."

"Why is that man here?" Elik tried to ask, but Skinner was jumpy and even more tense than she. He turned, started to leave, then turned again.

"You have fish in your pack?" he asked.

"Enough for the day."

"Not to eat." Skinner spoke as if she were a child.

"Give it to me." He put out his hand, then winced as he looked to the bruised skin below her eye. "Never mind. Do it yourself. Rub fish scales on your face. Make yourself look old and dirty."

"But—?"

"You want to be safe?" Skinner demanded, then he turned and slouched back to the stranger. Elik watched after him with concern. She had no idea who this man was, but Skinner should have known it wasn't a good thing, letting his fear show. He would do far better carrying his bow, telling this stranger he was a hunter.

As to the man, she already didn't trust him. His camp seemed too well established for a hunting camp. Unless he was passing through as a trader? But traders were polite and quiet and they headed through an empty route such as this, they didn't settle in.

Besides, why would Skinner, with his hungry eyes, be afraid of a trader?

Elik found a dry whitefish in her pack. The scales were dry and they sprang easily from the fish's belly into her hands, but they were too light to stay. She dug below the moss, scraped up some dirt, then patted it all together onto her cheeks.

It made her face feel tight and masklike, but there was a sense to it; a woman was seldom safe around the kind of man who traveled alone. And a man, especially a young man far from home, often did things that later, when others were about, he didn't like to tell.

By the time she picked her way over the hummocks to the camp, the two men were seated just inside the open flap of the tent. A smudge fire of rotten willows was lit and she smelled the tang, burning to keep away mosquitoes.

Behind the tent the dog stood at the end of its tether, pointed ears lifted, trying to decide who she might be. Behind the dog and down in a draw there was a creek, good for water perhaps, but from where she stood now, it seemed so narrow, she wondered how there could be fish inside. Small, low-lying tundra flowers flecked the ground. A mouse scurried by, brown and grey, its fur neatly groomed.

Had no one been here, Skinner might have picked the same spot for a camp. The wind was easy and it seemed the kind of place animals might come. The hunting might not be bad.

And yet, why would a man haul tent skins so large without the help of a boat? Even if the dog had helped pack some of the load, why go to all the trouble?

She set down her pack as near to the man's tent as was polite, but not so close they could accuse her of prying. Except that was what she tried to do, to listen, though all she could catch was their too-quick talking, the same as when Skinner and Allanaq had spoken together, too high and with the sounds all blurred together.

Skinner had been adamant about offering the man a feast, and so it was for her to decide how to prepare the meal, raw or cooked, land animal or sea—she had no wish to shame him.

And besides, with heavy, sweet-smelling food in her hand, she would have a better, more leisurely chance to listen.

Quickly, not wanting to go too far, she gathered cotton grass and dry twigs for tinder. She kept an eye on the man's black and silver long-eared dog, making sure it was tied. And she stole a longer glance around the camp, checking for anything she might grab if the men started fighting and she needed to run. Food. A fishing spear. If it meant surviving, she wouldn't be afraid to steal.

She was surprised when she returned with the tinder to find that one of the men—not Skinner, it had to be the stranger—had set out a mat for her to work on. On top of the mat lay a rack of caribou ribs. The meat was still fresh, no longer bloody, but soft enough.

That was surprising, she hadn't heard any movement. Unless the man had set the meat out earlier and she hadn't noticed. She must have grown more used to Skinner than she realized, with his loud, almost clumsy ways.

She glanced sideways at the man as she set up the fire. This Kaviaq looked younger than Skinner. Even sitting, he was tall, the way Allanaq had been tall. And he wore no labrets, as Skinner wore none. And everywhere on his cheeks, his temples, on the sharp bones of his face, were tattoos. Not like Skinner's, which reminded her of a walrus's whiskers. These were more like a bird's, with rows like feathers taking flight from center-lines of quills.

She pulled out her cutting knife, the last of Skinner's whale meat, and plain fish for her.

Skinner had already eaten whale meat that day, which meant it wouldn't be proper for him to also eat caribou. She didn't know what this Kaviaq needed, what foods he liked or what he was forbidden from eating, so she decided to cook them both, but not together, of course, and let the men take as they wished.

With a strike of her firestones, the dry cotton quickly caught. She fed it larger kindling then, shielding her eyes as if the smoke was burning, and moved closer where she could hear.

The men's voices had grown louder; there was anger in the words. The stranger seemed more adept at swallowing his thoughts. Skinner's face darkened. His fingers drummed nervously on his thigh.

She glanced back to the stranger and caught him watching her. Quickly she turned, lowered her gaze, but her heart was already pounding. The man's eyes were too strong, helping themselves where they weren't supposed to be. She didn't like that. No wonder Skinner was angry.

She made herself keep working. He had left a pair of forked sticks lying near the fire pit and she borrowed them, moved his cooking stones into the coals to heat. She laid the meat out to cook, long sections of ribs to one side, smoother whale meat to the other. She brought out Skinner's square bowl, and another, a finely painted bowl he had taken from Allanaq's boat. For her own meal she would use the rimmed woman's bowl she ate from every day.

Skinner had said the meal should be a feast, and so it would be. She didn't know what kind of rules this man's people followed, but she would do everything she knew that was proper, and then she would do more.

She would cook the two kinds of meat, land and sea, in two pots, and plan it so both could be ready at the same time. The ribs first, since they required more time. The whale next, but only after she had cleaned the pot and wiped the inside with ashes.

She would ask Skinner more about this man as soon as she had a chance, but for now there were certain things that everyone knew, no matter where a person traveled. Illness and death and bad luck—these things came when people ignored the proper rules of life. They came because people needed to eat meat in order to live, and to eat meat it was necessary to kill the bodies of animals who had souls, the same as people had souls. Forget, and the spirits brought illness. They stole your soul. They entered your body.

All children were taught this way by their elders, through stories, through the teaching of rules which must be honored.

These two animals, the caribou and the whale, they had never walked in the world together. It would be abhorrent if she tried to make them sleep in the same pot.

When the cooking was done Elik set the bowls on the ground in front of the men, along with seal oil and a few early berries she had picked along the way. She kept her gaze politely lowered, returned to the fire and chewed on a flake of her fish. But then, while they were busy with their food, she watched more curiously the way each man pulled out chunks of meat and ate and sucked his fingers.

And what she saw as the stranger ate, that Skinner with his face buried in his bowl missed, was the way Kaviaq ate the caribou, and accepted the bowl of whale meat when Skinner pushed it at him. But all Kaviaq did was suck his fingers, and belch without ever touching the whale. With the satisfied look of a well-fed man, he set the bowl down on the ground in front of Skinner.

Skinner smiled when he was done, until he looked in the bowl and his eyebrows lifted in surprise. He had expected Kaviaq's bowl to be empty. It was bad luck not to finish a meal, no different than if a hunter simply walked up to the carcass of a dead animal and bragged that its death wasn't needed. A man like that might as well lie down in his house and wait to die; no animal would come to his harpoon.

Flustered, Skinner turned to Elik. He lifted the bowl, motioned for her to come eat their leftovers, join the men.

Elik tucked her chin to her chest, pretending she hadn't heard. What was he thinking—that she would eat fresh caribou? How else did he think the spirits would judge him, if not by what they saw and heard?

She lifted her hood, fought the urge to rub away the fish scales; they felt stiff and tight and foolish. And now when she looked up, the man was watching again. Whatever she did, he followed. He kept watching.

She dropped another fire-heated rock into a pot of plain water, shredded in a bit of leaf.

"Sometimes," Kaviaq politely said, "a man grows thirsty?"

Skinner nearly jumped; he had forgotten to offer water. He motioned, and there was nothing Elik could do but bring the water bladder and stand between the two men. Just as she held it out, she looked down, noticed her hands. She had rubbed fish scales on the backs to make them look old. Foolish, childish thing to do. Why had she ever agreed to Skinner's idea?

Suddenly, the water slipped. Kaviaq reached, caught the container before it spilled. Skinner laughed uneasily and Elik reddened with embarrassment as he held it out. She took it back, and more carefully offered the ivory nozzle to Skinner, but the man kept watching, so closely, she pulled her hands inside her sleeves hoping to hide the fish scales.

She risked a glance, found him staring, but it wasn't her hands now, it was her parka. The designs in the pieced borders first, and then her belt, as if he was looking for something. What? Amulets? She hadn't returned them to her belt since the day Skinner hit her.

She backed away, this time taking care to notice his clothing. As ragged as the parka Skinner wore, that's how fine this Kaviaq's was. The fur from the soft white underbelly that had covered a caribou's heart was stitched in a line over his heart. Caribou ears hung from the hood, where his own ears would be covered. And there were amulets stitched to the chest, two round bones whose use she didn't know. And more on his belt, ivory and animal skins, miniature blades so tiny she wondered how he kept them on.

The men were finished. Elik removed their bowls, then sat down to her own meal. She mixed oil with dried fish. She drank water, and she listened. The sounds of their words had grown easier to understand. The man must have asked Skinner something he didn't want to hear. Skinner's fingers started tapping.

Elik wiped her bowl with a handful of grass, then set it carefully upside down against a rock so that later, nothing evil could sneak into the bowl, then inside of her.

"What does she do that for?"

Elik looked up in surprise, then quickly pushed the stick around the fire and stirred the ashes.

Skinner didn't turn to see. "Do what?" He asked uncomfortably.

"With the food?"

"What do I know what she does?" Skinner looked as wounded as if the man had insulted him. "I told you, the man I got her from wanted to trade. I needed a wife."

"She's a mother?"

Elik's stomach twisted to a knot.

"A mother?" Skinner coughed, then spat. And then he lied. "How could I know? I told you. She talks strange. She's hard to understand. Does a man ask a woman's vagina whose been living up inside?"

Kaviaq laughed, and Elik sent a thankful glance toward Skinner. He'd lied for her. She hadn't expected that.

"But if she's already old," Kaviaq spun about, caught Elik just as she turned. "Why rub fish scales on her face? And if she's not a mother, then why does she take such care with her things?"

"Things?" Skinner coughed, then frowned. "What things are those? I asked her just yesterday if she would fix my boots, and she said . . ."

Kaviaq grew impatient. "Not her sewing. Her food. Her cooking. Her bowl. She covers her head. She eats nothing raw. She won't touch your meat."

"Oh, that . . ." Skinner rubbed his hands together.

"How long have you had her?"

Elik reached for her pack. Nervously, she pulled out a handful of basket grass. She needed something in her hands, some work to hide behind. This man was too smart. She wanted this meal to be over, and them safely away.

"Oh, a long time," Skinner nodded vigorously as he answered. "I had her a very long time."

Kaviaq leaned into Skinner's face. "And you sleep with her? You have relations?"

"She is my wife," Skinner pretended surprise. "But . . . ah. Is that it?" He made a sign, hooked his fingers over his belt, pointed lewdly toward his crotch. "Is that what you want? A man grows cold, sleeping alone all season? He grows hungry for a different smell besides his own? If you like, I could lend her to you for a night?"

"I had a different thought."

"Different?" Skinner's voice lost its bluster. "What could be different? You want to exchange wives?"

Elik bit her tongue, not to speak. She had never trusted Skinner before, but now he'd lied for her. Twice.

Kaviaq laughed and slapped the ground as if Skinner had offered a joke. "And why would I want to be obligated to you?"

"I . . . I don't know," Skinner's voice grew smaller. He stared at his hands. "I suppose . . . you would not."

"And why would I want to call myself relative to such as you?"

"But I—I have obligations," Skinner tried to protest. "To her husband. We made promises . . ."

"And could you fill them, if you were dead?"

"Dead? No, no. Of course not," Skinner rose and then stood there. Elik looked up to see him pulling on his chin. His back was turned, she couldn't see his face, but he was looking now at the packs she had carried. He looked to the hills where his weapons and his own pack had been left.

Elik set down the grass. She made no pretense at work. Something was happening, too fast. The trust she had only moments earlier placed in Skinner fell quickly away.

"Not a partnership then? Of course," Skinner said.

"But you see, I was taking her back to the Seal People's village as it was. Because, you see . . . she is not Seal People, of course. You see. But she still sews, of course. It is useful having a woman. She sews. She isn't too ugly—"

Elik started to her feet, but Skinner stepped over, pressed her shoulder back down.

"She is not careless, is she?"

"No, no." Skinner sounded almost boastful now. As if he were discussing a bowl or a harpoon he'd made. A woman he had the right to trade. "You see for yourself, she minds what she eats. She minds everything."

Kaviaq nodded. "Where was your camp?" he asked.

"On the coast, the Place with Walrus Ivory."

"You stayed there the whole season?"

"Since I walked out from the Seal village, yes."

"Where is your bow? Your weapons? I see only what this woman carried."

"In the hills, there," Skinner pointed. "I didn't know who you were. We left our tent skins, extra food."

"Then go. Get them before I grow as greedy as a certain man I used to know . . . "

Skinner didn't wait. He took two swift steps, crouched in front of Elik's pack.

"Skinner?" Elik shook her head in disbelief. He tore open the top, quickly, sorting, piling, grabbing what he wished.

"You be quiet, and grateful," Skinner hissed.

Elik took his arm, but he shook her off. "What's happening? You aren't leaving?"

"You have nothing to complain about. He's able enough to provide for two wives already; he can feed one more. Better than me."

"But where are you going? Skinner—?"

Annoyed, Skinner pushed her away. He was too intent on the leftover meat, the bowls, the horn dipper—checking behind to see where Kaviaq stood.

"Don't be surprised," Skinner said, "if he throws you away. Unless you learn to be quieter for him than you were for me. And mind you listen when he tells you that Nuliaq is first wife and Little-Creek is in charge of the food. You remember that. She decides who eats, not you."

Kaviaq rose. He stood with arms folded, glaring at Skinner. "Perhaps you're ready now?"

Skinner's eyes widened. He stopped sorting. Instead, everything he'd pulled from Elik's pack he stuffed back in. Bowls, sewing things, he jammed quickly back inside. Then he stood, slung the pack over his shoulder, not just a share, not a portion, but everything she had carried. Everything she owned.

He started walking, quickly. Back toward the hill where they'd just come down.

Elik ran after him. "You can't leave me. How will I find you?"

"Go away!"

"Where are you going?" She grabbed his sleeve, but he tore it loose from her hand.

He glanced back to the camp. The dog was barking, pulling to be free, but Kaviaq remained where he was. "Go away," he warned. "You have a new husband, and I can go home. For once, I had something someone wanted. I'm alive. You understand?"

"Where will he take me? Is he Seal People?"

"Of course he's Seal People. Don't be a fool."

"But which of their villages? Where?"

"Let go. I've listened to enough of your questions. Your prattling. Be grateful. With him you won't starve."

Elik looked back to find Kaviaq with his fist in the scruff of the dog's neck, holding it back.

He stood tall and composed. He was looking at her. Directly at her. His eyes unguarded. Calm.

She swallowed, turned back around. Skinner was running, footsteps wide, hands clutched tight to the weight of his newly won pack, leaving her behind.

5

Elik refused to turn around.

The man called Kaviaq was standing somewhere behind her—next to his tent or with his dog, at his food rack. If she turned to look, he would gloat and imagine himself a powerful man to have acquired a woman so easily. He would laugh at the dirt-streak of tears smearing her face. If he was anything like Skinner, he was already thinking about where he could trade her again, how much seal oil she would bring, how many skins. He would drag her away and trade her before she even had a chance to learn where she was, which direction was home.

She sat, exactly where she was. She folded her legs and made herself comfortable beside the one basket Skinner had left behind. She opened the drawstring, found a layer of basket grass. Nothing but grass he'd left her. That was all she owned.

So be it, then. She reached in and pulled out a fistful. At least her hands could be busy while she watched Skinner's back turn into a line, then a dot, then a blur, as if he'd slipped into the empty space between the sky and the edge of the world. That was where he belonged.

She was angry and frightened and alone. Most of all alone. For all Skinner's foolishness and greed, at least he had been a relative, one of Allanaq's Seal People.

She separated out a few blades of grass, started coiling them to start a center for a bottom. She picked through the grass till she found a good wide blade, split it with her thumbnail, then flattened it between her teeth for a thread piece. She wrapped it around the skinny coil.

At least Skinner had come from the same village as Allanaq. He shared the same hatred for Red Fox. And though he lied easily about other things, she believed that he wanted to return home. Perhaps because he was cowardly, and surely for more reasons she didn't understand, he had honestly seen Allanaq as his hope.

No wonder he had been so careful avoiding people, if the first man they found sent him running like a frightened dog.

And where did that leave her? Tossed up on a stretch of valley, with no stories she knew to tell what happened here, what kind of place this was with its hills so numerous, they looked like beads strung together on a necklace.

And this man—she didn't have to look at his face to know what she'd already heard in his voice—that along with his large tent and ample meat supply, he was confident enough to think he could easily keep a woman fed. He could twist any bargain to his favor.

Skinner said he was Seal People, but did that mean he lived in the same village as Allanaq? Her own Real People moved and visited through any number of fish camps and small house sites, larger trading villages all along the coast.

But even if this man did come from the same village, that didn't mean he would go there soon. Or take her. Or that Allanaq's enemies would turn out to be the same as his.

And even if he did take her, and she found Allanaq, what if he'd already taken a new Seal woman for a wife? Or what if, as an infant, his parents had promised him to a girl. Maybe he never remembered to tell her? Maybe he would kill Red Fox, but afterward his thankful relatives would decide they didn't like the looks of his stranger-wife, with her flat nose and too-round face.

Maybe he was dead.

She wouldn't cry, she told herself. She wouldn't whine, the way women sometimes did. Not that she would rejoice. She would be quiet, she promised herself. Especially if she was alone, if she ran away.

There were always stories of women surviving through a winter, but not many. More often, they ended up stolen, spending the rest of their lives giving birth to children they didn't recognize, struggling to find a way home.

The wind slowly changed. A new layer of thick, flat-bottomed clouds moved in from the west. The sun circled slowly toward her other shoulder.

She finished pulling the thread piece out from the basket's growing bottom, stretched her back. Without turning, she listened, then realized that the sounds she'd kept track of earlier—his lifting the tent door flap, his occasional cough—she hadn't heard them in a while.

She held still, searching for a hint of where he was: *Nothing.*

She angled her chin, only a bit. *Not working at his*

tent. Not at his food rack. Her curiosity grew stronger. She lifted her gaze, slowly looked the other way.

This time she found him; he had walked off to the taller grass that grew nearer the creek. He was bent over at the waist, arms chopping up and down. He held a long digging stick, probably the kind with a sharpened bone end that anyone would use for chipping ice or digging in the ground. Gathering plants, that was all.

The knot in Elik shoulders loosened. The man was doing nothing more dangerous than gathering roots for a meal. *Masu,* most likely, if the season was the same here as at home. If he ate human food.

She was a wife again, traded this time, not shared— that much she had clearly understood from the men's arguing. Kaviaq had had no interest in being tied, through her, back to Skinner. Not through marriage, with its many family obligations. Not in a hunting partnership such as Allanaq and Drummer had made, with requirements of cooperation and food-sharing binding them together. Traded.

She almost laughed. If she was a man, most likely she would have made the same choice. A person had merely to look at Skinner, talk with him, to soon know he would always be content to settle for the smaller share of meat. To eat less rather than wake up early, have to hunt before his mouth was fed. What hunter wanted to be obligated to that?

But why was Skinner so frightened of a man who did nothing more than gather roots? Dig in the ground rather than hunt?

At home among Real People, it was women who did the gathering, men who hunted. Men who brought home meat, women who turned the meat into food, the skins into clothing.

But then again, as she sat and watched Kaviaq dig and pick, walk a few paces then dig again, she remembered—it wasn't completely true, what she'd just thought about work.

A man did whatever was necessary to stay alive, no less than a woman. The man who couldn't sew a patch in his boots was a man who died on the ice, alongside the seal he already caught. The woman who didn't know how to set a snare for ptarmigan or hare was a woman whose children would starve while they waited for a father to bring home his catch. They would already be dead.

The man lifted his sack to his shoulder, walked a few steps more.

Elik stiffened, then shifted her seat so she'd be able to watch more easily without being caught. But when she looked back to the work in her lap, she was surprised at how poorly it was done. The stitches were all uneven and the flat base of her basket curved higher on one side, lower and too loose on the other.

She lifted it to her teeth, bit sideways into the last stitch to pull it out and start again, properly this time. But then . . . no, she decided. Let the basket be ugly. Let this man wonder what kind of value he'd gotten for his trade, his promise not to kill Skinner if he left quickly. It didn't seem as if she had cost him very much.

The dog whined and Elik looked up to find Kaviaq back near the tent. He was untying the line from around its neck, murmuring dog-words too soft for her to understand. The dog's tail whipped the air. It licked his hand, then followed close beside as Kaviaq unrolled a mat and sat down in front of his tent. The dog sniffed around a while, then gave up when it realized there was no food of interest. Kaviaq pulled something out of his sack and the dog trotted off.

It wasn't *masu*, there was no long root in his hand. She'd guessed wrong. This was green and leafy. A moment later and Elik recognized the shape: it was the long-leafed *qanganaruaq*. Stinkweed. His hands would carry up its smell, the back of his throat would burn with the taste.

What was he doing? He sat with his legs straight out, pounding the dark leaves with a stone. He used a scooped-out bowl, the wood so large it could only have washed up along a beach. Not here.

He mixed the leaves with something that might have been seal oil, maybe water. And he kept rubbing them between his fingers, checking, trying to see if was done.

Then he rose. Elik's stomach twisted as she spun about. Surely, he knew she'd been watching—how could he not? Just as he must have been watching her.

And now she remembered what she looked like, with her face still smudged with fish scales. She felt as young and uncertain as the first time her grandmother led her into the center of the Bent Point village *qasgi* and she danced alone in front of the crowd.

She split a new blade of grass, started to thread it between two rows. She hadn't made one full loop when she heard a clacking sound. The shadows changed. She looked up to see Kaviaq standing in front of her, so close she could have moved a finger and touched his boot.

The clacking sound had come from two round amulets on his parka chest, but it was his belt that drew her attention. It was wrapped and stitched and cluttered with more amulets than she had ever seen on one man: a nose skin large enough to be a polar bear's. Feathers. Bones. An obsidian blade no larger than her finger. The head of a loon, not unlike the one Malluar had given her that was gone now. A chain of linked circles, again with the shape of a loon's head carved at the end, the entire piece from a single length of ivory. Allanaq had spent long days on similar pieces, but never for his own use, for his father's. His best work was always for his father.

And then, just like that, the man squatted in front of her. His knees grazed hers. He touched her shoulder and she startled, held her breath.

He took hold of her chin and she opened her mouth, ready to bite him, but he let go. He'd been ready for that.

Elik glowered, but she didn't let him see. She stared past his shoulder, watched his dog rooting beneath the food cache.

The man let a little while go by. Then again, he lifted his hand to her chin.

This time she allowed it. Better to stay alive and wait to find out what he wanted, what he was going to do.

His touch was light, gentler than she'd expected; he turned her chin toward him. She squeezed her eyes shut as he wiped something over the fish scales. Rubbing them off—was that all this was about?

She felt his fingers draw a circle around her eyes— enclosing the wound, that's what he was doing. Drawing a circle, like the sky. She smelled something:

the certain presence of urine. He was cleaning the wound, no differently than her grandmother might have done. She felt the soft nap of fur wiping her face, urine again, liquid dripping to her neck. That was all.

The man turned and Elik opened her eyes a slit. He was walking toward his tent.

Quickly, before he noticed, she felt along her face. A leaf clung to one cheek. Odd—she hadn't felt him put it there. The fish scales were gone.

With a new thought, she realized how lucky she was that Skinner had hit her. This Kaviaq would think he was healing a human wound. Skinner hadn't seen the wolverine scratch her face, and neither would Kaviaq. And what he didn't see, she wouldn't have to tell.

The tent flap opened and he stepped back out, this time with a dipper in his hand. When he knelt in front of her, she set her gaze back on the food rack. The dog had worried a fish off the line. It dragged the fish a short distance, then sniffed it, prodded it along the ground, then sniffed again.

Kaviaq dipped his fingers in the bowl. "Do you know what this is?"

Elik didn't answer. Her eyes took in only a part of his arm, the bowl, which was not the large one he'd started with, and a dark drip on his fingers of whatever he'd mixed.

"This will help the bruises heal," he said.

He lifted his hand nearer her face. "Do you know what this is?" he asked again.

Elik didn't answer.

"Can you hear me?"

The dog walked a tight circle around the fish, one

way first, then another. Finally, it settled itself into a ball and started chewing.

"Can you talk?"

"I can smell."

"Ah," the man's voice lifted, as if he'd won something. "I thought so. This is raven's berries, it's good for different kinds of pain. In your chest, or here . . ." he pointed to her stomach. "It's mixed with the *sarqiqruak* and then with fish oil.

"Not *sarqiqruak*," Elik said stubbornly. "*Qanganaruaq*. That's how you say it."

"*Qanganaruaq*?" The man shrugged. "If that's what you want to call it. I used it because I didn't know what was wrong with your face. If you eat too much of it you may vomit, but people say it always makes you well."

Elik glanced at his hands. "That bowl," she said. "It's mine."

"Of course it is. Anyone could see he was stealing your bowl. This is a woman's bowl. What use would he have for it?"

Surprise flared in Elik's eyes.

"That man—he isn't to be trusted. But tell me," Kaviaq asked, and there was no urgency in his voice, no pressure. "Why didn't you eat any of the food he offered? Surely you were hungry?"

Elik pressed her lips tight. She didn't want to answer. She would rather have run away. Somewhere. Anywhere. Except that his words were so different than she'd expected, she wondered what other words he had to say.

"He knew I had already eaten whale meat," she said, lying, but only a little, only to test what would happen. "My people don't insult the animals that way, mixing food of the land together with the sea. I had sworn once never to insult the souls of the caribou—"

Kaviaq leaned closer, his gaze so sudden and intent, she was glad she hadn't told the truer words: that the souls of her dead sons hovered so near, it was as if she was the lamp and they the moth, hungering for her light. She needed to be careful, always careful.

"I understand," Kaviaq said. "Among my Seal People it's the same. Especially when someone has a certain animal for a spirit helper, they take an oath not to eat that animal. Had a caribou's spirit spoken to you?"

Elik shook her head, surprised again. "No." She tried a different, halfway lie. "The oath was because of something my father once did, dishonoring a caribou. I took it on so the caribou would not remember his deed, so it would forgive my family."

"Not every woman accepts so difficult a taboo. This is a sign of strength."

"Skinner . . ." Elik muttered in surprise. "He took the meat I carried. My blankets. Everything."

"I know. I watched. But you needn't worry. There is plenty here. Tell me, how did he get you?"

Elik sighed. *We will be two husbands of the same wife,* Allanaq had promised Skinner. *Our sons will call each other brother.*

Kaviaq shifted his legs to sit more comfortably. "So?" he asked again. "Who was this husband Skinner traded you from?"

Something warned Elik not to answer. This man had known Skinner. And more than that, he knew the kind of man he was, in his heart, beneath his words. And if she spoke Allanaq's name . . . ?

If she spoke Allanaq's name, she remembered, nothing would happen, just as nothing happened the first time she said it to Skinner. She wouldn't have to lie. Allanaq had been named by Grey Owl. The Real People word meant A Stranger Who Becomes a Friend. It would mean nothing to Kaviaq. No more than *qanganaruaq* meant to him, or *sarqiqruak* to her. "Allanaq," she offered quietly. "His name was Allanaq."

"Allanaq?" Kaviaq repeated. The word seemed to come sideways from his mouth.

Elik tried not to smile. If he knew the name, he was doing a good job of lying.

"Skinner isn't the kind of man to go looking for a fight. Surely, he didn't steal you. But why would a man trade a woman such as you? Where is this first husband from?"

A woman such as you? Elik had no time to wonder what that meant. She searched for another answer. "Our home was on the Long Coast shore." She pointed through the pass, the way they'd come.

"How far? Did you see the end of the world?"

"No. I don't know. We were trading; we lost most of our goods in a storm, in our boat. In the end, my husband thought it was best for me, when Skinner came along. There would be food." Elik looked away.

"Why did Skinner try to hide you under fish scales?"

Elik laughed. "That Skinner! He didn't want to fight. In case you turned out to be the kind of man who prefers his wives new, and young. If I was old, he thought . . ." and she shrugged, hoping the rest seemed obvious enough and she wouldn't have to finish.

"Is he still alive then, this first husband?"

"I don't know." Elik answered truthfully, but Kaviaq misunderstood.

He reached over, touched her knee. "You mustn't fear," he said. "After death, a person comes back to their senses. After they are buried, safe and properly, their soul can see and understand again, more than we who are alive. It finds the path that leads to the Land of the Dead. Sometimes it's true, when the dead are afraid, they'll try to steal the soul of a living person. But if you took care, if you broke no burial rules, your husband would not do that. He will not come back. But now, tell me," Kaviaq had one more question. "What name do you use?"

"My name is Elik."

"Elik?" Kaviaq slowly moistened his lips. He nodded, more to himself then to her. He stared at the ground, then he rose and stood in front of her. "Do you know what that means?"

It was difficult not to look at him. His eyes were huge, dark, and shining. His long hair loose and clean. The tattoos on his face danced as his eyes crinkled, as he smiled as he wrinkled his nose.

"The name belonged to a relative," Elik said. "A cousin who lived in a village we call Fish River. At birth the soul, wishing to be reborn, enters the body along with its name. It is not the same for you?"

"It is the same. But your name, it means . . . ?"

"It means eye."

"In my language," Kaviaq said, "it also means eye. But it means more than the eye of a salmon which our children like to eat. And more than the eye we see through. It means vision, a certain kind of vision. It is the name we give someone who is gifted with inner sight. One Who Sees. Is that why they gave it to you?"

Elik muttered the first thing that came to mind: "At birth," she said, "a mother hopes for many things. Sometimes for her child to be gifted with a shaman's sight. More often, simply for health."

"There is a story I am reminded of," Kaviaq said. "A story of vision. From your name. It is the story of the blind boy who lived with his grandmother. Do you know it?"

Elik shook her head no.

"It is interesting. The boy, of course, could not hunt, so he and his grandmother were near starvation. Then one day, in the winter, a bear came and walked on their roof. The grandmother handed the boy a bow and arrow, and helped turn his hands in the right direction. The boy shot, and he heard the bear tumbling down. But when the grandmother came back from checking outside, she said the bear had run away. His arrow missed.

"All the rest of that winter the boy survived on worms and rotten meat, while secretly the grand-mother thrived. She was lying, you see. Keeping the rich meat to herself. Until summer came and one day, when the grandmother was not in the house, the boy heard his name called. He groped his way along, fol-lowing the voice until he came to a lake and something touched his hand. It was a Loon who had called. 'Hold tight around my neck,' the Loon said, 'and I will take you down under the water.'

"The boy did as the Loon said, until he grew fright-ened, and struggled and couldn't breathe. The Loon turned back for the surface, and as they broke through the water, the boy found he could see. Four times the Loon took him down and returned with him, and each time his vision grew stronger and clearer than it had been, even before he had gone blind.

"When the boy returned home, he saw the carcass of the bear with hardly more than a few strands of meat remaining after the winter. When his grandmother returned she grew frightened at his anger. 'Take the meat,' she cried. 'Eat all you like.' And the boy did. The next day he called his grandmother to go hunting with him, for a herd of beluga had made their way into a nearby lagoon. When the boy threw his harpoon, he tossed the line around his grandmother's legs. Her feet became tangled and the beluga pulled her into the water, where she drowned."

Kaviaq was done. He watched her a moment longer, then he quietly walked back to his tent. When he returned, he carried a large caribou-skin blanket. He left it in a roll just outside his door flap. He tied the dog back on its tether, then went back to his tent, alone. He closed the flap.

Elik waited till she realized he wasn't coming out again.

Her thoughts were heavy, too strange for her to sit there any longer. She took the blanket, carried it nearer his food cache, well beyond reach of the dog. Then she curled up inside, pulled her knees to her chest, and listened.

Inside his tent, Kaviaq was drumming. And there were footsteps: the sound of heavy dancing. He was dancing a circle around his tent. A small circle at first, then a larger one that was meant to enclose the camp.

It was the same ritual Malluar used to do when her legs were still strong and the rhythm of her drumming took hold.

Elik listened to the double beat, to his dance that drew a line, holding the entire valley inside a circle of safety. If there were any enemies, any harmful spirits who had followed her here, they would not have the power to enter his circle.

Finally, the drumming quieted. Elik lifted a corner of the blanket, wrapped it over her head, then fell asleep safe, shielded from whatever spirits slept in the damp ground below, the prying sky above.

Elik woke to a fog so thick, it seemed to have broken free of the sky. It crept over the ground, hiding the hump of land where for the last few days there had been a dark line of brush outlining the creek, a run of hills that were blue shadows in the morning, gold ribbons as the sun moved around the sky.

She sat up, pulled her parka and leggings on, then stuffed the blanket Kaviaq had loaned her into the crook of the food rack's corner pole, high up and safe beyond reach of the dog.

She lifted her arms skyward. "Eat well, spirits," she said, "you who dwell where I now walk." Then she turned, followed the smell of smoke.

In the fog, Kaviaq's tent seemed to have a floor but no roof. She heard a sound: stone hitting on stone? What was he doing? Striking a new blade from a flint core? Though his industry no longer surprised her, it still made her laugh to think of Skinner. How he would never rise first, never go off on a hunt unless she'd first served his food, stuffed fresh grass inside his boots. The only tools she ever saw in his hand were the ones Allanaq had made.

She found Kaviaq already seated on the ground out-side his tent, legs stretched straight in front of him. A skin bag filled with tools lay open on the ground. Elik leaned over, noticing how small the bag was. His tools all seemed well made, but few in number.

He was working on a piece of ivory, with a heavy scrap of skin on his lap and a smaller pad to protect his hand. He held the ivory braced in his left hand, a chisel burin in his right. Elik watched from behind his shoul-der as, with careful pressure, he drew the tool toward him. There was a small odor, almost like heat, like ivory burning.

A long section of walrus tusk remained on the ground beside him, white and new, large as the share a hunter earned when his harpoon struck first. Skinner was right in one thing, she decided. With this man, she need not fear starvation.

Kaviaq lowered his work. "There's a fire," he offered. "Sometimes a person feels hungry?"

"Thank you," Elik answered, uncertain even after these few days how much to say. She stole a glance to his face. Each time she saw him his tattoos seemed to change. And not only did they cover his face, as Allanaq's and Skinner's had, but they were on his hands also—two rows like tracks running from his middle finger to his wrist, more circling his wrist.

"I was thinking of hunting," Kaviaq said. "I waited till you were awake."

An empty water bladder leaned against his tent; Elik

picked it up. "I should get water," she offered. "And see if there are berries yet?"

"There's a gathering sack, and if you go near the creek," Kaviaq pointed, "you'll see where my raft is tied. There's good picking there."

Elik turned. She had taken no more than two steps, when: "Your face looks better," Kaviaq called from behind her. "Your bruise."

She lifted her hand partway to her cheek, then quickly lowered it, embarrassed. This man spoke so easily, as if he were used to women and visitors and talk. Too easily, she decided, and she made herself walk more quickly, without looking back.

Not until she was certain he was far enough away did she feel along the hard track of the scab.

It was true, she had forgotten—for the first time since Skinner left, she had woken without lifting her hand to her face, without worrying about the wound. And there was another thing to think about. Not once after Skinner started, not in all those nights they traveled together, had Skinner gone to sleep without first using her as a wife.

She didn't know yet if Kaviaq was being kind, or if he merely wanted her to look decent and whole, so that when he found another man he could more easily trade her, make a better deal.

The creek turned out to be wider and quicker than it seemed at first sight. It flowed below a cutbank, with slender roots poking where the dirt had fallen away. There were brown and grey willow and alder, moss and grass growing wherever it could.

There were birds in plenty flitting over the water, insects scooting along the surface. Elik took a deep breath. She would never tire of that smell: flowing water not yet locked in ice. The smell of rain and damp forming puddles in hummocky ground, moss that seemed to have no voice except in this, the shortest season of the year.

She found the raft hauled up above the creek, exactly as Kaviaq had said. It stood propped at an angle, a flat of lashed poles no different than a raft her father and brother would have built.

The poles were long and thin, too thick around for Kaviaq to have gotten them any place nearby. The limbs were all removed, the poles lined out in one direction, narrow at the bow, with a cross brace lashed across each. One end could be used as a platform, for hauling gear—which surely must have been the way he brought those heavy tent skins of his from his home, wherever that was.

Tucked under cover of the raft, she found a small kayak, the skins kept safe from the drying sun. He had hauled in rocks to keep it off the ground, and lashed it down in case of wind.

He hadn't told her there would be a kayak, but it made sense. If he lived in one of the Seal People villages, as Skinner said, then when he was ready to return, he would pole the raft along the stream to a river. Where the river ended in the sea he would cache the raft and climb into the kayak.

Elik jumped down the bank and squatted at the water's edge. She pulled the wood plug out from the bladder's nozzle and, carefully, held the end into the current, squeezing and pressing till it filled. Then she climbed back up, this time stopping for a better look at the kayak.

There were weapons stored beside it, harpoon shafts and an extra double-bladed paddle, a few empty baskets. Painted on the bow in a thick black line was the figure of a seal with its stomach, ribs, and bladder showing—patterns that were near doubles of the kind Allanaq also painted.

Even the shape of the kayak was narrower and longer than a boat her uncle would have made. This one had a solid bow and a point. And where her uncle's kayak would have lifted higher, this one cut straight.

Allanaq's designs, Kaviaq's designs, each no different from the other.

She tried to remember more names from the stories Allanaq used to tell, but the truth was, he seldom spoke of his first life before he came to her uncle, almost not at all. She hadn't heard of Skinner, who turned out to be a cousin. When he'd left, Allanaq had mentioned Ice Stick and another man, but she'd never heard him mention a man called Kaviaq.

Kaviaq wasn't there when she returned with the water. She set the bladder gently down, crossed to examine the fire. He'd taken the time to bank the coals with ash—he couldn't have gone far yet. He had said he was going hunting, but he hadn't said where, or for how long.

The flap door of his tent was shut, weighted on the outside with a rock. She was curious, but not enough to go inside. If he came back, she wouldn't want to be caught.

The ivory he'd been working was there still, tucked safely near the tent and covered with a skin. She glanced over her shoulder. The dog was gone. Kaviaq was nowhere in sight. She squatted down, lifted the cover from the ivory. She couldn't tell what he was making, but it took only a moment to recognize the start of the same kinds of smooth, openwork designs Allanaq would carve into ivory, just as the kayak had been the same. Beautiful, and strong.

Allanaq had long ago explained the care his people worked in the ivory and antler, that the figure carved with beauty pleased the animals more than the plain. That it called the spirits, drew their power the same way an amulet did, holding it, sharing it with the people when they were in need.

In the end, her Real People believed the same. The difference, if their labor was any sign, seemed to be that Allanaq and Kaviaq believed it more.

She picked up the ivory, touched the smooth surface to feel the curve. Then slowly, she began to feel something, a warmth flowing from the ivory into her skin. She stared a moment in surprise. The warmth grew more certain, almost hot.

Yes! She could feel it, deep inside the ivory, as if the tusk still breathed with life. As if she could feel from the surface to the heart inside, the core where the walrus's spirit-soul still clung to life inside of bone.

She closed her eyes. The warmth flowed through each of her fingers, through her hand and then higher, up through her arm, into her shoulders.

Elik shivered. She felt hot and cold, both at the same time.

She opened her eyes, lifted the ivory to her ear, and now she heard something. Inside the ivory. A change, as if a wind had turned. But this wasn't wind. It wasn't outside, it was there, against her ear.

She pulled it away. The sound faded. She brought it closer.

This time it was clearer than a wind. Almost a voice, speaking words. She was certain.

Her heart beat loudly, almost wildly now, but this wasn't her heart. She could tell the difference. And it wasn't the wind, that had been a different pitch, higher, farther away. This sound was definitely voices. Pauses. Sounds. Words.

Elik swallowed hard. She set the ivory down, carefully. She stared at it lying there, white against the darker fur wrapping.

Why did it always happen this way? Why, if she wasn't to speak to the spirits, did they keep coming back, calling to her?

She wanted the spirit inside the ivory to speak to her. She wanted to hear it as much as she had ever wanted anything. But all too clearly she remembered the oath she had sworn after the wolverine clawed her cheek.

Not to listen. Not to risk a trance. Always to go about as if she were blind.

And yet . . . she tried to think clearly. . . . Maybe there were differences? Maybe, though she hadn't been able to control the wolverine, not every spirit would threaten her the same?

She had called to the fish in the pond, and the fish had come. It had been only the smallest of songs, but nothing had gone wrong. The fish had not turned into a demon. It took no revenge. When the wolverine appeared, she had been angry. She had tried using the bone—which she had stolen—to call Allanaq. Perhaps against his will? She hadn't been angry when she sang for the fish. She wasn't angry now.

And she wouldn't be calling Allanaq now. She only wanted to hear the voice. This time, she wasn't trying to make something happen. Perhaps there was a difference, and that was why the trouble with the wolverine had started?

And what if she didn't use the wolverine's own song this time? She should have known not to do that. A song that came from the spirits was always the most powerful. She would do something different. Not with amulets—the only ones she had left since Skinner stole her pack were the oldest ones she stitched in the seam of every new parka. They'd been given to her when she was a girl, a baby, to help the sons she would one day have grow up strong.

Her stomach growled with hunger. She hadn't eaten, but there wasn't time. She stood, glanced carefully about: no sign of Kaviaq.

He had trusted her not to steal his kayak and run away. And he trusted her around his camp while he went hunting. Which meant, she hoped, that he wouldn't be back soon. If she hurried, there was time to try. Not a shaman's trance—she wasn't willing to risk that. But only the smallest song, the kind to help her concentrate. Only to listen.

With an air of calm that, even yesterday, she wouldn't have believed possible, she brought over her blanket, folded it, then sat on it.

At home, she would have used lamp-black to begin a ritual. Here she settled for wood ashes, rubbing them onto her nose, her chin, her cheeks. She closed her eyes.

Malluar had taught her that there was a place inside a person's thoughts that was equal to the greatest solitude of the mountains. It was a sacred place of silence, *qarrtsiluni*, where a person who was a shaman needed to visit, to wait until a powerful, inexplicable understanding came over her.

Malluar would have used her shaman's drum to start her trance, to find that place. She would have beat the drum, and called it *her little kayak*, and asked it to take her sailing under the sea. But Elik had never been permitted to make her own shaman drum. What she did have was a voice, and she could sing. Malluar had taught her that there was power inside words, hidden inside the sounds, and that with these words her tongue could be as strong as a blade.

Quickly then, before she thought of all the hundred little reasons to be afraid, not to try, Elik closed her eyes and, as if the words floated up, out of the ivory, into her blood then out her mouth, she sang: *"Aya iya aya ya-iya. Yai ya ayai ya."*

She repeated it. Again. And again. Over and over, till the rhythm filled her, rocked her, lulled her like a child with its tone.

She quieted finally but a sound remained, as if one last strain of the song lingered. It moved up out of the ivory, onto the wind.

She opened her eyes. She still heard the sound, but it had moved. It wasn't in the ivory now. Where had it gone?

Elik stood, turned her ear. She heard something, not so far away as the creek, but nearer. Slowly, she started walking. Stopped. Listened again. When she looked back, the rounded dome of Kaviaq's tent was smaller but still visible. And the sound . . . it was louder now.

She saw the caribou carcass before she saw the bear.

The empty ribs framed the ground and part of the sky. The meat was ripped back and one rear leg, intact, pointed upward, as if in death the animal had tried to walk along the sky. The carcass was headless; skull and antlers lay a few paces farther. It was not watching. The eyes were closed.

She only saw the bear when it lifted its face from inside the belly. Strands of pink meat trailed back out its mouth.

Unconcerned, it watched her as it ate, knowing the caribou was its own catch first. Not hers. The bear was a honey brown color, fat and contented with its summer feast.

It licked up the meat, leaving a sheen of blood on its muzzle. She was that close, enough to see its dark eyes and the curve of white, hard teeth showing as it opened and closed its mouth, as it chewed.

Elik hadn't yet moved. She didn't back away or make a sound. She didn't drop down and play dead or talk to it or do any of the things people warned each other to remember around a bear.

It wouldn't have mattered. If the bear wanted to kill her, she would be dead.

Finally though, it finished eating. The bear sat back on its haunches. It swerved its great head to one side, watching her now, just as she watched it.

She didn't know what it was thinking. It didn't speak. Instead, it dropped onto its feet and then turned, as if it were in no hurry, as if it knew she was a woman, weaponless, smelling of her woman's smell and it didn't care. Satiated with its meal, the bear ambled off across the open tundra, away toward thicker brush.

The moment the bear was far enough away, Elik stepped nearer for a look—at its tracks first, the huge, long size of its claws digging into the ground. But there was another motion. Something caught her eye and she turned toward the caribou.

Something was moving. Not the carcass, but off to one side. She waited, watched again. It was the head, the entire caribou head seemed to turn, seemed to follow where she'd gone.

She took a step, trying harder to see. The skull was moving. The skin, the eyes, the lips, all moving like grass in the wind. Crawling. No, not crawling. Not exactly. It was shimmering.

She glanced about. There was no sign of the bear, and none of Kaviaq or his dog. She couldn't leave—she was too frightened to go back alone. She knelt, then leaned forward, her weight on her wrists as she tried to see.

The next instant, she jumped suddenly back. She covered her mouth with her hands.

The entire head was swarming with wasps. Yellow, black, stinging wasps. They were layered thicker than fur, thicker than the matted shreds of flesh hidden beneath them.

They crawled over each other, scavenging, hungry, fighting for the meat. Hundreds of them. Hives of them. Lifting. Tasting. Hissing inside empty eye cavities. Crawling inside the mouth where lips no longer cried.

Elik stood. She held out her hand, searching for balance, but too quickly. The wasps felt her motion. One flew over. Another followed. They sensed her heat, then found her hand. They lit on her fingers. Those two, then another. Then more. She stared in bewilderment as they walked on her fingernails, sniffed at her wrist, crawled up inside the sleeve of her parka.

With her hand out in front of her, she stepped backward. That was when the first one stung. With the knife it kept in its mouth, she felt its prick. One, then another. On her wrist. Near her elbow. On her hand. Knife points stabbing. She could almost hear the sound.

Inside her ears, then deeper, as if they had found their way inside of her. Inside her mouth. With a thick dull taste that didn't stay there, but moved slowly. Everything seemed to slow. Except for the taste inside her mouth that was spreading. Down her throat. Into her lungs.

Tightening inside her lungs. Closing them, like a door . . .

By then, her legs had forgotten how to stand. One moment they held her. The next moment she was falling. The ground pressed against her face and the taste . . . Her throat closed tight, but the wasp-taste wanted to come out. And she was vomiting instead of breathing. That was all she knew.

That and blackness, and the slow drumbeat of her heart throbbing deep inside.

And then from somewhere else, a different sound touched her, also inside, but different.

It was a thin sound again, higher pitched than the

ivory sound, but also inside. Inside and then covering her. Warming wherever she was cold. And the world, it wasn't dark. It was summer, she remembered that now. Sunlight, and she could see.

Let it not be the bear, she prayed. She had no weapon. She could never fight its claws or teeth.

But there was no animal. Instead, the sound led her to a hummock, a thick mound of grass on the ground. The hummock looked the same as the roof of a sod-covered winterhouse.

She knelt to it, pressed her cheek to the dirt to see better. A small puff of smoke rose from inside.

She touched it and on one side, where she'd thought to find solid ground, there was a tiny polar-bear skin covering a door. The door gave way. It opened, and she found she was exactly the right size to crawl inside.

The tunnel was long and low, no different than in a human house, and there was a light shining at its end. She followed it, then found after a little while she could stand upright. She reached out, felt the walls. They were icy and hard and their cold touch brought another memory of a house such as this.

It was the Wolverine-spirit's house and she remembered where she'd been when she first found it: alone on her vision-quest. The one time Malluar had willingly allowed her to search for a spirit helper.

The feeling was the same, then and now. The way her arms and legs were delirious with exhaustion. She had been freezing in the wind, and frightened, until the man who was a Wolverine-spirit called her to come inside.

"Qamma."

Startled, Elik peered ahead. She'd heard a voice, someone inside the house, at the end of the cold-trap entry.

"*Qamma.*" She heard it again, the voice. And the word, more clearly. *Qamma.* It was a shaman word. Malluar had taught it to her. It was the word the spirits used when they summoned a human being.

Did someone want her?

Elik walked toward the lamplight. At the end of the tunnel she stepped up into a room. There was a floor without planking, and walls of upright driftwood logs. There were heavy log rafters to hold up the roof and a skyhole in its center, with a seal oil lamp burning below. And around the walls of the house were sleeping benches. And on the benches, four people sat watching her.

A Seal-woman with spotted brown hair and a round, dark-skinned nose, a parka fringed with seal claws. "*Qamma,*" she said, and Elik recognized the voice she'd heard outside. "You are wanted."

The man on the bench next to her was part beluga and part wolf. The split white tail that was his whale part hung over the bench and swept the floor as comfortably as it would have swept the waves. "We were calling you," he said.

In the center bench opposite the entry, a Loon held a bowl out toward Elik. It was a *qattaq*, the kind of woman's ceremonial bowl that a woman held to the moon each year requesting game, but the Loon didn't speak and so Elik didn't touch it. She didn't know what she was supposed to do.

The last person she saw was a Wolverine. He lifted his face, as if he had just caught her scent; he pulled back his lips to show his long teeth, smiling. "I know you," he said.

She cringed, remembering the burn of his claws. She nearly ran. She would have, except that . . . She began to notice, he was so finely dressed, his fur, his parka . . . he was a man now. Surely, he wouldn't hurt her?

They were people, all of them, though some of their animal parts still showed, their ears and mouths especially holding true to their animal shape.

The hood on the Wolverine-man's parka was his animal head pushed back, mouth open toward the wall behind him. His human nose was thin, not flat. His shoulders were lean, his back long and straight. "I'm thirsty," he said, and his voice came at her like a wind, not quite clear but biting and cold. And the smell he had about him was heady and strong. It filled her nostrils, made her dizzy with its scent.

"I'm thirsty," he repeated. "Can you bring water?"

She knew those words. All animals asked them. Human men of their wives. Animals of the hunter. They asked for water when they died. Seals and caribou, bears, whales, people—all were thirsty. It was a proper thing to ask.

The man stepped down from the bench and moved closer. He was so near, he needed to speak no louder than a whisper and she could hear. "I am glad you have come to my house," he said. "I have no wife. I'll bring you furs to keep you warm. I want to be inside you," he said, and Elik stared at his face as he spoke.

He was as beautiful as he had been the first time she saw him. His sleeping place was piled thick with the furs of a wealthy man. His parka was rich and warm. In this house, she would never be cold. She would never want for meat.

"What you will be," the Loon laughed from behind him, "is fat and pregnant with his animal children."

Elik stepped back in surprise.

"Your babies will be born with tails like their father and teeth so sharp, no human man would ever let them live."

"It isn't true," the Wolverine protested. "Your babies will be like the dog babies that started the Forest People, far away from here. They became a race of humans. Not dogs."

"Except for their noses," the Loon added. And it gestured with its hands, human hands, pointing vulgarly toward the Wolverine-man's face. "Their noses will look like that, like snouts, not flat and proper. And when they are naked, their fur will show in more places then just their crotch and armpits."

"Don't listen," the Wolverine hissed. "He only wants you for himself."

"You should go now," the Loon said. "Find yourself a better husband. After he's been inside of you awhile, come back and visit and perhaps we'll speak of more. This husband wouldn't know what to do with a woman such as you."

The Wolverine-man bared his teeth. He stepped toward the Loon, arguing, while Elik quietly started backing away. She felt with her foot till she found the entry-well, then quickly, hurrying now, she started down.

This time she had to crouch to fit. Now the smell of

the house made her throat sting. Her chest hurt and the smoke from their lamp followed her. It was difficult to breathe, to see. She started to cough, to cough again.

And then, someone was shaking her. Yelling at her to breathe, not to cough. Or else to keep coughing. She couldn't tell which.

There were arms and hands, firm hands that weren't the Wolverine's. They clutched her shoulders. Lifted her. Shook her.

Someone was shaking her. Holding her, forcing her head back. "What happened?"

Elik opened her eyes. Kaviaq's face was above hers, one arm around her shoulders, the other supporting her head. He breathed heavily, as if he'd been running, and his eyes were wide with concern. "Was it Skinner? Did he do this? I'll kill him if he comes back. Are you hurt?"

"Not Skinner, no." Elik shivered with cold and with shame. Her chin, her cheek, the ground where she had lain were covered in vomit. Kaviaq seemed not to care. He lifted a clump of hair away from her eyes.

"Are you ill?"

"I don't know." She felt hot and cold at the same time. Her forehead was damp with sweat.

"Did something happen?"

It took her a moment to remember, then: "It was there." She started to point, then stopped, confused. The thatch of grass that had been the roof of the house was gone now. The tiny door, the skyhole where the smoke had risen—nothing remained.

She looked farther, remembering the caribou. But when she tried to sit, pain flared as she leaned on her hand. "There," she said, and Kaviaq turned, following where she pointed.

The caribou skull lay as it had been, angled above the ground, part bone, part flesh, wasps as thick as skin surrounding it.

Kaviaq walked closer for a look. He stood over the skull, then crossed to where the ribcage lay, then back to the head again. "You were stung?" he asked, and Elik nodded.

She found a handful of moss, pulled it up to wipe her mouth, her neck and face. She dug up a handful of cool dirt from the layer below, pressed it on her hand where the swelling hurt.

Kaviaq made a cutting motion with his arms, separating the ground where they stood from the skull, so nothing could come near. Then he started kicking about the ground, walking a larger circle.

Was he looking for a weapon, Elik wondered? A flint point buried in the ground? Finally, he walked back to where she sat, but he wasn't satisfied yet. He patted the moss, separated the grass to keep searching. "What were you doing?" he asked.

Elik lifted the cake of dirt to look at her hand. It had swollen from her fingers nearly to her elbow, as if she had no wrist, as if while her eyes were closed, someone had painted her skin a new and darker color.

How was she supposed to answer? Kaviaq's eyes held concern more than fear, curiosity more than the anger she'd learned to expect from Skinner, or even from Allanaq for that matter.

Why should she trust him? Because he healed her face? Because he came running when she fell? She wrapped her good hand under her armpit. "I was dreaming," she said.

"Of who?"

Elik tightened her mouth. Skinner had accused her of asking too many questions, but this man—he was no better than she.

Something on the ground caught her eye, not far. It was Kaviaq's birding spear, the bone prongs tilting above the ground. He must have been hunting, then heard her scream. He'd caught two fat birds; she could see them lashed above their webbed feet to the barbs. He must have thrown it on the ground when he saw her lying there.

"It was relatives of mine, in the dream," she told him. "I was remembering the way we girls would visit from house to house when we were young. We played all day, until finally one of the elders called for help, for someone to bring clean snow to melt for water."

"And you went?"

"Of course."

"We do that also," he said. "Our children are taught to help the elders, to learn from them, since they know so much more. But there are different kinds of elders. And not all children hear. Tell me, these people in your dream—what words did they call you with?"

Elik hesitated. This man was like no one she had ever met. The way his thoughts followed hers, as if he could hear, as if he could see . . .

She had to answer, but all she could think of was the way Malluar grew so easily annoyed. When Elik asked too many questions, she'd toss out answers in slanted words with double meanings. Nothing true, but never all a lie.

"You mean, what did they say?"

"I mean the word," he pressed. "The word they used?"

Say it, Elik dared herself. This man with his too-quick words and his odd way of talking—why would he know one of Malluar's secret words? Or even the sound, or the meaning?

"Qamma," she said, only the one word, then she waited.

Kaviaq walked the few steps back to the caribou skull. He nudged it with the crimped front of one boot. Then, without any fear of the cloud of wasps that darted suddenly this way and that, he squatted down beside it.

The wasps lifted in a cloud, almost as if they were birds, one bird joined in a single, winged body. They licked at Kaviaq's knees, tasted his leg, even his hand. He didn't move or flinch. He didn't breathe until they settled again. They fell back to their frenzied eating, a thousand separate insects, too intent on their hunger to trouble with a man.

Kaviaq stood and·looked at her; that was all he did, but she couldn't return his gaze. She grew uncomfortable, all too aware of the dirt on her hair, her face, her swollen hand.

Gently then, in a voice as soft as water, he said, "What animal would not call to a woman such as you? What spirit would not come to a light so bright as yours? Even your hair is like the feather on a loon's long neck."

He stopped, shook his head. "I am being foolish, I think . . . I think I have been alone here too long."

He started toward his bird spear, then changed his mind, stepped back again. "Did you think I wouldn't recognize a sacred word? Or that I wouldn't see for myself . . . You are a shaman. It flows from you, the way you step over every stone with care. The way the wind touches you, differently than it touches another. The way birds fly near you, anxious to hear your voice."

Elik was standing now; she had seen his lips move. Her ears had heard the sounds. But his words . . . could he possibly have spoken those words?

"Tell me," he asked. "This relative who called *Qamma* and said that you were wanted, did she bring you into her house?"

Elik nodded.

"Was this the first time?"

Elik crossed her arms over her breasts. "No."

"Who else tried? When?"

"Wolverine." She couldn't hold the name inside. "A Wolverine-spirit also tried."

Kaviaq waited while Elik composed herself. "Is it difficult to speak?"

Elik nodded. He has such long fingers, she noticed, long hands, and a circle of tattoos drawn around his wrists. What does it mean, so many lines?

"Is it me you are afraid of?" he asked. "Or spirits— Those Who Must Be Questioned?"

"Both," she answered truthfully.

"Perhaps it's best," Kaviaq said. Then, after a moment: "Everything that lives has a spirit. Every child knows this. You cannot walk or hunt or eat, but see its truth."

Elik nodded. "We're not so different, your people and mine."

"I see that, you're right. And so your people

understand also that everything has a name. The tent door. The lake. The berry that grows from the bush—all have names, and inside the names all have spirits, and all must be respected. But can you answer one more question, only a small thing? I need to know, were you trained as a shaman?"

"Perhaps a little," she whispered. "Malluar, from my home, my teacher—she said it was the work of a lifetime, learning to be a shaman."

"Your Malluar sounds wise."

"She is."

Kaviaq smiled, then dipped his head. "I too once heard the spirits call out *Qamma*," he said. "I too was once what my people call 'a new man.'"

"You are a shaman." Elik looked up, met his eyes. It was no longer a question.

"I am. And like you, I was not allowed to eat of the tongue, or the head, or the heart of any animal while I waited to learn. I could not suck marrow from any bone. If I did this, I was told, Those Who Must Be Questioned would never speak to me. They would not answer."

"Is that why Skinner was afraid of you, because you are a shaman?"

"Skinner? That man is afraid of everything." Kaviaq flicked his hand dismisivly. "But I want to hear about your Malluar. You said she is a woman, not a man? You're sure?"

"Yes, of course. But, why—?"

"Nothing, no." Kaviaq hushed her. "I just wanted to know. Sometimes, there are jealousies. I would not want to interfere. She is from your home?" He waited till Elik nodded, then: "Tell me, how is it that someone wise enough to believe in patience could also leave you alone, prey to the spirits? But no, you needn't answer. I understand. I've also known elders who forgot how it feels to be young, to be watched by unseen spirits. Followed in the dark, by animals, by the sky. It does things to a person. It leaves him . . ." Kaviaq paused.

"Helpless," Elik finished.

"Yes. That's it. Helpless and begging for the few lessons only an elder, stronger shaman can grant. Songs and words and amulets. There are so few things we have that help us against the world. And yet," Kaviaq looked softly at her, "your teacher was also right. It would be foolish to believe a novice could control the spirits. It can be as dangerous as sending a child out alone in a kayak, steering through a storm."

Elik pulled her gaze from his eyes. She wanted to drink his words, to swallow them, make them a part of her. Like his hand that had touched her cheek, healing the wolverine's scratch, she wanted his words to do the same, to teach her. Heal her.

And yet . . . she forced her thoughts to slow. She was not so young a girl as she once had been, to go running after any promise, any hope without thought of the consequences. Be wary, she told herself. The wolverine also wore a coat of softest fur. And this man, for all his words, could still trade her, or desert her. He could kill her as easily as that, and no one, not Skinner, not Allanaq, not Grey Owl waiting at home for her return, would ever know.

Elik looked toward his tent. Large though it was, it was only a summerhouse, not sturdy enough for shelter against the winter cold. The tent was held by a frame of flexing willow poles he must have brought on the raft, planning on staying. And the caribou skins; she counted six at least, stretching from the domed roof to the ground. No man on a hunting trip carried so much weight.

The flap of his tent was always closed. She hadn't yet been inside. All she had ever seen on the outside were a few fishing spears. A bird-hunting bola he hung on the tent. The one tool kit with its beaver-toothed engraving tools, the burin, the awl. No more than the simplest man would keep.

Among her own Real People the strongest shamans surrounded themselves with wealth: weapons, skins, seal pokes filled with oil. Kaviaq had the air of a shaman, a look in his eyes. The cast of his shoulders. Why not the wealth?

"How did you come to be here?" she asked. "Alone on the tundra when my own people would be at their fish camps or hunting caribou. Why are you alone?"

He hesitated, long enough that she thought he wouldn't answer. When she was young, a question so direct would have brought her father's cuff on her ears. But if he was a shaman, a Seal People shaman, then perhaps he was running from Red Fox, the same as Skinner had run? Or perhaps he'd been chased, the way Allanaq and his father were? Was that what he didn't want to tell?

Kaviaq squatted on his heels. He lifted a few stones, setting them in a pattern: a dot in the center, a wider circle without. "I only came here to wait," he said slowly, "because of a vision. A dream came to me. In it, one of my helping spirits told me to come to this place—a river valley between two hills. The dream told me to wait and see what I would find."

Elik lifted her eyes in surprise. "How long have you been here?"

"Since spring, the last time the moon shone in the sky. But all this while, I thought I'd been summoned to meet a new spirit helper." He reached across, touched her hand. "I think now, the vision was of you."

It was a moment before Elik remembered how to move. She took back her hand, forced herself to breathe, to think clearly, slowly. "I too have had visions," she said.

"Of this wolverine?" Kaviaq asked encouragingly.

"No. I mean, yes. I mean . . ." Elik stopped. She wanted to be careful but the words were there, pressing, pushing to come out. "There is more. I didn't tell everything. There were other spirits in the house. But the wolverine—him I knew from an earlier time."

"Tell me—?"

Elik glanced to his eyes. They were clear; there was no sign of guile or deceit. And she was so hungry—she hadn't realized till now—she was so lonely for someone she could speak with.

Please, she sent out a prayer. *Let this man not be lying. Let me not regret this day.*

She swallowed, then went on. "It was the first time Malluar sent me on a vision-quest. It was late winter. I ate no food for five days. I walked, I wandered. I don't know where I slept. How I found the strength. It was a Wolverine who finally came. He called me into his house. I almost stayed, I would have, except a part of me remembered that I would die if I became his wife, that no human woman could stay alive in that place. I left him, and ran away."

"I have heard of this, how sometimes a spirit is so attracted to a woman's light, he grows more interested in marriage than in food."

"I thought I could stop him. I thought I could be stronger."

"Did your Malluar give you no songs? No secret words? You should tell me if there were. I could help."

"No. No songs."

"Ah, the Wolverine must have sensed this."

"But if it's true, and I'll never be strong enough to stop him."

"But if you weren't strong, why should he care?"

Elik stood very quiet. She still didn't know whether she should laugh or cry, embrace this man or run and hide.

"Take courage," he whispered. "It is not everyone who the spirits will serve. Now listen, I can help. There are amulets I have, and songs and magical words, *ser-ratit* from the First Times when tongues had power. They are strong enough to prevent this Wolverine from hurting you. Only tell me, just a little more. What else did your Malluar teach?"

What else? Elik thought of all her frustrations. The words Malluar had spoken, the stories, the talk. So much talk. "She said that the most important skill a shaman can learn is how to send the soul out of the body, freely journeying."

"Journeying—yes. This is true. But did she tell you where?"

"Where? Why, wherever it's necessary. To search for game. To find the cause for illness."

"Yes. It's the same for a shaman of the Seal People," Kaviaq said. "We learn in order to help. The shaman speaks to the Weather, begging it to be gentle. He travels to the Moon in times of hunger, when someone has neglected the spirits and they are offended. He begs the souls of the animals to return so that people may hunt. You see these amulets?"

He held up the two on his chest, small circles like the sun and the moon, Elik saw now, sliced from a vertebra, smoothed and rounded.

"I have heard of Alignuk," she said. "The brother of the Sun. And I have also heard that only the most powerful shamans succeed in going there, speaking to him. But isn't it true," Elik reasoned, "that to acquire a spirit's help and reach the Moon, a shaman must already be powerful?"

"And you are."

"Perhaps, but only a little."

Kaviaq smiled. "Your modesty is rare. It becomes you. But I can help. Though you mustn't be upset if you don't succeed fully, not at the beginning."

"Help me? How?"

"I can give you helping spirits."

"But what if the Wolverine comes again?"

"It's true, a shaman doesn't choose which spirit appears. But it's also true that the more of them you call, the more powerful you become. The stronger the light inside of you, the more spirits come. I can show you how to invite them into you. To send your free-soul journeying, while they come and sit inside your chest. I will teach you to see into the future, and to heal. Perhaps, like the greatest shamans of old, you will someday be able to breathe life back into the dead."

Elik forced herself to think. Be cautious, not hasty. "Why? Why are you telling me this?"

Kaviaq chuckled. "You are right to ask," he said. "I think . . . I think there is another reason, beyond the vision that told me that if I waited here, something would come." He looked at his hands, then gave another laugh, louder this time.

"I see myself in you. I too once longed to be a shaman, to understand what was happening, each time I went out on the ice, fishing or hunting. Why, when other men spoke of tracks, I saw the deeper shadow within. When they looked to the sky to see the weather, I saw eyes, faces looking down at me. And like you, I also once had a teacher. And my teacher promised great things. He said, do not go out hunting with your father, stay with me and I will give you magical songs so strong, the seal will come to you even without a harpoon. The walrus will lie down for you."

Kaviaq waited a moment, then said, "You are too beautiful, too modest. You shouldn't have to wait a lifetime."

"Then teach me." Elik straightened her shoulders.

Kaviaq watched her closely. "You truly aren't afraid?"

"I already was."

Kaviaq chuckled, but then a moment later she heard him sigh and rub his face as if he was tired suddenly, his thoughts drawn elsewhere.

Elik grew worried. Had she said something wrong? Had she been too forward again? But no; Kaviaq looked up and he was smiling again.

"You must promise to remember," he said. "Never to try these things without me. You could die—it is that dangerous. When you learn to trance—at first, of course—I must be there when your spirit leaves your body. And you must always wait for me to be there to help guide it back in. You understand?"

"Yes."

"Good. Then we can begin. Listen to my voice, and do only as I say."

"Yes, of course. Now?" Elik smiled brightly.

"Hush. My voice—listen only to my voice," Kaviaq firmly repeated. "Do not speak, or move. Do only what I say. Can you remember that?"

Elik nodded.

"That's better. Now, first we make you safe." Kaviaq motioned Elik to follow back toward the tent. He entered it, returned a moment later with his arms full. He set down a large, flat shaman's drum Elik hadn't seen before and a pair of sealskin pants, which he folded and told her to sit on.

"Now," he said, and he sat down so close she could almost feel his knees against hers. "You must be very still. I will hide your soul so it cannot be hurt.

"Later, not today, I will allow whatever spirit wishes, to come and see the shaman-light inside of you. That way they will learn to recognize you. When you call, they will follow your light. But for now, you must only close your eyes."

Elik did as she was told.

"Can you hear me?"

"Yes."

"I want you to sit, and wait, and not to move."

Elik breathed deeply. She let her eyes grow heavier. She waited, till little by little she felt a stillness come over her, then a wind lightly lift her hair. Kaviaq began to hum, and she listened to both him and the sounds of songbirds. A robin. And in the distance, a thrush.

She felt Kaviaq nearby, a warmth rising from his skin, his breathing near her. His whisper: *Do only as I say, and nothing more.*

"I am pulling your soul out through your eyes," he said, and she felt it—something light and soft like a feather. It grazed her cheeks, tickled her eyes. "Don't be afraid," he said. "Don't open your eyes. I want you to put your finger in your mouth. Lick it. Let the water that covers your skin listen to mine."

Elik's hand lifted to her mouth. She licked her finger, then lowered her hand to her lap. She felt the wind taste the saliva, cool the finger.

She heard shuffling, and then a loud beat—Kaviaq's drum. And then a droning song, words and sounds repeated so many times they became a part of the wind, a single, echoing sound.

Until finally, like an echoing sound, they faded.

Elik tried to open her eyes. She couldn't. Until a moment later, Kaviaq allowed the words: "Open your eyes."

And now she could. She did as he said. She rubbed her eyes. They felt sandy and rough, as if she'd been asleep. She blinked, and the next time she looked, there was a rock in front of her, a flat, grey rock half-buried in the ground. She didn't remember it being there before.

"Turn it over," Kaviaq said. "No questions now, just do as I say."

Elik dug her fingers under the rock, scratching for a grip. She pried, the rock budged, and then rolled backward. Below it, on the cool ground, a mass of earthworms stretched, crawled, knotted themselves together.

"*Kupillerok!*" Elik curled her lips in revulsion.

Kaviaq leaned over to watch. "The worm eats into flesh. Into fish. Into the skin of a caribou," he said. "When it dies it is born again, and so because of this, it also gives power. This is their test. If the shaman-light inside you is genuine the worm becomes your helper. Push back your sleeve."

Elik stared at Kaviaq. "Must I?"

"You said you wanted this."

"I do."

"Then push up your sleeve, unless you are afraid?" Kaviaq asked, and there was no softness in his voice. "Put in your hand."

"Which one?" Elik asked. Kaviaq pointed to the arm that was already swollen from the wasp stings. The skin was tender, the entire arm stiff, but Elik forced herself to open her hand, lay her fingers flat. She lowered her arm to the worms.

Her throat closed. She started to choke at the touch, the feel of their soft bodies moving as they started crawling between her fingers, then up on her wrist, exploring through the thin, fine hairs, tasting her skin. They dragged their mud with them, like tattoos marking her arms. Her mouth curled in disgust.

"Now watch," Kaviaq said. "Lift your arm and the worms will fall away."

Gladly, Elik pulled away and it was true—the worms did as he said. They slid and fell, nearly flew from her arm. They curled and burrowed deeper into the ground, exactly as Kaviaq said they would.

Elik stared with gratitude at her arm. It felt numb,

more dead than alive. Where the worms had been there were tracks now, brown ribbons outlining her veins.

"You see there," Kaviaq said. "That is their sign, their promise that someday you will be as the greatest shamans of old. You will be able to transform your body. You will learn to see inside yourself, as if you were a skeleton. Your flesh will disappear and your bones will become visible. You will learn to name them by their shaman-names, and you will be lighter than air. Only then will you truly be a shaman. Now put your hand back in."

Elik hesitated. She looked to Kaviaq.

"You must," he said. "This is a great gift. This is what you wanted, isn't it?"

Elik's lips drew back, her eyes narrowed to slits, but she made herself do it. She lay her arm back in the hollow. Somehow, thankfully, only a few of the worms noticed this time. They lifted their ends. Heads? Tails? She hardly knew. They tasted her skin, then mounted the curve of her arm.

Doglike, they sniffed again at her hand. Elik clenched her jaw, forced herself to watch. There was no pain. She wasn't hurt. No matter the trails of their mud or the numbness of her arm—she was whole, and he was right. This was what she wanted, and she would do anything to learn, anything he asked.

The next moment though, she must have moved. The worms fell and curled, then straightened, then quickly started burrowing into the ground.

Worriedly, she looked to Kaviaq but he hadn't seen. "Look," he whispered, and Elik turned, followed his gaze. No more than a few paces away, a large grey ground squirrel stood on its haunches, watching what she did. Its tiny forelegs were lifted near its chest. Its ears perked up.

"What does it mean?" Elik whispered.

"The squirrel is a spirit," Kaviaq said, and he spoke slowly, respectfully. "What it means is that you are one who is able to cross the path and return alive. The squirrel heard what you did, and it came. And now, the wolverine will not hurt you anymore. The worm has accepted you, and now the squirrel will be one of your helping spirits. It came because it witnessed your strength. It will do as you ask."

Kaviaq leaned over and coughed. He forced up a sound in the back of his throat, and then spit. The white saliva lit on the worms on the ground, and on Elik's arm. He spit in her eyes, even before she realized what he was doing. Her soul was returned.

"Now go and see what the squirrel offers."

Elik approached the squirrel. For a single moment, she thought the animal might stay, that it would allow her touch. Its nose twitched, it watched as she squatted, till she reached her arm and suddenly, it dropped its forelegs to the ground and darted away.

Elik looked at the empty space where the squirrel had sat. There was a hole, she noticed, and a tunnel beneath. She felt around with her one good hand as far as she could reach. With a stick from the fire, she opened the tunnel. In a pocket deep inside lay a cache of seeds, browns and greys, large and small. They smelled of damp soil and wet fur.

She filled her hand and brought it to her mouth. The taste of the seeds was sweet, different than fish, pleasing. When she turned back to Kaviaq, he had pushed the rock back over the worms and was watching her. "Now give thanks," he said, "to your newest spirit helper."

Elik lay down in the bed she had made for herself near the base of Kaviaq's food rack. She pulled the blankets over her head, covering the silhouette of hanging fish, the empty sky above.

There were no northern lights yet this season. No distant wolves howling to frighten her away. It didn't matter. She could not sleep.

She rolled over, watched the way the dog lay, with its legs twitching, dreaming of a hare. She turned on her other side. She smelled the drifting smoke from the smudge fire Kaviaq burned to keep the insects away. Too easily, she heard the soft motion of his steps as he walked around the camp. And then the rustling of tent skins as he let himself in. A soft sound that might be bedding furs being readied for the night. And something else. Something was different.

Elik stood up. With the fur robe clasped around her shoulder, she turned and looked about.

It was his tent, she realized. The door flap had been left open. A small light shone invitingly from inside.

She walked slowly nearer, till she stood in the open shadow of the door, the robe still covering her shoulders. Inside, Kaviaq sat beside a small fire; only his leggings were on, no parka, no boots. As soon as he saw her he set down the drum he had just picked up, and he smiled. He had none of the hungry look that had never left Skinner's face. Nor did his eyes remind her of

Allanaq's, the way he watched constantly for a day that never came.

He wasn't going to hurt her, was he? And wasn't there a certain risk for both of them, being strangers, being shaman?

She stepped inside the tent, looked around. There were shaman things everywhere, more than she had imagined. Sucking tubes and another drum. A spirit mask made of driftwood, paint, and bone. Another with a willow hoop beyond the face. She looked up to find she was standing under a pair of sealskin boots hanging from the sky of the tent. They were a hunter's winter boots, with bottoms of bearded sealskins. Somewhere a woman had chewed folds into the thick skin, urging it to the shape of a foot. The stitches were invisible, all in a perfect straight line, and the boot tops were pieced with changing squares of black and white caribou, all with the finest stitchwork. Somewhere, the boots said, there is a woman who cares.

Elik let the blanket fall from her shoulders. She stood with her arms at her sides, a little shy, modest, while she felt his eyes watching her.

"You are a mother?" he asked.

Elik shrank back; she drew the blankets to her waist to hide. She had forgotten about the folds of skin her stomach revealed. She didn't want to think of those others now, the dead. But if she lied, he would know that too. She lifted her chin. "I was," she answered.

"When?"

She prayed it wouldn't matter. "One winter ago."

"Where is the child?"

"Dead."

Kaviaq looked beyond her, outside the tent. He seemed to be thinking, counting the seasons, the need for concern. "A full year now?" He repeated. "That should be enough time."

"It was early in the winter. The birthing—" Elik didn't want to explain. "It went wrong."

"Even so, among my people, a woman keeps the prohibitions for only a month, two at the most."

"Malluar said I must. Isn't it better to live carefully?"

"Yes. But anyone can see—there is no death left clinging to you. The worm would not have touched you. The wolverine would have felt no desire."

Kaviaq rose and walked around her to the door. He pulled down the rock that held it open, smoothed the flap tight against the floor. He sat down again on the blankets.

Elik turned to find him watching her, his eyes taking in the full length of her body, her legs, buttocks. "You are a woman of honor," he said. "You live with care."

"It doesn't matter to you, that I was Skinner's wife?"

"Why should it matter? People often have husbands or wives elsewhere."

"Do you?" Elik glanced to the boots again.

"Yes. Two wives. You will meet them."

With a smile playing on her mouth now, she said, "In my home, we provide shaman with payment for their services. If they help us find something lost. Or change the weather. We give them something they are needing."

"And what do you have that I could need?" Kaviaq reached out and took hold of her foot. His hand was large and warm as it circled her ankle.

He pulled and she slid closer. She folded her legs,

sat beside him on the bedding. He moved his hand up from her ankle, higher, to her calves, her thighs.

This was Kaviaq, she whispered to herself. A good man. She had nearly forgotten the way a good man could feel.

He moved to face her, lifting himself till his chest grazed her breasts. Till he eased her back, down to the soft furs. He hushed her fears with his weight, his warmth. She closed her eyes and then, instead of hushing her, he brought a quiet sigh from her lips.

6

Elik woke the next day with the scent of Kaviaq's skin lingering on her hands, in her hair. She imagined his voice again, the words and sounds he'd murmured during the night and that she heard again in her morning dreams.

She remembered his long-fingered hands. And the way his shoulders tightened when he lifted her, softened when he lay on top of her, and then behind her, and then again side by side until finally, exhausted, they had fallen asleep.

She had wanted to please him. She hoped she had.

There was so much to think about, not only the way she had felt last night, but the way it turned out that Kaviaq was a shaman.

How strange the world so often was. She, who had always longed to be a shaman, had once, before she was married with Allanaq, been loved by a shaman, Malluar's cousin, a man far older than Kaviaq. And Allanaq's father was a shaman. And it was Allanaq's pursuit of another shaman that had brought her here to this one.

Qamma, they all had said to her. *You are wanted.*

Elik reached out to touch him. The tent was dark;

only a thin seam of light outlined the door flap, the skyhole in the roof overhead.

She stretched farther, felt again—his sleeping place was empty. Surprised, she pushed aside the heavy blankets, sat upright. What a childish thing that was for her to do, sleeping later than a man. What if he thought her lazy? Or childish? What if he decided he didn't need a woman who . . .

No. She stopped herself. She mustn't think that way, letting fear creep back in. Kaviaq was not Skinner. He wanted her because he had sensed she was a shaman, not because he was poor and needed a woman to trade. He would not use her and then throw her away.

She untangled her clothes from the sleeping skins at her feet. She dressed quickly, then stepped outside into the bright, windy day.

His dog had stretched itself out to watch two long-beaked eagles fishing near the stream. Kaviaq sat closer. His hood was lifted, his chin pressed against his chest. He was carving, she guessed from the walrus ivory in his hands. In the fire pit a few steps away, a fire was already lit.

Elik swallowed her embarrassment, crossed to the hearth. She found a stitched-together birchbark bowl balanced against the stones. The bowl was filled with a broth, warm still, and sweet with the smell of fish. Her own bowl lay upside down on the ground where she had left it.

Taking small, gracious steps she carried the bowl to Kaviaq.

His back was towards her and she gave a slight cough. He looked up from his carving and smiled broadly when he saw her; his eyes seemed to glow with the same memory that had wakened her.

Shyly, she returned the smile. She had grown used to his face, she decided, a man without labrets, with none of Skinner's boxlike chin. None of the sharp teeth she'd once seen inside a Forest man's open mouth. If anything, he looked like a slightly older Allanaq, with deeper creases around his eyes.

He set aside his beaver-toothed carving tool, took the bowl, and drank.

Elik watched as the wind rustled his hair. Then she leaned over, and playfully pointed to the carving. "What do you call this?" she asked.

"Something made by hand."

"No," she laughed. "I know that, but why this way? Behind the neck, where the backbone would be. Why not just make it smooth and be done? Why cut through the legs, and waste so much ivory?"

This time it was Kaviaq who laughed. "For beauty," he said. "And strength. Somewhere a walrus died and sent this gift. I could have used it for a drag handle and tied a cord to help drag a seal home over the ice. Or made it into any number of cord attachers. Or a box lid. A harpoon head. But the ivory told me to look deeper before I made those things and so I did. I took my knife and brought out the spirit that was hiding under the skin, the hidden shape. This one is a loon, and the walrus is more pleased."

Kaviaq handed back the bowl, then he made a gesture with his hands. He drew a circle in front of his eyes, one eye first, then the other.

"What is that you do now?"

"What? This?" Kaviaq pointed to the end of the ivory where he'd been working.

"No, the motion," Elik said, but then her smile fell.

Kaviaq bristled, wrinkled his nose. "How could you not know?" he asked. "This is how we clear our vision. All Seal People do this. Whenever we drink, we clear our sight, otherwise we would never find any animals, no matter if they were right in front of us. They would stay invisible.

"Did you think I was like Skinner, a man who squanders his sight on his wife, staring at her buttocks instead of hunting, then trading her stitchwork for the meat he never caught?"

Kaviaq started to say more, but he stopped, held back by the confusion on her face. More gently, he said, "Come here," and he took her hand, pulled her closer. He reached behind her parka, lifted the hood to cover her head.

"There are things you need to remember," he said. "A woman of the Seal People goes around with her hood raised. She doesn't want to be noticed by the Wind, the Weather, even the Rock you stand on—all have spirits. All are watching you.

"Perhaps where you come from, or with Skinner, you were allowed to live as a child. But you are Seal People now. You must learn to walk properly in the world. Do you understand?"

Cautiously, Elik nodded.

With the backs of his fingers, Kaviaq brushed her cheek where the bruises had disappeared. "Go," he said. "Find some work."

"I could learn a song, to thank the Squirrel? I was thinking about how if I sat and waited and—"

"No." Kaviaq motioned her away. "Better not. That Squirrel-spirit might find my carving instead. Better to save it for another time."

Elik thought she understood. "Will you hunt today?"

"Why, no." Kaviaq looked up and chuckled. He spoke as indulgently as a father correcting his child. "This is my work, here. It's a loon. You see this mark, this will be the length of the beak, and here later, I'll add eyes to show the power of its vision. Of all the spirits, the loon is most important to a shaman. See here, below the neck, the open links are like the bones of a shaman who dies when he begins his trance, then wakes and returns to life. When it's done, I'll trade my own small human sight for the loon's magical eyes. It will help me hunt." He looked up, smiled. "Meat for your belly when we're home, and skins for the cold."

"Home?" She stuttered; the word had taken her by surprise.

"What, did you think we would stay here forever?"

"But . . . is it far?"

Kaviaq picked out a spur from one of the ivory's curves. "Some, yes. More than two days."

"Your village, has it a name?"

"We are Seal People. We live in the Seal People's Place."

"But, I mean, is there only the one village? Or are there others, smaller ones along the rivers? Near caribou-crossings?"

"You ask so much," Kaviaq said. "I forget how little you know. Have I frightened you, speaking of a village you've never seen? Is that why you ask?"

"Yes," Elik whispered, then she turned aside. She

prayed he wouldn't ask more, uncertain how she'd answer if he did.

He didn't. His thoughts had moved in their own direction. "I suppose," he said, "I would be lying if I didn't tell you I have enemies. I am not always safe. But then again," he allowed a smile, "what shaman is? We beg for spirits such as the loon to come and speak with us. We risk our lives to do this. And if we don't, the risk is just as great. The caribou grow angry. The seal hides, and people's hope turns into blame. This is no easy life you've taken on," he said, and his voice lowered, turned almost sad. "I am sorry."

"Don't say that," Elik shook her head. "It isn't so. It doesn't matter, easy or hard. Safe or not. To be a shaman—it's a path I've never denied, no more than I could deny my lungs a breath of air."

"You are good," Kaviaq said. "And you are right, but you are also young. You have never faced a starving winter, a village full of people turning to you for help, for food.

"But—" he shook his head. "Enough with all this talk. Words have strength, but we waste it with our worrying. I need to finish this carving, and to do that, my youngest wife, I need quiet."

Elik nodded, just as relieved to slip away. Her tongue felt as if it had suddenly gone thick, her hands turned too clumsy to do anything but take back the bowl, return it to the fire.

Kaviaq had frightened her, but not by speaking of enemies or spirits, as he seemed to think. What troubled her, what made her stomach rise, was the realizing that it might be time to leave soon.

She didn't want to leave. She wasn't ready. It was so

much simpler, staying here. Living as Kaviaq's wife. Listening to his words.

Allanaq was far away. Alive, she hoped, for his own sake. For hers, she wasn't sure. There had been so little room left for her anymore.

Except here. Hidden from Skinner's quick anger and Allanaq's tight fears, she could almost be content.

She knew it was odd to feel that way, when not so long ago she had run after Skinner, as frightened as a child for her mother's hand. Begging a man she hated to take her back. Not to leave her with a man she didn't know.

She slowed the fire with wet moss, then moved to escape the smoke. One thing else was true; the wind had reminded her. Whatever else Kaviaq said, the season was turning. Food needed to be gathered and put aside. A grown woman needed to think about that before all else. It made no difference if her family was only as large as the appetite of one small woman and one man. She still needed to plan for food, for the coming winter.

And what was beginning to look true was that Kaviaq gave most of his attention to his ivory and his private thoughts. Yesterday, the same as today, perhaps the same tomorrow.

Not that she meant to complain—she need do no more than think back to his tent last night, and she felt a lightness inside that made her want to giggle and run to her sister Naiya, and laugh as if they both were girls again. That feeling wasn't going to leave.

It was just that she had never known a man who didn't worry about his hunting. Yet here was Kaviaq, satisfied with whatever small catch came home, hare or ptarmigan, fish from the stream. Not that he was the same as Skinner, who was always hungry but lazy. Kaviaq seemed not to care.

He had no secret stores he was hiding, no dried salmon, no frozen pit-cache such as she'd dug for the beluga. Only the upright drying rack, hung with remnants of the caribou he'd caught or traded, sometime before she arrived. The problem wasn't the lack of meat today, it was how little preparation he'd made for winter.

She had seen no woven willow nets for catching larger fish runs. No nets of any kind. No beating sticks such as women used when blueberries came in season. And while it was true that no one liked to be burdened with too much weight, she had seen only one or two flints to replace the few arrows, knives, and harpoon tips he did carry.

Could Kaviaq be so wealthy, or so great a hunter, like the wolverine, he had no need to worry about his meat?

Without turning back for permission, Elik borrowed his barbed fishing spear. He could call her back if it mattered, but he sat in the same position, legs out straight, only his hands moving over his work.

At the stream where his raft was tied, Elik walked until she found a likely-looking place for fish. There had been more rain the last few days, some of it even turning to snow, and the stream was high. It talked as it rushed by, singing and dancing with colors that were blue and brown, silver and green. There was an eddy, and a turn where brush had packed in with silt and debris. A slow pool had built up, deep but not clear.

She waded into the shallower, ankle-deep water first. The current was slow and the pressure pushed lightly around her legs. Her footing felt solid. She lifted the fish spear till her hand was above her ear, the prongs pointed above the grey water. And then she waited.

The wind lifted. It blew loose strands of hair across her eyes. She waded in a little deeper, then back to the edge. There were whitefish, she had already seen one dart just beyond the spear's reach.

She would catch more than a day's worth. She would clean them, and bring them back to Kaviaq, and without taking the time to cook it, he would eat it then look at her, not with that glimpse of impatience from the morning, but with kindness.

He would take her hand and they would walk together into his tent, and he would make love to her the way he had last night.

She wanted that, the solid feel of his arms, his urgency chasing away her fears. She wanted his voice and his words, the surprise of finding him here, as if this valley was the center of the earth.

A fish's tail cut the water. Elik followed its line, then struck. Water splashed her face and hands and she yanked out the weight of a fat, jerking whitefish.

The center, and one of the outer barbed prongs pierced its middle. Blood ran from its wound-holes, down along its sparkling sides. On the bank, she freed the fish with her foot, hit it with a stone to help it die quickly and with thanks. She tucked it safely behind the rock, then waded into the stream again.

When the water reached as high as the knots on her

boot top, she speared a second. Then another. Then a full hand's count. Then more.

The day passed. The wind changed, turned the thin streams of clouds to a thicker band, grey on the bottom, billowing white above. Not until her arms felt the tug of so much work and her stomach begged for food, did she quit her fishing.

Using the antler-handled knife she had borrowed from Kaviaq, she scraped the large scales from the fish. She fixed the heads so they wouldn't slip, then cut beneath the neck, behind the gill, along the length. She yanked out the stomach and organs and gave those parts back to the water. She piled the eggs to one side; then, with the head still attached to the spine, she pulled back the meat so it was ready to dry.

Quietly, not to seem proud, she counted them again. *Qula malruk.* Two hands' count plus two more. She strung a line through the gill holes, then carried them all, wet and slapping her shoulders, as she walked back to camp.

The dog yipped excitedly when she returned, and she tossed it a handful of the guts she'd saved, then warned it to stay back. The rest was for the drying rack. Then she called toward the tent, smiling with the story of her catch. The tent was dark, hushed, and empty. Kaviaq wasn't there.

Not there, and not toward the south, the way she and Skinner had come. She shielded her eyes from the sun and watched to the east, the west.

Her stomach knotted tighter as she circled the camp.

His ivory and his carving tools were gone also. She searched beneath his blankets, behind his baskets.

The one good harpoon she knew of was gone. Had he taken a bola? The braided throwing-stones were small enough, he could take them or not, she wouldn't know. She wasn't sure enough of what he owned to say what was gone.

Surely, he'd changed his mind and decided to try hunting. He'd taken his ivory, but carving didn't mean he couldn't hunt. Any other man would.

Maybe he had finally noticed the season? There had been frost that morning, a crust of white covering the grass. It had thawed, but surely he had noticed.

She smiled, and chased her fear away. The frost had turned his thoughts to hunting. That was all. Most likely, he had known all along of a caribou herd. He'd only been waiting. And now, with so much meat, he might even consider the chance of staying. If there was a caribou-crossing place, he could easily catch enough for the two of them. She could fish and trap. They could stay as long as they liked. There was no reason to leave.

Elik's thoughts danced ahead. She could help by doubling up the skins of the tent, cover them over with sod. Banked with snow, it would be almost as warm as a dug-out winterhouse. Or what if she started a new house? Two days with both of them working and the digging would be done. For corners, they could use the same willow poles as the tent. Or the raft—they could take it apart for roof beams, cover it with sod and snow. She knew how to chink the holes, make it warm. They had little seal oil, but she could catch more fish. She wanted to stay here with him. She hadn't realized how much till now.

She still couldn't guess which way he might have

gone, but it wouldn't matter. Even with this new layer of night in the evening sky, he could walk almost as long as he liked. Allanaq often hunted that way for caribou or seal, going off for a few days at a time. And her brother used to, when he was alive. He would leave his wife at home, and Kimik wouldn't complain, she would visit around. There were always cousins, sisters, friends.

True, she was alone. But it would only be for a little while. He would come back. And in the meantime, there was this fish to dry. Whitefish needed good smudge fires to keep away the flies, and a hand's count of days to dry before they were ready to string.

She could make a willow net while she waited, the narrow kind for trapping fish. Maybe, if she worked hard enough, she could make another net for ice fishing. Everyone knew of times when hunters failed to find seal, and a family lived on a woman's more dependable catch of fish and ptarmigan, or rabbit. Maybe even voles, if she found enough.

He still hadn't returned when the last fish was hung with its tail to the sky, and the slime wiped from her hands. She ate a little, the finger-sized roots Kaviaq had dug earlier, and half a dried fish, not today's. She worked on her grass basket till her eyes burned too sharply to finish another row.

By night, Kaviaq still hadn't come back. Elik crawled into the tent, into his sleeping furs, and lay quietly, looking about.

One of the water bladders was missing, she noticed. Which meant Kaviaq had planned on being gone at least a full day, if not more.

Then again, his extra boots still hung on the frame overhead, which meant, she hoped, that he wouldn't go far. She settled back into the warmth of his bed. By then, she was weary from her long day's work, tired enough so that sleep came and settled over her thoughts.

In the morning, he still wasn't there. Nor that evening, nor the next day. She spent her time cutting and stripping willow, weaving it into a net to trap ptarmigan. She speared more whitefish and killed a hare with a rock, then scraped and stretched the skin.

It was on the third day after that, as she walked back to the camp with two fat ptarmigans she caught in her newest net. She set them inside the circle of the fire pit, then turned to find that the tent flap she'd left open was closed again.

Instantly, her heart leapt.

She looked about. The dog was untied, though it hadn't barked. It was chewing on a haunch of meat. Kaviaq had gone hunting. He'd tossed the dog meat— of course it wouldn't bark. It was too busy, too content.

For a moment she wasn't certain what to do—call first, or go to him in the tent? But no—the flap was closed. Perhaps he wanted to be alone.

She would build a fire, with those rocks of his that came from a place he said was called *Ikniq. Keneq,* she had said, for fire. *Ikniq,* he had laughed, and told her to go and practice his way.

She took out a small bit of dry willow-cotton rubbed with charcoal from an older fire. She stretched the cotton between her fingers, thinning it. Then the spark. *Ikniq,* she mouthed the word. I have to remember to say *ikniq* if he asks.

When the fire grew hot enough to trust, she pierced one of the birds with a stick. She forced the narrow end into the ptarmigan, up and angled from the chest toward its back, wedging it so it wouldn't slip. The thicker end of the stick she planted into the ground. Then she sat with it, singeing the feathers, turning it to make certain the skin didn't burn.

Finally, she heard a rustling sound. With her best, most patient manners, she first checked that the glossy fat was dripping along the stick. She wiped it, licked her fingers. They tasted sweet. She leaned the wide breast closer toward the heat, then turned to greet him.

Kaviaq stood with the sun's light full on one side of his face; the other side was in shadow.

She offered him a smile and leaned the stick toward him. The bird seemed to bow, to offer its scent.

Kaviaq knelt on his heels beside her. He peeled back the browned skin, licked his fingers. But instead of eating, he let the meal wait. He looked instead to Elik. "I dreamt of you," he said.

Her face warmed. "I was here all along. I also dreamt of you."

Kaviaq let his gaze take in the camp, the crowded food rack, the tent, as if he'd been gone a very long time. He turned back to Elik, but by then a different look was on his face.

"The dream was sweet," he said, "but the trance that came over me wasn't."

Elik's brows knit. "What trance? Didn't you leave to hunt? The dog was eating your catch."

"Your fish. That's all. The dog was so happy to see me, I looked for a treat. But why worry about my hunting, when the fish come so willingly for you? We need so little."

Elik pushed aside her disappointment, trying to understand. "What was wrong then, with your trance?"

Kaviaq took his time answering. He drew the stick to his face, bit off a mouthful. He chewed, and thought, and then finally, with his cheeks glistening with grease, he said, "What went wrong was that nothing happened, and it should have."

"What should have happened?"

"Something. That's what I'm telling you. I drummed and I sang. I called on my spirit helpers and they told me that something is going to happen. I waited, but it didn't. But it will. We have to be ready." He pulled a shred of meat from the bird's breastbone, pushed it for an offering into the ashes.

"Remember what I said?" he continued. "About how a vision led me to this place. I was told someone would come. Not you, but someone who died on the ice?"

"My brother?" Elik asked excitedly. "My brother never returned from a hunting trip."

Kaviaq cocked his head to one side. "Maybe. When did he die?"

"Three winters ago. But maybe he isn't dead. Maybe he only—?"

"No. That wouldn't be it. I'm sorry." Kaviaq's features softened. He lifted his hand, his fingers glided along her neck. He took her arm, and she came to him. She closed her eyes as he pulled her down, there on the ground beside him.

For one sweet moment, he buried his face in the curve of her neck. His breath warmed her. His hands moved to her waist, then higher up inside her parka, as high as her shoulders. He lifted her toward him, and she moved her arms to take hold, but he sighed.

Elik looked to his face just as he stiffened. He laid her back on the ground, shifted so his legs no longer touched hers.

"We mustn't," he said. "Something is going to happen. And we, not just me, but you also must be ready."

Elik edged free of him. She sat up, disappointed, confused.

Had she done something wrong? Offended him, made a mistake? But no. There was a look, almost of sadness, on his face. He pulled a strand of dry grass from her hair, then stood.

Elik set the ptarmigan back down atop the rocks, then followed him into the tent. He smoothed the door flap shut behind them, sat on the blankets, then motioned for her to do the same. Then, without ceremony, without warning, he said, "It's time you learned the first part of the shaman's journey to the moon."

"Now?" Elik asked in surprise, but then she stopped and pressed her hands to her knees, not to move, not to do anything but listen, do as he said.

"A shaman needs someone," he said. "Not simply a helper to hand him his drum, but someone worthy enough to inherit his songs. I have never had such a person. At home there were families who approached me, children who were offered, but they showed none of the signs I hoped to find. And if one thing is true, it's that the spirits a shaman hopes to control are too dangerous for ordinary people. I wanted no families angered, no deaths blamed on me. Though perhaps—"

Kaviaq paused, remembering. "Perhaps there were times when I was too jealous, when I guarded my secrets too closely. Now I am not so young. And here you have come to me, out of this valley, almost out of the air. You are already gifted. You have no reason to challenge me."

"Why would I challenge you?" Elik protested.

"You won't," Kaviaq said. "I have been thinking about this since Skinner first brought you here. You have no reason to disobey. They say it's best when a man marries a woman from a family he knows, but I think not. Not everything that happens between relatives is peaceful. Since you are not Seal People, there is no one to push an older claim on you. Except Skinner—and he's weak enough, I have no fear. I won't need to watch behind my back because of you."

"Is that how you learned to be a shaman? From a relative?"

"No. My skills were learned, not inherited. Though there are also other ways. Not all of them are good. And you?"

"The same," Elik said. "My father was the poorest hunter. No one in my mother's family heard the spirits speak; if anything, they warned me away from shamans. I wasn't related to Malluar. I had to beg, then wait years, till she agreed to teach."

"It was the same for me," Kaviaq said. "So much the same. I begged, not because I was greedy, but for the sake of the spirits I heard. And finally another shaman took me in. But the peace did not last."

"Why?" Elik asked. "Was he jealous?"

"We fought, mostly over a woman. It didn't start with her, but there it ended. The jealousies started years before, when I was young, an orphan living with my grandmother. Even when I was a child, people saw that I had uncanny abilities. That I woke from strange dreams, and found myself in different places from where I first lay down. That the spirits spoke to me, while others heard only the wind. I was able to find food when others, even other shamans, found none."

"Yes," Elik whispered. "That was the same for me. But not anymore."

"And yet, there is more," Kaviaq said. "Much more that I can teach you. Not only to bind the spirits so they'll speak to you, but to fly with them to the house in the moon where the souls of the animals live. So that someday when food is scarce—and someday, it always is—you will know how to find your way. You will be able to help."

"What will I have to do? Fight the wolverine?"

"No. No wolverine anymore. I will guard you."

"You'll be with me?"

Kaviaq took a moment before he answered. He looked toward the door flap, then the skyhole overhead. "You ask so many questions," he said. "I will not come all the way, but you must remember—you would not be able to begin a trance without me. You are too new, still. You will hear me, my song and my drum. And you'll be safe, I promise. If you do as I say, and only as I say, then no harm will come. You said you know the story of Suqunuq who became the sun, and her brother Aliganak, who lives in the moon?"

"I know the story, but no more than that."

Kaviaq nodded. "The land there is very beautiful; I will teach you to see it. There are rivers and lakes, and villages. The animals live there and so do the souls of the dead. When we cannot see the moon, it's because Aliganak is guiding the animals down to earth to be born again.

"Except it also happens," he said, "that sometimes people fail to honor the *inuas*. They refuse to confess their wrongs, and because of this the animals refuse to be hunted. That is when the shaman must help. In the deepest trance, he travels to the moon and begs them to return.

"Now listen, when you first arrive you will see a land no different than the earth, except that the grass grows downward, and it is filled with snow. And here and there in the grass you will see lakes that shine, a great many small lakes. They are the stars in the sky above and around you. The souls of dead people and animals will be there, but they will not come near you. They will not see you until you climb through the star-holes and enter the house.

"For this first time, I can allow you no more, it would be dangerous. You will see the house, the way it is covered in white caribou skins. There will be an enormous walrus, which you must guard yourself from."

Kaviaq smiled at Elik. "If you are careful, it won't hurt you," he said gently. "And you are not to go inside this time. Not until I say. You are not to ask for anything. Do you understand?"

Elik nodded and Kaviaq secured the door flap. He closed the small opening in the roof, every place where light could see in and ruin his secrets. Finally, he sat and folded his legs. He tucked his penis between his thighs.

He leaned forward and gave her his own pants to sit

on. He lifted her hood, tugged it so it covered her eyes, her face, so she could not see.

By then the air had already changed. He took up his drum and the stick he used for a beater. He began with the words first, before his drum, rising from a breath to a chant: *"You moon up there,"* he sang . . .

> *You who shine.*
> *You who live in the sky,*
> *Someone is coming.*
> *You who live in the sky.*
> *Someone is calling. Someone is near.*

He repeated the words. The darkness thickened. Elik felt it tighten like the hood, shutting her out from the rest of the world. Twice, when she turned aside—only for a moment, a heart's beat—he stopped. He made her open her eyes and watch as he beat the drum rim. For the longest time this went on, until he permitted her to close her eyes, and to listen. He started again.

This time, finally, as his drum grew louder, her eyes grew heavier. Her ears rang. The tent was gone.

Where it had been daylight outside, it was night now, wherever she looked. She could see stars, lights twinkling wherever she turned.

One memory came back to her: that day long ago when Malluar allowed her to trance. She had been alone that time, lost and hungry. She didn't feel that way now. She felt alive, tight as a bowstring waiting to release. She felt light, and air, and awe.

Time passed. She had no way of knowing how long. Except that the stars were still out, everywhere surrounding her. She was no longer sitting in Kaviaq's tent, no longer standing on the earth at all.

She kept very still. From far away, she could hear the sound of Kaviaq's song, thinner but still with her, exactly as he'd promised.

Except that now, as she tried to listen, the song began to blur. She heard his words—*You moon up there*—but they no longer had meaning. Only the pulsing rhythm remained. The drumbeat. Beautiful. Lower pitched. Like water, rushing beneath layers of newly frozen ice.

Later, she told herself, she would ask how that was done. How it was possible for anyone merely human to drum so loud. The beat of it changed her feet, made them lighter than smoke, changed her eyes so they were clear enough they could see through night . . .

Elik opened her eyes. Something was happening. The song had faded, but her sight seemed to broaden. There was light, no end to it. Nothing too far or too thick she couldn't see through it. Nothing hidden but she could find it. Nothing secret, but she would learn its name.

She turned at a sound, thinking she would find Kaviaq. But it wasn't him at all.

She heard it again before she saw it, the outstretched wings of a Loon flying in the distance below her. It moved quickly, not close over the chop of the sea, but upward, though it held its head low as if, no matter that it was flying up to meet her, a part of it would always be looking toward the sea.

For one frightening moment, she realized she was cold, numb with cold, and dizzy. The earth was below her—the tent, the land, the river and oceans to the north.

And the Loon, it was below her now, the dark and white of its wings spread wide. It looked up, long enough for her to see its eyes, not black the way another loon's would have been, but white and thick, and shining as if they were made of polished ivory.

She opened her arms. The Loon passed under her, and the next moment she was stretched out on its back, arms around its neck. She wasn't going to fall, the Loon wouldn't let her. And besides, she was too light for that, as if her bones were as hollow as any bird's, her skin like feathers.

And light. There was a light surrounding her. *Qaumaneq.* The light of a shaman's vision, burning both inside of her and without, revealing the sky and the stars and all the worlds for her to see.

And what she saw now was the moon, growing larger and closer in front of her. The Loon hovered nearby so she could see the house, exactly as Kaviaq had promised. It was a sod house, no different than any she knew, except that it was huge and white and the souls of the seals were inside. But so many? They were pressed together, shoulder to shoulder. She wondered how there could be any left for people to hunt in the sea.

She opened her mouth, thinking she would call to see if the man was there, if he could tell her why he kept the *inuas* of the seals up there, but the Loon dipped its wing, veered, and pulled away.

Tightly, she clung to its neck. Her hair blew free, blending with the blacks and whites of the Loon's sleek feathers. Gracefully, it turned its head. So beautiful, there was no room for fear. The Loon looked at her with its eyes of ivory, and she wasn't afraid anymore. She could see . . .

She was alone when she woke up. The silence in the tent was so thick, Elik lifted her hand and felt to make certain where the floor was, where the walls. Kaviaq was gone. There was no sound of breathing beyond her own.

She turned until a crack of light took shape, outlining the door.

One shoulder ached and she was sore down along her side, as if she'd fallen. It didn't matter. She crawled forward, felt for which way the flap opened. She pushed it, then sat there, nearly blinded in the brighter light.

She must have made more noise than she realized, because suddenly, Kaviaq was there. He'd been crouching over the fire pit, the smoke of a newly raised fire billowing around him. "You're awake?" he asked. He sounded surprised.

Elik shielded her eyes, waited for his smile.

"You woke up?" he repeated. "But, how? I mean— without me? Didn't I tell you not to do anything without me?"

She shivered, looked down. She was naked, clothed only in her short inside trousers. She squeezed her arms over her breasts. She remembered Kaviaq removing his clothes, but she had been wearing her parka, hadn't she?

The look on his face as he fixed the rock to the door flap was solemn, unreadable. He stepped around her, then in. He squatted in the center of the tent, waited for Elik to join him.

"So. Tell me. What did you see?"

For a moment, Elik couldn't think how to answer. She remembered everything with absolute clarity. But was it true? Had Kaviaq also seen the moon? Or had he stayed behind, guarding the openings in her nose and eyes, the way he'd guarded her soul the first time?

"I saw it," she said, and her voice sounded dull with sleep. "The moon. The house where Alignuk lives. I did only what you said, I never went in. I never saw him."

"Ah, but that's good." Kaviaq smiled indulgently. He passed her her parka. *Put it on*, he motioned, then: "Did you see nothing else? Did you see caribou? Or seals? A year of plenty? Did you see the stars?"

"The stars, yes. But no other animals. Except for the Loon," she smiled, remembering.

"A loon?" the suddenness of his voice stopped her. "What loon?"

"The Loon carried me on its back, to the house in the moon."

"You mean a cormorant?"

"No. It was—"

"A bird, of course. They're both dark. But a loon, I don't think so. A loon is powerful, sacred. It comes only to those who . . . no. Never mind. In the dark, I'm sure you were mistaken."

A flash of white from the carved ivory loon on Kaviaq's belt caught her eye. Next to that lay another loon amulet.

Kaviaq followed Elik's gaze. "You were thinking of this one, perhaps?"

"No." Elik shook her head. He was frightening her, his questions, his loudness. Why should she lie? "It saw me, and it flew, with its webbed feet back, its neck outstretched. The beak wasn't hooked at an angle, the way a cormorant's is. And its wings were slower, you could hear . . . "

"What color?"

"The Loon? Its summer colors. It hadn't yet turned to winter brown."

"And did it sing for you?" he asked. "Did you think to be initiated without me?" His voice was pinched, his mouth angry.

Elik lowered her gaze. "No, it didn't do that," she said. "I mean, I thought it almost did. Laughing, the way a Loon does. But I was wrong. It didn't."

"Why?"

"Why what?" Elik couldn't follow his thoughts. A Loon had come and carried her to the moon—if that wasn't what he wanted, why didn't he explain? And now that she thought about it, hadn't she dreamt of a loon that same day Skinner had struck her? Just before the wolverine came, she had pulled out her amulet pouch and the loon Malluar had given her tumbled out first. And there was another loon amulet, the one Allanaq had given her, also missing.

"Why so easily?"

"Easily? I don't understand. You said I was gifted. Why shouldn't I have seen it? Wasn't I supposed to?"

Kaviaq was silent for a moment. He sighed, and then he shook his head as if she were a child, incautious and without the sense to understand danger. "You're young, not wise. I told you to wait," he said and he started to rise, then hesitated. "Tell me. This loon, did it speak to you? Give you any words to say?"

"Nothing," Elik swore, and she looked away from his eyes. They were too much like Malluar's, probing, hinting and hiding all at the same time. "Nothing," she said again. "It said nothing at all."

The summer season had passed. Evenings and dusk and the rippling colors of autumn took its place. There was no mistaking the difference, from the full dark of night to the smallest berries, already ripened, already fallen to the ground.

Some days now, the wind swept in from the north with a bite and a chill that grew as the evening deepened, and then held on in the morning, a hard frost lingering past dawn, waiting on the paler sun.

Stars returned, for the first time since the winter ice went out along the Long Coast shore. Elik found the definite outline of Tuktu, the Caribou, and the three straight stars in a row that Malluar had once told her were stretching posts that the women in the Sky World used for braiding and stretching rawhide lines.

She remembered how as a young girl, she had made a name for this time of year. The Laughing Moon she had called it because that was how it made her feel. The wind lifting its fingers and tickling, teasing her braids. The jaegers, auklets, and cormorants filling the sky as brightly as a row of dancers in the *qasgi*.

She remembered how in this season the mosquitoes would have all disappeared and the youngest girls played outside, naked and laughing. The touch of frosted air would waken her breath as she ran. But that had been when she was a child.

As for this frost, it was early still. Winter would come later, squeezing at her chest, burning frozen circles on her cheeks.

Winter.

She would worry about it less if she knew where she would find herself when it arrived. If they were staying, why wouldn't Kaviaq start the digging for a house? Unless he assumed that if she wanted one, she would start the work herself? Like the fishing, the trapping. And the clothes. They would both soon need skins for a new set of winter clothes.

Even boots—Allanaq used to need as many as five pairs of sealskin boots in a winter. Kaviaq had not even enough skins for one. She would have, they wouldn't have had to worry, if Skinner hadn't stolen what she owned.

When she tried to ask about it, Kaviaq pointed toward the neat rows of gutted salmon she had hung along the food rack. They were large, and packed close, and with the frozen pit she'd already filled with more, what need was there to worry?

While Kaviaq worked his adze smoothly over his ivory, Elik felt the thickness on the marmot skin she was scraping. Along with the hare and ground squirrel, she had five of the soft pelts already, all found in a single, tunneled village with grassy dens.

She watched Kaviaq a moment, then went back to her work. She had lived at his side long enough now to know he didn't like to talk while he carved. But she also knew that if she spoke softly, allowing a woman's fears to creep into her voice, eventually he would answer.

"Look at this," she said. "The flint end of the scraping tool is nicked. It's put a hole in the marmot skin."

Kaviaq nodded without looking up. He had five links now, and at their end, the slender beak and rounded head of a loon. This was his second chain since she had come.

"I was thinking about these skins," Elik said. "The marmot is good for trim, but maybe I should trade some for sealskin for boots?"

This time Kaviaq paused. His gaze fell on Elik's braids. She had twisted them carefully, oiled and tied them as she did each day, with a soft, narrow strip of rawhide and a hollow bone for a bead.

"You would be beautiful," Kaviaq said, "with more tattoos. Every man who looks at you will want you. I'll have to be careful when we are home."

"Home?" Elik stopped. "We are leaving?"

"Did I ever say we were staying?"

"No," Elik covered her dismay. "You never did. You didn't. But you also didn't say which way you meant? I was wondering, that's all. Along the river? Or toward the coast."

Kaviaq chuckled. "We are Seal People, I told you. Not Forest People. Not Dog People."

"The same Seal People as Skinner?"

"Yes. You knew that."

"I forgot. Will it take long, reaching your home?"

"If we leave before the first slush ice begins to form, maybe not." Kaviaq lifted his face. He smelled the air. "If the seas are high, the passage will be rougher. It depends."

"Will we pass other villages? You never told me—have you relatives elsewhere?"

Her question brought a laugh. "What man doesn't have relatives?"

Elik smiled. He was a good man, and if he sometimes spoke to her as if she was a child, she wasn't annoyed. Better to be a child and coddled, than hit and ignored the way her father used to hit her mother.

"Wait. I see—" Kaviaq said. "I know. You are wondering about other women? You mustn't worry. They'll treat you as well as I tell them. My first wife, she has one son. A small boy. She'll be glad of your hands to help her work. And my second wife, she's old and far too worried herself about being put out. She'll make no trouble." Kaviaq chuckled. "It might take her a while to get used to living with a man wealthy enough to support three wives, but she won't make trouble. She has nowhere else to go."

The morning after that was a white-faced day, with a wind that rose before dawn and pricked the stream with a shiver of ripples.

Elik woke early. She built a fire out of willow brush, pushed the cooking stones into the center to heat. Kaviaq had slept poorly through the night. He had sat up fitfully and stared toward the skyhole so often, she hardly slept herself. She hoped to feed him now, calm him with a meal made from fish eggs and blueberries.

She untied her braids, worked her fingers through the knots, then retied them. She hoped she hadn't been the cause of his long night. Whether all her questions had reminded him of winter, or of relatives he didn't want to know.

Finally he stepped outside. He turned in the direction of the sun, breathed deeply, then sang his morning song.

She waited till he relieved himself, then quietly, she offered a dipper full of cold water. He took it, but he seemed too moody to care. He wanted no food, never even glanced to the sweet mixture she spooned into his bowl. Nor did he notice her hair, or the warming fire, or whether she was there or not.

Instead, he ducked back inside the tent, returned a moment later with one of the small boxes he kept on a peg in the tent. It didn't seem to matter that she saw. He opened the hinged lid and removed a small egg-shaped clump of red ochre.

Squatting on his heels, he licked the paint and started rubbing it on his face. All along the left side, from his chin to his forehead. The red streaked into splotches of dark and lighter shades that he didn't take the trouble to rub out evenly.

He took a lump of charcoal from the fire, added black lines like the tracks of an eagle walking on a wet sand beach.

He painted them on the right side of his face only, not the red. Then he stood. "I'll be back," he said, as simply as that. His voice was flat, his expression unreadable.

Elik rose in protest, too late: Kaviaq was already walking away. She started after him, then stopped. His hands were empty. He'd left the box. Taken no weapons. Chasing him would be worse then useless.

She stood with the wind in her eyes, watching till he disappeared. As if the earth had eaten him, he turned into a tiny dot, and then no more.

Methodically, Elik walked around the camp. A light rain began to fall. At the drying rack, she flipped over the newest row of fish, shooed the flies away.

She smothered the fire; the rain would put it out anyway. And she tucked his uneaten food into the cold storage hole she'd dug beneath the moss. She took a digging stick and started walking.

If they did leave, as Kaviaq said, and she would be third wife in a house that wasn't hers, then it was impossible to say what share of a husband's catch she could own. As husband, Kaviaq might think he could order his wives to share. But he wouldn't be the third wife, living in that house. He wouldn't know how it would feel.

Nor did he know when they would leave. He had only said it depended. Weather changed. Food grew scarce. Storms came early. What if she got sick? What if he changed his mind, and decided not to go?

Elik turned back for camp. She passed the rest of the day scraping the marmot hide, hanging and stretching a squirrel skin, and pulling out the leg bones for needles.

Kaviaq didn't return that night. Nor was he there the next morning when Elik climbed from the tent to find another frost covering the land. All in one day it seemed, the tundra flowers turned from red to brown. Blueberries softened on the bushes.

The camp seemed smaller, now that it was cold, an insubstantial shelter. This was not the first time, she reminded herself, that Kaviaq had gone. Women were often left alone.

But the truth was, though she saw no bears, no wolves, no sign of people, with Kaviaq she felt safe. Alone, she felt small.

Without him it didn't seem to matter whether she built a fire, or picked berries. Whether she dressed or combed her hair. They had been alone together for so long, he had become father to her, teacher, husband, uncle, and brother, all together inside one man.

She missed him, and she knew it. Not only because she was alone, but because she couldn't stop thinking about the way his foot always searched for hers before he fell asleep. The way his skin was dark, and in a few places near his shoulder and along his ribs, so soft she could feel it even now, under her hand. She remembered how he laughed. The way he lifted himself over her.

By the time the second day was finished, the marmot skins were scraped free of fat and hanging to dry. She had a full two hands' count of squirrel pelts hanging on the food rack. The dog was well fed on the scraps and heads she tossed him. Her hands ached from the work, but it was better to work than to think about, or risk, or dare, the kind of trance she had tried when she called for Allanaq.

Besides, she told herself, if something happened to Kaviaq, if he was hurt or killed—she would know it. The shaman-light he had taught her to kindle was bright as a torch that would enable her to find him, even if he were far away. She would see him. Even into the future, she would know.

But what if he did die? Could she find her way home? It wasn't traveling alone that worried her so much as being found by strangers. And somehow, she doubted Skinner had gone back to his first camp. Or that Allanaq would be sitting at the beluga camp. If she could find the beluga camp. What a fool she had been not to make better plans.

At the end of the second day, when Kaviaq still

hadn't returned, she walked around the camp, counting his weapons, wondering where he had gone.

He had not even taken his fish spear this time; that still leaned against the tent. The bird-dart too. His shaman drum was gone, though. And when she searched for his newest ivory carving, she couldn't find it. Not among his sleeping robes. Not tucked inside the extra pair of boots he hung from the roof of the tent.

She took them down, reached inside. She was surprised how stiff they were. He must have hung them up while they were wet. With no woman to help soften them properly, no wonder he didn't wear them. Too bad they were so ruined. They looked to have been beautiful once.

On the morning of the third day, Elik woke with a start from a dream. Malluar was dead. It was true. She had seen her walking toward the sky. Her parka was stitched over with amulets, ivory, and shells.

They swayed and struck each other as she walked. And they should have been loud. They should have rung with the power of their noise, except Elik couldn't hear them.

Malluar carried a water bladder and a grass basket filled with cut-up meat. But though she had food and drink she seemed restless. She wandered, retraced her steps.

In the dream, Elik saw the souls of other people who had died. Her father, her grandmother—still coughing. She saw a man who had once come on a trading trip to their village, then died two days later.

Elik yanked back her blankets; she was overheated. Her heart beat too quickly. She felt along the floor, found her boots, and pulled them on. She was shaking.

Malluar had turned to her. She had put down her food and, from somewhere in the grass, she found a wooden spirit-mask. She put it on. Elik remembered that now. Malluar had put on the mask and looked at her through the cut-out eyeholes. She had whistled through the mouth. And then she'd spoken: "Drink full," she said, "you spirits who gave so that I might walk." That was all.

Elik hurried out of the tent. She walked off a small distance, squatted to relieve herself. She lifted the hood of her parka and walked the required circle, moving in the same direction as the sun.

When she came back, Kaviaq's drum was there, leaning against the tent. A harpoon was tossed beside the hearth, and a pack she didn't know he owned.

He must have returned last night and slept outside. Or else he walked up quietly from the other direction. He was back, that was what mattered. She didn't care how.

She smiled broadly as she lifted the door flap, stepped inside. His back was to her. He didn't turn, but then, a man could be tired after three days. If he had been hunting he might have gone without sleep. Or if he tranced—?

He stood just off the center of the floor, his face lifted toward the highest curve. "Quiet," he hushed her before she could speak. "They're moving."

"What are?"

"The boots. Wait and watch. You'll see. I came in. I put down the two hares. There, you can see them yourself."

Elik glanced down; two brown hares had been

tossed on a grass mat. They lay with their skins intact, legs cocked stiffly at an angle.

"I lay them down, just now, thinking what a fine present I had brought my wife. But then, as I stood, the tent started talking to me. Everything. You weren't here, so you couldn't know, but it was singing. Everything was singing."

"Singing?" Elik felt a restless unease.

"'Look up.' That was what I heard. 'Look up.' And I did. And the voice was right."

Kaviaq's eyes were dark, closed circles. The skin beneath seemed hollow from exhaustion. "Each day," he said, "for three years now, I have watched for a sign of motion, swaying. Some sign to tell me whether the man they belonged to was alive."

"They aren't your boots?"

"Of course not. How could they be?"

"It's just that—"

"What?" Kaviaq seemed genuinely surprised at the thought. "Hanging all this time without being worn?"

Elik pressed her lips together. She squatted on the floor beside the hares and locked her arms around her knees and waited, watching to see the boots move.

They didn't. Nor sway, nor spin, nor anything.

After what seemed a long while, Elik looked to Kaviaq. "Malluar is dead," she said. "I learned it in a dream. I feel . . . I feel troubled."

"Don't be," Kaviaq said, but he was distracted, his thoughts elsewhere. "Someday, her soul will yearn to be born again. It will grow bored among the dead."

"But what of all the things she promised to teach when I came home? I was to learn from her. I was . . . "

"And you will," Kaviaq muttered, "you will." But he

still wasn't paying attention. He stepped to the door, looked to see if possibly it was the wind that had shaken the tent. But no, the grass lay quiet, sparkling and bent with the morning frost. And on the roof, there was no squirrel or bird who'd come looking for a perch.

He turned back inside, looked to Elik. "Life is endless," he said. "And your Malluar will be reborn, but the souls of people may return as animals. Animals as people. As to Anguta . . . ?" he shrugged, wet his lips. "The boots feel him, the sound of his footsteps. Maybe close. Maybe far. He is ready to come home. Finally, there are two things that I know, after all this time."

"Anguta?" Elik repeated the name, but with a slur in the sounds, the way he had pronounced it. "Anguta." She tried it again.

"Hush. Don't speak so loud. We shouldn't use that name. He could be here. Anywhere. Alive and longing to find me dead."

Elik held quiet. He was scaring her now, his strange, distracted words, his tight mouth. She knew that name. *Anguta*. Though Kaviaq made the sound too thin. The name belonged to Allanaq's father. Surely, though, it was only coincidence. In every village there was more than one child named for the same person. She was not the only Elik.

Kaviaq stared at the boots, at the pattern of black and white caribou furs stitched in perfect, tiny squares along the top.

He glanced to Elik, back to the boots again. He winced, and sputtered, and wiped his mouth.

The boots still hadn't moved. He grew annoyed, then angry, then finally, in disgust, he walked to the door, "Come," he said, and he grabbed Elik by the arm, hurried her outside with him.

At the dog's post he stopped abruptly, released his grip. "Stand there," he ordered. Then, as Elik stepped cautiously aside, he untied the dog and slapped its rump until it trotted off a pace, then whined and sat itself down to watch.

The ground was bare where the dog had stood. Inside its scratched-up circle were scattered piles of turds and a few gnawed bones. The frost was heavy enough, the dog's shit was frozen. Kaviaq surveyed the piles, looking for one turd, exactly the one he wanted. His hand hovered a moment, and then he snatched one.

Quickly then, he started rubbing, rolling the frozen turd along the right arm of his parka sleeve, down his left. From the cuff as high as the shoulder. Again. One time singing. Another time not.

The instant he was done, he tossed the turd over his shoulder. Then he looked for a different spot where the moss grew thicker, untrammeled by the dog's daily pacing.

As if he were a caribou crazy with the buzzing and stinging of a thousand mosquitoes, he dropped and rolled. As if he were a dog, he rocked on his back, rubbed his arms, waved his legs. Till finally, he slowed. He remembered Elik.

She was backing away, moving beyond his reach. Her face was twisted, her gaze darting about.

"Don't leave," he warned sharply. "I don't want something getting at me through you. A wife of mine— you wouldn't be safe. Not with Anguta, possibly even Qajak near."

"Qajak?" Elik's heart caught.

"The dog scent is for earth smell," he said, mistaking her fear. It will hide me from any spirits Anguta might send. I'll be invisible."

She wasn't listening. She didn't care just now about dogs or smells or hiding. "Qajak?" She forced herself to say the name. "Who is that? What does it mean?"

Kaviaq stood up. Calmer now, he straightened the hem of his parka. "It's a boat, the small, decked boat. Don't you know?"

"Yes. Yes of course. We have such names. I know what a kayak is." With perfect clarity, Elik remembered Allanaq paddling away from her in the umiak. His back rose straight and stiff above the gunwale, while Skinner with his newfound treasure smiled broadly. The skin boat lifted on a wave, then carried Allanaq down, hiding him inside a widening trough of water.

She turned to keep the thought from Kaviaq's prying eyes. But already another thought, deeper and far colder, moved in to take its place.

Qajak was the name Skinner also used for Allanaq. And Kaviaq called Qajak enemy. He named Anguta. The father. His enemy.

She looked directly at the man in front of her. "And your name?" she asked. "Surely you have more than one?" She swallowed her breath, stood without moving. "What does Kaviaq mean?"

"Fox. But why do you ask. You understand most of what I say."

"Which fox?"

"Silver. Or Cross Fox. Red Fox."

He walked towards her. He seemed calmer now, but still distracted enough that he didn't notice how she shrank from his touch. He led her into the tent and she stumbled through the door, then stood there, hands against her sides to keep them from shaking, as he pulled off his parka and shook it toward each of the walls, shook it so the smell of the dog would hide the tent, hide their human smell inside.

Time went by, Elik didn't know how much.

While Kaviaq watched the boots, she sat with her head between her knees. More than anything else, she prayed she could go to sleep, no longer think. She wanted to make herself numb and small, to find a place where she never heard any more names. A place where she could hide from whatever was going to happen next.

Kaviaq tapped her on the shoulder. She looked up to see him pointing. The boots were swaying, dangling from the cord that tied them to the frame. First one, then the other, exactly as if somewhere, the two human feet that belonged to them were walking. In the same gait that any man would walk. The right boot swayed, and then the left.

"If he's near," Kaviaq said, "if he's near, then my waiting is done. But if not . . ." Kaviaq pulled on his chin, "if not, it means he has gained a new spirit helper. Or found an amulet that brought new strength." He turned to Elik. "Do you think?"

"No." Elik said, too loudly. "I don't know."

"No. Of course you don't. I've frightened you. I'm sorry." Kaviaq stepped nearer. He smoothed her hair.

"It was the same with my brother," Elik leapt for a truth, a story she could tell. "We hung his boots to learn if he was alive. He'd been seal hunting on the winter ice pack. Did I tell you? He had gone out with my father. The next day my father returned alone."

"Yet you looked to those boots with hope? And so you see, you needn't be frightened of these."

"You think he's alive?"

"That man?" Kaviaq studied the boots again. "If he is dead, they could not move. And while it's true that the souls of evil men may haunt their burial place, unless he died in this very spot—and that I doubt—he would have no power here. They would not move."

Elik made a sound, a sigh, louder than she should have.

Kaviaq turned to look at her. In the tent's dim light, his tattoos made his face look like a bramble of bushes and leaves. He smiled to see her sitting so patiently, gentle and a little afraid.

His smile grew. He turned and moved aside the two dead hares. He glanced purposefully from her to the bed. He motioned for her to come and sit, join him. When she didn't move, he laughed playfully. He took her hand, pulled her to lie beside him.

"The man who wore those boots," he whispered as he nuzzled her ear. "He never heard your name. Whatever strength he has, he used it to search for me, not you. You're safe. I'll take care of you."

He pulled off his leggings and tossed them behind him. Then his boots. Then, naked, he lay down beside her. His legs stretched alongside hers. His hands held her breasts.

She clenched her teeth, not to scream. She forced herself not to stiffen, not to seem different as he settled himself to lie over her. Not to make any sound at all.

He moved to position himself, then closed his eyes and sighed. "I longed for you," he whispered. "When I was alone. I needed you. My thoughts wandered. My hand pretended."

She squeezed her eyes shut as his weight pressed down on hers. He moved her legs further apart. She let him. He fit himself into the places inside of her. His tongue. His fingers. All the places she had allowed him to touch. To know.

Red Fox. Kaviaq. Qajak. Allanaq.

His rhythm drummed the names inside her.

Red Fox. Kaviaq. Qajak. Allanaq. Until finally, his rocking ceased. He pulled himself away, rolled to the furs beside her. Carefully, she edged away, not to touch him. Not to do anything except wait, hold her breath, pray he fell asleep.

And he did, quickly but not deeply; restlessly, so that each time she moved, he opened his eyes and murmured. He felt for her arm. She waited.

There was no hope of sleep, and only one certainty that kept her from running in terror: he had no hint, in all the world, not a clue who she was.

She was safe, but only for now. Come night, another morning? How long till he found out?

Little by little, Kaviaq's sleep deepened. She freed her legs the rest of the way from the heavy furs, grabbed another, and wrapped it over her shivering arms. She stepped quietly across the floor, lifted the spear he had leaned beside the entry, then crossed to stand beneath the patch of afternoon light falling through the skyhole overhead.

For what seemed the longest while, she watched the boots. They didn't move. Nothing happened. She lifted the butt end of the spear, nudged them, tapped them, then watched as they swayed lightly above her.

They had moved before, while Kaviaq watched. She had seen it for herself. But why? If they were Allanaq's boots, she would have understood. The boots would have felt his steps; he was close enough. But they weren't Allanaq's. They were Anguta's. Kaviaq had no reason to lie, nor could he be mistaken.

Kaviaq—Red Fox—he could easily have helped himself to his enemy's boots, and anything else he wanted, simply taken it from their empty house. She knew the story. He had tied their hands. His four cousins towed them out in a boat to the open seas. What relative left behind would dare protest if Red Fox took one pair of boots?

But Anguta was dead. How could the boots have moved . . . unless it was her?

Was that possible? She'd never known Anguta alive. He was already dead when Grey Owl brought Allanaq home.

It was true she had once seen his body. Not the body, but the shroud of burial skins covering it. She and Allanaq had dragged the body . . .

His bones.

Elik shuddered. She pulled her hand from the spear, stared at it, at her fingers.

She had stolen a bone from Allanaq's pouch, from Anguta's hand. She had held the bones in her hand, the same hand she had touched the boots with just yesterday. She had reached in and felt the stitches, the cracking fur, stiffened soles.

Her stomach sank. It was because of her the boots had swayed. Kaviaq would find out. He would use the boots, speak to them somehow. He would work his way backward to find the bone. In her pouch. In her . . .

No. Wait. Where were they, the bones? Where was her amulet pouch?

She glanced to Kaviaq; his eyes were shut, his breathing steady. Gingerly, she lifted her parka from its peg, reached up inside, feeling along the seams.

If he woke, she would say she was cold. Or going outside to piss—a lie, but surely, he would believe it.

He could do things to her if he wanted. He was powerful, a shaman. He could use thought to make things happen.

But he wouldn't. He wouldn't hurt her, so long as he didn't know.

She felt along the hem, along each seam. No light was needed. Her hands knew the touch of every amulet she carried. But all that was there was the patch of salmon skin and the same small amulets she'd carried since she was born.

She didn't need to search. She remembered now. Skinner had stolen her baskets, and with her baskets, her pouch. The bone was inside.

And all this time, she'd been so intent on Kaviaq, she hadn't thought about the pouch. Even the loon necklace Allanaq had given her was gone. She had taken it off when the wolverine scratched her face. She'd put it in the pouch, the pouch in the basket . . .

And what if Skinner hadn't taken her things? When Red Fox looked to the boots, where would they have pointed then, with Anguta's bone inside her pouch? Allanaq's loon around her neck?

Elik woke the next morning on the floor of the tent. A caribou robe had been thrown over her shoulders. She lifted her head to find Kaviaq's sleeping place already empty.

She sat up, listened till she heard him outside, muttering or singing; she couldn't tell which. She dressed quickly, retied her braids with a crisscrossing of rawhide, then stepped outside to the cool, morning light.

There was frost again, she saw that first. Ice had formed on the few shallow ponds that were visible from where she stood.

Kaviaq was seated on a sealskin mat. His legs were folded, his back to the tent. He was talking to himself, leaning forward and doing something with his hands.

Elik let out her breath in disappointment. The way he talked, she had prayed there was someone else here. Even Skinner would have been welcome. But no. Nothing had changed since the night before.

She lifted her hood to cover her head properly, then slowly approached. In between Kaviaq's knees, on the sealskin mat, lay a series of small animal figures, none any larger than a salmonberry. They were divining stones; she'd seen their like before, though she had never tried forecasting herself.

As she watched, Kaviaq swept them up. He lifted them to his mouth and licked them, spread his saliva so they would recognize his name. Then he tossed them, let them sprawl and roll and fall which way they might.

The tiny shapes of seal and caribou, fish and wolf tumbled, then slowed. When they stopped, their heads and tails pointed in every direction. Not one of them touched another.

Kaviaq studied them intently before glancing over his shoulder. "You see these," he said without a greeting. "They have never failed me, never."

Elik fixed a smile on her face, nodded.

"Until now. I have been trying since daybreak to understand. I ask them what they know about the boots. Why they walk? Where is Anguta? But all they speak about is caribou—the herd that came down from north of the Igiasisauq River. You see how this one turns its legs to the north? But why should they speak of caribou, when it's boots I ask about? I was wondering—" He hesitated. He seemed uncomfortable. "Tell me again, how long it's been since that miscarriage you had?"

"Miscarriage?" Elik's hand moved to her stomach. "It was done a year ago," she said. "I told you. The moon after the first hard snow. A year ago."

Thoughtful, Kaviaq pulled on his chin. "So you said."

"Is something wrong?"

"No. I'm sorry," he looked at her with the same forgiving face he had shown yesterday. "You are innocent. It's not the miscarriage that troubles the stones. It's just that I wondered, only for a moment, if those spirits still clung, then maybe . . . but no. It's too long ago. It isn't that."

Kaviaq scooped up the pieces, blew on them this time instead of spitting. He tossed them out, sent them tumbling.

When they fell, the fish's tail lay over the caribou. Wolf and seal rolled further. Kaviaq considered them a moment, then: "It's time," he said.

"Time?" Elik studied the figures, but if there was

meaning, it didn't speak to her.

"To go home. You see how the fish points north, toward the Seal People's Place?"

"Your village, yes."

"It won't take long. We follow the stream, then the sea until we come to the Place of White Whales. From there we follow the land past Akulaaq, a large lagoon, then to the Place Where Raven Made Dry Land." Abruptly, Kaviaq rose. Elik lurched out of his way.

A chill wind lifted the lightest piece, a wolf figure made of rotted wood. The wind sent it rolling, over and again, till the wolf hit against a blade of grass.

"The wind will be even louder along the river," Kaviaq said. "Soon there'll be ice and the route more difficult. We need to leave either now, or much later, when the ice is landfast and safe again." He walked past her and stood in front of the tent. He seemed to be figuring: the skins to be taken down, the poles to store away, the food they would have to carry.

"With the winter coming," he said, "it will be time to open the *qasgi*. Perhaps the fish is right. Anguta is not here, but he is somewhere. Searching for me. I think now it would have been better if I'd killed him from the start, and cut off his head so his spirit wouldn't find me. I should be home."

Elik watched as Kaviaq felt along his belt to his newest amulet. He had finished the cut-through ivory links, and the loon's head carved at its end. There were eyes in the loon now, inset stone of darkest black.

She felt lightheaded suddenly, confused. She didn't want to travel with him. She didn't want to stay. She didn't know what she wanted, other than what she had yesterday, before Red Fox came and took Kaviaq away.

She tried to think of something to say: "Will we hunt? In case we get stranded. Shouldn't we have more meat?"

"We have enough," Kaviaq said. "There'll be a run of late-season whitefish as we reach the mouth of the river."

"But you have more wives," Elik tried to stall. "What if I'm poorly treated?"

"Hush," Kaviaq looked at her. "You mustn't worry. You will have everything. I will tell them you are a wife, not an orphan. You have a right to food shares."

"What if your wife . . . what if . . ." Elik stopped. Her tongue felt thick. She swallowed, but already he misunderstood.

"If there are children from our coupling," he said, "they would be welcome, as all children are welcome."

"You have children?"

Kaviaq stepped closer. She started to back away, then stopped, held herself rigid. He reached out and laid his hand flat on top of her belly, low down in the place a child would grow. "I will have more," he said. "And so will you."

"What if—" Elik took the tiniest step away. "What if there is death on me? What if your wives—"

"Hush. You worry too much," he said. His voice grew louder. He cocked his head, looked at her slant-wise.

"When we get there, will you teach me?" The words jumped from Elik's mouth. "There is so much you promised. So much—"

Kaviaq stopped her. "So much you need to learn," he said. "Proper behavior first. A woman doesn't ask questions so directly. She keeps her eyes lowered. She never steps over a man. Never wastes food, or drinks sloppily or loud. Everything you do, everything, will affect my family. Not only you. You understand?"

"Yes," Elik whispered.

Kaviaq watched her closely. "I have allowed you much freedom," he said. "When we are home, you will not be allowed to follow your own mind. It would not be good for the Seal People. You understand?"

Calmly, Elik nodded, then turned and hid her eyes.

Elik spent the remainder of that day taking down the camp. The sun stayed cold, hidden behind a white sky that changed to grey as the day wore on, a snow-sky filled with heavy moisture that even the birds seemed to taste. They passed overhead, geese in long V-shaped formations flying south, swans and louder cranes lifting from the ponds, joining the flocks that had already gone ahead.

By the time Elik rolled the tent skins and tied the bedding, the sky had changed again. What she thought would be snow turned instead to a dry frost that hardened the moss and left the lichens crackling each time she carried another load to the raft.

Her own belongings were few. She had but a single needle case that she wore in a pouch on her belt, a few strands of sinew. She rolled together the hare, the squirrel, and the marmot hides she had trapped herself. All else belonged to Kaviaq.

She saw now what she hadn't been willing to recognize before, though the signs had been there all along. This had never been a summer fish camp, with cakes of roe laid out on rocks to dry. It was never meant to be a place where a wife counted out the salmon that would feed her family through the year. She was the one who had tried to make it so. Kaviaq never had.

He was smiling as he lowered the raft into the stream, pleased as any hunter sharing out his first fresh seal meat of the year.

She set her loads along the bank while Kaviaq checked the lashings. He cinched them, and knotted them, and added a few new knots. Then together they maneuvered the loads onto the raft.

He had built crosspieces into a platform atop the wide stern end, for a place to dry off tent skins, or his drum. Her fish. Atop those they piled the kayak, upside down and secured across the deck. Kaviaq untied the raft from its mooring, then took up his place on the bow. The dog climbed on last.

Elik leaned her pole into the gravel bottom while Kaviaq pushed toward the center. On her second push the gravel gave way to a soft, thicker mud and they turned into the slow current, downstream.

They poled the raft and floated during the remaining daylight, then camped without a fire. It was the next morning that they reached the river that Kaviaq called Inmachuk—one of the rivers Skinner had also mentioned. Along its edge a brittle membrane of ice already clung. Where there were willow and alder, the leaves had turned to gold and brown.

Elik was glad when he told her to take the position behind him on the raft. He had seemed content when they first left, but he'd woken in a sullen mood, nearly as quiet as she. All through that day, whenever they came around a bend he stiffened and slowed the raft and searched for sign of a fire, a camp, a place where his enemy could trap him.

For her own part, Elik kept her eye on his fishing spear. It was packed at the very top of their gear. The shaft was lashed down, but with a wrapping that only circled twice, no knots. She could easily pull it out if she needed it.

She didn't know if he would kill her when he found out who she was. But he could, if he wanted to, as easily as a man killed a fish—pierced it, then gutted it. He could sever her tendons as if she were an enemy whose ghost he wanted to destroy.

He was strong enough to do it, and worried in a way he hadn't been before. All day as they poled, she watched the way his shoulders moved, and the way he bent his legs for balance as he peered around every shallow bend.

Two times, maybe three, she caught him checking his knives. There was one in each boot, and he'd slipped another in his sleeve. But as the day wore on and they found no trace of camp fires, he grew less wary again.

He steered to avoid the shallow sand bars more than an enemy, and he kept to the center where the current was strong. He seemed to know the swift course and he held it, through the second night they camped, then into the third.

It was then, midway into the third day, that the river ended. It broadened suddenly, like the wing-tips of a bird it fanned out, poured itself into a sandy beach, and then before long, into the sea.

She smelled the salt air before she saw it. The cold wind, the changing wisps of clouds, the open view. Along the shore, everywhere, there were beach ridges and knee-high grass, crusted, all of it, in a white glaze of frost.

In the hazy distance, blue mountains rimmed the northern and eastern edges of land. The farthest she could see was into the west, a low bar of land that must have been a long, pointing cape. The world in front of her was sea. Salt water stretching, then falling away, beyond the stone pillars that held up the earth.

The tide went out as they unloaded the raft. Red, orange, and slick purple starfish lay like tundra flowers along the backwash gullies. Anemones. Sea cucumbers. Crabs, all seemed to be watching, to see what the sky brought in.

That night they set a simple camp, a shelter made of the skins tied from the kayak they'd unloaded, to the raft.

The next morning, they unloaded the rest of the gear and sorted it. They stowed the raft upright, so it might be easier to find again. The heavy tent skins he left behind, piled safely over the raft.

All they kept was the skin-covered kayak. Narrow. Built for one.

Kaviaq lashed their sleeping skins midway along the deck, secured them with lines and cord attachers.

Into the narrow stern end he pushed as much of their food and carry-sacks as the boat could hold. Harpoons were slipped into mounts alongside the deck, secured with rawhide tie-downs, one harpoon to each side. When the loading was done, he surveyed the boat, then looked to the open water, the height of the waves, the direction of the wind.

"Climb in," Kaviaq said.

"In?" Elik stared at the round hole in the deck. One place to sit. One place to steer.

"Inside. Where the dog sat, past my feet. Hurry. We'll lose the wind." Kaviaq didn't wait to hear her answer. He bent over the dog, patted its head, ruffled its fur.

Excitedly, the dog's tail whisked the air. It yipped and side-stepped, yipped again. Kaviaq whispered something in its ear, then threw a fish. He threw it inland, as far as his arm could send it. As soon as the dog started running he turned to Elik.

"Inside," he hurried her. "Get in."

7

Kaviaq stood behind her on the shore.

He shielded his eyes, studied two sea gulls as they arched their wings, veered, and then settled into a glide. "Go on," he urged her. "You see how the birds also hurry? The weather calls them home. Get in."

Elik hesitated. One of the gulls cast a shadow over the kayak. The shadow skimmed the deck, the damp sand behind her, then disappeared.

One last time, she glanced to the river's mouth, the grassy shore that led away in each direction. She pushed it into her memory. Inmachuk, he had named the river, where the sandy beach opened to the sea. In the far distance there was bluff, not large enough to be mountain, but a hill perhaps, a place someone might live. She pushed it into her memory. Inmachuk back to the Noxapaga, back to the Kuzitrin. Home.

Finally, without a word, she gripped the hatch rim and stepped inside. Like a dead otter, the kayak listed to one side.

Kaviaq grabbed for the stern and steadied the boat against his legs. "Move slowly," he warned.

Elik didn't answer. She knelt on the grass matting

below his seat, pulled her body into a tight crouch, then slipped inside.

The last two sounds she heard were the dog's high-pitched bark, its whining as it realized she had taken its place. And then the hollow sound of her own breath as she pushed with her arms, slid deeper inside.

Her shoulders pressed against wooden ribs. Her feet searched for the bow.

Far above her head, the wind disappeared, traded its voice for the muffled sound of waves. In place of the sky, the faded color of stitched-together hides formed a roof above her head.

The boat lurched. For one moment the light remained, dull and close, not like sun but not like darkness either. Then Kaviaq climbed in and her back rippled against the shallow sea.

His feet grazed her head. She shrank away, forced herself into a smaller ball, not to touch him. She pressed her knees tighter into the boatskins, in between two ribs. She shifted till her hand found her parka hood and she closed it over her head, away from his feet, so that no part of him touched her, not anywhere.

He could kill her, as easily as if she were a sea gull and he a child playing with a rock. And all those words he had whispered of his love, all his promises about shaman's wisdom and sharing, they would rise like smoke toward the moon. Empty. Like nothing at all.

The boat rose then fell with the changing swells. She felt sick remembering the little sounds that had escaped her mouth as he slipped between her legs. The way she had met his body, urged him as he moved inside her.

She swallowed a sharp breath of air, then started to cry. This time, at least, she didn't need to hide it. He wouldn't hear her down in the bowels of the boat. He wouldn't know.

And maybe it wouldn't matter. Maybe she was already dead but she didn't know it. Maybe, sometime when they'd been in his tent, he had taken a knife and cut into the woman parts of her, gouging them out, turning her invisible. Barren. Dead.

She forced her shoulders against one side of the kayak, turned till she saw the black soles of his boots nearly touching her face.

If she had a knife, she would kill him for all his lying. It wouldn't even have to be a stone knife—bone would do, sharpened to the finest point. She would make it herself. She would jab it up, inside through the soft skin of his feet. A hole so deep, the blood that flowed out would surely carry his soul away. It would kill him the way, a year ago, he had killed her. Her children.

She moved her hands to her stomach. Clutched the empty woman-parts inside, and cried.

Elik pressed the bite of oil-soaked meat into Allanaq's mouth. He smiled as he chewed. She fed him another.

Hatch, he said in his Seal People's language. *Pai*, she repeated for the opening of the kayak in hers.

Stem, he shaped the word with his lips.

Amuvik, she said in hers. Then *stum*, she tried repeating, but the word came out wrong and he laughed at her.

Seal, he said in his language, and he shaped his

mouth like a seal's, opening it for a breath of air. When she started to try, he wouldn't allow her the chance. He pressed his mouth over hers, breathing his seal-air into her lungs.

Choking her. Too tight. Too hot. Too sick . . .

A grating sound pulled Elik from her dreams.

She'd been sleeping. She didn't know how long, only that she still lay wedged inside the kayak. She tried to move but her right leg was cramped with cold. She craned her neck, trying to see; Kaviaq's boot soles and leggings covered her like the lid of a box.

The kayak scraped bottom and she rolled with it, her knees dug into one length of ribs, her shoulders pressed into the other.

In the water outside, hardly more than a hand's width from her face, Kaviaq anchored his paddle into shallow mud.

Twice that first day he had pulled the kayak in to shore, let her out to wince in the glaring sky. Each time he walked off and left her alone as he scouted the area. Each time he came back, he showed off whatever stones or shells or driftwood treasure he'd gathered along the way.

He pointed out places where she could gather berries, cranberries mostly, because they were sweetest after a frost. While he sat down to check the boat, Elik took a small basket and followed the drainages inland to whatever likely field she found. She picked berries, but only enough to show him she had tried.

Mostly what she did was check to make sure he hadn't followed, and then work to memorize the land.

At the highest vantage points, she counted off sand-bars, cliffs, river-mouths, whatever inland hills were visible through the haze.

When winter came she wouldn't need to keep to the rivers; she would have more choices. The snows would be hardened by wind. She could run away on snow-shoes—that would be easier than now, through the bog. Or, if it was too rugged, she could follow the ice along the shore. She would have to be careful of polar bears. And she would have to carry food, unless she stopped often enough to fish.

Later, before climbing back in the boat, she asked him to name the places, saying it was important for her to learn about her new home. And he did: Qinaugaq, for Where the Land Points Like a Nose, and the spring seal hunt was always good. And Taqtu, for the Place Where the Mountain is Red, and caribou like to graze. He told her to stay away from Atnaq, the Hunting Bag Strap, because there, an entire village had been abandoned after two families died, all of them—father, two mothers, grandmothers, and children all at the same time.

She used her fingers to count the nights they slept, the places they hauled in, filled their water bags with fresh lake water.

She told herself that if he hit her, she would run away. If he asked about Allanaq. Or too many questions about a husband. About the miscarriage. Or where Skinner got her—she would run away.

Either she would try to find this route again, or another; either way, she would return. In winter, the land would look completely different. In a storm, or fog, she might as well be blind. Or if she was walking instead of kayaking. Snowshoeing instead of walking. If she died here, maybe she would find her brother. And the two of them would try to make their way together to the Land Above the Sky.

It was near a round, clearwater pond that she found the clay, the same kind she and her mother and her grandmother liked to use for making pots.

She knelt to the ground when she saw it, the soft brown color as familiar as her hand. She felt it, scraped it up with her fingernail to be sure. It was pot-dirt, the same as they used at home for lamps and cooking pots. At home they would clean out the larger rocks, mix the clay with ptarmigan feathers to strengthen the bowl. When she was a girl, it was one of her favorite chores to be allowed to decorate the outside with paddle-marks.

But it wasn't making the pots that tugged her memory—it was something Allanaq had said the very first time they met. She had stumbled into her cousin's house, thinking to find Two Ravens nursing her baby. Instead, there Allanaq stood, as frightened of her village as she was now of Kaviaq.

He had picked up a clay pot from her cousin's hearth. "We don't make these in my home," he said. "We don't make these . . ."

"But we do," she said now, and she started to cry. "Real People use clay."

She wiped her nose, glanced over her shoulder to make sure she wasn't followed. Though really, she knew, it wouldn't be necessary. Kaviaq wouldn't accuse her of anything. It was clay, she would tell him if he asked. Pot-dirt. The same as she had once told Allanaq.

Using her hands, Elik scraped up as much of the brown muck as she could easily carry. She pressed it into the basket she had brought for berries, then made her way back to the beach.

Kaviaq scarcely looked up. She hid the basket in among her pile of skins, covered it back over. With the clay safely wrapped, she felt safe again, secure, as if she had stretched a long brown line connecting her back to the Long Coast shore. Its weight cleared her thoughts, reminded her that patience would help her plan.

If nothing else, she should at least pay attention to the shore. That's what her brother Iluperaq would have done. If he was stranded, he would search for a hiding place, a cave, in case there was a storm. He would learn where there was fresh water in summer, driftwood, flints to make into tools.

Learn the winds first—that was how the elders taught the boys. The wind, and then the ice. The ice, and then the ways of the animals. Learn enough, and even a woman might have a chance of surviving.

The next time Elik climbed into the kayak, she hid a stone knife in her hand. She waited till Kaviaq paddled the boat out beyond the breakers and the kayak's rocking smoothed to a forward motion.

Turning onto one shoulder, and with her hands above her head, her nose nearly pressed against his boot soles, she reached for the seam along the bottom edge of his parka. The side seam, where two skins overlapped. He wouldn't notice.

She worked slowly; one tug, and Kaviaq would

think she had simply moved to get more comfortable.
A second, and he might wonder.

She held his parka out, away from his leg, then
began to cut. A steady sawing motion, back and forth,
pausing only when his paddle changed.

The flaked knife edge was sharp, but not so sharp as
the bite his own parka would take when she turned it
against him, used it—perhaps with a magical song?—
against him.

Patiently, she kept sawing until an edge came loose,
the smallest piece, hardly longer than her little finger.
That was all she needed. She pushed it in the only hiding place she could reach, down in the bottom of her
boot sole, tucked in with the grass padding.

Elik woke to the now-familiar sound of scraping gravel,
the press of the sea bottom rippling along her spine.

She opened her eyes to see droplets of water on the
outside of the boatskins, lit up by the sun. The droplets
ran and joined and separated into streams of browns
and greys.

She arched her back, watching as Kaviaq climbed
from the hatch. His legs seemed bodiless above her, as
if after so many days, that was all he had become, a
demon *tunraq* dressed in furs. A spirit with no arms, no
head attached.

Finally though, there was light, a cooler air to
breathe.

Elik shimmied away from the bow-end and reached
for the hard curve of the hatch. The first thing she saw
as she lifted her shoulders above the deck was a beach
as flat as the sea. Tiny patches of sand and grass already

dried by the winter frost. The coarse gravel of the Seal People's shore.

And then Kaviaq; he was kneeling on the gravel. His back was straight, his chin uplifted, and on his face, a look of gratitude, thanksgiving. He opened his mouth, swallowing the light and wind in prayer. "I am not asleep," she heard him say. "I am alive."

She freed her legs from the kayak, curious as she watched him scoop up handfuls of dirt, rub it into the shoulders of his parka, along the sleeves.

He smiled when he found her watching. "The dirt," he called. "It's a barrier. If Anguta's spirit helpers search the kayak, they'll find nothing but the smell of land. A beach, no different than any other—that's all they'll find."

Elik turned back to help unload the boat. Skins, baskets, food. Her pile of squirrel pelts; would they be safe left here, or should she keep them with her? In spite of Kaviaq's promises, she didn't really know whether she would be given a place by herself, or share a hearth with another woman. A bed with a different man?

Kaviaq hadn't noticed her hesitation. He stood where he was, watching beyond the beach. His face was lit, his smile broader than she had seen since the day the boots had moved.

She let out her breath, then covered her mouth in case he heard her sigh. She turned, followed his gaze. Without a ridge to climb, the village stretched itself full length: an expanse of sod-covered houses lined up on a beach so low she wondered a storm didn't come and wash them out to sea.

There were kayaks on rows of stands, some built of

driftwood the same as Real People would use, some of stones piled high off the ground.

Quickly, she searched the row in case a certain umiak was there. She would recognize it, easily. If it was here. If Allanaq was alive. If Skinner hadn't lied and there *was* a route along the coast.

But no. The boat wasn't there and somehow, she wasn't surprised, not at that. What did surprise her was the relief she felt.

Allanaq wasn't here for Red Fox to kill. He might live another day more.

She turned, lifted her gaze beyond the boat racks. There were women standing on scaffoldings, working over the tallest driftwood frames she had ever seen. Square frames, with walrus skins stretched tight around each side. And not one frame, but three. And two women on each, knives and scraping tools in their hands, shoulders leaning to their work as they split each hide in two.

And beyond them, the village. Food caches. Storage racks with long braids of pink intestine, inflated seal pokes ballooning full of air. There were whale bones, ribs and jaws poking toward the sky. And again, the mounded shape of roofs. More houses than she had ever seen at once.

Kaviaq's voice lifted with pride. "The land comes out like this," he said, and he opened his hand to show her. "A finger that points to the sea. The Seal People's place. If the weather's good tomorrow, I'll show you where a whale turned into the first dry land in the world. It's nearby. You'll see."

Elik touched his arm and Kaviaq stopped. Three men had risen from the shelter of an upturned umiak.

Even from a distance, they seemed to know it was Kaviaq, not an enemy. They stood politely about, pretending disinterest.

"Do you know them?" Elik asked.

"It's Bird's Mouth, my oldest cousin, and Samik, his brother. They need to hear about Anguta. The other brothers will want to know." He turned back to the boat, finished tying off the lines.

Elik unstrapped the remaining straps from the upper deck and, with the roll of pelts held to her chest, she followed two cautious steps behind Kaviaq.

They passed a long row of food racks with strips of dark meat hanging toward the ground. Thick white polar bear hides draped another rack, legs to each side, flies buzzing near the eyeholes.

Elik watched everywhere; boats, dogs, houses, and people—she tried taking it all in at once. But it was a raised scaffolding that stopped her, a mountain of white and browned skulls heaped atop a driftwood platform, high above ground. "What is that?" She stepped back, more than a little surprised.

"Where?" Kaviaq followed her glance. "The seal skull mound?"

"You save them? All?" Elik stared openly as they approached. The mound was so deep, the skull of one seal was nearly indistinguishable from the jaw of another. Small ringed and spotted seals, larger *ugruk*— the bearded seal—she couldn't tell them all apart. Some were recent kills, others obviously older. She made out the longer snout of a polar bear but no caribou, no antler of any kind, and no part of the seals but the heads, massing as if they were carried on a wave, surging through breaking foam.

Or as if they moved on a cloud? White shapes tumbling inside the clouds of a summer storm? She had seen that somewhere before, hadn't she? The shapes of seal skulls, outlined in clouds? She couldn't remember where.

"Save them?" Kaviaq lifted an eyebrow, surprised at another of her Real People questions. "Of course. These are the skulls of seals taken the past year. We save them to honor their spirits. If we butchered them, or left them carelessly on the ground, they would be angered. When they were born again they would never come here. To someone else's shores perhaps, not ours.

"It's part of the winter Bladder Feast. We feast the seal's bladder, where the soul resides. We compose new songs, wear new clothes, drink from new bowls and dippers. On the last day we return the bladders here to their skulls on the mound. Only because we honor them are they willing to give their flesh to us. You don't do this?"

"No. We do. We give them water, for their thirst. But a mound—so large? We never save so many . . ." She picked out one of them, followed its empty gaze toward the houses. Another stared toward the ground. Others to the sky, the boats, the neck or eye or jaw of another skull, all heaped and tumbled without direction.

She would have stayed there, she hadn't had enough, but Kaviaq motioned her to follow. The knot of men who'd been watching since they landed were close enough now, he lifted his arm in greeting. But then, with a concerned glance, he turned to Elik. "Tell me—" he asked. "Is there a chance? Could you be carrying a child?"

Elik froze. Thoughts of the skull mound fled. "What? A child? No." The question caught her off guard and she protested, but even so, her thoughts rushed back, counting off the time. It wasn't possible. She hadn't bled—she would remember—not since the death of her sons. "Not since my last pregnancy."

Kaviaq nodded. "It's best for now," he said. "A pregnant woman. There are so many troubles. But listen . . ." He leaned closer. "You be careful. These men—don't let them see you acting like a stranger. Keep your mind awake. Say nothing wrong—no. Better yet, say nothing at all."

"Who are they?"

"Bird's Mouth is the heavier, round-faced man. I knew he would come. Samik, in the winter parka, is one of his three younger brothers, my cousins. The third is Ice Stick."

"Is he a relative?"

"Not mine," Kaviaq said, then: "Wait here. You see that path? A woman died there once. Be careful. It isn't safe. And there," he pointed. "There's a pond, and beyond it the graves. Don't wander that way. You stay near, but not too close, understand?"

Elik nodded, and almost thanked him. He was right to tell her those things. How could she know, alone, which people were safe, which paths were dangerous?

She repeated the names. Bird's Mouth. Samik. Ice Stick—was that one of the names Allanaq had mentioned? That man with the long legs and skinny shoulders? If he wasn't Kaviaq's relative, did that mean he might be Allanaq's, or not?

She squatted where she was, settled her few bundles

to lean against her legs. The men drew Kaviaq into a circle and instantly the talk grew louder, enough that she was able to understand a few of the words: *tuktu*, she heard, the word for caribou, and the word invisible. Two of the men seemed worried, the skinny one angry.

The gladness drained from Kaviaq's face. Only for a moment, then he smoothed his eyes again, composed his mouth. "He may be dead," she heard him say. "He may be alive. I came back because I learned that Anguta will return. If it's also true that the caribou hid, it must be because of that. He is alive. He seeks his vengeance."

Kaviaq's voice dipped and though he went on speaking, Elik heard no more. What she caught instead was the glance the two men who he said were brothers exchanged behind his back. A lifted eyebrow, a pursed look on the mouth of one of them. Did they doubt his word?

Elik edged nearer, but the other man—was it Ice Stick?—he caught her motion, turned, and watched a little too long in her direction. Elik pretended to swat a mosquito. She lifted her hood, covered her head.

Kaviaq was right. She needed to be careful here, and quiet. She attracted enough attention simply being what she was, a strange woman climbing from Red Fox's kayak.

Kaviaq had also caught the man's pointed glance. "Show me what you have," he said, and Elik watched as he took hold of the man's sleeve, guiding him away but also, she understood, protecting her from probing eyes.

Elik rose to follow behind the small group. At the food rack where they stopped, she noticed what she hadn't seen before: the wind-darkened strips of dried meat were mostly seal—small seal, not the prized bearded seal.

The caribou ribs, back meat, and legs that should have hung with their hooves intact—there were few, too few for this time of year, for a village so large.

It was food the men were talking about. And perhaps not just talking. Perhaps, if their pointed glances told any tale—perhaps they were looking for someone to blame.

She hoped not. It was dangerous walking into a village that felt nervous, fretful of the winter lying ahead. There were stories, everyone knew them, of the way fear could ruin a man's aim, just as he loosed his arrow. The way hunger robbed a woman's wisdom, tricked her into forgetting where her own food cache lay, buried under a drift of snow.

Abruptly, the men's talk ended. The two who were brothers turned in one direction, skinny Ice Stick in another. Kaviaq picked a path between houses and Elik grabbed up her load. She followed a few steps, but then a light near the boats caught her eyes. She turned to see the spark of a fire.

"Look," she called. She motioned toward the women who had left off scraping the walrus skins and were bending over their kayak now. "What are they doing?"

Kaviaq glanced, then kept on walking.

"There's a fire," Elik said, loud as she dared.

"It's on the ground, not the boat," Kaviaq walked back and grabbed her sleeve, tugged to keep her moving. "They've lit a smudge pot to burn out evil. But stop staring. Keep walking."

Elik quickened her steps. "Are they afraid of me?"

"It's not about you. It's about me."

They passed by more people now but Kaviaq walked with the gait of a man who didn't want to be stopped. There were women working outside houses, children running naked, oblivious of the chill. A pack of fat-bellied boys threw rocks and two little girls with berry baskets in their hands played in the gravel. The haunches of meat on their food racks may have been few, but to her eye the village and the people seemed rich.

None of the dogs she saw had mange, and a few curious puppies were allowed to wander free. There were fox pelts and skinned birds hanging by their necks. There were pintails and cranes, taken before they fled the winter skies. Outside each house were food-drying racks, and whether they were full or empty just now, their crosspieces were so long, only pride would have built them so large, not waste.

Finally, Kaviaq stopped outside one of the houses. Its outside door was framed in driftwood. The opening watched in the same direction as all the other houses they had passed: westward toward the sea. The mounded roof was covered in blocks of dark sod, the shape like a wasp hive, with only its outermost layer allowed to show.

Elik followed in behind Kaviaq. She searched with her foot, expecting to find herself in a long tunnel as she would have at home, but instead there was only a short entry. Two steps and her foot struck wood. Kaviaq slipped through the heavy polar bear door hide; she took it from him, then stepped inside.

No seal oil lamp had been left for light, but the house smelled alive, of fish and sod and wood fires and a urine pot.

The very first thing, Kaviaq crossed to the sleeping bench. He ran his hand along the ledge. In the dark, Elik heard the familiar scrape of willow branches shifting under a layer of grass matting and bedding furs. Kaviaq turned in surprise, as if he had expected someone to be there. "I'll call someone," he said to Elik. "I'll have one of the girls bring coals from another house."

Elik bent to the fire pit in the center of the floor; the square of stones was still warm. A soft layer of ash covered a morning fire. "Wait," she said. "I'll open the skyhole." She stepped onto the largest stone, balanced, then found exactly what she had expected: a small, gut-skin framework covering the hole from the outside. She pushed and it slid aside, opening a window to the sun.

Immediately, a square of light filled the floor. The house was large, that was what she noticed first. Two people could have spread their arms and still not touched more than one wall at a time. There were raised sleeping benches built along three sides, with room for storage under each. It was a square house, and except for having no entry tunnel, not so different from her own. Touching the outside of the sleeping benches were four heavy posts to help hold up the roof. The walls behind the benches leaned a little toward the center. The floor was planked with wood, which meant that the house was well cared for. Not so new that the owners had had only time to dig a gravel floor. Not so weathered that the boards showed signs of rot.

There was a smell also, the daily smell of raw meat and fish and rendered fat. And other smells on top, dried plants that were different from those Elik had been taught to find. And baskets, boxes, containers—more than her father's house with its four women had ever known.

It was a woman's house, she decided, not a man's. A large drying rack stretched neatly above the hearth, another beside the entry wall. And there were cooking stones. A urine-tub that was emptied. Stitched-together birchbark pots and food trays rather than hunting gear. Sewing scraps rather than flintknapping tools. The only thing missing was a woman's seal oil lamp. There was none, just as she had known.

One thing else about the house she noticed: it was a shaman's house. Along the roof ridge were masks, more than a hunter ever kept. Wooden spirit masks with the eyeholes cut through, their cheeks painted red and black. A bird-faced mask with pointed bill, a jaw that opened and closed. A shaman drum hung on the wall to her side, and the frame of another, without any gut covering, lay pegged behind that. And on the floor a basket filled with driftwood, ivory, and a round whale vertebra waiting to be carved.

Kaviaq leaned against the bench. He seemed settled, as if everything that was new to Elik was familiar to him. "What I don't understand," he said, "is how they could have caught no caribou, when I led them to a herd. If the caribou hid, it was after I left. The vision took me away; I told you. The fault isn't mine."

"Is that what they said?"

"That the spring hunt never happened, yes. They told the same story, all three of them. Bird's Mouth said that after I left, the few caribou they had taken must have grown angry. They told their brothers to flee. Or to stay north, in the mountains. No one knew why."

"Someone must have done wrong? Disrespected the caribou?"

"After I left, perhaps. But I was there, at the caribou-crossing place. I saw signs of trampled ground. Moss eaten everywhere. We sighted more than a few early males. Why would a herd turn aside?"

"What did they say of their fall hunt?"

"You saw their meat racks."

Elik nodded. "Is it bad?"

"Maybe. Not yet. Unless they allow their fears to grow ahead of them. They've been waiting for my return so the *qasgi* can be opened for the new season. They want to sing, to pray."

Kaviaq grew thoughtful. He lowered his voice. "The only thing I should have done, perhaps, was to wait longer before I left for the river valley. But how could I know? A vision came and I needed to follow it. The same as when I found the caribou in the first place. If I waited in the village, as they say I should have waited at the crossing place, then not only would they have had no caribou, but I would not have found you." He quieted for a moment, then stepped closer. "Elik."

Kaviaq lifted his hand to her face. With a slow touch, he traced his fingers over the three blue-black tattoo lines on her chin.

Elik locked her gaze on the wall behind his shoulder. *Don't fight. Stay alive . . .*

He pulled her in by the belt around her waist, then lower. He pressed her hips against him. But then he paused. "You're frightened?"

"No. I . . ."

"You're shaking. What is it? This house? Those men?"

She risked a glance at his face; his eyes were as soft as the first time she'd stepped into his tent. There was no threat, no lies.

She took a breath. Her shoulders loosened.

Kaviaq smiled. "That's it, then? The men? But you mustn't be afraid. I like you brave, the way you are. I will tell them you are my wife. No one will hurt you while I'm gone."

"Gone? Where are you going?"

"Only to the *qasgi*. I told you, they need me to call the winter, invite it in. But the ceremony lasts three days. And all that while . . ." his voice softened again, "it's forbidden for a man to lie with a woman.

"A man," he continued, "a shaman especially, must be strong, directed. When I touch you—" he pulled her back with him, leaned against the sleeping bench— "you flutter, like a bird's wing. But I am the weaker one. Every time I am near you, I forget what I am about. I think only of you."

Elik didn't dare speak. She didn't protest or make a sound. He lifted her to the bench, and rolled so that the soft caribou bedding was beneath her and he above. Then somehow, her own parka was off, her fur trousers tossed along with his and hers and the bedding.

He slowed. He held himself over her, but so gently, he seemed afraid he might crush her. His long hair mixed with her own. He lowered his face, warmed his lips against her neck. He brought his weight down. Slowly and so carefully; she couldn't remember him ever being so slow before. In long, deep strokes, he moved into her.

I'm alive, she told herself. *Alone in a village of strangers, and not once has this man treated me roughly.*

Her hand grabbed for something to hold: sleeping furs—she dragged them closer. A neat roll of fawn skins, the hair so soft, they could only have been taken in the spring. Someone was getting ready to sew. Someone wealthy enough to claim the lightest, warmest skins for clothing.

Kaviaq sighed and Elik let go the furs. She moved her hands around his back.

She was alive and she hadn't expected to be. Not here. In this village. Lying in the arms of a man who, according to everything she knew, should have terrified her.

Except, the odd thing was, she didn't feel afraid. Tired, yes. And lonely. Yesterday she had been afraid, but not now.

She felt the scratching softness of caribou bedding. She was in the shelter of a sod-roofed house. She had enough food, she wouldn't starve. And after all her worrying at the river camp, she saw now why he hadn't troubled himself with the winter's food. He was already wealthy in fur and meat shares. He was a shaman and people would always trade their oil and skins for his power.

She closed her eyes. She willed her muscles to untie themselves, to loosen. She let her body move upward. She would not fight. She was not going to die.

He murmured and his rhythm quickened, but now from outside the house she heard the sound of a dog's hungry bark, and then quiet. Someone had tossed it food. Footsteps circled from the rear of the house toward the entry.

Kaviaq's sighing changed to short huffing sounds and he kept on, but Elik freed a hand, grabbed the bedding, and plumped it so her face was hidden but she still could see.

The door flap lifted and a figure moved slowly in. The curved hem and the parka's long tail told her it was a woman. Tall, narrow shouldered, and when the woman lowered her hood, Elik opened her mouth in surprise at her piercing, beautiful eyes.

The woman glanced directly to the bench, as if already she had heard the gossip. A smile flickered across her mouth, then hid. Elik drew back inside the furs as the woman's prying gaze lifted to catch a glimpse of her hair, a breast, a hand she couldn't hide.

The door flap lifted again, and another woman entered, an older woman. Her glance moved quickly to the bed, but unlike the first woman she watched only till she was certain someone was there. She entered, moved along the wall. She was a tiny woman, too small to hide the young boy who peeked out from behind her legs.

With his eyes round as moons, the boy leaned forward, "Who is it? Is it *aapa*, my father?" he asked.

As soon as he heard the voice, Kaviaq looked up and smiled broadly at the boy.

Protectively, the younger woman took hold of the child's shoulders and pulled him close. She fixed her glance on Kaviaq's face and held it, far longer than Elik would have expected a woman to dare. But the boy wiggled and pulled at her, till finally she lowered her eyes, helped him pull off his parka. "It's your *aapa*," she said. "Now go and sit."

With a shy, playful smile toward Kaviaq, the boy burrowed into the farthest corner of the sleeping bench and pulled out a stick-doll dressed in a little coat. Quickly, he lost himself in the pile of furs.

Elik rolled out from under Kaviaq and sat up, before the two women decided she was no better than the youngest fool of a girl. She covered her lap with the blanket.

Kaviaq wiped the sweat from his face, but he set his hand on Elik's shoulder, a loud motion. He meant it to be seen.

While the younger woman busied herself shaking the snow from the boy's parka, the older woman squatted beside the hearth. She slid a horn box out from her sleeve, tilted it till a live coal fell to the ashes. She bent low, her cheek nearly resting on the stones, and she puffed and coughed and worked the fire. All the while she peeked under her arm, over her shoulder, snatching glances at the few baskets and skins Elik had carried into the house.

"So. You're back," the younger woman said. "And this is what you brought us?" She lifted her chin in Elik's direction.

The woman's voice surprised her. It was so strong and confident, she nearly expected Kaviaq to raise a fist, threaten the woman the way Skinner had threatened her each time she had spoken so loudly. Elik glanced between the women; as far as she could tell, they both belonged here. And hadn't Skinner and Kaviaq said there would be two wives, the younger wife with a son?

Kaviaq opened his mouth in a half smile. "I didn't bring her for you," he said. "I traded for her. She's mine."

"Then let her stay with your relatives. Mitik could use her."

"Or Pintail?" the older woman offered. And though her manners were more careful and guarded than the younger woman's, she was the one Kaviaq turned on, silencing her with a glance.

"She lives here." He jabbed a finger toward the floor. "In this house. She is my wife."

"What kind of wife?" The younger woman asked.

Kaviaq's mouth tightened in annoyance. "Third wife. And you will be considerate toward her. Both of you. She keeps food-taboos—more than a few."

The younger woman lifted her brows. "Why? Is she a widow?"

"She had a husband."

"Had? Who? If he was Seal People, I would know him."

Kaviaq took a moment before he answered. "The husband I got her from was Seal People. At least, when I saw him he claimed to still be. I traded her from Skinner."

"Skinner?" The older woman eyes lifted in surprise, then just as quickly she turned, hid her face.

Kaviaq ignored her. With a reassuring gesture, he reached for Elik's hand.

Elik glanced about the house. Something had just happened, she wasn't sure what. She waited, but no one was speaking plainly. Everyone seemed to understand but her.

The little boy poked his head from the bedding, peered at the adults. The younger woman climbed to the bench beside him, carefully away from Kaviaq. She lifted her parka, made a space for him to wiggle up inside. But then, as if she'd forgotten how large the child had grown, she worked her parka the rest of the way over her head, then crossed her legs for the boy to more easily climb in her lap.

With one hand he took hold of her shoulder and with the other he lifted her breast to his mouth.

Kaviaq climbed down. He stood in the middle of the floor, naked, watching the back of the boy's head. "Ivalu?" he called gently.

The boy turned, stretching his mother's breast till it fell from his mouth.

"Come here."

Brightly, as if he'd been hoping for just such an invitation, the boy leaped into Kaviaq's arms. They stood there a moment, the two of them with their naked bellies pressed together, the little boy's legs wrapped around Kaviaq's waist.

Kaviaq smiled nearly as brightly as the boy. "You want to come with the men to the *qasgi*? We're going to have a ceremony. We're going to clean it and then open it. Every bucket and container that was left from last year, we'll turn upside down so that anything evil will be caught. And we'll kill it. We'll make huge noises. You can too—anything that tries to hurt you, we'll find it and send it away. And we'll ask for good weather, and a good hunt. Look here, I brought you a strong piece of driftwood. We'll make a bow for you. Maybe this year you'll catch your first seal."

The boy twisted from Kaviaq's arms, ran back to his mother. "Yes? Can I go?"

"You don't have to ask her," Kaviaq teased. "You come with the men, you're almost big now."

"And what about that one?" the mother asked. "Does she speak?"

"She speaks. And I'll tell you this—" his voice flared with authority. "When she does, the *inuas* of the animals listen. She has looked with the eyes of a shaman on the house in the moon."

Elik lowered her gaze to the fire pit while the woman's scrutinizing glance walked over her.

"She is a shaman?" The woman's voice lifted in surprise.

"She is—she will be. She is my wife," Kaviaq said. "And you will make certain she has everything new. Bowls, spoons, pelts for sewing. Whatever a woman needs. She must not have anything used, anything touched by another person's breath."

The house grew quiet as Kaviaq dressed himself. But when he turned to leave, the older woman grabbed hold of his arm. "He is alive?" she asked.

"I told you, yes."

She wouldn't let go. "Did he say anything?"

"No." Kaviaq wrenched his arm away. "He ran so quickly when he saw me, his only thought was staying that way."

Kaviaq motioned, and the boy followed. Behind them, the door flap scraped heavily into place. Cooler air slid across the floor, searched for the walls.

Elik remained where she was, watching as the older

woman worried over the fire. She had a thick, hacking cough that reminded Elik of her grandmother. But behind that and behind the swirl of tattoos, she wasn't so old as Elik had thought at first, nowhere near so ancient as Malluar. Closer to the age her mother had been when she died.

The younger woman brought a large grass basket out from the storage area below the bench. She sat back with it on her lap.

The older woman dropped a stiffly curled tomcod into a bowl and reached for a knife. Elik leaned forward to see what she used. The rounded blade and simple antler handle attached to the middle were no different than any woman's knife Elik would have used herself.

The younger woman rummaged through the basket, pulled out a rolled-up hide, and turned it to find a starting place. With one end in her teeth and a knife in her hand, she started slicing away the ragged outer edge.

Back and forth, she cut an even strip. The strip grew like a worm, inching beside the woman's knee, till finally it dropped away.

The older woman looked up from her work. "Do you need that?"

"What, the scrap?"

"There's plenty left. I could use it."

"It's thin. There are holes along the length."

"You don't need it?"

"Take it."

"I can sew it to another," she said, and she put it away in a basket nearer the door. She rose, pulled a water bladder down from a peg on the wall, aimed the spout and squeezed a stream of water into a smaller birchbark pot.

From another seal poke she pulled out a mass of what looked to be sourdock leaves stored in a coating of oil. The smell was pungent and sweet, and Elik stared at the fish. She hadn't eaten yet that day; she'd hardly drunk any water.

Was she supposed to ask for food first? Or would that be impolite, and was she expected to wait till it was offered?

Should she help? Or did they hate her already because Kaviaq had brought another woman in the house?

She looked to their clothing. Their parkas were nearly the same as any woman of the Real People might have worn, not straight-hemmed like the men's, but modestly long-tailed in the back. The younger woman's leggings and outer parka were made from sealskin trimmed with finely stitched caribou. A row of puffin beaks clacked across the chest. Wolverine tufts decorated the seams.

The older woman's parka, though she also wore a double layer for the cold, was plainer, the outside a layer of caribou with the fur turned out. The younger woman's boots were better made; the crimped soles shaped from beluga or walrus.

The older woman opened another container, scooped out a handful of creamy white fat. As Elik watched she whipped the fat through her strong hands, then chopped the fish into smaller bits, tossed in those and the sourdock, and then—best of all—berries, glistening, almost black. Their juice mixed with the froth of fat, all together in the bowl.

Elik reminded herself not to stare. But what if, in spite of Kaviaq's warnings, they didn't want to share? Was she supposed to wait until he came back and ordered them to feed her?

A husband could hope his wives would live together peacefully. As loudly and as often as he liked, he could instruct them to share. He could beat them. Holler at them. Send them out of his house.

But the truth was, a husband was home less often than a wife. What he said, what he wanted—all could easily be ignored.

She thought of Allanaq, of his first year among Real People. How had he kept himself alive? When he hunted seals and returned empty-handed, the men called him a fool. When he caught two, and they caught one, they blamed him. If he ate too fast or too slowly. Whether he refused their daughters or took them. Whenever they looked at him, they saw a man who was different, not Real People, like them.

The younger woman had taken out new work—a skin for boot soles, Elik guessed. A winter pair with the hair left on so the bottom would last longer. Elik followed the woman's hands, watching how she worked. "Those look like good fall skins," she said, trying a compliment.

"It's bearded seal. Hindquarters," the woman answered proudly. She rearranged the hide on her lap, then sprinkled on water to moisten the raw skin.

"You're making boots?"

"A new pair for Red Fox."

Red Fox. Elik frowned at the name, then lowered her eyes to hide her distaste.

The skin made a crackling sound as the woman started scraping it, working her tool in a back and forth motion. "You leave the fat layer on when you flense the skin?" Elik asked.

"Some of it."

"We do too. It makes it easier to work that way."

"And the hair? You leave that on?"

"Sometimes." Elik made certain she sounded polite. "It depends on what you're sewing. Sometimes we use ashes to help remove the hair."

"We do that. What else?"

"When I do it, I have to watch the edges," Elik shook her head the way a young girl might, uncertain of her skill, gossiping. "They get tight and curl if it isn't moist enough, and then it's more difficult. So many times I have to do the edges again, they get brittle if I don't fix it."

"That's why you need to do the edges first."

"First?" Elik lifted her voice. "I didn't know that. I just start in the middle."

"Oh, no. You have to be careful." The woman lifted her glance, showed the first hint of a smile.

"I always cut myself when I do it like you," Elik said, "on my lap instead of a hard board."

"A board is good, but it's faster this way. Besides, it's your tools that are most important. You have to have a good sharp bone from a polar bear. The lower forearm is best."

"Yours looks very sharp—" Elik said, then she stopped. The older woman was sifting through Elik's basket. Her pile of marmot and squirrel skins sprawled haphazardly on the floor.

"I brought those—" Elik tried not to jump.

The woman's mouth was tight. "Show us what you have."

Elik blanched. It was impossible to refuse. *It doesn't matter*, she told herself. *There's only the few skins.*

The older woman held the basket toward Elik.

Elik squatted on the floor. She pushed aside the wrapped packet of clay, hoping they wouldn't care. She straightened the squirrel hides, the marmot and hare. She set out the ptarmigan wings. The few strands of whale sinew.

The younger woman ran a quick glance over the pile. "So. He makes you third wife?"

Uncertainly, Elik offered a half smile.

"These are soft," the older woman ran her hand along the nap of squirrel pelts. "But you're lucky. There's one thing you can be certain of as Red Fox's wife—in this house, you won't starve."

She turned and before Elik realized it, her own bowl sat on the floor in front of her, brim full with fish and broth.

"*Quyana*," Elik said quietly. *Thank you.* She lifted the bowl; it was not the berry-sweetened fat the woman had been preparing—that would go to the men in the *qasgi*, but a simple cod stew, the one meal Elik would have wished for.

She drank the broth first, then pushed a few chunks of the fish into her mouth. It was warm and tasty and she ate without speaking. Only when she had eaten her fill did it strike her that somehow, the anger she'd expected to hear hadn't happened. They were three women, talking. That was all.

She looked to the older woman again. For the first time, she saw how strangely her fingertips were colored: not brown, as the most hands were, but lighter, as if she were cold. As if her fingers had no blood inside. Elik said nothing about it, instead: "I owned more things, but my belongings were . . . lost," she said, as she caught herself.

The older woman stiffened, then coughed. The cough was deep and refused to stop. It was a while before she could speak. "And when was that?" she asked.

"The man I traveled with—"

"Skinner?"

"Yes. He took them when—"

"Red Fox told the truth? He is alive?"

"Yes." Elik remembered the scratches on her cheeks. There were other memories also. Most were not pleasant, but a few—like the way he had lied for her to Kaviaq—had surprised her.

"I was sure he was dead. But I wasn't troubled. Either he died violently, I told myself, or by his own hand. Either way, he would feast in the afterlife. He would have meat, and plenty. But the day would come—I knew this—when he would tire of it all. He would find a suitable child and climb inside its body. He would be reborn."

The woman laughed at some private joke. "What did he do, push you onto Red Fox the moment he realized the man was interested?"

Elik nodded in surprise at her accuracy.

"How did you find him?"

"Kaviaq—you mean Red Fox? He was camped in a valley."

"No, Skinner. How did you come to be with Skinner?"

328 c~ ELYSE GUTTENBERG

Elik hesitated, and the younger woman tried to help: "Did Red Fox tell you anything about Skinner?"

"Should he have?"

"Red Fox might have, for instance, told you that after he kicked Skinner out of the Seal People's village, he took Little-Creek into his house?"

This time, Elik understood. "You are Little-Creek? Skinner's first wife?"

The older woman lowered her head, but not before Elik recognized the quiet sadness, the resignation that was so different from the way the younger woman sat, her shoulders straight, full of pride.

"I am called Nuliaq," the younger woman said. "I am Red Fox's second wife."

"Second wife? But didn't he say I was to be third, after Little-Creek? Who is first?"

Nuliaq shook her head. "Long ago he had a young wife, a child, really. She was given to him the day he took his first bear. He lived with her family, since she was so young. She was still hardly a woman when she died in labor, along with the child. We don't usually count her.

"I also had a first husband," Nuliaq continued, warming to the talk. "He died in a hunting accident. We had no children who survived, and I was married again, not to Red Fox. A different man before Red Fox. They quarreled over me. Once, they even wrestled with fists, though Red Fox was far younger. Relatives put a stop to it—that time." She tossed her head, lost for a moment in the memory.

"Red Fox has a habit of collecting women who weren't his." Little-Creek said. Then she straightened her shoulders, mimicked Red Fox's stance: "'Isn't it a man's obligation?' That's what he said when I came here. 'Wouldn't I be talked about, the center of gossip, if I didn't take you in? Didn't provide for you?' Ha! Not much longer. I have relatives in another village. Next spring, or sooner—before the ice goes out—I'm going to find them."

"And you?" Nuliaq asked. "You had a first husband, someplace you came from?"

"I had," Elik said without offering a name.

Neither woman seemed to notice. "You have children?" Nuliaq asked, and Elik glanced at her breasts. One lay round and full against her ribs; the other slack from her boy's sucking. "No," she answered. "No children."

"You mustn't worry," Nuliaq said sincerely. "So many children die. So many never begin. I have my son now, but sometimes I thought he never would get born. When he's here, we can all enjoy him. We can share his laughter. We are co-wives, *aipaq-aipaq* to each other. Once you come to live with us, that never changes, no matter which of us Red Fox favors."

"No matter whether *we* favor some certain, unnamed man?" Little-Creek turned a teasing smile on Nuliaq, but the younger woman shushed her.

"Red Fox is afraid," Nuliaq said to Elik.

"Of what?"

"Of what people might be saying about a shaman whose spirit helpers no longer listen to him. And if he's not worried yet, he will be. The more people see him, the more they'll talk. Red Fox knows this, better than others. Memories change when the meat grows small."

Elik remembered the pointed stares two of the men had exchanged behind Kaviaq's back. She wondered if

Nuliaq knew who they were, but before she could ask, Little-Creek stopped the talk. She pointed toward the skyhole. There were footsteps outside, above them and then near the entry.

Elik listened, hoping the heavy step would bring Kaviaq's familiar face. But no—a moment later and two women entered the house. They pulled down their hoods, laughed as they said something about the wind, but Elik didn't hear. She stared at her hands, surprised by her own disappointment.

The two women squatted on the floor. One of them immediately started taking out her sewing, buried her face inside her basket.

The second woman brought out a bowl filled with fat. For a gift, Elik saw, though none of them mentioned it. She simply pushed it under the sleeping bench, out of their way. "The house was cold," was all she said. "We brought our work." Then she took out a stiff boot sole and started softening the edge with her teeth.

Little-Creek nodded, then busied herself again with cooking for the *qasgi*. She dragged a sack in from outside: fermented seal flippers that had been left in the ground to age. She tested them to see if the skin fell away from the bones and the meat was ready. She smiled at the pungent smell, then took out another bowl of fat and another of berries.

Elik gathered up the basket Little-Creek had opened and took out a square of woven grass. She started twisting the strands into the unfinished row, peering over the top to catch a look at the women.

The one with the food was nearly the same age as Little-Creek; the one with the round face who was still fumbling through her basket was closer to Nuliaq's age. Her eyes were small, hidden inside a corner fold of skin, and busy as she spent more time peering around the fire for a look at Elik than settling into her sewing.

Nuliaq leaned closer. "These are relatives," she whispered to Elik. "Higjik is the older one. Spider squints. You'll want to remember who you can share with."

Elik looked at them again. The older woman, Higjik, wore an amulet pinned to her chest, an owl's foot, Elik guessed. Among her Real People, that would give keen sight. A piece of sealgut was tied around her belt, for a healthy stomach. She wore other amulets also—as did Spider—pinned to her belt, sleeves, and chest. Caribou teeth and tiny harpoon heads, for strong hunting for their sons. Something shriveled, perhaps the ear of hare, for good hearing. Amulets, the same as her aunt or her mother, or any woman she had ever known, would also wear.

Little-Creek reached under the sleeping bench, rummaged around in the dark. She came back out with a knife, but when she sat up the coughing started again. It took hold of her shoulders and shook them. Her face darkened and the coughing went on, till finally Nuliaq rose and fetched her a drink of water.

No one spoke until the coughing was done. Little-Creek dried her mouth, passed the water to Higjik. Higjik also drank, then passed the cup along to Spider, but the woman shook her head no.

She had emptied her basket on the floor, fanned her things in a haphazard sprawl. Elik craned her neck to see: an antler boot-sole crimper, a bone scraping tool curved to fit her hand. An unfinished boot sole. Braided sinew. "I can't find my sewing awl," Spider said. She seemed flustered, annoyed with herself. "I made certain that I brought it. I thought I did."

"Maybe you left it with the parka you were sewing for Ice Stick?"

Ice Stick. That was the man Kaviaq had pulled away outside. And the older woman's name—Higjik? Wasn't that another name Allanaq had mentioned? What if he was here, hiding—and one of these women knew it?

Elik glanced around the room. Nuliaq was Red Fox's wife. That didn't surprise her—she was beautiful, strong-willed but also kind. And Little-Creek. She was tiny, the size of a child really. Other than the cough, she seemed strong. Anyone had but to look at her arms to see her strength, the years a woman spent hauling, stooping, and butchering. And if the way Little-Creek asked for Nuliaq's scraps was any sign, then certainly there'd been nothing soft in her life with Skinner, nothing easy.

"No. The awl was stolen," Spider said emphatically. "Someone stole it."

"It could be lost?" Nuliaq offered.

"That was my favorite. The beaver bone stayed sharp."

"You dropped it once before," Higjik reminded her. "In the floorboards in the house."

Without planning it, without thinking, Elik lifted her voice. "Possibly," she offered, "there are some small ways for finding lost awls and needles?"

Spider's eyebrows lifted in surprise. Higjik and Little-Creek both looked to Nuliaq. There was a thin, stretching quiet, then: "Is that what Red Fox meant," Nuliaq asked, "saying you were a shaman?"

Politely, Elik lowered her eyes to the floor. "When I was young, I was the kind of child who fainted easily. They said I had falling spells."

"Ah, that's difficult," Little-Creek said sympathetically. "I have heard of more than one child who died that way. You were lucky. How did they stop?"

"They didn't, exactly. They changed. It was around the time I first became a woman. A shaman took me in. An elder woman in my village. Now, it seems, I have the smallest bit of sight."

Nuliaq and Little-Creek exchanged glances. "What will you try?"

"Have you wild celery to burn?"

Nuliaq hesitated, long enough for Little-Creek to reach across her for one of the storage baskets. "We have, yes," she said, and she pushed it closer to Elik.

"Can the house be darkened?"

"Yes."

Carefully, Elik chose her words. None of the women even pretended anymore to care about their work. They had come to see her. To find out who she was, bring a little gossip back to their own houses. She prayed she wasn't making a mistake.

"I have spirit helpers," she said. "If I ask, they may show me where the awl is."

Little-Creek looked to Nuliaq; Nuliaq fixed her gaze on Elik's hands till finally, slowly, she nodded her assent.

With slow, deliberate motions Elik rose and dusted the dry celery over the fire. She set a handful inside, waited till the leaves smoked and raised a cleansing air. "In my home," she said, "we call this *canraq*. Its smoke carries away bad air. It purifies the house."

Nuliaq stepped onto the stones. She reached through the skyhole, covered it over with the boards that lay on the roof, outside. The house folded itself into darkness.

Elik sat on the floor, closest to Spider. She couldn't see her face, only a rose-colored shadow lit up by the fire.

"You must first tell me," Elik said, "if you have an open wound, and you have eaten raw food before it is healed—"

"I don't. I wouldn't."

Elik smiled to herself. *It was the same, the rules for these people, the same as for her own.* "And you know that seal must never be eaten with caribou, no whale or wolf together?"

"We don't," Nuliaq whispered, and the other women murmured their agreement.

"Who can say," Elik continued, "why something happens? Why one man grows ill, another man lives? The one thing we can know for certain is that what we say, what we do, affects the world."

In the dark, Elik felt for Little-Creek's bowl. She dropped a bit of fish into the fire. "For you spirits," she began. "For your thirst." Then she started to sing, quietly at first, curious to hear if they talked.

"She's young to sound so wise," one of the women— Higjik was it?—whispered to another.

"Respectful."

"Red Fox said she is a shaman?" That from Spider.

"Falling spells?" Elik recognized Nuliaq's voice. "She

is modest. Red Fox would have boasted that they proved he was a shaman, that he died, then was restored to life."

"What can she do?"

"I don't know. He says she's to have a full wife's share."

"She's pretty. What man wouldn't want to fill that pot?"

"Did you hear what else he said?"

Curious, Elik waited till she heard the answer: "Anguta is alive—" then she coughed to get their attention. "I'll need something of yours to hold," she said to Spider.

The other women quieted as Spider shuffled closer. Elik felt her hand first, then the soft fur of Spider's parka. She took hold of the hem, rested it in her lap as Spider sat back.

Firmly, she willed her thoughts not to run away, not to be frightened or shy of where they needed to go. It was true she had sworn to Red Fox that she would attempt no trance without him. But she didn't mean for this to be a trance. Even Malluar had said lesser shamans had certain abilities: to see into the future, to search for lost possessions. She could do this for Spider, surely it was a small thing. Red Fox wouldn't be upset.

In the beginning, Elik merely rubbed the parka between her fingers, inviting its soft touch to enter into her. Then she started to hum, a song she remembered from Malluar. She let the words fill her thoughts, the way Malluar had taught. But then a thought occurred to her, a fear really, that words alone would not be enough. A drum would have helped, but she had none.

Nor did she have Red Fox's echoing voice, telling her what to see.

She was alone, she realized, without Red Fox or Malluar to help. But did that mean she shouldn't try? Surely, she could search for the woman's awl; it was no great thing. She swallowed her breath, closed her eyes, and let the words grow to a clear, strong voice:

> *I will visit*
> *Unknown woman,*
> *Search out hidden things*
> *Behind the man.*
> *Let the boot-thong hang loose—*
> *Seek thou under man*
> *And under woman!*
> *Spirit from the Air*
> *Come, come swiftly hither.*
> *Thy shaman here*
> *Is calling thee.*

She repeated the verses, let the house fill with their rhythm, their sound. Till slowly, little by little, Elik's own breathing began to change, to slow and then to deepen.

Her shoulders slumped. Her head grew heavier.

She knew nothing, except for the one word she had wanted to call: "*Cikik,*" for the Squirrel. She shaped it on her lips, started to give it sound. But another name came in its place. *Qerqauq,* the Loon, louder, pushing aside the other.

The Loon came and lifted her up, as if her legs were wrapped around its back again. As if, with her arms clinging to its neck, she looked down and saw from far away the river valley where Kaviaq's tent had stood above a stream. She saw the rock under which the worms had waited, and a short distance away a small animal lifted its head. *Cikik.* The Squirrel. It lifted its dark eye and looked directly toward her, but if it meant to speak, it had no chance. The Loon took her farther, and this time she saw the umiak she had been in, with Allanaq still seated in the rear. His harpoon was readied, aimed closely toward the sea. But the seal he waited for wasn't there. She could see it clearly in the distance where it had surfaced.

Its bright eyes signaled a greeting. It had been waiting for her all this while. *"Come to us,"* the seal sang. *"And we will come to you. Quench our thirst, and we will fill your food racks. We will show you, teach you, reveal what you long to know. If only you will help us see . . ."*

Someone raised a light, and Elik was suddenly awake. Faces, women she didn't know, hovered worriedly around her. Except now she recognized the smallest woman, Little-Creek. Her arms were around Elik's shoulders, helping her to sit. Her warm breasts pressed the back of her neck.

Above her stood a woman, a beautiful woman. Her black hair caught the fire's light. Her flat teeth showed when she smiled. Nuliaq. She remembered now. The woman angled a water dipper, held it for her to drink.

"There now. You're fine," Little-Creek crooned in her ear.

There was another woman also. Her face looked soft, chin and cheek tattoo marks like ribs on a leaf. "I'm sorry," Elik apologized. "I couldn't find the awl."

"Couldn't find it?" Little-Creek laughed. "But you did. Here's Spider, just back from her house."

Elik sat higher. She was dizzy, but there was the woman, Spider, just as Little-Creek had said. She was smiling and out of breath, and she wasn't alone. Three more women, different women, crowded up against the sleeping bench. One was younger than Elik, the other two she couldn't tell. Their parkas were dusted with snow. They smiled, then hid their faces, laughed and stole glances trying to see.

"It was in my boy's bowl," Spider sang out. "Just as she said. I didn't even remember, I had been wiping the bowl when Higjik called. He was playing with my things. It wasn't stolen, it was there."

"And what of you?" Nuliaq asked. "What happened?"

Elik shook her head. With so many women watching, staring at her, it was difficult to remember. "I'm not sure," she said. "The room was darkened. I called on the Squirrel—one of my helping spirits."

"No, no," Higjik called. "We heard wings."

"Wings. It's true," Little-Creek insisted. "Large wings. They sounded so close, if I touched your hand, it would have been feathers I felt, not a hand."

A shiver ran through Elik, a weak coldness. She hadn't meant to trance, not so deeply she no longer heard the same sounds the other women heard. She remembered the dark look on Kaviaq's face when she told how a loon had carried her to the moon. How angry he had seemed.

Was this the Loon again? Or the Squirrel, pulling her into a trance without Red Fox? "I don't know," she said truthfully, and she reached for a longer drink of water. "I remember nothing."

"You fainted," Higjik said. "Just like you said, when you were young. But first, you made something happen."

Elik turned to look at her. *Higjik,* she memorized the name, along with the pattern on her parka, the rows of tightly fit caribou teeth stitched sideways on her belt. The way the wolverine ruff on her hood turned into fox tails, into squirrel pelts and caribou, all blending as perfectly as if they were one.

"Higjik is married to one of my cousins," Nuliaq leaned closer to help. "And Spider is a cousin through an aunt."

"Cousins?" Elik repeated. And then suddenly, realizing her chance, she quickly asked, "I heard of a cousin, is he here? A man named Allanaq?"

"Allanaq?" Nuliaq turned a blank look toward Little-Creek, then to Higjik. "Do you know a man named Allanaq?"

"He might have come in, trading. Earlier in the season?"

Little-Creek shook her head no. Spider thought a moment, but none of them could place the name.

By then, Elik had realized her mistake. Qajak. She should have said Qajak, the way they would know his name. But somehow the chance had fled. Her throat closed when she tried to say the name.

She looked to the women, all sitting with their eyes lowered, too polite to let her down. She let out the breath she'd forgotten she was holding. Let it wait, she warned herself.

Higjik saw her face change, started talking to cover

the silence. "If you are counted as one of Red Fox's wives," she said, "it'll be good for your children, any children that will come. They'll be related through Nuliaq on one side, Red Fox on another. You'll see, it's not so confusing. There's Mitik, who's married with Bird's Mouth, and Pintail, who's married with Samik, and One Pot. She's—"

"Please," Elik stopped her. She felt overwhelmed suddenly. So much had changed in one day. So much had happened. "Wait. You won't tell Red Fox, will you? About the awl, I mean. And the wings you said you heard. If he knew, he'd be angry with me. He'll—"

"Don't worry," Little-Creek said, and she took Elik's arm. "Red Fox will hear nothing. I don't know what kind of women you know, but here we know how to keep our secrets."

Elik nodded. She leaned back against Little-Creek. The next thing she knew, Nuliaq was standing beside the entry as her little boy, Ivalu, skipped into the house. The women began filing out, the newer ones first, and then Higjik. Spider glanced back, nodding her thanks to Elik as she left.

It was late when she finally lay down on the caribou furs to sleep. She breathed deeply, took in the smells of the house, familiar as childhood, of dry willow, grass mats, and furs, thick, warm caribou furs to wrap herself inside.

"Do you know the story," Little-Creek called. "The story of how Eagle First Brought the Gift of Feast and Song to the People?"

Elik smiled in the dark. "We do. We tell that story."

"It's about a village near a river where a young son

went hunting. One time, he looked up in the sky, and there was a mighty eagle circling overhead. The eagle landed and drew back his hood so the boy could see the human soul inside. It swore to the boy it would kill him, the same way it killed his older brothers, unless he promised to hold a great song festival when he returned home. The boy said he would, except that he didn't understand. 'What is song?' he asked. 'What is festival?'

"The eagle returned to its bird shape and carried him up to the mountains where his mother lived. The first thing the boy heard was a great hammering sound. 'That is my mother's heart,' the eagle explained, and he took the boy inside the house to meet her. The house was the same as a human house, only larger, and the mother eagle climbed from her bed and showed the boy how a *qasgi* must be built, larger than a house, enough so that an entire village of people could come together. And the mother eagle taught the boy to make a drum, and how to put words together to make a song, and last of all how to dance.

"When the boy returned home, he told his father what he had learned, and together they built a house larger than any ever before. The first people who came were animal-people, wolf and fox, wolverine and caribou, all manner of people. They came and sat together. Food was shared, and gifts. And as they sang and drummed, the boy heard again the heart of the eagle mother beating. This is the story. This is how people learned, from the animals who taught them."

"It's the same," Elik answered, then she waited to see

if Little-Creek would tell another, the way her grandmother always did in winter, never one alone.

But she didn't. In a little while more, from the low
shelf of the sleeping bench opposite hers, Elik heard
Little-Creek's breathing grow heavier. A deep sound
came up out of the back of her throat each time she
took in air. Nuliaq's little boy had also fallen asleep. He
lay on the center bed, an extra hump curled in beside
his mother.

They were three women sharing one house. Talking
about the skins they needed to sew, the luck of the
men's hunt, about stories and relatives and food.

Climbing out of that kayak, she had expected many
things. Kindness had not been one of them.

The stiff hide brushed the floor as Red Fox entered the
house. Cool air followed in. The small fire wavered,
then straightened itself.

Elik looked up from her stitchwork and watched as
he wiped the snow from his eyelashes, then blinked,
waiting until he could see.

She lowered her eyes, surprised at the way she could
feel both anxious and relieved to see his familiar face
after two nights alone. She glanced toward Nuliaq, to
see if she'd been watched, but Nuliaq's gaze was lowered, her hands already busy filling Red Fox's bowl
with fish broth and meat.

Little-Creek had also risen. With her snow-beating
stick, she stood behind Red Fox, waiting to take his
parka and dry the skins before they stiffened.

Red Fox.

Without speaking, Elik moved her lips, practicing

the shape of the sound. It was going to be difficult for her to use that name. Red Fox was a man she had never known. He was a story to her, an enemy, the kind of ghost story that mothers told their children, hoping to keep them near at home.

Kaviaq she had known. The man who found her in the river valley.

"I did everything," Red Fox said. "The same as any other man in the late autumn season. I went out in my kayak."

Elik laid aside her sewing, folded her hands. She felt awkward, uncertain what her place was. If Ivalu had been here then Nuliaq would have cared for the boy, and Little-Creek the food. She would have been the one to dry Red Fox's parka.

Kaviaq stood in the center of the room, unsettled. As if he wasn't any more certain what to do with himself than Elik was. He asked for water. Nuliaq fetched it. He drank down a huge, gulping mouthful. He squatted by the fire, asked for meat. Nuliaq passed a strip of frozen fish.

"We went out early, hunting seals," he started his story again. "As soon as it was light enough to see. Samik was in the distance in his own kayak. No Bird already caught one seal; he made a huge noise dragging it up on the deck. Everyone could hear."

Red Fox chewed on the fish, sliced off another section. "I used my throwing stick, a barbed dart head on the harpoon. I sang my oldest hunting songs."

Elik nodded, but Red Fox shook his head. "One seal came to see who I was. Only one. I threw the harpoon and missed. It never returned."

"You can eat, and rest," Nuliaq offered. "Then try again. It was only one hunt."

"The slush ice is already forming. And the men are waiting for me to open the *qasgi*," he said. "The boys have brought a thin sheet of ice from the pond between the lagoons. They've already set it over the skyhole. Clear light fills the floor, and I have no first seal. Samik caught one. And No Bird. Did I tell you that already?"

"But not every hunter, surely?"

"No. But people were watching. Their shaman caught no seal, and he should have. That's what they're saying. I was out there as long as the light lasted."

Red Fox glared in annoyance as a fit of coughing took hold of Little-Creek. She set his parka down and covered her mouth, turned to the wall until her coughing turned to a wheeze.

Red Fox passed his empty bowl to Nuliaq, then glanced about the house. "Where is Ivalu?" he asked.

"He's playing out, with his cousins."

"He's a good boy," Elik said, hoping to add a brighter thought. "He has your face . . ."

Nuliaq eyes widened. She sent a hand signal: *Bad luck. Don't speak so . . .*

Red Fox turned on Little-Creek. "Did you say something?" he asked.

Little-Creek hung her head. "Nothing," she apologized. "No." But Red Fox's gaze followed her. Each time she moved, whether to set his parka to dry above the fire, or to take care of the food bowls, she seemed to annoy him.

Finally, she piled together the bowls of food she'd prepared before he came. "I'll bring these to the *qasgi*," she said and she stepped toward the entry. "And then I'll go help Nanogak; with both daughters dead and three sons, she has more work than she can do alone."

Red Fox grew quieter with Little-Creek gone, but no more reassured. He rose, then he sat. He stared around the house. He checked the amulets on his belt, the sun and moon circles stitched on his parka's chest.

"Ice Stick kept looking back to see what I'd caught, all the way home. He even slowed his paddling, so my kayak would draw near and he could stare. And I could hear the men, maybe not my closest cousins, but there were others. They're all talking about the caribou hunt last spring. Some of them say that maybe it wasn't caribou I saw, but something else, hidden in the caribou's skin. What if they're right? It's possible, isn't it? Someone else's thoughtless action could bring a spirit in. What if a spirit tried to trick me?"

Red Fox climbed to the sleeping bench, but instead of lying down, his gaze lit on Nuliaq's broad *ulu* and he picked it up, ran his fingers along the edge.

Dull, the knife drew no blood. He licked it, wet the edge, then watched as the flint turned a lighter grey. Then he reached for a clump of his hair, a long strand. He brought it forward around his face, in front of his chin.

In slow, deliberate strokes, he started cutting, hacking off finger-length strands of his hair.

Elik stopped sewing till Nuliaq reached across, nudged her arm. *Keep working. He doesn't like it when people stare.*

Elik did as she was told. She lowered her head, but

out of the corner of her eyes she kept watching as Red
Fox twisted the hair around his finger, then ate it. He
sucked it, worked it around his mouth, and a moment
later swallowed it down.

Elik shifted toward Nuliaq. "What is he doing?" She
mouthed the question.

"Catching his strength back," Nuliaq whispered, "so
it doesn't escape. Hair is most alive, in all a man's body.
He sees it grow. He eats it to stay strong."

"Is he growing weak?"

Nuliaq's eyes widened. "Hush," she warned. "Never
say such things."

Elik stole another glance. Red Fox sat with his eyes
closed now, waiting, she guessed, to feel the hair
inside. It wasn't a good thing for a man to come home
empty-handed, to miss a shot. She'd seen what it did to
Allanaq, as if he opened his hand and let his luck fall
out, as if he scooped up fear instead.

She looked to the new winter boots she had started
for herself just that morning. The sealskin had been a
generous gift from Nuliaq. The hair had already been
removed to make them waterproof, and some of the fat
had been left on to soften the skin. Nuliaq had also
given her a fine scraping tool made from a polar bear's
lower forearm, and a pouch filled with caribou sinew
that was stronger, easier to use than her own brittle
beluga sinew would have been.

Not only were the gifts generous, they were a sign
that all was well. Whatever luck Red Fox had, there
were still fish and meat and skins to feed the house.
Surely, just because he had missed one seal didn't mean
he wouldn't catch another. And surely, as a shaman,
people would always trade meat for his services.

She dampened the sinew in fish oil to help it slip, then stole another glance at Kaviaq. He was seated on the bench still, doing nothing more than looking around the house. She followed his gaze from the rafters to the wall pegs to the drying rack above the fire pit.

But now there was something else in the way he stared that troubled her, a nervousness that reminded her of something her father used to say: that a person could always know if a man had killed someone by his eyes, by the way he watched other men around him, to see if they were watching him, planning something back.

Red Fox looked up just as she remembered to roll the sinew against her cheek to sharpen the point. "Where are they?" he asked.

Nuliaq and Elik exchanged glances. "Where are what?" Nuliaq asked, but Red Fox ignored her. He looked only at Elik. "The boots," he said. "I haven't seen them since we unloaded the kayak. Did you bring them?"

"Under the bench," Elik answered softly.

"What boots?" Nuliaq asked.

Red Fox lifted his hand, warning her to hush. He rose, nodded for Elik to bring them out; then he stepped back, as if he expected an entire living enemy, not just his boots, to climb out from under the bench.

Elik unrolled the hide. The boots were in the center, laid out flat. The brittle ties wrapped the pair together.

"What if he's here?" Red Fox asked.

Nuliaq's eyes widened as she glanced from Red Fox to Elik. She inched her way to the back wall of her sleeping place, pulled in her knees, stayed out of the way.

Cautiously, Red Fox touched the boots. "My enemy," he said. "He's here. Somewhere in this village. I feel his hatred through the wall. His jealousy walks upright, like a man."

Elik swallowed, made her voice as calm as possible. "What will you do?"

"Hang them. Let them speak," Red Fox said, and this time, with a sudden motion, he rolled them back in their outer skins.

It wasn't until he passed the boots to Elik to hold that he stopped, noticed her face. "You're frightened," he said. "I'm sorry. I shouldn't have brought my anger here, inside. It's just that—I don't want him to find you. He would take you and use you, and then kill you for no other reason than to laugh at my grief."

He turned then, narrowed his eyes as he gazed about the house, this time noticing the pots, the baskets full of food, sewing—women's things, everywhere.

"Not here," he said. "There is a safer place to hang the boots. I want that man to die. But I don't want him to know your name. I want him to be dead, forever. Without hope of coming back."

"Carry the skin," he pointed. "I'll bring my drum, a mat to sit on."

Elik paused as she followed him outside the house. The sky outside was bright with the later morning light. The sea had a different color than when they arrived, greyer with the newly formed slush ice. It caught the sun, flattened the rays on the near shore side, left them sparkling beyond.

It was beautiful. The lick of open water separated the world into parts: dark sea below, land and sky above. As familiar as her childhood, the tastes, the sounds, the smells.

She wondered if the late winter sea ice would be louder here when it cracked than it was at home, but then she decided, no.

It was the same world. The winds would be different, the currents, the shore, but that was only their shape. Just as at home, the hills beyond the Fish River village might have a different shape than the more distant hills behind the Long Coast shore. Or the way the current surrounding the Bent Point village where she had grown up was quieter than the Long Coast currents, where she lived with Allanaq. All was ice, still. And sea. All places, animals, and people had spirits. All were alive.

She looked around, hurried to catch up to Red Fox. "Where are we going?"

"Somewhere he walked. Someplace that knew him." Red Fox stopped, turned to reassure her: "Not the graves," he said. "You needn't fear."

She merely nodded, then followed behind, weaving in and out of the houses. She thought at first he was following a certain path, but the longer he walked, the more she realized the only pattern to his steps was that there was no pattern.

In between two houses, then around them again. Nowhere near the seal skull mound. Nowhere near the burials. If something was following, he meant to deceive it. If a spirit watched, he wanted it lost.

He stopped to wait while two ravens played in the wind above the *qasgi*, another three of the dark birds considered whether to land on a food rack.

He waited till they flew away, then turned along a path that followed the spit. The path carried them a good distance, till he stopped abruptly, and Elik drew up behind him. She found herself looking out on a long expanse of bones, upright caribou ribs and walrus tusks, pointing skyward like a hedge of grass along a beach.

Red Fox smiled at her confusion. "There was a war here, in my father's time," he said. "We were attacked by Forest People. Fools. They thought they'd wait for dawn, then sneak in with lances and their bows. They didn't know we set out sharpened spikes, waiting for them to come. They'd taken off their boots, disguised the noise of their footsteps," Red Fox smiled at the thought. "Their bloodied, cut-up feet marked a path that lasted till the rainy season washed it to the ground. But we remember. We never forget. You have wars, among your people?"

"We have raids. Smaller raids," Elik said, and she shook her head trying to picture the scene.

"There are more stories, more raids. I'll tell you about them later, when we have time. Now we try this way . . ."

Red Fox turned, and without explanation followed the same path back toward the village again, then twisting through a different set of houses. Past the large house that Bird's Mouth and Samik shared with their wives, Mitik and Pintail. Past the house the younger brothers, Mink and No Bird shared with their wives, White Smoke and Sister.

The next houses were grouped close beside each other, set back farther from the sea than Red Fox's four cousins' houses. He pointed out one where he said a man named Old Sheshalik lived with his nephew, a tall man who had a reputation as a fast runner. Inuk was his name. And Red Fox was thinking that maybe he should talk to Nuliaq about her brother's young daughter Chikigak, who would be thinking about a husband soon.

And another house, with a boat storage rack built nearly over the roof, that he said belonged to Okpik, who was related to Nuliaq's first husband. And another house where the naked poles of a summer tent still sat outside the entry. Nuna lived there, he said, a man who had tried giving his son to Red Fox years ago to train as a shaman. But the boy was sickly, too sickly to endure the hardship of a trance, and Red Fox had sent the boy home.

There were more houses, and more names. Names for the children who stared curiously after her. And names she was beginning to recognize. And more names for relatives, cousins, partners who were gone hunting, and others who were visiting in different villages.

At last, feeling thoroughly confused, she stopped behind Red Fox outside an old house she didn't remember seeing before.

Red Fox hesitated, glanced back to see if anyone had followed, but no—the few people outside paid no more attention to him than to the ravens. A fallen beam blocked the entry and Red Fox had to first lift his foot to step across, then lower his head to clear another beam.

Elik followed after him. An inner door held a hide flap that still hung over the opening, so stiff and chewed by dogs and mice, she wondered how anyone could be so poor.

There was no light inside and no fire, no smell of cooking or warmth to wake a smell. Elik pushed back her hood, listened to the hollow sound of wind trapped in empty walls, air so cold it echoed without moving.

Red Fox stood beneath the skyhole in the smallest beam of light. He set down his shaman drum, took the skins from Elik, and set those beside the drum.

Elik put her hand out for balance and a web of hoarfrost disintegrated at her touch. She wrinkled her nose. "What is this place?" she whispered.

"It's abandoned," Red Fox said. "Be careful." He knelt to the floor, started reassembling the hearthstones into the shape of a square.

"Did it collapse? From snow?" In the uneven shadows, Elik made out the shape of driftwood beams fallen from the roof. The wall opposite the entry lay nearly flat upon the bench, rotted from rain, from spring runoff. "Did someone die here?" she asked, and she stepped closer. She set her hand on Red Fox's shoulder, leaned against his back.

"No," Red Fox whispered as he started on a fire. He pulled a horn box from his belt. Fire rocks, oil-soaked shavings for tinder. He hunched over the stones and before long a small fire broadened the circle of light.

The outer rim of the floor was edged in a broken line of seal skulls. One touching on the other, all empty-eyed, open-mouthed. All facing inward and toward the sea, waiting to greet their brothers when they returned. It was the one thing about the house that struck her as right, as whole and fitting—that the seals still looked to the sea.

"No one comes in here," Red Fox said. "This was Anguta's house."

Elik pulled away from Red Fox. She had heard stories of this place, of the last night Allanaq had slept here. The way his father had stood—where?—The door . . . it must have been there, before it collapsed. His father had stood with his songs and his amulets suddenly useless while Red Fox's cousins dropped down through the skyhole.

Red Fox reached to take her hand. "Don't be afraid; you're with me," he said.

Elik looked past his shoulder to the fire pit. Cooking stones. Food tray. A dipper left on the floor. Anguta had had a young wife, but it didn't appear as if she'd ever come back for her things. Had anything here been touched, she wondered, even once since that last day?

"Keep watch on the fire," Red Fox said. "I don't want to stay any longer than we need."

Elik did as he said. She crouched beside the stones but she turned, unable to keep from watching as he pulled out the same pair of boots that had hung all those nights above her head.

He held them carefully, making sure they didn't rub against his skin, against his parka. He looked about the walls till he found a peg high and secure enough that the boots could sway without falling.

Elik searched her memory. She didn't remember Allanaq ever naming the four cousins who jumped through the skyhole, but it didn't matter. She knew them now, Bird's Mouth and Samik, Mink and No Bird.

The strange thing, though, was that they had turned out not to be evil. Their wives had brought their sewing and sat in the house, as curious to see a newcomer as any of the other women had been.

They brought their children. White Smoke had a new baby in her parka. Brown eyes, pink lips. He was no different, no more a demon, than her own sister's son had been. And Bird's Mouth, though she had hardly been around him, wasn't a bad man. He had come into their house once, for Little-Creek. She had had a coughing fit while visiting in another house, and Bird's Mouth had been the one to come with a message for Nuliaq, asking for her help. He had stood in the center of the floor, his eyes too polite to stare at Elik as she bent and lifted the heavy robes Nuliaq sent back with him for Little-Creek.

She could see now, Allanaq had had no chance of killing them. Woken from sleep. Four men against one, fighting in the tight confines of these walls.

Anguta, Allanaq had told her, never raised his arm to stop them. He had stood at the door with his shaman rattle and drum and sung—that was the only weapon his father used.

Elik studied the ruined skyhole, picturing the way it must have fallen.

And would they kill her, she wondered, those cousins, if they found out who she was?

"If the boots don't move now," Red Fox said, "it will mean he's dead."

Elik turned her attention back to the fire. "That will be good?" she asked. "Is that what you want?"

"Sometimes I've wondered. If he's alive, I could fight him again. By now he's an old man. I could win.

I could kill him properly, sever the tendons in his ankles so his spirit cannot find the way back. If he's dead, who knows what that means? Whether he's buried?

"It's possible—" Red Fox paused as the light caught the boots. When nothing happened, he continued. "It's possible I did the wrong thing, sending him away to die. Did I tell you the words he spat at me as he left: *'You will not see me dead now.'* That's what he said. But what it means—I've never known. I think about them, the words. They must have been a curse. He wants me dead, forever. He'll come back, any way he can."

Without taking his glance from the boots, Red Fox walked a circle around the floor, watched from one angle first, and then another. He cocked his head, looked away, then back again, as if to trick them into moving. He squatted and watched the shadow they made on the walls, creeping along the ceiling.

Elik crossed her arms over her chest. She made her face as still as a mask. Anguta was dead. She knew that, but Red Fox didn't. The one reason she had discovered for why the boots had swayed in the tent was because of her, because they had felt the nearness of Anguta's bone, the smell of his son on her skin.

But now—both were gone. Long gone. If the boots didn't move, that would prove she was right.

She watched with Red Fox. No motion. No swaying.

When she looked to the fire, a spark caught her eye, something gleaming on the far side of the stones. She looked again and this time saw it wasn't a spark, but something that had caught the light. Something small.

Red Fox wasn't watching. She stretched out her hand.

"At first, after he was gone," Red Fox continued, "my days were all at peace. That winter the animals gave themselves joyously. They came to the Seal People. Our racks hung heavy with meat and we feasted and celebrated and hunted."

Elik brushed the top layer of ash and dust. Below it on the floor lay the scattered flakes from a man's flint-knapping. She glanced up. Red Fox wasn't watching. Smoothly, slowly, she closed her hand around the flakes.

"In death," Red Fox said, "a spirit often lingers near its belongings, near its graves. That's why I sent him away—to spare the Seal People. So his spirit wouldn't come back, try to visit his weapons, the bowls he ate from. His boots—"

Elik looked at the tiny shards in her hand. Obsidian flakes, edges sharp as knives. The color wavered, from black to the color of water. Clear.

Allanaq had made these, struck them with a hammerstone from a core. She remembered, he had told her how he cut himself free of the thongs with his amulet knife, a blade so small they hadn't thought to steal it from his belt.

"What was that?" Red Fox turned suddenly to the door.

Elik whipped in her hand, closed her fist tight. Instantly, she felt the sharp, hair-thin edge of a flake slicing through her skin. She sucked in her breath, refusing to look. "There's nothing," was all she said. "You are worried."

He stared intently at the ruined door. "If he were a

ghost, he would be powerful. But how would he return. In human form? In the shape of an animal? A demon?"

Elik waited till Red Fox turned back to the boots before opening her hand. Her long finger and her palm were cut in two places. A sliver of stone was imbedded in her skin. She pulled it out, lifted her finger to her mouth and sucked till the blood stopped flowing.

Red Fox kept watching. "For a while," he said, "I was at peace. I told you that—"

Elik nodded, listened again.

"But then something changed. My nights—he started invading my nights. My dreams. I saw him walking along a straight, long beach. I saw a small village of houses, all with their faces, their doors, turned away from the sea. Why would he go to a place like that?" Red Fox turned, looked for Elik to answer.

She shook her head, shrugged. *Was that the Long Coast village he'd seen? Was it possible? In a dream?*

"I started searching again. After all that time. I tranced and I sang. I had to know if he was dead. Whether we were safe or if I'd succeeded only in postponing his vengeance. Nothing more.

"Eventually, one of my helping spirits, the bear, found him. While I lay in the *qasgi*, in a trance so deep they thought I might die, my helping spirit found a den where another bear, this one a mother, lay sleeping.

"The bear knew Anguta. She reeked of his smell, it was on her fur, in her claws, the way a woman smells of a man after she has lain with him."

"Carayak!" Elik covered her mouth with her hands.

"I saw him," Red Fox said. "Through the eyes of my

helping spirit, I looked out through the eyes of that sow. She was dreaming of him, of the smell of a human hunter. He had been stalking her. From the autumn season when I—she—built her den and he first found her, digging out the underbrush for a house. Then into the winter, while we slept and dreamt, and my children . . . hers, I mean . . ." Red Fox shook his head. "Her cubs grew inside her belly.

"The trance was stronger than any I'd felt in all my life. She—Elik, I became that bear, before it died. If you only knew what it was like to be that mother, to lose two children inside of you . . . I felt them, unborn, nursing inside my womb. Sucking the milk I fed them, even before their birth.

"I felt the sleep of winter. The warmth, like food, of my own fur, the frozen ground that was hard, but sheltering. To a human it would have seemed crusted, too cold for sleep. But I was the bear, and inside the bear's fur, in its skin of fat and muscle, no ground was cold. No shelter anything but warm.

"I would have slept in that bed, filling my dreams with thoughts of fish and berries. Sun and water sparkling with play. I would have. I would have slept forever, but his scent came back. He woke me, tugged me out of that sleep that had been so sweet. It was him, the human smell of my enemy. And yet, his scent—it was deceitful, so sweet, I let it draw me . . .

"What did a bear know of human guile? All I knew was his smell. It woke me from the sweet dreams of summer, a stream full of spawning salmon, red and sweet and oily salmon I would have fed to my children."

Red Fox sucked in his breath, as if he'd been struck. His hand lifted to his chest, to his neck. "He killed me," he said. "Stabbed the heart that beat inside my breast. I grew cold—I who had never known such a thing. And yet—that alone, I could have endured. But in that trance, I was the bear, and what he did, what he killed, it was my unborn cubs.

"I was dying, and I did the only thing I could do. I lashed out. I breathed his scent inside of me. His name. His face. And as I died, as the breath soul went out of me, it killed his sons. Two sons.

"By then, the trance was weakening. My own soul returned to this body. I woke. I was human again. A man, not a bear. Here, in my own village.

"And yet it was fair, it was right. He killed my two bear-sons, I killed his. But now—look. You see how the boots never sway? He may have been alive then, but he is dead now. There is no soul left to find. Still . . ." he stopped, a look of confusion on his face. "If the boots swayed then, at the river camp . . . where was he then?"

Elik didn't answer. She locked her eyes on the fire, pulled her knees to her chest, and leaned back against a fallen beam that once must have supported Allanaq's sleeping bench.

An aching exhaustion moved through her. She dropped the slivered flakes into the dust, let them lie there, forgotten.

"Unless it was the son. Could he be alive?" Red Fox grew quiet. He seemed to consider the thought. "Qajak. It is possible. What if his father taught him his most powerful shaman-songs, and he means to use them? What if the father is dead, but the son means to take revenge? The son—that's it. Anguta is dead. Qajak is alive."

Red Fox suddenly stopped. He held still, cocked his head. "What is that?"

Elik looked to the door. "What is what?" she asked. She heard nothing. No footsteps or crunching snow. She turned a nervous eye to Red Fox.

He was looking at her, at her hands. "That light?" he said.

Elik pulled her hands behind her back, out of the fire's orange light. "It's the fire. That's all. I'm hot."

"No. Heat isn't that color, not on skin. There was something—a light. Your hands. Show me what you have."

"Show you what?" Elik rose on shaking legs. She stepped away.

"Your hands." Red Fox reached out for her. She stepped back, but he followed, pressed her nearly to the wall.

There was little she could do. He touched her shoulder. Her heart beat furiously. She brought her hands out from behind. The bleeding had stopped, but the brown stain remained.

"Your hands," Red Fox said. "I saw them glowing."

"I cut it. You saw a spark, that's all. You see—it's gone now. Nothing's here."

"No, it was you. Not the fire," Red Fox disagreed. "Your hands were glowing. This is what happens when a person is a shaman."

Elik shook her head; she pulled from his arms. "Please, can we leave? I don't like it here. I want to leave."

"Of course we can leave. You're right, it's dangerous

here." Protectively, Kaviaq pulled her in, pressed her against his chest.

Elik lowered her head into the fold of his shoulder, tried not to breathe while he held her, smoothed the top of her hair.

8

Nuliaq pulled the last bit of sinew through the thick layers of skin, then cut the remaining length with her teeth. Beside her on the floor, Elik softened a caribou hide, chewing then wringing it, folding then chewing again.

Both women sat with their legs outstretched, faces turned to catch the light of Elik's seal oil lamp.

"This is the part of the story I remember best," Nuliaq said. "I learned it from my grandmother Anuga when I was young. It goes like this: There was a very old woman who was put out from her village. She was abandoned. Maybe the people were starving, maybe her husband died and there was no one to hunt for her. I'm not sure why."

"No no," Elik laughed. "It isn't right to interrupt a story telling what you don't know. You need to say it through."

"But I *don't* know," Nuliaq laughed back. "Was she ill? Maybe she stole something from the dead, then tried to hurt someone with it? Maybe someone died because of her?"

"But a story isn't gossip. You have to learn it right, the way it's told, otherwise no one will listen when you sing it during the feasts. They'll laugh at you."

Nuliaq smiled, shook her head. "I'm not a story-teller. I'm not an old grandmother. I'll explain that I only know part. Or I'll be quiet, if I can't be accurate."

"That's all right, so long as you say so before you begin, or at the end. Not in the middle, once you started."

Nuliaq checked the seam on the one-piece parka she was sewing for Ivalu. "Very well, I'll try. But I'd be just as content to listen." She lay the parka across her lap.

"So. There was a very old woman who was put out from her village. The grandmother was left to survive alone with her young granddaughter. There was no man with them, no one to help. And so what could one old woman do? She had to hunt. The child needed to eat. Each day the grandmother woke, and with the power of a secret song she transformed herself into a man."

"And as a man," Elik recited with Nuliaq, "she lay with her granddaughter at night, as if the girl were a wife."

"And the girl took care of their sewing," Nuliaq continued. "She melted snow for water. She kept a fire, and cooked. The grandmother, because she had no antler or ivory to make into weapons, cut off her toes and these became her harpoons. She cut off her fingernail and this became a dog, and the dog helped when she hunted on the moving ice pack; it sniffed until it found a seal's breathing holes, and in this way the old woman was able to hunt. She was powerful when she was a man, and the small family survived. But whenever she came home and turned into a grandmother again, she was tired. She became very small. The granddaughter had to chew the seal meat her husband-grandmother had caught, and feed it into the old woman's mouth. Then she would have strength again and when the next day came, she could hunt."

"You see?" Elik said. "You told it well. All of it— though you're right. It is a hard story to understand. Did the girl have babies? What happened when their relatives found out?"

"I don't know," Nuliaq shrugged. "At least the grandmother was able to hunt. Why should they have to die, just because no one took care of them?"

"Tell another," Elik said. "My grandmother used to say that one story always needs a second, so it doesn't fall down."

"But it's your turn," Nuliaq tapped Elik's foot. "You tell."

Elik thought a moment. She reached over and fixed the wick in the seal oil lamp she had made from the clay only a short while ago. The bowl of the lamp was shallow, the same shape as she would have made in the Long Coast village, with a lip to hold in the oil and a slot to keep the wick in place. The lamp had surprised Nuliaq, the way it sputtered when fat dripped to the wick, and gave off a yellow light instead of a flame, like wood.

Elik lifted her eyes, watched the heat rise toward the skyhole. It was closed now, covered with strips of stitched-together sealgut. The white gut was clear enough to see light through, not so easily as in the *qasgi* where a thin sheet of clear lake ice had been placed over the window for the opening ceremony, but enough so it seemed to her as if the roof of their house was like the sky outside, the same as the sky was a roof over the ground. The same as the ice that covered the sea was a roof over the ocean floor. The same as—" Elik stopped, chuckled at her dizzying thoughts.

"What is it?" Nuliaq asked.

Elik shook her head. "I was wondering what the underside of the ice looks like to the Seal People in their village on the ocean bottom. Do you think it looks the same to them as our sky does for us? And if it does, then does the topside of our sky look like the ground to the spirits, and to the dead people walking above?

"Do you think they look down sometimes and try to see who's walking below their feet?" Elik stopped talking long enough to catch the expression on Nuliaq's face, her smile opening to a laugh.

"No one I have ever met talks like you, sister-wife."

"So you keep saying," Elik said, and she pushed aside her seriousness. "But I still don't understand how you can sleep with all that noise the dwarf-people make beneath this house." Elik cocked her ear, and made a face to listen. "Don't you hear it?"

Nuliaq reached to Elik and gave her a push for her foolishness. And for one more moment they laughed together, no differently than if they were two young girls.

But the moment couldn't last. Nuliaq caught her breath, remembering herself. "We mustn't joke while our husband is seal hunting," she said. "The men say the spotted seal turns cranky, and the ringed seal is shy and quiet. Our voices are like thunder to them. Red Fox is hoping for bearded seal most of all, and we have to be mindful.

"If we fall asleep, then Red Fox will also grow tired.

If we are quiet, the seal will also be quiet, it won't put up a fight. When he comes home, we'll take the head of the bearded seal into the house, and honor it until the Bladder Feast."

"The Bladder Feast," Elik repeated. "We don't have that."

Nuliaq looked over in surprise. "You say your people honor the seals, but you don't celebrate the Bladder Feast? You are strange. Wise and foolish at the same time."

"So are the young," Elik said. "But they grow. They learn. Tell me about your feast. What do you do with the bladders?"

"Each year," Nuliaq said, "We make peace with the animals, otherwise they wouldn't come when we hunted. In a year like this, when hunting is poor—"

"Shh!" Elik stopped her. "Don't say bad things. Your words make them true."

"Now I'm the one who forgets herself," Nuliaq apologized. "But the feast—we bring the heads of the seals to the mound outside, but it is their souls that live inside the bladders that are the most important. We save them, and feast them, and on the last day of the ceremony, we unite them with their skulls. As we treat them, so they treat us." Nuliaq stopped. She cocked her head, looked to the skyhole. "Do you hear that?"

Elik held still, listening. "Someone is drumming?"

"It's Inuk—I mean his uncle. Sheshalik, I know his drum. It has that deep sound. It must be Red Fox is back. None of the other men are still out."

Elik set aside the hides. "Should we call Little-Creek?"

"No, let her be. Her coughing only angers him. She's better off in Higjik's house."

"And Ivalu?"

"Let him play, at least till we know if there's food. Make sure you bring your best knife. And fresh water, and that dipper. If he has a bearded seal we'll celebrate his First Catch of the season. If not . . . ?"

"Don't talk about *if not*," Elik said. "Tomorrow, he'll go hunting again, the same as yesterday. The same as every man."

A snow had begun to fall, tiny flakes falling at a slant. The sun was a low white circle against a whiter sky. Elik lifted her hood and followed Nuliaq past the houses, the *qasgi*, the near-empty food racks that she didn't allow herself to see, to worry about.

Old Sheshalik had already quit his drumming and disappeared down the pole-ladder that reached from the skyhole into his house. His nephew Inuk remained, seated on his ankles and watching—a little too closely, Elik thought—the entire way as they followed the path between the houses, then down to where the rougher shore ice covered what had once been beach and sea.

Winter had settled in since Elik arrived. The autumn storms that had brought their harvest of mussels and tomcod were gone now. Behind the storms the slush ice had come, settling in against the land, hardening into thick, young ice. Spreading outward from an apron that clutched the shore, into fields and hills of bent and heaved-up pressure ridges, and then beyond, to the edge of the pack ice.

Red Fox was no larger than a dot in the distance when Elik tapped Nuliaq's arm, pointed out the darker line of a seal scudding its path behind the man.

Nuliaq shielded her eyes. "Is it large?" she asked. "I can't see."

"It's too far to know."

"Don't forget, if it's bearded seal," Nuliaq said, "we won't be able to eat it ourselves. His first seal of the year must be shared, the meat and the fat and the skin."

"And the bladder?"

"The soul lives inside the bladder. Red Fox gives that back to the seal; it's never eaten," Nuliaq said, but by then her voice had fallen. Red Fox was near enough now, they could see the seal was small. Large enough to eat, but not to rejoice.

Nuliaq rubbed her hands along the front of her parka, hiding her disappointment. Neither she nor Elik had eaten more than one small meal a day since Red Fox left. It wouldn't have been seemly, eating more than two small women needed, while their husband was out on the ice. Ivalu had eaten—a child wasn't expected to be patient with hunger. And Elik had quickly caught on to the way Nuliaq pretended not to notice when Little-Creek sometimes hid a haunch of caribou meat under her parka or dried fish beneath her bedding.

Red Fox dragged the seal by a towline around his chest; he pulled with his weight leaning forward. He stopped often, checking for firm footing with his ice-testing stick, glancing toward the houses to see who had come to meet him on the ice.

It seemed to Elik she had stood this way before,

lined out with women waiting in a row. Sometimes singing, sometimes holding quiet while the hunters dragged their catch home to wives, sisters, mothers. It was a familiar sight, the blue shadow of a pressure ridge heaved up high as a mountain, the distant grey of an open lead reflecting darkly in the clouds.

She wondered if Allanaq had been as careful in the boat as Red Fox was walking on the ice now. She didn't know. She didn't know if he was dead or alive, lost or found somewhere, adopted by another family.

What she did know was that each day he didn't appear, each day there was no news of a trader approaching the village overland, that was another day she was certain he was dead.

Nuliaq walked ahead to meet Red Fox. She took the drag handle from his bulky mitten, pulled the seal along till Elik came and helped, gripping it by its rear flippers, pushing while Nuliaq dragged it to a level shelf just below the beach.

Elik pulled the dipper from her belt, then nodded toward Red Fox. She wanted him to see her smile, to know that she was glad for this seal, for any seal, but he didn't look her way.

He was too intent on watching Nuliaq, staring pointedly at the top of her hood as she leaned over the seal, at her dark braids as they swayed, almost touching the rise of its chest.

He set down his ice-testing stick and harpoon. When finally he did look to Elik, his eyes were a flat color, his mouth pinched and tight. "It's a small seal," he said. "But it came. It did come. It came to its breathing hole."

Elik stole a second glance to his face. Why did he

sound so disappointed? Because it wasn't the bearded seal he hoped for, but a small seal? That didn't make sense. Even *natchiq* the ringed seal would give them a few days of food and oil, clothing and lines for rope making.

Nuliaq hadn't noticed. She bent over the seal, held its slippery grey head so the mouth was lifted. Elik filled the dipper with the fresh water they'd brought from the house, passed it to Nuliaq who, with the honor due a first wife, poured a few drops into the seal's thin mouth.

"We are giving you water for your thirst," Nuliaq sang. *"Pure water, so you will tell others of your kind, there is good water here. Fresh water to quench the thirst in their souls."*

Nuliaq scraped up a fistful of snow, sprinkled it near the seal's mouth, its joints, front and back, its flippers—five places to calm the spirit for its journey.

"I was sitting on an ice block, waiting, no different than any other time," Red Fox said, and this time, his voice sounded so oddly insistent, Nuliaq stopped her work. She glanced to his face, found the same pinched mouth, the troubled eyes Elik had seen.

Nuliaq nudged Elik's arm. *Get the dipper. Walk near me.*

Red Fox waited while the women took up the towline. Then he followed behind, talking all the while. "All I could think," he said, "when I started out, was that if I had committed a wrong, no seal would come. They would leave at the sight of me. The same way the caribou left. Even if I didn't understand, at least I would see it for myself.

"But I worried too much. Even before I left to hunt,

while the other men sat in the *qasgi* waiting for dawn and talking of who had caught their first seal of the year, and who had caught two, I sat with a robe over my shoulders, worrying.

"But then finally, I did find a seal's breathing hole. Half a day's walk," he waited for Nuliaq to stop, then pointed to show the direction.

"The dome of its breathing hole was moist with the seal's breath; the ice covering the hole had hardly formed. I felt lucky. It was a good hole, the seal was still using it. I sang my hunting songs. I sang secret shaman-songs. I prepared my harpoon, and I set a feather to help show motion, the same as every other time. And then I sat, through a night and another day. And almost—" he stopped, waited.

Nuliaq held her shoulders rigid and tight. She sent a worried glance to Elik, signaled her to stand and listen, the same as she did.

"—Almost the seal didn't come. Almost, I gave up and returned home empty-handed. But I didn't give in. I didn't sleep. I did nothing but wait until morning came, when I stood and turned in the direction of the sun. I took five breaths, as I always do, and then just before I sat back down, I felt something." He moved to look directly at Nuliaq. "Do you know what that was?"

Nuliaq stared at the white ground. The seal slid nearer her feet, its pointy nose lifted to smell the air.

"I felt the wind reach up inside my parka," Red Fox said. "I heard it whistling a song. To me. Accusing me of being a careless man. Me, a foolish man. A man who thinks so little of the wind that he mocks it. Forgets the importance of respect. The whistling grew and I felt a spot of cold, a knife prick of cold, cutting to my skin. Here. Look at this."

Red Fox stepped up to Nuliaq. He turned the bottom hem of his parka out, holding it for her to see where a piece had been smoothly cut, not torn, from the side seam below his arm.

Nuliaq lifted her hand to touch, but Elik couldn't move. She didn't dare. Her face drained of blood. She had forgotten—how could she have forgotten? The hole she'd cut in his parka, while they were in the kayak. She had meant to use it against him. And the scrap—if he found it, and he would—he would know she'd tried to kill him. He would know—

If there had been any confusion in Red Fox's voice, it was gone now. He was angry and accusing, not disappointed. "It wasn't my enemy at all," he said. "But someone who isn't afraid to use a knife against stitches. A woman who can easily get to her husband's parka . . . ?"

Nuliaq jerked her hands away. "I didn't do this."

"No?"

"I have nothing to gain with you dead. You know that."

Elik stared toward the horizon. Ice blending into sky, a single line where the land fell away.

Desperately, she searched back through the days. What had she done with the scrap? She remembered the way she'd felt in the kayak, so afraid, she could taste it in her mouth. The way Red Fox's boots had been so close, it seemed the entire earth was standing on her head. She had reached past his feet to his parka.

She remembered how tightly the kayak squeezed, the deck like a skin growing over her own skin.

Changing her to a seal. A dead seal. She had made the cut, and then twisted, worked her arms back along her sides. And hid it—that's what she had done. She had hidden the knife inside her boot.

And the scrap of his fur—she had wedged it inside. It had worked its way into her boot toe. She hadn't taken it out. It was there, all this time. She looked up.

Red Fox stood with his head inclined, his fingers exploring the nick in the seam. "How do I know you don't want another man? I was gone a long time. A woman without a man . . . ?" Rudely, Red Fox licked his lips.

Nuliaq's face burned. "If I wanted to leave, I would," she answered stubbornly. "I don't need to use charms or bits of your flesh. I can walk away."

"Brave words," Red Fox said. "For a woman. But what if there is a man?"

"There is no man."

Red Fox ignored the denial. "But what if there is and he's too afraid to steal you while I'm still alive?"

"I have brothers, uncles who would take me in. Two Legs and Sigluna."

"And where are they? In Paatitaaq, the wild-onion village?"

"Yes."

"And when was the last time you saw them?"

"What is this about? Are you still searching for secrets I never had? I told you. If I wanted to leave, I have feet. I know how to walk."

Elik wiggled her toes inside her boot. Not the left. It had been the right boot. The right foot. She could feel it now. The tiniest hump inside the smooth grass sock.

She glanced to Red Fox. His face was dark with

anger, but not at her. He stood a hand's breadth from Nuliaq, accusing, daring her to say more.

Cautiously, Elik leaned onto her toes. She could feel it, the scrap. It had crept against the thick seam-work, tucked itself into a hump. Red Fox knew nothing.

Nuliaq lifted her chin. "And what would I say to my son?" she asked. "If he thought I wanted his father's death?"

Red Fox held her gaze a moment longer, then shook his head. "He's a child. Whatever a mother tells him, that's what he'll believe."

"When he's young, perhaps. But he also has ears. What would I tell him later, when he heard people whisper? All his life he would hear their whispers."

"It sounds to me like you've been thinking." Red Fox curled his mouth in annoyance, but he turned from Nuliaq. His eyes moved across the mounds of each house, so intent, he seemed to be naming each person and where they were related, where their loyalties were born and who their partners were.

"There's Ice Stick. He'll never stop hating me. He could do anything. But there's also my cousin Bird's Mouth. He would never go against me. He does too well, having me alive. As do his brothers behind him. Samik. Mink. No Bird . . . ? He's young. He might not remember so well. Sheshalik's old. He'll soon be gone. Without him, his nephew Inuk would leave. He has no woman here yet, and more relatives in other villages. And Grayling, and Owl? They'll stand together, perhaps not with Ice Stick. But which way?"

Nuliaq turned from the houses and exchanged a worried glance with Elik, till Red Fox turned, caught them both with their mouths open, their gestures pointing his way. He looked from Nuliaq to Elik as if noticing them both for the first time. "Where is Little-Creek?"

Guardedly, Nuliaq signaled Elik: *Hush. Don't tell.*

"Why didn't she come meet me?"

Elik bent over the seal and started rubbing shards of icy snow onto its fur, scrubbing the blood from the harpoon wound.

"What kind of wife doesn't help with a husband's seal?"

Neither woman spoke.

Red Fox watched Nuliaq retie the dragline through a slice in the seal's fore flipper, then settle the line over her shoulders, across her chest.

They trudged back in a heavy silence, faces hidden deep inside their hoods. With a crablike side step, Elik walked behind Nuliaq, prodding the seal whenever it skidded the wrong way. She prayed that Red Fox's anger would quiet, that the scrap in her boot would not give her away.

Outside their house, all was as quiet as when they'd left. The skyhole gave no sign of smoke, no sign if Little-Creek had returned.

Elik moved toward the entry, then looked up in surprise as Nuliaq continued dragging the seal around the back of the house, then up the slope of the snow-covered roof.

Nuliaq gestured for Elik to follow, then, as they stood together on the top of the roof: "Quiet," she said. "Look back."

On the path behind Red Fox, two men, Samik and Inuk—he must have climbed down from his roof for a better look—walked together out from the *qasgi* and along the same path they had just taken. The two men called no greeting but it was easy to see they had purposefully changed their direction, chosen this one for the chance it gave them to check the size of Red Fox's one small seal.

Red Fox pretended not to notice. With his shoulders tight, refusing to see the men, he looked nowhere but at the door. Nuliaq too pretended not to see them.

"What's going on?" Elik whispered.

"We lower the seal through the skyhole, not through an ordinary door."

"But it's not a bearded seal," Elik asked. "I thought you gave the First Catch rights only to the *ugruk*."

"But think—" Nuliaq passed Elik the line attached to the seal's mouth. "What if he catches no other? You see how Samik lowered his glance. He doesn't gloat. He's as frightened as Red Fox, seeing his cousin bring home a small boy's catch."

"Inuk too?"

Nuliaq's gaze dropped to her boots.

"Inuk looks with different eyes," she said. "Don't look at him. Just go around inside. Help me bring this seal down."

The two men were gone by the time Elik climbed through the front entry. Inside the house, she kept a careful distance away from Red Fox. She stepped onto the fire pit rocks, lifted her arms to help guide the seal as Nuliaq lowered it down from the roof. With the skyhole left open for light, she pushed the seal onto a scrap of hide. Then she stepped back, expecting Red Fox to make the first cut, severing the head from the body.

He didn't.

Even before Nuliaq was inside, he had crossed to Little-Creek's side of the bench—the cold side, nearest the door. He flung back the sleeping furs, the woven grass mat below. Whatever he was looking for, he didn't find.

On hands and knees he bent to her storage baskets beneath the bench. Pushing. Toppling. Searching.

Nuliaq entered, and he shoved a basket toward her feet. "Who but a wife could cut a man's clothes?" he argued. "What about my food? What if she poisoned it? What if she cut my hair while I was sleeping, used it in some evil, something against me?"

Red Fox sniffed at the inside of a large bowl. "Was she cooking? She might have tricked me into eating something." He looked up. "What if she was jealous because I brought Elik in the house?"

Nuliaq tried to make her voice sound pleasant: "Was I jealous when Little-Creek moved in?"

"You? You're not that kind of woman. You're too proud. Maybe it scared her, having to share with another woman, not just one. Where is she? Hiding?" He stepped to Nuliaq, not Elik.

"You haven't seen the men," he said. "The way they sit in the *qasgi*? They're watching me. Did I tell you that? Each time a man comes in from hunting, any man, and he's caught no seal, they all turn to see what I'll do. As if I'm the cause."

Red Fox pointed toward Little-Creek's empty sleeping place. "Find her," he said. "Tell her if she tries to run away, I'll kill her. I spared her husband, but her . . ." He tapped his hands, thought a moment. "Wait. Better yet, I'll find her, and you will help."

"Now?" Nuliaq stood with her knife at her side. "What about the seal?"

Red Fox looked down. Water was already puddling on the floor, dripping from the seal's fur to the mat. "The seal can wait," Red Fox said. "I want her, now. I want her curse away from me."

Elik squatted at the fire pit, hoping that if she looked busy, she could stay and destroy the scrap of fur when no one was about. She tried to make her voice sound small, a little frightened. "Need I come?" she asked.

Red Fox turned. He let out his breath, set down the bowl he'd been holding. "You should," he nodded. "It's safest. There's no way of knowing what else she'd try, what else is hiding in these walls. I don't want you hurt."

Elik brushed off her knees and stood. She felt almost embarrassed by his kindness; she didn't deserve it. No more than Little-Creek deserved his anger.

Behind them, Nuliaq crouched beside the seal. With a flick of her curved woman's knife, she slit the eyelids. The right one first, then the left.

"I told you to leave it," Red Fox said. "What are you doing?"

"You don't want demons and curses inside the house, and I don't want the seal to see your anger. There's too much anger here."

"Then find her," Red Fox glared. "Make her undo whatever she's begun, or there will be demons, and shouting, louder than this."

He turned to Elik. "You see what I live with?" He caught his breath, lowered his voice. "Someone attacks me, yet I'm accused of anger. Of course the *inuas* see. Of course they know."

Outside in the wind again, Red Fox hurried them along. He stopped in front of different houses, choosing the path with a smoldering care. The nearest house to theirs was shared by Bird's Mouth and Samik, the next house by their brothers. Relatives, all of them, people who Red Fox trusted. He had no need to search inside. Little-Creek would never stay there.

It was at Ice Stick and Spider's house, the next one beyond those, that he motioned for them to wait. A thin layer of smoke spread like a cloud above the sky-hole. Red Fox looked to Nuliaq: "In here?" he asked, but she only shrugged. Red Fox threw her a look of disgust, then pushed inside, not even troubling to call or be polite.

By the time Elik stepped in behind them, the house had folded itself into a stony silence. Elik had been here before, but only for short visits when Nuliaq asked her to fetch water or coals for their fire. The inside was smaller than their house, but neat and busy with tools and baskets. There was no planking on the walls, only a layer of grass matting hanging to cover the sod. Four larger posts met the corners of the sleeping bench that ran along all but the entry wall. The sleeping bench stood as high as Elik's waist and wide enough for a man with his head toward the fire to stretch out and only have to bend his legs a little if he didn't want to touch the outside wall.

But there were no men, only women inside. Spider and Higjik, who were always together. And Nanogak, whose husband Grayling was Ice Stick's brother. She was a round woman with no waist left after giving birth to five children. The straightest lines of her body were on her face, where her nostrils flared sharply and the line of her nose pointed directly into her chin.

One Pot was there also, an elderly woman who lived on the shares her relatives brought—this was the first time Elik had seen her outside her own small house.

On the floor, Ivalu played with two other children, Little Eyes and a girl named Raven. The boy glanced up, smiled at his mother, then went back to the wooden stick-people they had piled on the floor.

They were relatives—Elik saw it for herself this time, clearly enough she didn't have to be told. There was a resemblance, something in the way Spider and Higjik's eyes narrowed in the corner, the way Nanogak and One Pot both had high foreheads. Small differences, but they were there, enough to tell them apart from the people Red Fox named as family. And different again from Elik's rounder-faced Real People.

Spider and Higjik both sat with their legs straight in front of them, awls and bone needles in their hands, the same guarded expression on both their faces. Spider moved to the fire pit, where she kept a container of water dangling from a rope, the rope from the roof beam overhead. A smell of fish and oil and women filled the house. And then one thing more.

From the sleeping bench along the middle wall, under a mound of furs, came the sound of coughing. It was Little-Creek, with a raspier, more bruising noise than Elik had heard before.

Spider waited till the coughing passed. Then politely, she nodded to Red Fox. "Come," she said. "You're welcome to eat."

Red Fox stood with his feet set firm. "I came for my wife."

"She is asleep," Spider said. She held out a bowl of food: dried fish, a few choice lumps of a darker meat.

Red Fox ignored it. "Wake her."

"She is ill."

"If you believed that, all these people wouldn't be here. They wouldn't let their children near. You don't look afraid." Red Fox drew himself taller. "Wake her."

The blankets moved. The hump beneath them turned into the shoulders, drawn face, and loose strands of Little-Creek's damp hair.

"So," she wiped her mouth, tried to joke, "my second husband longs for his wife's tight legs. Were you afraid I ran away with another man?" Little-Creek laughed, then coughed, then smiled as if it was all a joke.

Red Fox kept his hands tight against his sides. "Run later, as you will."

Little-Creek narrowed her eyes. "What do you want?"

"Payment," Red Fox said. "For a certain parka that someone's teeth, or knife, or maybe fingernails destroyed."

Elik pressed herself against the shadow of the wall. Should she say something, call out that she was the one? Or wait only a little longer, and Red Fox would see that nothing happened. Another day, maybe two, and he would catch a bearded seal. His luck would come back. He would go back to ignoring Little-Creek.

Little-Creek looked to Nuliaq. "What is he saying? Is he in a trance—?"

Nuliaq moved toward the bench, but she never reached it. Red Fox reeled and pushed her out of his way. Without stopping to see where she'd fallen, he crossed the floor. Higjik and Nanogak jumped from his reach.

He grabbed Little-Creek by her hair, twisted it around his fist, and pulled her, up and out of the furs. He forced her from the bench.

With the furs dragging from her legs, Little-Creek stumbled and fell. She grabbed for Red Fox's parka, trying to climb, to stand while he held her head yanked back by her hair.

Elik crouched where she was, opening her arms for Ivalu to jump to safety. She passed the wide-eyed boy to Nuliaq, who was standing now, pressed against the wall. The other women also held back, too afraid to stop him.

"I didn't do it," Little-Creek fought for breath. "Nothing. Whatever you said."

"Who did?"

"Did what?" she begged. "How can I know?" Her cheeks were blotchy, pale and dark at the same time.

Red Fox tugged harder on her hair. He forced her up from the floor, onto her knees. He pulled back her head.

Little-Creek pursed her lips and hurled a line of spit flying to his chin, his cheek, his mouth.

Furious, Red Fox lifted his fist and struck the side of her face. He reached to hit her again, but the coughing started, so deep this time, Little-Creek's knees buckled. She doubled over, head toward the floor.

Red Fox wiped his mouth. He waited, doing nothing while Little-Creek wrapped her arms over her thin breasts, calmed her breathing. By then his anger had already slipped, turned to annoyance, frustration.

The other women stood as they were, waiting, keeping out of his reach. As soon as Little-Creek quieted he nudged her with his foot. "You come with me," he ordered. Elik stepped up to her, wrapped a fur robe around her shoulders. She helped her stand, lifted the robe to cover her head.

Red Fox turned for the door but Nuliaq called him back. "I need to stay here," she said. Firmly, she kept her hands on Ivalu's shoulders, holding the boy close. She sent a signal to Elik: *You go. Don't leave Little-Creek alone.*

Elik nodded her agreement.

Red Fox felt the weight of the women's gazes, daring him to strike Nuliaq too, but he wouldn't do it. Let them talk as they might, he wouldn't give in to their gossip, their stares.

Instead, he ducked outside, waited until he heard the crunching sounds of Little-Creek's, then Elik's, boots stepping onto snow. He didn't say a word, none of them did, until they were inside their own house again, safe from prying eyes.

This time the house felt cool; the skyhole had been left open, the fire still unlit. Little-Creek stared in surprise at her baskets, emptied and strewn about the floor. When she saw the seal, she glanced to Elik: *Is that his problem?* She lifted her chin toward the seal. *His catch came home too small?*

Be careful, Elik whispered. *He's angrier than that.*

Little-Creek answered with a nod, then squatted beside the fire pit. Using her fingers, she began patting cold ashes from the hearth on the side of her face that was swelling now, dark with bruises from his hand.

Red Fox paid her no attention. He motioned for Elik to help him out of his parka. Awkwardly, he stood with arms lifted, his lip curling each time the ruined parka slid along his skin.

With a last pull, Elik held the parka in her hands. She hung it on the drying rack above the fire, then removed her own parka, both the outer and inner layers, but not her leggings, and certainly not her boots. She wedged herself into the farthest corner of the sleeping bench, pulled a large caribou robe over her shoulders.

As soon as Red Fox left, she would pull the scrap out of her boot and destroy it.

If only he stopped worrying over her, watching as carefully as if she were a child, wanting her near his side.

She might be able to swallow the scrap, it was small enough. She could chew it if he didn't leave. If he kept watching her. She would wait and shit it out later. Hide it again after that, unless she was lucky, and there was nothing left to hide.

Little-Creek hadn't moved. She sat with her shoulders hunched, chin tucked in against her chest as if waiting for Red Fox to strike her again.

Except he didn't. With Little-Creek and Elik both where he could see them, his anger didn't return. More properly, he turned his attention to the seal again. He squatted beside it and, with his sharpest butchering knife, he made the first circling cut, east to west around the base of the skull, the same direction as the sun rises and then sets.

Elik edged closer to watch the way he cut through the bone, then snapped the spine. Below the neck, above the shoulders, exactly so.

When the head was free of the body, he placed it on

the mat, then began skinning it, pulling the fur off like a mask, whiskers still attached. He set the naked head to one side, then went on to care for the body.

The meat and fat he removed together, separating the strips into piles. All of this First Catch was to be given away, the choicest bits for the eldest women, small cuts for the children. The bladder would be cleaned and saved for the feast, the head would be boiled and set with the others on the mound. The rest would be divided among relatives.

Red Fox wiped his hands when he was done. With an air of calm, he studied Little-Creek's back. "Take your things," he said. His voice was level, almost flat. "Get out. You're not my wife anymore."

Little-Creek lifted her eyes in disbelief. "I can leave?"

"Find some other hunter to feed you. Someone you hate less than me."

"You won't follow me?" She asked. Her voice was shocked, as if she couldn't believe such luck.

"Have I ever?"

She thought about that. "I'm dying."

"No you're not. And neither am I. But you tried to bring demons into this house, against me. When you leave me alone, they will leave you. I have seen this. I no longer fear what you've done."

Little-Creek pushed herself up from the floor. Elik could see the effort it took her, straightening, swallowing her breath with small grabbing sounds, not to cough.

"Just mind what you take." Red Fox said. "If Nuliaq complains . . ."

"She'll have no complaints," Little-Creek said quickly. "Ask her later, you'll see." Her eyes were dancing when she looked to Elik. She nodded, hid her smile. Then she started gathering up the seal pokes, baskets, the roll of pelts she kept beneath the bench.

All the while she sorted she talked aloud. "One. Two. Five. One hand's count. Another. Three. Four. Two hands'. I'll keep the twenty strips of sealgut I traded for the oil. Enough to make a waterproof coat and trade it into meat."

She stopped suddenly, turned to Elik: "Mind you, count what you own," she warned. "I always have, not because someone might steal, but because of what you need. You never know what you need. Tell Nuliaq these were mine." She pulled the roll of pelts against the larger basket. "I earned them from a parka I stitched for Old Sheshalik. And this pile for the boots I made for Ice Stick when Spider's new baby made her too sick to sew. That's why he took me in," she flashed a look toward Red Fox. "Not out of kindness. Because he knew I'd cost him nothing. He could brag to others how he took pity on me."

Red Fox wrinkled his nose. "The dog stays," he said.

"What?" Little-Creek looked surprised. "That dog was mine. It came with me."

"I've grown fond of it. You don't feed it."

Little-Creek looked to Elik, then shrugged. "Keep it then. Feed it. See what use it does you."

After that, it didn't take long. Little-Creek had come to Red Fox's house owning little; she carried out but a little bit more. With a cautioning glance to Elik, and a cough that she swallowed behind her hand, Little-Creek stepped through the door.

No sooner had the flap slid back into place than Red Fox turned to Elik. "So," he said. "Every day since we returned, I searched for the trouble, and here it was, all along. You see how she did that? How she made it sound as if I was the selfish one, taking her in? As if Nuliaq didn't have to share meat, not only out of her mouth, but out of Ivalu's? As if I never had pity, never gave her sleeping furs, pots, the sewing awls she claims like a hunter's weapon?"

He opened his hands, as if to show Elik all the riches of his house. "I was reasonable," he went on. "But she thanked me with hate. Look here—what is this?"

Red Fox's gaze happened on Elik's clay lamp. The shallow bowl was filled with oil. Another chunk of fat waited to melt. Curious, Red Fox dipped his finger in the oil, tasted it. "Seal? Not fish. What was Little-Creek doing?"

"It's a lamp," Elik tried to explain.

"A lamp? She burns oil that could be eaten? Doesn't she think of the seal that gave its life for hers?"

"It isn't disrespect," Elik said. "If the oil were needed for food instead of light, I wouldn't burn it."

"You?"

Elik bit down on her lip. She wouldn't lie. Red Fox had allowed Little-Creek to leave, but what if he changed his mind? "The lamp is mine," she said.

Red Fox touched the slick moss wick. "I've seen these," he said, and now he nodded as if he'd only just remembered. "At trading fairs. But we don't use them. Your Real People make these?"

"It's clay," Elik said. And then, glad for something, anything to talk about, she said, "We mix the clay with ptarmigan feathers and rock-powder. We burn fish oil or seal for light. If food were scarce, we would burn driftwood instead. It doesn't have to be wasteful." She took a moment to show him, lighting the wick, twisting it to burn brighter.

"And where did you get this clay? Not here?"

Elik stared at the floor. "I found it when we were coming home. Back, I mean. Here. One time when I picked berries."

She watched him, waiting for his suspicions to finally grow, but all he did was shrug, and turn instead to the ruined parka in the drying rack.

"For now," he said, and the lamp was all forgotten, "the best thing we could do is to destroy that. Soon. Now. Cut away its power. Burn it. I will wear an older parka, or borrow one. Who knows what other poison she rubbed in the seams? Maybe that's what made her ill. I want you to burn it, then sew me another, in time for the Bladder Feast."

Elik hid her relief. Here, out of Red Fox's own words, was more than she dared hope. He hadn't hurt Little-Creek; she seemed more than happy to leave. And now he claimed that the parka couldn't hurt him anymore. She wouldn't have to speak, and Little-Creek wouldn't be in danger because of her.

She stepped wide of the seal skull. Later, she would boil the meat off the bone, and then save the skull to honor in the mound.

This time, as she climbed back on the sleeping place with his parka, she removed her boots. Both of them, as simply and calmly as if this were any other day of the year. She set his parka on her lap, then found her sewing kit tucked in against the wall.

She looked up. Red Fox was watching.

With a show of calm, she pulled out her curved woman's knife. She smoothed the parka over her legs, flattened the front and the sides. Little-Creek had made the parka; she recognized the work now, stitches small and neat as the woman who made them, tight and perfectly spaced. No wind would ever reach the man who wore these skins. No wonder he had found the hole.

She stole another glance. Red Fox had leaned back against the bench, his head heavy on his shoulder. His eyes were closed—of course. He hadn't slept since his hunt. Perhaps not even in the *qasgi*, the long night before.

And now, as if nothing in the world were amiss, she reached inside her boots. All the way inside. She pulled out the inner grass sock. Reached and felt again. And now her fingers found it, the smallest strip of fur clinging to the welted seam above the toe. It had worked its way through the hole it widened in the sock.

The fur stuck, then peeled away, flattened after so much wear. Quietly, so quietly, she placed the scrap inside Red Fox's parka, up against the side seam where it once had lived. She reached for the knife, then stopped. Red Fox coughed and her hand froze. "I thought you were asleep," she muttered.

Red Fox shook his head. "I lied," he said, and he was smiling, no matter that his voice was husky, thick with exhaustion. "To Little-Creek. Just now. She never was jealous of you. I knew that. It was me. I'm the one who doesn't want to share you. Not with her, or Nuliaq. Not with anyone. I want to come into my house and eat food that has been cooked by your hand, no one else's. I want to wear a parka stitched by your needle. You and no one else."

Elik's hands started to shake, as if they had a spirit inside, all separate from her own. She set the knife down. She didn't trust it.

Red Fox rose, then stood in front of her. He pushed the parka from her lap, out of the way. He set his hands on her knees, then slowly slid them higher, to the edge of her inside trousers. His fingers played beneath the fur.

Wherever his hands moved, her skin felt as if it were on fire. She closed her eyes. Her breath caught.

"Are you cold?" he asked. "You're shivering."

If he wanted her to answer in words, she couldn't. She shook her head no.

"I want you to be warm," he said, and he pushed her legs apart, climbed up in between. He leaned over her and pressed her down to the bedding, moved his hands above her shoulders.

And then again, as if there were a small fluttering spirit living inside her hands, reminding them what to do, how it felt, she reached behind his shoulders, clung tightly to his back.

"I want you to be wealthy," he whispered. "With furs and oil and meat and babies. I want to hear you sing."

Elik waited until Red Fox was asleep before she climbed out from under him. Carefully, she freed her legs first, and then her arms. She rolled him to his side, the way he liked to sleep.

As soon as his breathing quieted, she wiped her thighs, and then the sweat between her breasts where he had fallen asleep on top of her. She was thirsty but she didn't want to risk the chance of making noise, waking him. If he woke and spoke to her, she didn't know what she would say.

She slid the parka out from behind his legs where it was buried. She felt around for her knife, found it lying beside his ear, then she climbed from the sleeping bench.

She made the first cut following the seam, slicing the blade through the run of stitches. The next cut was a narrow strip alongside, through the hairs and skin this time, from the neck to the hem. White and brown hairs came away on her legs. She worked her way around the front, cutting strip after strip.

Red Fox started snoring just as she began the arm-hole, slicing from the shoulder to the cuff. One end in her teeth, tugging with the knife, tearing to hurry her work.

He was still sleeping when she stepped to the hearth and began feeding dry grass into the buried coals to raise a flame. Then bark, then larger sticks.

While she waited for the fire, she dragged the separate piles of seal intestine, meat, skin, and flippers outside to the raised food cache where it would freeze. The head she kept inside, leaving it to clean till the parka was done. For now, she fed it five drops of water, so it would think kindly on their house, forget the anger it had seen. And then with another thought, as if the seal had whispered its request, she turned the head to face the sea.

The fire was ready. With her eye on the flame, she started feeding in the strips of hide, slowly, so the flame wouldn't smother, so the smell of singed fur wouldn't waken Red Fox, wouldn't draw his thoughts back to her, the way hers kept returning to him.

To Kaviaq. Red Fox. Kaviaq. Red Fox.

Which man was he, she wanted to know.

Kaviaq, who she had loved at the river camp? Or Red Fox, lashing out with fears that seemed to grow with the winter, the darkness inside him matching the darkening days.

Was it from Anguta? Or because of the men, whispering behind his back, worried—as much as he was— why the caribou had fled, why their shaman caught but one small seal?

And yet . . . he was still Kaviaq to her. In his gestures. His eyes. The way he spoke when no one else could hear.

She tried, and then failed, to remember a time when Allanaq's need for her had been so urgent.

She remembered the first time she and Allanaq had made love, with his father's dead skeleton beside them, wrapped inside hides, waiting for burial. Even that had not been enough to stop their hands from grabbing for each other, rushing aside their clothes.

But since then? How long since the last time Allanaq had touched her? She knew the day, exactly. It was just before the bear hunt, before the two sons died. A year ago now. Maybe more?

It was true he'd been forbidden. But it wasn't the prohibitions that came between them. It was a different kind of forbidding: how long since Allanaq had wanted her, spoken to her the way Kaviaq did?

But what if Kaviaq turned again into Red Fox? What if Red Fox turned on her, the way he had on Little-Creek? Of if someone convinced him that a stranger in their village could bring trouble? Demons and illness? It had happened to Allanaq among her people. Couldn't it just as easily happen to her in his?

And if it did, what would happen to her when all that remained of the man she had called husband at the river camp were his eyes, and his voice? Would all the promises he had made be gone? No different in the end than the promises Malluar had made? Words that turned into smoke, disappeared into air?

Elik sighed. The parka was finished burning. No hint remained but a smell in the air, smoke lingering near the roof hole. Red Fox had stretched himself into a comfortable sleep, one arm covering his eyes, the other cushioning his head.

For her, there was no chance of sleep. From the storage area beneath the bench, she counted out the long, rolled strips of gut she would need for his new parka. Twice around the house, and more than that to start with. A shaman's parka made out of the waterproof membrane, for the power it contained. That which had been the animal's inside skin, becoming the shaman's outside skin. That which was dead adding strength to his life.

Twenty strips, stitched together, measured from her elbow to her fingers for the body, then more added for Red Fox's larger size. She measured out her hands for the size of his chest, checked and measured again for what would become the straight-bottomed hem.

And then she started sewing, one white weightless strip stitched to the next. Two threads together, carrying the sinew in a running stitch, a welting of grass to swell inside the needle-holes, make them waterproof, help Red Fox to dive and swim and live, as the seal once lived.

Elik was the one who was sleeping when morning came. Some time earlier, while a grey dawn filtered slowly into the house, Red Fox had woken and left to begin the *qasgi's* opening ceremony.

Sometime later, when she was sure he was gone, Nuliaq had returned. Gently, she tapped Elik's shoulder. "There'll be light for a little while," she said. "We need to bring food to the *qasgi*."

Elik woke with a start. She glanced to the fire, then to the sleeping bench.

"He's gone," Nuliaq said.

Elik gathered together the long strips that had fallen from her lap. "What did he tell you?"

"Nothing. I didn't want to see him. But Little-Creek brought her things to Higjik's house. Owl said she was welcome to stay with them and grow fat on his catch, if he could be warm in the skins she scraped."

"Was that all? Did she tell you about the parka? It's burnt now. He told me to burn it."

"Little-Creek will be fine. She's always been the strongest woman I know, taking care of Skinner as well as herself. But come. The light's already turned. The men will be taking their sweat bath, then there'll be stories and talk all night. Take the bowls. I'll carry the fish."

Elik slipped on her parka and followed Nuliaq outside. On the paths along the way, there were other women carrying food as they were. Wooden bowls that had been made just for the new season. Seal pokes filled with fish and oil, berries and birds. Whatever they had in their storage pits and raised caches, that was how much they brought.

The *qasgi*'s sunken entrance was built low, with a tunnel that was similar enough to her Real People's houses, it brought a smile to her face. With a sense of familiarity, Elik bent low and crawled in behind Nuliaq. She had been in here only once before, and that time the walls had been dark, the fire hidden by a cluster of men. She hadn't seen the huge whale jaw-bones built into the framework of the entry, or the rich smooth planking on the floor and walls that were lit up for today.

At the end of the tunnel she passed the food up to Nuliaq, then checked that her parka lay flat, her belt was modestly tied. Nothing lewd, nothing open for the men to talk about.

She climbed up through the round entry-well, into the smell of burning celery, hushed voices, walls and rafters that were hung with animal masks and spirit masks. An air of food and smoke and the smell of the sea.

Nuliaq had to nudge her, remind her to stop staring and move along. But then, as they came to the wall where the food was laid out, it was Nuliaq who slowed as she added her string of fish to the pile. It was an immense pile, bowls balanced one atop the other, stretching in long rows, and filled to overflowing with the choicest bits of fish and meat. Nuliaq nodded, smiled at the feast.

It was for this the two women had been careful not to eat too much at home. The more they shared here, the more the seals would see how well the gift of their flesh had been appreciated. The more they would be willing to give tomorrow.

Other women were entering behind them now and making their way to the women's bench along the rear wall. Nuliaq picked their seats on the bench beside Higjik, next to Spider. Elik removed her parka, then leaned forward and looked to the sides: Mitik and Pintail, White Smoke and Sister all sat together on her right, talking, laughing. Pintail held her baby's head against her breast, and White Smoke brushed the top of her little girl's hair when she saw Elik lean out. She returned the smile. They were relatives on Red Fox's side, the wives of his cousins. As were the women Nuliaq sat among, her cousins, from the oldest, One Pot, to Nuliaq's unmarried niece, Chikigak.

And the men also. They were grouped around the fire by family first, and then by age. Elik sat back, nodded to herself. Were people everywhere the same, she wondered? She could have closed her eyes and heard her own sister's voice in place of the sweet, prattling woman they called Sister, it wasn't difficult. Or her aunt Nua instead of Nuliaq. Kimik would have worn a new necklace such as the one Spider was wearing now, showing everyone in reach the shells and ivory hanging between her breasts. Even among the men, Bear Hand, who used to give Allanaq so much trouble, could be sitting there in place of Red Fox's eldest cousin, Bird's Mouth, silently judging the pelts on each man's parka.

Red Fox had risen. Elik reeled her thoughts back in, leaned to one side for a better view. The center floor had emptied as the men moved aside to give him room. They took up their drums as he stood under the skyhole.

His chest was bare. Light shimmered through the ice window. Shoots of red, yellow, and blue played across his face, his shoulders and the floor around his feet. He was dressed plainly in his leggings, and but for the sunlight, he wore no paint on his face, no mask of any kind.

From a band around his forehead, the skin of a fox's head leaned against his chin. It moved when he moved, danced as he bent to take up his drum, start the songs that would begin the winter, invite the animals back to their shores.

"*Spirit from the Air*," he sang, then repeated the verse. "*Spirit from the Air, come swiftly hither. Thy shaman calls, is calling you, Come bite ill-luck to death. Come swiftly . . .*"

Elik sighed and leaned back. She wasn't listening so much as watching him, the way he danced with his feet stomping the floor, knees bent with each strong motion. His hands like knives, precise and strong, and also beautiful.

How strange it was, to feel so many different things at the same time. As if each time she saw him, he wore a different face. And toward each face, a different feeling leapt from in her breast.

She watched him, let her eyes fill with the sight of him. She had loved him, feared him, respected him. How was that possible?

The drummers slowed their beat, enough that she caught a few of his words.

"Thy shaman calls. Come bite ill-luck to death."

That was odd, the way the words sounded so familiar. Not something recent, but from long ago. They reminded her of Malluar. Not the voice. His was deeper, his tone stronger. But something in the way he called on the *inuas* of the air, asking them to recognize his power as a shaman, so they would help . . .

Wasn't that the same as what Malluar asked, not once but many times, whether she drummed or sang, prayed or closed her eyes in trance?

And now that she thought about it, they were alike in other ways also. Both were her teachers. Both tempted her with promises.

Malluar had died without keeping hers. What of Red Fox?

The rhythm of his dance had slowed to a quieter pace. He bent his knees, lifted his hands to tell the story of a journey overland, tracking caribou at a river crossing. "These Are the Animals We Call to Hunt," he began, and she watched him, but she was wondering if anything had changed, from Malluar's promises to his. From her first frightened search for a spirit helper till now, today.

A shudder came over her, a thought she didn't like.

It traced a path from Malluar's promises to Red Fox's, to her. What if Red Fox died without teaching more? What if she tried to reach the house in the moon, but couldn't finish the journey without him?

What if Allanaq never returned?

The *qasgi* quieted. Red Fox's dancing was finished, the drums returned to the floor. People began talking again, visiting, whispering. One young girl looked clearly in her direction, then turned to the woman nearest her on the bench. "Is that her?" the girl asked.

Elik couldn't help but see the way the girl pulled on Sister's arm. "Ask her if she'll help."

"That isn't polite, hush."

"But she's a shaman?"

"I told you, yes. Now hush."

Elik lifted her gaze; on the floor where the men were sitting, the young man Inuk was watching her. Uncomfortably, she shifted in her seat. Had the young girl's talk reached as far as the men? Did everyone hear?

Nuliaq sent her a pointed stare, but Elik wasn't certain what it meant.

The men grew noisier, discussing which of the dances would go next, and which of the stories. A few of the women rose, walked about. Then, unexpectedly, Elik looked up to find the same girl standing with a small dish stretched out in her hand. Surprised, Elik took the bowl. It was filled with a broth, a thin stew. Chunks of meat settled at the bottom.

Elik thought she had seen the girl before, but she wasn't certain. And that in itself surprised her. She had been here long enough, she thought she'd met everyone there was. Unless the girl had only just become a woman? In which case she might have been in confinement—they had done that with Elik for a month, kept her in the house the first time she bled.

The girl was too shy to speak first, and so Elik politely thanked her.

"It's only a small portion." The girl's eyes flicked to Elik, then even more quickly away.

"But you are kind, and the smell is sweet. Was there something you wanted?"

"I heard you find things?" she asked. "You change the weather, and bring good luck?"

"Oh, no. That's too much . . ." Elik didn't know if she should smile at such proud talk, or frown. "Did you lose something?" Elik took a bite of the meat, it had been cooked a long time and the taste was lighter than she had expected.

"An amulet I had, yes." She watched proudly as Elik ate. "Do you like the loon?"

"What loon?" Elik looked up.

"The stew meat?" The girl repeated. "It's loon. Do you like it?"

Elik's mouth thickened around her tongue. She started to gag on the piece she had swallowed. She spit out the bite in her mouth. There were people everywhere, watching her, staring.

"Loon?" She looked for water, desperate to chase away the taste.

"It's mild, like seal, there's sour leaves in it too. And blood soup. See how much fat there is?"

The smell of the meat reached for her, thick as smoke. Was that a head floating in the broth? Was that the loon's eyes? Elik winced, pulled away.

"I don't eat loon," she tried to say, but was that true? She had sworn a prohibition—hadn't she?

She felt ill suddenly, the voices around her too high, thin and strange. She felt for balance, forced her feet to straighten, support her weight, but the moment she stood her stomach twisted and then heaved. She clamped her hands over her mouth.

Miscarriage, someone whispered. *Trance and dead and Red Fox and needles. Shaman and miscarriage. Food and shaman.*

And then she didn't hear anymore. She was out in the wind, doubled over and vomiting in the snow, against the *qasgi* wall. The women's voices whistling like spirits in her ear. *Miscarriage and shaman, food and trance and dead.*

She straightened when she was done, wiped her mouth, and spit into the snow. She shouldn't be surprised, she told herself. She could no more have eaten that loon than Malluar could eat the bear meat Allanaq had slid in front of her. She smoothed the front of her parka, reached for her hood, but then she stopped. Had she heard something, a sound carried through the wind?

She turned but no one was there; no one had followed her out of the *qasgi*. The only thing nearby were the tall legs and platform of the seal skull mound; and angled against one of the legs, a large grey rock showed above the newest layer of snow.

It wasn't till she brushed the snow from the rock that she saw it was one of the seal skulls. It must have fallen somehow, loosened by the wind. The head had been severed just above the first vertebra; the bony eye sockets were round and dry. This one was small, a ringed seal probably, though she couldn't say for sure. What mattered more was the way it seemed to look at her, and the way the wind changed as she stepped to one side, and then the other.

And the way, when she lifted the skull toward her ear, the hollow wind sound changed. It almost sounded like a woman's voice, calling to her friends along the shore.

She would have climbed up the scaffolding if she thought she could reach the mound, return the skull before a dog dragged it off. But no. The scaffolding leaned precariously. She wasn't certain how it stood under the weight of so many skulls, let alone her own off-centered weight. She could toss it up, but that seemed disrespectful. And she was no raven, to fly away with a shiny prize.

In the end, she set the skull back against the drift-wood pole, in the same position as she'd found it. But then, with a different thought, she turned it so the hollows of the eyes were facing toward the seal's home, the sea. That seemed better. She packed the snow tightly in around the bone, and then spit. "Drink well," she whispered. "Until the Bladder Feast." Then she turned and made her way back to the house.

Elik watched the white hide of the door flap lift as Red Fox stepped inside the house. She had been waiting for him since she left the *qasgi* yesterday, and again through an entire day, planning how to ask her question.

His face was covered in a thick layer of frost and he wiped his eyelashes and cheeks, then smiled as he realized she was alone. "I just was thinking," he said, "of that day we spent inside the tent. It was raining and you'd caught whitefish and brought it inside. You remember?"

Elik rose and returned the smile. "I remember," she said, then she moved to help as he sat down, lifted his foot for her to pull off his boots and damp mittens. The boots she put back outside to freeze; later she would beat the ice from the fur. She sat down with his mittens, checking to see if they needed repair. Until she glanced up, realized he'd been watching her. He smiled again, a hint this time.

And now, she realized what he'd meant, not praising her for the fish, but remembering what they'd done after, inside the tent.

"I was fishing again," she said quickly. "Ice fishing with the women."

"I heard that," Red Fox said. "I meant to thank you. Word has been going around, how well you do."

Politely, Elik disagreed. "It was only a small string of tomcod."

"Mitik says it was more than she brought home, and she was sitting at the ice hole just past yours. She wasn't jealous—she didn't say that. Only that you caught more than the other women."

"I tried to show Nuliaq. It was only the way I wrapped the squirrel tooth to the line. The way my mother taught. It was a little different."

"Yes, but you see, it's better this way. You're fishing goes well. But you're polite. You do it in a way that shames no one, and you're willing to share. You help me more than you understand. Things are bad enough this winter, you see. What if I had brought home a stranger-wife who no one could trust? Or a lazy woman?"

Red Fox smiled at the thought—she was already caring for his clothes. And talking about the skill of her catch. She was no lazy woman. She was a good wife. A beautiful woman. He stretched his arms, and yawned, and turned suggestively toward the piled furs on the sleeping bench.

She saw where his thoughts were leading; another moment and he would ask for water, then grab for her belt. She set the mittens in her lap.

"Sometimes one wonders," she spoke quickly, but politely. "A person wonders if perhaps this isn't a good time, and we might talk about the journey you started to teach—in that very tent. I had caught fish, and you spoke of the shaman's flight to the moon. But—we didn't finish?"

"That's true, we didn't. But—why now?"

Elik calmed her voice, not to sound as if she was begging. Not to sound as if she challenged him. "Sometimes, a woman grows afraid," she said. "A woman who is still a stranger. She asks herself—what if something happened and she was alone and she didn't know the right things to do, to say? If she needed help from the spirits, needed to ask the moon to fill a poor woman's pot, and—"

Red Fox lifted his hand, motioning to her to stop. "Hush," he whispered, "I understand. Mitik told me, you were shyer than most women. She said, with more tattoos you might be prettier, and then feel better around the other women. But she doesn't know you as well as I do. And I see, she was partly right when she spoke to me. But it's more than that you want. Come here. Sit."

Elik's heart beat against the walls of her stomach. Without waiting to be told twice, she folded her legs, took a seat on the grass mat opposite him. But Red Fox was in no hurry.

He gulped down a large drink of water, ate a little from the raw fish she laid out. He looked about the house, nodded when he saw that the skull of his seal had been boiled clean and that she had turned it so its eye sockets faced the sea.

"Have I told you," he asked, "how much you remind me of myself when I was young? No matter that you are a woman, and I was a boy. I remember how I was filled with yearning.

"The shaman who taught me—have I spoken about

him? He made promises. He predicted greatness for me. Much the way, I think, your Malluar hinted at what she would someday teach you, and what you might become.

"I believed him, of course. Everything he said. And I waited. And all the while he kept promising that someday the time would be right and the inner vision necessary to become a powerful shaman would be mine. He would teach me words, he promised. Songs so powerful, the spirits would make themselves visible. And not just one spirit would become my helper, but many.

"Yet each time he promised, something more important found a way of happening. Seasons went by and always there was a new reason why the time wasn't right. Someone was ill, and their lost soul was wandering. Or someone had died, and too many spirits were near. Or the caribou came, or they didn't. Or the seals. Or the walrus. There was always an important reason to wait.

"Through all that, I remained the dutiful son, the patient pupil. What else could I have done? I served my teacher, cut his meat, fetched his water, and waited for the portion that was mine.

"It never came. He lied. Those songs he promised, in the end he refused to share. Still, I was able to earn the respect of a few *inuas* who became my spirit helpers. One winter, while the village's catch was poor and fear of hunger was thicker than the taste of meat, the spirits gave me a vision of the place a bowhead whale had died. To my teacher, they showed nothing. It was soon after that, his jealousy grew worse.

"He refused me even the smallest amulet he'd

promised I would inherit. He claimed that I would never be more than an *ibrukok,* a lesser shaman, good for divination and predicting the weather but with no means to change it. It didn't matter that for years he had complimented me, called me *Tarejumak,* the Shadowmaker. The older he grew, the more jealous he became.

"He tried to steal my wife. He was even, I think, jealous of his son."

"His son?"

Red Fox lifted a questioning glance at Elik, but then he went on. "His son. He never taught him even the smallest part of what he taught me. Only to be a flint-knapper, which was all the boy knew to ask for. How to twist sinew around a bow and where to aim at a caribou, for a heart shot. Never the inner sight that would have turned him into a shaman.

"I don't want you to live that way," he said. "Withering beneath another shaman's jealousies. If you are ready, you should not be denied."

"I am ready," Elik whispered, then again: "I am."

Red Fox glanced to the skyhole. Higher, beyond the roof, the brief day had darkened into night. The wind tapped against the gut window, but it wasn't strong enough to enter the sod house.

"This is a good time," Red Fox said. "Without daylight, the men will sleep late in the *qasgi.* The women will all be busy lapping up a meal of Little-Creek's gossip. While you . . ." he smiled at Elik. "You will be starting a different journey. Tell me, have you eaten?"

"No."

"Good. Unbind your braids. You must have no knots anywhere."

Elik nodded, and while Red Fox pushed away the water and the food, she pulled the lacing from her hair, then waited with a nervous anticipation. The house was warm though only her seal oil lamp was burning. She felt no chill, only a hunger, a longing deeper than she could explain.

Red Fox plunged his hands into the cold ashes of the fire pit. When he pulled them out, his skin looked as though it had been changed into a tighter, grey-white glove.

Gravely, he wiped his fingers across Elik's eyes, then below, on her cheeks, her chin, her throat. "I will give you the gift of a word," he said. "In the shaman's secret language. When I tell you, you must repeat it over and over, a hundred times over, until the sound fills you and it is all you hear."

"With this word, you will feel as if the entire house is lifting. It will open and you will rise on the air and travel to the moon. This is the word, *torngrarzuk*. It is old, from the times when animals could talk, and it is strong because it is old. Now say it."

"*Torngrarzuk*, she repeated, and a chill passed over, as surely as if a wind had entered the house. "What does it mean?"

Red Fox narrowed his lower lip and turned aside, almost as if hiding his thoughts. Then quietly: "I don't know. I only know you must say it over and over. It will keep you safe. It will guide your journey. There is but one thing I require. If you should hear a song, or a word, any sound, you must tell me when you return."

"I will," she promised. "I swear."

Red Fox reached over, touched her knee. "Of course you do," he said. "Because you understand, don't you?

Just as you said before, you do not want to grow afraid . . .
There is much to fear. You would not want to lie.

"Now, say the word, repeat it, but listen also.
Sometimes a shaman visits the bottom of the sea,
where the animals live in their villages, the same as
people. And sometimes he travels to the moon. That
last time when I began you on your journey, I told you
only to climb through the star-holes and look at the
house in the moon. You were not to go inside."

"I didn't—" Elik started to say, but Red Fox stopped
her.

"Don't speak. I told you, only listen. Repeat the
word. More. Again. Listen to me now: This time you
may look inside the house. What you will see are the
souls of the animals there. Do not go in the house.
Only look. There will be a gut window in the wall.
When you look through it, you will see a bench covered with grass mats. It is there that the souls of the
dead sit and rest. They divide themselves, sea mammals in a pool on one side, the land animals on the
other. Do not go in, and do not, above all, try to
speak to the dead. They could steal your soul, and
you would never come back alive. Now close your
eyes."

Red Fox said no more. He took his drum, and as
Elik repeated the word, he began the double beat, so
close, Elik could feel it beneath her skin, inside her
blood. Heavier. Shorter. Louder. Quicker.

"*Torngrarzuk*," she repeated through it all.

"*Torngrarzuk*," he whispered with her.

And the longer the drum went on, the deeper the
darkness grew. Her closed eyes felt thicker, heavier,
until there was nothing but the drumming that filled

her ears, and the word that had no meaning surrounding her thoughts.

But that too began to change. The sound of the word turned into a different sound, something she already recognized.

There was a wind, a trilling in the air. And then laughter, human, but more than that, part animal and human and spirit all together in the rush of the Loon's high voice.

The sky surrounding her was dark, the stars as thick as snow. The Loon was with her. As if nothing had happened between that last time she had clung to its back and now. She found herself suddenly lifted again, the Loon's wings stretched to each side. She felt its strength surround her, the warmth of its heartbeat against her chest.

Past stars, through dark and wind, the Loon flew higher. Until a moment came and Elik realized the bird had slowed. The Loon shook its head once, then again. It brought one of its wings around, held it like a hand in front of its face. Then it trembled, shook its long beaked head; and now held in its feathers, as if they were a hand, were the Loon's two eyes.

Carefully, so they wouldn't fall, the Loon passed its eyes back to Elik, then waited as she shook her head, removed her eyes, and replaced them with the Loon's.

She blinked, closed then opened her new eyes as she tried to settle their fit. She heard the Loon laughing in that voice it had, not unlike her own woman's voice. It was laughing as it looked back down to the earth, saw the ice that covered the ocean, snow on houses, the brown dots that were caribou, roving over the tundra far below.

And now with the Loon's dark eyes lending sight, she saw the moon, more beautiful than it had ever appeared.

The fear she had felt that first time—that she would fall if she didn't hold tight—she didn't feel that now. Instead, there was an ecstasy inside her. A knowledge, that if the Loon chose not to carry her, if it let go, it wouldn't matter. She would not fall. It had taught her to spread her arms like wings, to see with its own clear vision, not only things that were near but things that were hidden, invisible, lost, or dead.

The moon was below her now, and the Loon set her down directly in front of the house, then disappeared. She pushed through the thick, white bear hide, and stepped inside to find the house far larger than it had seemed from the earth, below. She looked up, and there on the beams supporting the house, she saw the souls of the land animals, caribou and wolf, sheep and fox. They sat side by side and they were smiling, as if they were content. She would have smiled a greeting, but she turned, and found a pool in the floor of the house, a large pool filled with clear water, and surrounding it were the souls of the seals, all pushing and angling for a chance to see into the pool.

But so many! And she remembered now the last time she had seen this house. It had been only a glimpse, but enough to know there were too many seals. They had been pressed together so tightly there wasn't room for them all on the bench. They weren't singing and there wasn't any joy. She had tried to ask what was the matter, but the Loon had carried her away.

This time, she was determined to find out what was

wrong. She squeezed in among them, made her way past their slick bodies and flippers. On hands and knees she joined them at the pool's rim. "What are you looking at?" she asked.

"The sea," they answered. And it seemed to her it was true; the ocean was down there, below the sky, and below the ice. Huge waves moved within the pool. She glanced to the seals around her, and saw that that was all they wanted to do, to look at the sea. The same way all the doors on the Seal People's houses were facing toward the sea. The same as the seal skulls in Allanaq's house were turned toward the sea.

"We long to go home," the seals said. "But our way is blocked."

Elik looked through the pool again to see what was wrong, but all she saw was the village, the houses no larger than if they belonged to a vole. She saw the larger mound of the *qasgi*. And the skulls on the seal mound, mostly hidden beneath the snow. "Are you thirsty?" she asked, because she couldn't see what was wrong.

"No," they said, and though they all spoke, their voices sounded as if they were one voice. "It is our souls that thirst," they said. "We yearn to leave this house and return home to swim again, but the path is blocked. We cannot see the way."

Elik wanted to speak with them more, to ask what she could do, but she caught a reflection in the water. She rose and turned to find Alignuk, the man whose house this was.

He was standing behind her, but he didn't seem to notice. She walked toward him, but he looked through her as if she were invisible. She remembered what Red

Fox had asked, that if he spoke to her, if she heard any word or song of power, she was to tell him. But the man didn't speak, and she was just as glad, because his face was bright, and far too frightening to look at for long.

She turned away, and now she saw another hole. This one was covered by the large, white bone of a caribou shoulder, but only partially, so that a crack was open, and the earth could be seen far below.

She would have gone to the hole and looked down to see the village again, but she become aware of something else behind her. It was a bench she hadn't noticed before. The bench was covered in bear hides, sleek and thick and soft. And seated on the bench were the souls of dead people, some newly arrived, some visiting from villages where they lived.

Among all those souls, two were dressed like children, small and each as like to the other as two hands could be. Nor were they naked, as some of the other people were, but dressed in a parka of clean, white feathers.

And here was the strange thing: One of them wore the legs, and was naked from the waist up, while the other wore the jacket, and his legs, penis, and feet were all uncovered. And it was from the feather parka that she recognized them, her two small sons.

They seemed tired, as if they had just woken from sleep. She opened her mouth to greet them, to tell them who she was, but just at that moment a shadow moved across their faces. She looked up and saw that the shadow was made from a bird's wing. It was the Loon, but it was too large to fit in the door. She had to cross back to the hole and push aside the caribou shoulder bone to see it waiting outside.

But now, before she realized what was happening, her two tiny sons were falling through the hole. Falling, and the Loon was catching them. First in its mouth, then guiding them around to its back.

The two souls clung to its neck, exactly as she had done, exactly as if they were the Loon's own young in their first days of life. And they were happy, that was what she saw. They had become tired of being too young even to hunt, and they were ready to be born again.

Somewhere there were two infants, newborn, longing for a name. And the two souls were pulled toward them, laughing, hungry already, at the idea of being born again.

One moment she saw them. She saw the Loon nudge them to safety with its beak. She saw their faces lit and shining. Their arms lifted, pointing, voices as filled with laughter as any child.

And then they were gone, and the Loon was returning again, ready to carry her home. And the one thing she was certain of was this: That no matter where she searched, inside the ground, on the earth, or above, the souls of her two sons were no longer among the dead. Somewhere, in a village, in a house, in a birth hut, they would be born again.

Red Fox watched closely as Elik slowly pushed herself up to a sitting position. "You were gone," he said. He sounded concerned.

Elik rubbed her eyes and face as she waited for the

room to clear. There was a mound of coals in the fire pit. Red-centered and glowing, they gave off a golden light and a heat that reached upward, filled the house. There had been no fire when they began.

"There have been stories of shamans who stayed in their trances longer than four days, and never woke. It seemed a long while."

"Did it?" Elik stared at the coals. Slowly, the sense of exhilaration returned, the awe at finding her vision so wide and strong.

Elik wet her lips. "There was—" she began. "There was—" But then she stopped, trying to find the words to explain, to tell what she had seen.

Red Fox grew uncomfortable, more anxious the longer she hesitated. "What did you see?" he asked. "The Loon again?"

Elik nodded.

"The Loon? And did it sing?" He had thought he was teasing, until he saw Elik's face. He drew back. His expression fell. "Who told you to say that?"

"Say what?"

"That it was a loon."

"No one." Elik shook her head.

"But it was the same? The same as before?"

"The same. Yes. I swear it—"

"But it didn't speak? It gave you no song?"

"Nothing, no. I would tell you."

Red Fox moved to stand behind Elik's shoulder, out of her line of sight. His fingers drummed his sides. She couldn't tell if he was angry, or afraid. "You know, don't you, if a song were given to you in a vision, it would be powerful? It could make a man into the greatest hunter. It would destroy an enemy's bow, even at a distance. I would be willing, if there was such a song, to trade great gifts for it. You would tell me?" He waited for Elik to nod. "And you saw nothing else?"

Elik hesitated. She didn't understand him when he was like this, uncertain, more than half-afraid. "I saw the house," she said, hoping more of the story would satisfy him. "Just as you described. The souls of the animals were there. And a pool. I saw the souls of the sea animals, and on the bench, my two sons were there."

"Two sons?" Red Fox stopped her. "What two?"

"I told you," Elik said, confused now. "The sons who died."

"You told me of one."

"Did I?" Elik searched her memory. "I don't recall."

"When we were at the river camp. You told me there was one." Red Fox stared at Elik's disheveled hair. "After Skinner left. I asked your name—"

"Yes. You asked if I had given birth. And I told you I had, and that was why I was careful what food I ate."

"One. You told me you had one. You said you ate no caribou because of your father."

"That's true. But I had two miscarriages. One years before, a dead-birth that never began."

"Which was it then? One son, or two?"

"It was born dead. I—" Elik stopped. The lies were growing, folding themselves around her tongue too fast. She didn't know what she was saying. What Red Fox wanted to hear. "No. I meant two. I'm sorry. I'm confused. The trance—it was deep. The rest—it doesn't matter, does it?"

"No," Red Fox leaned back, he took a deep breath. "It doesn't matter. You went far. I'm proud for you. But

I need to leave now. I waited for you a long while. I have to go to the *qasgi*, but I want you to stay inside." He took a longer look at her, made sure she understood. "It would not be a good idea if you went visiting just now. I'll send Nuliaq home so you have someone to talk to."

"Where is she?" Elik glanced to the sleeping bench. "Is something wrong?"

"No, of course not. I'll send her. Don't worry."

Elik shook her head. "I won't. I'll wait," she promised. But she sat still only until she heard his footsteps disappearing through the entry, till she was sure he would not return. Then she stood.

She looked for a drink but the water bladder and pots they melted snow in were all empty. She stared at the door flap. "I don't want to be here," she said aloud. "I don't want to be alone."

She walked back to the sleeping bench. She tried lying down but she felt too uncomfortable. And Nuliaq still hadn't come. She looked for food, but nothing she would eat had been brought inside.

Her hands were cold. She shook them. Her arms shivered. She grabbed her parka, put it on.

On the floor between the planking and the wall, a vole's quick scuttling caught her eye. She watched as it sniffed its way along the wall, beneath the bench, then out again toward the fire pit. It was searching for something. But what—? Some smell it wanted from among Red Fox's things?

No, not Red Fox's things. But not hers, and not Nuliaq's either. There was another name the vole brought to mind. Allanaq.

He was alive—it came to her suddenly. A knowing.

A certainty. Though no spirit had whispered his name. Only the vole, but even the smallest animal had a voice.

Allanaq was nearby and she had to find a way to reach him, tell him she was here.

In his house, the abandoned house. That was it. Either she would find him hiding, or she would find some way to reach him. The tiny flakes that had cut her hand—surely they were his. Struck from a core, forgotten among the ashes. Somehow, she would be able to use them.

Quickly then, before Nuliaq returned, she poured the oil out of her lamp, packed it along with the wick and a small chunk of fat and the fire stones she kept in a pouch. Within moments she was outside, watching and waiting.

If someone saw her walking alone between the houses, she would lie and say she'd been foolish and let the fire go out, that she needed to borrow coals from someone's hearth. She threw a chunk of fish to Red Fox's dog to quiet it, then started walking, slowly, as though nothing was amiss.

The sky was dark, but there was enough moonlight not to stumble off the hard-edged path. The house itself was easier to find than she remembered. With its empty food rack and fallen boat stand, it was a broken shell compared to all the others.

On the ground beside her, just tall enough to show their flattened heads above the snow, a circle of pegs hammered into the ground marked the place where a sealskin had once been stretched.

It was empty now. Gone the hide. Gone the strands of membrane, scraps of fat and hair. Only this outline of a circle remained: a peg, then space. A peg, then empty space again.

She stared at the shape, puzzling out what it reminded her of: a seal poke emptied of oil? Or a seal bladder, inflated till it ballooned, then never used. It gave her a lonely feeling, as of something wasted, a gift dishonored. She turned away from it, ducked her head, and felt for the fallen pole she remembered having to step over.

What she didn't remember as she straightened into the house was the darkness. There'd been shadows when she and Red Fox had entered, a hazy light from the skyhole.

This time it was different. The dark was dense and cold. A wind echoed through her ears, a shushing sound. Something moved—another vole?

With her heart pounding, Elik lowered herself to her hands and feet. She started crawling along the floor, one hand stretched in front of her, feeling for the fire pit as if she were blind.

Her knee struck a stone first, before her hand, but she managed not to cry. She set out her lamp and fire starter rocks. The braided moss wick was slick with oil, and her spark quickly jumped, then caught. She sat there, minding the wick till the light settled, planning what to try once she found Allanaq's flints again.

She was just reaching toward the ash pile when she heard it. A sound. A footstep in the snow outside. A shiver ran along her neck and she stiffened, turned to look behind her.

Her heart beat almost too loudly to hear, but there it was again. A sound just outside the door. And then a voice, muted and too careful to shout.

A whisper followed, a woman's voice. "Are you there?" A moment later and Nuliaq straightened through the ruined door frame. She blinked, caught in the flare of Elik's light. Her mouth opened and closed in a look of surprise. She fumbled with the rolled bundle of furs she'd carried in her arm. And then, before Elik could say a word, Nuliaq was gone, through the door frame and into the night, leaving Elik with her own unsettling thoughts.

There were voices, a cough that didn't sound like Nuliaq's. Long moments passed until finally Nuliaq stepped in again. She no longer held the roll of furs in her arms. Her face was flushed, but controlled again. She moved closer into the light, this time taking in the sight of the fallen corner posts, the rotten flooring and tilted sleeping bench

Elik looked behind her toward the door. "Where is Red Fox?"

"In the *qasgi*."

Elik waited, but Nuliaq seemed in no hurry to say more. "Did he send you?" Elik asked her. "Did you follow me?"

Nuliaq shook her head no, then: "Yes." She rushed to change her mind. "I saw footprints leading away from the house. I was worried, so I followed. That's all."

"You needn't have been. I was fine. I was looking for Little-Creek and I got lost . . ."

"Here?" This time it was Nuliaq who was skeptical. She looked to the lamp, to Elik again. "You knew where you were," she disagreed. "What are you looking for?"

Elik listened toward the entry, waited in case

someone was still there. Then: "If I tell you, how do I know you won't tell others?"

"What? Is this about Anguta again?"

"No. It isn't. But tell me first, if Red Fox asks, would you tell?"

Nuliaq moved slowly along the length of the sleeping bench. She touched the fallen supports, the shreds of what had once been woven grass bedding. Her lips moved soundlessly, as if she were talking to each abandoned object she touched.

Finally, she turned back around. "You and I are co-wives," she said. "Even if Red Fox threw my belongings out in the snow as he did with Little-Creek, even if . . . Even if I lived in another village with a different husband, you and I would still be sisters. That will never change unless we let it."

"Red Fox wouldn't put you out. Not you."

Nuliaq laughed guardedly. "He wouldn't beat me, the way he did Little-Creek. He knows I'll raise my fist back. I can bite. Or scratch. I've done it before." She straightened her shoulders. "He knows there are men, my brothers, who would take me in. Maybe men who aren't my brothers? He's threatened, but he holds back his hand. And he wonders, he never stops wondering whether I'm hiding something, secrets he would trade anything to know."

"What kind of secrets?"

Nuliaq shrugged, pushed the question aside without answering. "Mostly though, it doesn't sit well with him, the idea of killing the mother of his son."

Nuliaq pulled off her mitten, wiped her fingers over the platform ledge, then lifted them to her nose. There was no smell; the house had been frozen too long.

"What are you looking for?"

"No," Nuliaq said. "You tell me. Why did you come here?"

"You tell me something first."

Carefully, the two women watched each other until one of them smiled, and then the other. Both shook their heads, then laughed. "Very well," Nuliaq said. "I'll start. The man who lived here last was a shaman."

"I knew that. Red Fox brought me here before. Tell me something else."

"All right. Did you know that the shaman had a wife?"

Elik nodded. "Yes. Did you also know he had a grown son?"

"Did you know the wife had a son?"

"The wife?" Elik had to think a moment. "No. What was his name."

"Whose name? The son's, or the wife's child?"

Confused, Elik shook her head. "Which wife are we talking about?"

Nuliaq sighed. Her mitten was still off and she held her arm out, looked at her hand. "It shows age, doesn't it? Your hands are smoother. Still young. My hands, when they were young—there were other men they held. Do you know, I've lived with three husbands, and shared a night with more men than I remember, and from all of them, I have but one son."

"Red Fox is your third husband." Elik said. Nuliaq had told her that the first day they met.

"A man called Tooth was first. But I was very young then. He had come in a umiak from the place called Big Island, looking for a wife. He'd brought hides, so many, walrus and bearded seal. He was tall, but he was ugly. He had the smallest of noses, and a very flat face."

"But the second—" Elik asked. "The second was Anguta?"

"Don't say his name in this house." Nuliaq warned. "It brings bad luck."

"He is dead. He isn't here."

"So Red Fox has been hoping. But now, it's your turn. What do you want in here? What does this house have to do with you?"

Elik gave a small, shy shrug. "I am married with his son."

"Qajak?" Nuliaq's eyes widened. "He's alive?"

"I don't know anymore. But then . . . you are the wife who both shaman fought over—I should have realized that. But if you were here that last day, how could you . . . why did you help Red Fox?"

Nuliaq lifted her hands in protest. "Who told you that? You have heard too many stories, I think. You have to understand—they fought over me. Both men. I was stolen from the bed of one. Kidnapped, almost while my legs were still wrapped around the other. Do you think either of those men ever asked me what I wanted?"

"But why did they fight? Couldn't they have shared you? It wouldn't have been the first time two men shared a woman."

"Those two? Their real fight was never about me. You can see that. But once the older shaman decided he needed me, do you think Red Fox could keep his thoughts from wondering why? His thoughts and then his eyes, his hands, and then the rest of his body?

"The first night after Qajak and his father were gone

and Red Fox climbed beneath my blankets, he didn't even want me. He pulled me close, he bit my neck, he held my breasts, but then he sat up. Do you know what he wanted? Anguta's shaman secrets. He thought I might have overheard them."

"Did you?"

"Anguta was no fool. No stray word ever escaped his mouth. Never."

"What of Ivalu then? Whose son is he?"

"He has my face, more than his father's." Nuliaq smiled. "Which is why Red Fox is never really certain. The boy could easily have been growing inside me when the other shaman died.

"For months after Ivalu was born, he wouldn't stop crying, raising his knees to his belly as if there was a pain in there. I wondered if we had given him the wrong name, and he was trying to shake it off. Red Fox took the name from an uncle in another village who had died. He refused to consider whether another soul, a certain shaman's soul, could have entered the baby.

"But wouldn't any child cry, given the wrong name? Red Fox has never stopped being afraid that shaman would come back."

Elik nodded, then quietly she asked, "Who was that outside?"

Nuliaq glanced to the door. "I was looking for some-one. A man."

Elik thought back to the *qasgi*. There had been a man. She had thought he was staring. But it wasn't at her, it was Nuliaq. "Inuk?"

Nuliaq nodded. "My husband was gone a long time this summer," she said, and a smile came to her mouth. She pushed it away. "But you, Elik—you need to be careful. People are no longer simply curious about you. There's more than a few women have been whispering about your power. They say that your helping spirits are strong, that you can change the weather, call the seals. But too much need in a village isn't always safe for a shaman. The same as too many men isn't safe for a woman. Until the hunt improves, we both need to be careful. Red Fox also has hopes."

9

Long strips. Narrow strips. *Qiluu.* The name for the
white, weightless sealgut when it was still part of the
seal, alive and in the sea. *Immar enin.* The name for
the same length of gut after it had been dried and the
tube slit open, stitched and worked and changed into
a different skin, a covering to protect the human life
that borrowed it. Wore it. Danced in it during the
Bladder Feast that would, in turn, thank the seal that
returned to life in the sea.

Elik crawled along the sections of sealgut she'd laid
out in rows. Much of the work was already finished,
the early cleaning and drying, the pattern that Nuliaq,
since she was more familiar with Red Fox's size, had
helped to lay out.

Six hands across for the width needed to cover Red
Fox's chest, shoulder to shoulder. Nine hands for the
length of his arm. Then the hood with its drawstring.
And then the sewing; the first few horizontal strips had
already been joined with the same waterproof boat
stitch Elik already knew, the first line grabbing partway
into one layer, the second an overcast stitch sealing the
fold.

Later, she would add rows of orange puffin beaks,

stitched into the welting between rows. Bright and loud, they would hang from his shoulder, his chest, and wrist.

Red Fox would like that. The rattling sound the beaks made as he danced would set up a clatter, loud enough to frighten any evil away. Each stitch she took was important: the better her work today, the more it would strengthen his shaman-sight later.

Elik slowed her hand; a sound came from outside, footsteps on the roof overhead.

Nuliaq called a greeting; the footsteps moved to the front entry and a moment later Spider climbed into the house. Her son Little Eyes hid behind her legs, and behind him Ivalu tumbled in, then jumped to his mother's lap. "You're wet," Nuliaq laughed as she smoothed his hair.

Spider lifted two round-chested ptarmigans to show her catch. "My nets were good to me today," she said, and she set one of the birds beside the fire pit for a gift, the other by the cool floor near the door.

"Thank you," Nuliaq said. "Who else had luck?"

"Nanogak's been fishing as long as there's light. And Mitik found a fox in her nets. It's a good thing; the women's small catch looks to be more dependable than seals for the men."

"It's often that way. The men have to wait for the weather to clear. The women's traps aren't so far. Sometimes it's easier."

"The snow's blowing harder. The sky's grey and low." Spider brushed the flakes from her hood. "Some of the men say it grows worse. It's surprising for a trader to come in weather like this."

Elik froze. "A trader?"

Nuliaq pulled Ivalu closer. She glanced sideways at Elik. "Often traders come," she said to calm her. "Even now. It's not so unusual . . ."

"A trader?" Elik repeated, but her voice cracked and her hands began to shake. Quickly, before Spider noticed, she set her needle down, pressed her hands flat on her legs.

"That's what I came to show you. Here, let go." Spider nudged her boy toward Ivalu. "Perhaps there's a bite of fish for two helpful boys?"

"There's tomcod," Nuliaq offered as Ivalu wiggled from her arms. She climbed from the sleeping bench, pulled a curled, dry fish from a basket.

Elik cleared the parka strips from the floor. It couldn't be Allanaq, could it? The season was wrong. Traders arriving by boat were supposed to come earlier, when the ice was still open, the way she and Allanaq had planned.

Or later—she had been thinking about that. The winter trails were always better after the snow was hardened by wind. But not during a storm.

"You have to come and see," Spider said.

"See what?"

"Is it a secret?" Nuliaq asked.

"No. Yes," Spider teased. She lifted her hand and felt inside her parka hood. But whatever was there, she wouldn't show. "You have to come and see."

"But it is a man?" Elik pressed for more. "A Seal Person, or a stranger?"

Spider squinted as she smiled, then, drawing out her game, she lifted her thumb and showed a small section of necklace.

Elik caught a glimpse of bone beads and shell. "You

had a different necklace on, another new one in the *qasgi*."

"That one was a gift from Ice Stick," Spider said. "These are from the *qasgi*. But I won't tell you any more." Spider said. "It's late in the season, so everyone was surprised. And Ice Stick says he doesn't think any good will come of it. But he's quick, my husband. He traded so fast, no one else had a chance."

With her eyes still dancing in jest, Spider pulled a pouch from her belt, squatted, and opened it over a grass mat.

Nuliaq kept her hand on Elik's shoulder as they crawled closer for a look. Two things spilled from Spider's pouch, the first the dark grain of antler, the second a lighter flash of ivory.

Nuliaq picked up the antler piece—a bag handle carved with the head of a beluga whale on one end, turning into the head of a wolf on the other. Eye dots, and skeleton lines that showed not only the outer form, but the inner as well. None of it was different than others the Seal People carved, except for the detail, the fineness of the line. Whale baleen bristled above the rib line. Two holes were cleanly bored through the center to take a cord.

"I saw one like this yesterday," Nuliaq said.

"Yesterday?" Spider sounded surprised. "But he— these—just arrived. Ice Stick said he was the first to trade."

Elik's hand hovered over the ivory without touching it. The round eyes and thick features of a bear's face shaped a handle. Below, the smooth ivory was cut into a row of teeth. A comb. Her comb. The comb Allanaq had carved for a present when she first learned she was pregnant.

Nuliaq glanced with worry to Elik's tightened face. "What is it?" she whispered.

"My comb."

"What did you say?" Spider asked.

Nuliaq shook her head in warning, but Elik couldn't sit still. "It's him," she said, and she rose. She stared at the soot-darkened walls of the house. Red Fox's house. His bed. His spears, harpoons, and knives. His house. His wife.

"This trader," Nuliaq asked Spider. "Where is he now?"

"With the other men, passing the day in the *qasgi*. And he's brought more things. Skins. Spoons. Carvings. Perhaps Red Fox will find a gift for you?"

"Elik?" Nuliaq leveled her voice. "Perhaps we might bring food to our husband?"

Elik nodded but she didn't answer. She couldn't speak. She felt too light, as if at any moment a wind would blow into the house and lift her, send her tumbling away. Falling, then tumbling as if she were no more than the lightest thread of wild cotton, tumbling away.

What if someone had already told Allanaq she had married with his enemy? And if he didn't know, how could she bring herself to tell?

Her gaze happened on her clay seal oil lamp. Maybe she would be lucky and Spider was wrong, and Allanaq had already left the *qasgi*? Maybe she wouldn't have a chance to speak to him. She could send the lamp as a message, warn him that she was here.

She couldn't lie. Sooner or later he would learn she was sleeping in Red Fox's bed. Perhaps though, the lamp would say what she could not: that no matter what he heard, she was still a woman of the Real People. A wife. And if she was a wife, then wasn't he still a husband? Unless the husband didn't want her anymore.

Elik poured the small bit of oil out of the lamp base into their cooking pot. She swiped the inside dry with an old duck wing, then tucked the lamp inside her belt. She left after that, she and Spider and the two boys, Nuliaq with a second bowl of fish.

The walk in the afternoon dusk was hardly long enough to settle her fears. They hit her, along with the falling snow, like little pinpricks on her face, in her eyes.

The *qasgi* was dimly lit when they arrived. The air was thick and over-warm from an earlier sweat bath the men had taken. Stiffly, she climbed in behind Spider and Nuliaq, hid her gaze then lifted it, searched the men's shadowed backs, then searched again.

Nuliaq sat and so did she, shoulder to shoulder between the other women on the bench behind the men. Spider climbed in beside One Pot and arranged her son with a place to play. Nuliaq's niece Chikigak, the one who had just become a woman, was there— was that another new necklace she wore? She wondered which of the men had given it to her so soon. Farther along the women's bench, White Smoke and Pintail, with her baby on her breast, leaned and smiled a greeting as Elik settled herself.

She nodded, but she would have preferred it if just this once they didn't all have to look at her, check to see what she wore, what she'd brought for food. She pulled off her parka and rolled it into a pillow against the wall. She leaned back and felt the sharp angles of the lamp pressing through her fur. Slowly—she wanted no one to see—she pulled it out, set it where it could easily be reached.

Her bones felt as if they'd turned soft inside her body as she tried to sit forward and study the men. They crowded together on the *qasgi*'s floor, each man according to his place. The men formed a circle, the eldest in the honored seat closest to the fire, the youngest nearer the women's bench. Old Sheshalik she knew from his skinny shoulders. His son Inuk sat beside him, and this time she didn't miss the quick flare of Nuliaq's eyes as Inuk turned, glanced to see who'd entered.

Elik looked away. It could be just as dangerous for someone to catch her following Inuk's eyes back to Nuliaq as it would be for Nuliaq herself to watch Inuk.

Red Fox sat in the center of the row. She would have recognized him no matter if he wore a mask or a full-sized robe of wolf hide. The other men took her longer to name. Since the colder weather had settled in, she spent most of her time either with Nuliaq in their own house, or carrying their sewing to sit with the other women, while the men spent their days in the *qasgi*.

She recognized Red Fox's oldest cousin, the heavyset Bird's Mouth, because of where he sat, nearest to Red Fox's shoulder. And Spider's husband Ice Stick, and then his brother Grayling, who was married with Nanogak.

In her Long Coast village it had always been easy to pick Allanaq out. There, her Seal People husband had been taller than the men of the Real People. He walked differently. Spoke differently. Wore tattoos like no other man. She leaned forward, started again along the line.

Then she found him, the smaller man in the circle farthest from Red Fox. Shadows flicked across his face, hiding him. Her mouth opened in surprise. It was Skinner. Not Allanaq. Skinner!

Elik sank back against the wall and almost laughed out loud. She felt relieved, not disappointed. She had been terrified, expecting to find Red Fox with a knife pointing at Allanaq's throat. And relieved again, because she had been equally frightened that Red Fox would be the one on the floor, dead in a pool of blood. Allanaq standing over him, or dead himself, with Bird's Mouth's knife in his chest.

Her breath fluttered, caught against her ribs as she tried to understand what she hadn't been willing to think about before.

She wanted neither man dead. Not Allanaq. Not Red Fox. She wanted both of them. She wanted them alive.

"You're safe," Nuliaq touched her arm reassuringly.

"Not yet," Elik disagreed. "Skinner can't be trusted. There are names, things he could easily tell."

"He's looking at you," Spider whispered in her other ear.

"He's looking for Little-Creek," Nuliaq said.

Spider smiled at the chance to gossip. "He's already been there. He came in last night, just when the wind turned louder." Then she added another thought: "It's odd, isn't it? Skinner home just now, when Little-Creek grows more ill?"

Nuliaq made a cutting motion in the air, chasing the evil away.

Elik's thoughts leapt in a hundred directions. Skinner was hungry, that's why he returned. Most likely he grew worried when he realized another winter was near. And if he had already visited Little-Creek in Higjik's house then surely he knew she was here.

And maybe, now that Skinner knew that Red Fox had kept her, he hoped to gain more from his trade, make a better bargain?

Did he plan on sharing Little-Creek's bed in Higjik's house now? Little-Creek had said that a cousin of hers from a place called Sandy Spit was staying there, along with his wife and her mother. What if Little-Creek's illness didn't let go of her? Would Skinner expect to share *her* bed?

From what she could tell, Red Fox seemed to be ignoring Skinner now. They sat opposite each other, Red Fox scooping fresh-caught fish out of the bowl Nuliaq had brought. He patted his stomach, belched, acted less like a shaman and more like a man who needed to brag and lie about the number of seal bladders he'd bring to the feast.

Skinner sat with no guest bowl in front of him. He waited to drink till a water bladder made its way around the line. The dry fish he chewed came from the long, common tray in the center of the floor. He chewed and belched as loudly as Red Fox, polite as any man. Until he was done, and this time he took his turn staring at each of the women along the bench.

He nodded briefly at those related to Little-Creek, to Spider, whose eyes darted nervously to her husband. He nodded to Nuliaq. Then he found Elik and his gaze stopped. A knowing smile fit itself to the corners of his mouth.

Elik shifted uncomfortably. For a man who always lacked for something, Skinner seemed too pleased, too sure of himself. What did he think—that Red Fox would pay more for her now? Hides, oil, and meat because without him, Red Fox would never have found his newest wife?

Or would Skinner ask something of her? Some gift in exchange for his silence?

She looked away, caught the grim line of Red Fox's clenched jaw as he watched Skinner watching her.

Don't look at me, she sent Skinner a silent plea. *Don't think my name.*

But it was already too late. Red Fox had seen enough. There was no reason for him to be patient with a noisy, bragging man. Certainly not after what he thought Little-Creek had done to his parka. And now here was Skinner watching Elik so closely, so lewdly— had a summer alone taught him nothing? His manners hadn't changed. They had always been something no shaman should have to tolerate.

"So." Red Fox broke the silence. "It must be the first chill of winter brought you back?"

Skinner faced Red Fox without shrinking. "Why risk a winter alone?" he shrugged, as if it was all so obvious. "When in a village there are hunting partners and relatives with meat to share?"

"For a man who hunts," Red Fox baited him. "A man with his own skins and seal bladders to count."

Skinner winced, but he wasn't certain whether he'd been insulted. "I brought back gifts," he countered, and a few of the women nodded, glanced toward his pile of baskets.

Spider pointed the baskets out for Nuliaq, and Elik looked too, but then her face fell. She hadn't noticed there were baskets in the center of the floor. But they weren't Skinner's. They were hers. The very ones he had stolen when he left her with Red Fox.

And all the other trade goods he had come home bragging about, the harpoon heads, points and scrapers and knives that would be inside—those were Allanaq's, the gifts Skinner had so greedily hoarded on the shore.

"Take them," Skinner went on, thinking to compliment Red Fox. "You have a household, growing. And a new wife . . . perhaps a new son?" he laughed, but it came out too knowing, a little too familiar for Red Fox's taste.

"I have a new wife," Red Fox agreed.

"This one looks fatter than I remember. But then again," Skinner slipped his hand inside his belt, lowered his thumbs suggestively toward his crotch, "sometimes a man needs two wives to help him up in the morning, not like the rest of us men, who must rise for only one."

Nuliaq set her hand over Elik's

Skinner chuckled and looked to the other men, inviting them to laugh along with his joke. Till a moment passed, and he realized no one else had smiled. The men shifted uncomfortably in their seats. Ice Stick pressed a warning to Skinner's shoulder.

Red Fox offered no smile. He picked up a drum, but not a beating stick. "I'm only a poor hunter," he said. "Sometimes my thoughts stray, it's true. But then, so do the thoughts of other men when they should be hunting. And instead, their eyes are in their hands, and their hands between their legs. They hold tight and wonder maybe, if they had a woman, the seals would recognize the smell?"

Skinner paled as he listened. He reached for another drum, ready to answer Red Fox's insult with one of his own, but again, Ice Stick's ready warning held him back.

Ice Stick took the drum from Skinner's hand, returned it to the floor. He nodded toward Spider on the women's bench, obviously afraid.

Skinner glowered, but then he caught the worried look on the women's faces. Whatever he was going to say, he seemed to change his mind. He shook out his shoulders. "That storm," he said. "It's rising. I saw it all the while I pulled my poor, empty sledge. I was in a village with a man called The Ear, a fat man with a woman's eyes, you remember him?"

He looked to Ice Stick, slowly took back the drum. "The Ear said that the weather knows why the animals leave. But it won't always tell. He said . . ."

The talking and confusion grew louder.

Elik couldn't hear, but she did see Ice Stick, and now Inuk and even Bird's Mouth, lean forward to stop Skinner's arguing.

Her stomach twisted. She felt helpless. Skinner was going to tell. The more he talked, the more likely it was that her name would jump from his mouth, and she could do nothing to stop it. He would tell where he got her. He would name Allanaq. He would point to her.

The tension rose higher. Skinner glanced anxiously along the bench, searched the empty spot where Little-Creek usually sat. If anyone could calm Skinner, talk him into reason, she could.

But Little-Creek's illness had grown steadily worse since Red Fox put her out. And here was another thought that kept troubling Elik. If Little-Creek was ill, wasn't the fault partly hers? If a spirit had climbed inside her body and chased away her soul, then wasn't she obligated to try and get it back out?

The Squirrel-spirit had helped her find that sewing awl. And the Loon might be willing to come and learn why Little-Creek's soul had fled. It was possible. She wasn't certain, but it was possible.

Elik glanced around the *qasgi*. There wasn't a person there but their attention was riveted on Red Fox and Skinner. She could slip outside; even if people saw, they wouldn't care enough to follow, not if it meant missing the excitement of an insult-match, or wrestling. Or worse.

With a finger to her lips, hushing Nuliaq, begging Spider not to follow, she picked up her parka, made her way slowly along the women's line.

Little-Creek needed to be well, and Elik owed it to her to cure her. If she wasn't sick, then Skinner would be calmer. If she stayed sick, Red Fox might accuse her of wrongdoing.

But sickness would not enter the heart of a woman who wasn't evil. Elik could cure her, help prove she wasn't evil.

And if she was well, Skinner would be content. She would explain, and he would be more careful not to challenge Red Fox. Then Red Fox would leave Skinner alone. And if he left Skinner alone, then Skinner would have no reason to tell. He would be too busy helping Little-Creek recover to worry about Elik.

The wind bristled sharply against Elik's face as she stood outside Higjik's house, trying to listen through the door. "Let the girl do the work, then she'll learn," a woman's voice said.

"Yes, but the boots were so wet," a huskier voice said. "They were already ruined. I can save the fur, but I don't know about the sole."

There was laughter, then the first voice again: "His sister broke a tooth. I don't know what made her cry more, the pain or the insult of not being able to finish the song."

Someone else spoke—the first voice?—Elik wasn't certain. The sound of coughing stopped their talk: Little-Creek's coughing. Elik had been waiting to hear it. She lowered her hood and pushed in through the door flap.

The first thing she saw was Nanogak seated on the floor beside the fire pit, softening strands of sinew in her mouth. Higjik sat on the edge of the sleeping bench above her, repairing a hole in a seam of her husband's large boots.

Little-Creek coughed loudly behind her, hacking, knees pulled to her chest. She seemed a slight thing, so small the blankets hardly lifted with her cough. She wasn't sleeping though. She heard the shifting voices, the change inside the house. With an effort, she sat up and smiled when she saw Elik. "Did you hear?" she asked. "Some people are saying there is an old man come in along the winter trail?"

"I did more than only hear," Elik said warmly. "I saw."

"Not before I did." Little-Creek's smile broadened even wider. "Did I tell you? Old gossip that I am, did I tell you I dreamed of my husband's smell? I always used to know when he came home. How could I not, when I shared a bed with the man since before he knew what a bed was for?"

Higjik climbed from the platform and offered Elik a dipper full of water. "Drink," she said. "Tell us the talk. You were in the *qasgi*? Red Fox saw Skinner?"

Elik nodded. "Both were there."

"Was there any word when the Bladder Feast would begin?"

"Red Fox won't do it," Nanogak announced. "He's too afraid, since he's caught so little."

"He's afraid of me," Little-Creek joked. "Now that my husband is back."

"Skinner tried to joke, and Red Fox grew angry. I can't say he was afraid."

"Ah," said Higjik, and she patted a grass mat for Elik to sit. "That's because you're still new here, you don't see with the same eyes as other people. I'm older; I know fear when I see it, and it's all around, gathering like smoke."

"People are afraid of Red Fox?" Elik asked.

"They are afraid more of the weather, and what it brings."

"And what it doesn't bring. And also that Red Fox will fail against it," Nanogak said. "When my boys go playing around other houses, that's what I hear from them. There's talk about this storm. It's holding too long."

"Do people blame Red Fox for that?" Elik asked. "As if he was evil?"

"Human," Higjik said wisely. "Like any man, not simply good or evil. If he catches no seal, then something is wrong. The wind rises, so we see it's true."

"And in the middle of that, this old woman grew ill." Little-Creek tapped her chest as she whispered. "In his house."

"The good shaman," Higjik said, "is the one who brings good weather. The one whose songs are strongest."

Elik folded her hands, then politely, in a small voice, she said, "I was thinking about that. About Little-Creek and her cough . . ."

"The cough will go away," Little-Creek said stubbornly. "I've done nothing wrong. It's true."

"And yet, people wonder," Elik said. "They wonder if there's a spirit inside, making you ill. And if it's inside you, they are afraid it could easily climb inside them. I am only a small shaman," Elik added. "And new."

Higjik lifted her brows.

"I would like to try to help."

"What are you asking for? Payment?"

"No." Elik looked up in surprise.

"We've known shamans before," Nanogak echoed Higjik's sudden suspicion. "They seek wealth. They demand skins and meat. Gifts. Is that what you want?"

"I have nothing to pay with," Little-Creek said. "She knows that. Red Fox put me out. The same as he put my Skinner out. Empty-handed. For no other reason than that his foolishness bothered the man."

"You know who I am," Elik said. "What could I want that hasn't already been given? And yet, you are right. There is something I want. I want Skinner left alone, as much as you. Every time Red Fox remembers that you're ill, he'll wonder what evil is hovering near. He'll think he was right accusing you of cursing his parka, though I know it wasn't you. He'll begin to think that perhaps he shouldn't have

forgiven you. And thinking, he'll worry more about
Skinner."

"Why do you care?" Higjik ask.

Elik stared at her hands, planning how to answer.
"You know that it was Skinner who brought me to Red
Fox."

Little-Creek leaned forward.

"There are things Skinner knows about me, I don't
want him to tell."

"Ah," Nanogak glanced to Higjik as if she'd been
certain all along there was more to Elik's story.

"I cannot tell everything now," Elik said, "but later I
will. If Skinner is safe, then so am I."

"It's true," Little-Creek agreed. "And is that any different from the same thing I ask? To be left alone to
live?"

"But what will you do?" Higjik asked Elik. "Finding
a soul that's ill is not the same as finding a lost needle."

"Then I will try harder," Elik said. "I will try a full
trance."

Little-Creek freed her legs from the heavy robes and
moved to the edge of the platform. "If someone in this
village has done this to me, I will turn myself into a
weasel and follow the thief who stole my soul."

"I've heard of that," Nanogak said. "I heard of a
woman who grew ill, not because she broke any taboos
but only because she refused to marry a shaman. He
was so angry he stole her soul, and another shaman
had to search for it to keep her alive. He searched all
the way to the edge of the earth. That's where the first
shaman hid it. This happened long ago in my mother's
village. She said she was there when the shaman
brought back her soul, so I know it's true."

"How did he trance?" Elik asked.

"The house was darkened."

"A shaman always prefers dark," Higjik said.

"But this shaman, he was gone a long while. He had been tied, his knees and his ankles bound in knots— no man could have gotten out. My mother described the sounds she heard, strange sounds like nothing she had ever heard. That was how they knew his spirit had left his body. But he came back."

"Is that what you're going to do?" Higjik asked. "Tie your hands and feet? That's what Red Fox does. And the shaman before him."

"No—" Elik exclaimed. "I won't do that. I'm—"

"But Red Fox says, if he didn't, he fears what would happen to his soul. That if his body was free while he tranced, there was no telling what it could do. His soul could get lost."

"I have never bound my hands and feet," Elik said slowly, trying to think through everything she knew, everything she remembered. "If I were to lie on the floor, and writhe, and fight myself, the way Red Fox does—I don't know. Perhaps because I'm a woman, I feel too modest. Also," she said, "I don't know what's safe. Without Red Fox here . . . ?"

"That woman," Higjik asked. "Did she live?" She had taken up a ptarmigan wing and was using it to clear the floor. She stretched out a grass mat for Little Creek to lie on.

"Yes, but the shaman was in that trance for four days. He almost didn't come back."

"Will it take that long?" Little-Creek asked.

"I don't know," Elik answered honestly. "But I'd like a robe to borrow, to cover my head. Whatever happens will not be of my choosing. I don't know which spirits, if any, will come or what they'll reveal."

"Do you want the light put out?" Higjik asked.

"Yes, the skyhole first."

Nanogak glanced back to the door. "You brought no drum?"

"No. I have never been allowed to make my own."

"No ceremonial gloves? Red Fox seldom goes bare-handed."

Elik shook her head, but then, while Higjik replaced the gut window with a few planks of wood, the question lingered, troubling her. It was true. Red Fox bound his hands and legs before he tranced, as had Malluar, though not as often, and not at all when she was older. But both of them always drummed as they sang themselves into a trance.

And both had promised she would someday be allowed to make a shaman's drum. *Both had promised.*

"Red Fox says you've stood inside the house in the moon?" Nanogak peered down her sharp nose. "Can you do that? Call the caribou and seals, ask them to give themselves to our hunters?"

"It was only once," Elik apologized.

"Once doesn't matter," Little-Creek interrupted. "This cough in here, it doesn't live in a place called Once. It lives here," she hit her chest. "Inside these bones. Tell me what you want, and I'll do it."

Elik smiled at Little-Creek. "I don't know if my spirit helpers will come—"

"Try," Little-Creek said. "Otherwise, how will you know?"

"Will you lie down?"

Little-Creek lowered herself to the floor. Then, with

only her inside trousers and a simple, twisted belt left on, she stretched herself slowly onto the mat.

Higjik and Nanogak retreated to the safety of the bench.

"I'm going to touch you now. Here—" Elik set the palm of one hand gently on Little-Creek's breastbone, the other alongside her stomach.

Little-Creek stared toward the roof. "Do you know the story," she asked, "of the first two shamans? They were brothers, and they searched everywhere for a mother who would give birth to them. The older brother found one—she was shiny all over. He moved inside her body as if it were a house, except it was small and cramped. He lived there anyway, staying till he heard someone call from the entry that it was time to come out. That was the birth canal. He fell out of his shining mother, into another world where there were worms everywhere. They ate all his flesh, till he was nothing but a skeleton. Then he fell to another earth and by then he was the greatest shaman—that's something they say a shaman has to do, learn to see his bones beneath his skin. I don't know how they do that. But listen," she lifted herself on her elbows. "I was thinking, I don't want you doing that. Climbing inside me. Falling back out my vagina."

"Leave her be," Nanogak called from the sleeping bench. "Let her work. Besides, you're no shining mother. What would she want inside you?"

Little-Creek laughed, then nodded her consent. She lay back down and Elik touched her lightly. "I learned this with my brother's wife, when she was pregnant. That's all."

"There's no baby in there. I'm an old woman."

"I know," Elik smiled to reassure her. "I'm just searching."

"For what?"

"That I don't know—yet. But if you can keep from coughing, I'll feel your stomach. If I press here—" Elik slowly moved her hand, pushing in, releasing. "I can feel where it's hard—"

"Something's there," Nanogak chirped. "Will you sing it away? Or maybe use a sucking tube? I've seen Red Fox pull sickness out of a body, he pulls it right up inside the hollow of the bone tube. He throws it away and then—"

"No." Elik hushed Nanogak's questions. "I don't know. Maybe." Elik pressed along the opposite side. "It's softer here."

Little-Creek tried to see. "What does softer mean?"

"I have to listen. Lie down." Elik's hands hovered now, palms down, only a hair's breadth above Little-Creek's stomach. She held still, feeling the warmth rise from the woman's skin. She listened to the rasping waves inside her lungs.

Just as she was ready to begin, they heard a commotion outside the house, voices and footsteps. Higjik jumped to her feet as the door flap opened and Spider, looking relieved to be out of the *qasgi*, came in with her husband Ice Stick. Skinner followed sheepishly, then Nuliaq, and last of all, Higjik's husband Owl filed in.

One after the other they peered at Elik, then Little-Creek; then they lifted their eyes to find Higjik motioning them to be quiet, to take a seat well enough away so they could watch as long as they didn't interfere.

Skinner was no more than one step inside the house

when he stopped. As Elik watched, his shoulders, his gaze, even his hands seemed to lose their strength. All his bluster fell into worry at the sight of Little-Creek lying in the center of the floor.

Higjik took his hand, whispered some reassuring word, then led him to a place beside Ice Stick.

Owl checked both directions outside before stepping in. He fitted the door flap tightly against the floor. He nodded to Higjik, then crowded in against Ice Stick's shoulder.

Elik watched as Skinner took his seat. It was all she could do not to walk straight up to him and shake his shoulder, ask him where Allanaq was. But how could she with all these people here? And what if he didn't know?

Elik glanced measuringly along the row. Owl frightened her. His pocked skin and the long scar that ran the length of his face gave him a cruel, angry appearance that was masked again by his gentle voice and careful manners.

They had never exchanged any words. How could she trust him? Or Ice Stick, for that matter, the way he kept his gaze carefully lowered, as if he was even more afraid to look at her than she was at him?

"Could you put out the fire?" she asked, and Higjik moved to cover the coals. The house darkened.

Elik lifted the heavy caribou robe over her shoulders and head. She opened the front slit a crack, enough to reach through. Gently then, she rested her hand on Little-Creek's stomach. She waited till she felt Little-Creek's tension ease.

In the hushed darkness, an exhaustion came over her, an ache that pulled on her skin, made her breasts feel heavy and full. The caribou robe weighed her down. The heat. The rasp of heavy breathing all around.

For a little while more, she was aware of the house outside the robe. Little-Creek's abrasive chest. A sound that might have been Skinner's.

Smaller and tighter, she narrowed her attention, until her own breathing matched exactly the quake of Little-Creek's chest. Rising. Falling, no different than Red Fox's drum. A beat and then a quieter one. A beat and then a pause.

That was all she allowed herself to know. Little-Creek and her breathing. The flow of blood inside the small, resolute woman, and her breathing.

All else she pushed aside. The house. The women on the bench, men on the floor. Her own small fears and hopes. Away. She flung them all away.

And in their place she felt a heaviness, not the freedom of flight that had taken her to the moon, but more as if she were immersed in water. As if something heavier than the robe were pressing her down, down into the sea.

She kept on traveling, she didn't know how long. Except that after what seemed a great while, she began to see lights flickering on and off. And then more lights, so many they were like a rope pieced together with ivory cord attachers, longer than any retrieving line a man would need for his harpoon.

Down she journeyed, through the thick blackness, until at last she came to a country where the sun was only a small, white dot above the sky. She felt cold— not as if it were winter, for there wasn't any snow, but neither was there warmth. She felt awake also, as if all her oldest memories had become sharp again, while the small everyday things of life were shadowed and obscure.

Far away and very small, she saw two people cleaning the meat off a huge polar bear hide. Back and forth their pulled their scraping tools, their rhythm never faltering. They must have noticed her because they looked up, and she saw that one of them was the soul of her mother, and the other was her dead grandmother.

They waved a greeting though they came no closer, and the one clear thing she heard was their warning to her not to drink the water, for she was under the sea now and everything was salt.

Elik looked about and realized it was true. She was in a place she had never been before. What she had thought were rocks were houses, and what she had thought was grass she saw now were the upright poles of food racks. She was in a village, the same as any human village she had ever been in.

She made her way toward one of the houses, the only one with a light glowing behind the door. She slipped inside and there, seated around the floor as if they had been waiting for her, were people, Loon and Wolverine, Seal and Beluga and the Squirrel. They were dressed as they had been the last time she saw them, the Seal-woman with spotted brown hair. The Squirrel with a parka trimmed with thick, grey tails. But the man who was the Loon wore the most beautiful clothes of all: a parka pieced with black and white feathers, and a headband strung with beads so smoothly shaped, they looked like eyes, a hundred eyes all ringed around his throat.

"Come, sit with us," the Loon said, and Elik joined them on the floor. But now, though the Loon kept talking, it became harder to hear. Behind her and in the corners of the house, overhead and everywhere, there was a strange frightening noise of tearing and scraping.

"What is that?" she asked.

"Someone was sewing during a ceremony when it was forbidden," the Loon said. "And so the noise is painful and loud down here. We were hoping you would come and stop it."

"What should I do?"

"Look up," the Loon said, and Elik did. She saw the long rope of lights again, except that this time it was leading up. There was a house in the sky above them, Higjik's house, and in the center of the floor, Little-Creek was lying very still.

"She isn't dead yet," the Loon said. "Only asleep. But she is hungry for something. Look around. What else do you see?"

Elik turned from Little-Creek and began searching the house, and the longer she looked, the more she was able to see. She made out the shapes of people, tiny people who were hiding, crowded in beneath the sleeping bench, behind the baskets, along the roof beams.

A great loneliness came over her as she realized these were dead people. And it seemed as if years had gone by, years and years of her life, and these were her relatives, those who were already dead and those who were not yet born, and all of them were worried, frightened that their souls might be stolen.

Without planning it, she reached for the tray in the center of the floor. There was food inside, or what looked to be food, dried pieces of blackened fish and meat, she didn't know what kind.

She grabbed one of the pieces, a dark, shapeless thing, and she tossed it up, right through the skyhole, all the way toward Little-Creek's hard bed. She watched while the pieces fell and scattered, then disappeared.

The Loon nodded, smiled toward Elik. But when she asked what had happened, it wouldn't speak.

She looked to the others, Wolverine and Squirrel. They all sat quietly, unable to speak, until she noticed that their mouths were opening and closing for want of water. But she hadn't brought any, nor had she brought any dipper, nor did she see any containers for water.

She leaned over, thinking she could spit into their mouths, offer her own saliva to quench their thirst. But the Loon backed away, as did the Seal and the others too. "No," the Seal stopped her. "Even if you gave us a drink, our thirst would not be quenched. We are too afraid to leave this *qasgi*. The dead seals in the moon cannot find the path to come down. We have not enough souls to be born again. We cannot allow your men to hunt us."

Elik's hands wouldn't move. They felt cold and useless, as if a hundred stone points were pricking her skin.

She opened her eyes to darkness, blinked, then tried to sit. Her hands were asleep, crushed beneath the weight of her chest. She was in Higjik's house, she remembered as she pushed back the caribou robe, freed her shoulders.

She was being watched. Nuliaq and Skinner, Spider and Ice Stick and Higjik and Owl and Nanogak, all tensely watching her. Nuliaq dropped to Elik's side. "You're awake?" she asked.

Elik had to think before she could answer. "I went . . . it was somewhere far. I saw . . ."

"You lay without moving."

"Where is Little-Creek. Is she gone?"

Nuliaq pointed toward the bench. "Asleep. It was a long time. She woke, and asked for something cold to drink. We didn't know if we should touch you. Skinner said he'd seen you like this before. He said we should wait, if we wanted Little-Creek to stay well, we shouldn't interfere."

"I'm awake," Little-Creek called, and her voice sounded thin, not from illness but more as if it needed practice remembering how the words were supposed to sound. "And I'm strong. Look," she said, and she thumped herself on the hard bone of her chest. No cough came out.

"Show her your tongue," Nuliaq said, then to Elik: "Go see. It didn't look that way before, as if it was painted."

"Painted?" Elik rose shakily. Spider moved aside, opening a space for Elik to climb to the bench. Little-Creek opened her mouth to a wide circle. When she stuck her tongue out it was splotched with shapes of black, dry and with a bad odor.

"What is it?" Nuliaq asked.

"I don't know. But I saw something black where I went. I thought it was food. It was small and dark and I threw it up to Little-Creek, I remember that. And then . . ."

Nuliaq's eyes widened. "That was it. Her soul. You found her soul. You sent it back."

The house quieted. Spider stole a glance to Elik's face, then quickly away. The men lowered their eyes.

Elik gathered her thoughts. She remembered throwing the black lumps up toward the sky—into Higjik's house. It seemed as if more had happened, but she wasn't sure. Still, to have helped Little-Creek—that would suffice.

"Something was inside you," she said. "Something came and stole your breath. It came in through the holes you opened. In your stitches. You must have been sewing when it wasn't allowed."

"No," Little-Creek denied the accusation. "I was careful. I never did that. When?"

"During the *qasgi* opening, perhaps?"

Nuliaq nodded. "It's true. If you sewed on a sealskin, then the seals might have felt your needle. Especially during a ceremony, if one grew angry enough, it could come in. Make you sick."

"Yes, but I wasn't sewing then. I was already sick."

"Then who—?" Elik asked, but no sooner was the question spoken than Skinner jumped briskly from his seat.

"It was Spider," he said. "I saw her when I first arrived."

Spider wrinkled her nose, looked to Ice Stick. "I was making you those dance boots," she said slowly. "But I was done, before . . . ?"

Skinner shook his head. "No. No. I came back and you were still working, but parts of the ceremony weren't over. You were home, so you wouldn't know, sitting with the women, what the men were doing. And so it's possible."

"What should I do?" Spider turned to Elik.

"My cough is gone," Little-Creek said. "The first day you came to us, I told Nuliaq there was something about you. A person could see it, just by looking in your eyes."

Elik looked away, not to seem proud or too content. "There was a house under the sea," she told them. "And the *inuas* were the ones who helped. They showed me Little-Creek's soul. Without them, I wouldn't have been able to return it. The house looked the same as most human houses. It was lit, and there was a skyhole. That's all, except that now you are well."

Elik listened as Red Fox's breathing changed, from the slow inhalation of sleep to a lighter catch.

He would waken soon, this man who was her husband. The wind would be strong today. She could hear its gravelly voice on the gut window overhead. She pushed her feet out from the furs, turned toward the small square of light that filtered to the floor.

Nuliaq, on the opposite side of the sleeping bench from Elik, had already relieved herself in the urine pot, brought clean snow in to melt, and climbed back in to sleep.

Kaviaq stirred. He moved an arm out from the blankets, then rolled toward her side. Somehow, Elik wasn't surprised as she felt his foot slide up against his leg. A questioning move first, and then a firmer touch.

She sighed, then smiled, though she didn't think his eyes were open.

She would call him Kaviaq today, she had already decided. Kaviaq. Not Red Fox.

When she first woke, she had been thinking about

how it was the food she cooked that filled his belly. His house that sheltered her. Her clothing that kept him warm. His stories that filled her dreams.

She wondered why it was that some days she could think of nothing but going home to the Long Coast village. Other days, it seemed she had always lived here, as if she had taken off the clothing of her Real People and slipped on the skins of Kaviaq's Seal People, so easily she couldn't remember when or how it happened.

He settled his leg over her knee. His toes brushed her ankle. She opened her legs a little farther, letting him know.

It was like a naming game she played without anyone hearing. Some days she called him Kaviaq. Some days he woke first and turned into Red Fox. Some days she called him husband, other times shaman. Some days enemy. Sometimes friend.

Today was a good morning, no matter the cold wind that crept in the house.

He would be Kaviaq, and she would give thanks for the feeling of safety she had woken with. She even felt a little proud of herself, though boasting was never seemly in a woman—not in anyone for that matter. And yet . . . she did feel content.

Little-Creek's cough had seemed to fly out of her chest and disappear just as Elik's trance ended. And the trance itself, the way it had come over her, carried her down to the bottom of the sea. She had understood the language of the Loon. She had sat in its house with Loon and Wolverine, Caribou and Ground Squirrel. And they had shown her the way to send Little-Creek's soul though the skyhole.

A warmth flowed through her as Kaviaq reached

across the small space between them. His hand found her breast, played with it, and then moved lower.

She closed her eyes, breathed slowly as he touched her belly. Her navel. He walked his fingers down, teasing now, playing his way to her thighs. His other hand moved behind her buttocks, pulled her closer.

There was a smell on him—Nuliaq's woman smell. She smiled as she recognized it in his hair, on his neck, as he settled himself on top of her. Through half the night she had lain awake and listened to their sounds: Kaviaq's throaty murmurs, Nuliaq's sighing that was almost a song.

That was how they sounded, the two of them together. Husband breathing out. Wife sighing in. She had lain there, curled in her furs, listening and thinking about how much she had to give thanks for, even here so far from home.

It was nothing like the stories her mother used to warn her with. How there were some women who could share a husband, and though both of them were wives, they shared nothing else. No friendship. No food. They would divide a house, and sometimes the husband never guessed, though they would even build two hearths.

They separated oil, and the seals he brought home were divided, one by one, and never shared. They even grew angry if one of the children asked for food from the wrong mother's pot.

Not here. Kaviaq, for all his other fears, gave them no cause to be jealous. She had gone to sleep wanting it to be her turn, and now it was. She pressed her mouth against the salt-oil-sweat of his neck.

Red Fox pulled back and smiled. "Little Wife," he

whispered, and she reached her arms around his back, brought him down, closer, tighter against her.

She lifted her hips to meet his, and he did, but not with the force she expected. There was a quiet about him—it wasn't hard to tell—even as he moved inside of her. Not a passion but a rhythm, almost holding back. It reminded her of herself, the way she had moved before she understood that it was possible to love someone and fear them at the same time.

Then suddenly, he was done. She hardly knew it had happened.

Elik lay still until he freed himself, then she sat up. She turned to hide her disappointment. She ran her fingers through the tangle of her hair, smoothing it to start a braid. Where had his thoughts gone, she wondered? Was something wrong?

Nuliaq was already busy near the hearth, her own gaze quiet on the fire, on the food she would serve if Kaviaq was hungry. Ivalu played with the wooden stick-dolls he liked to set up in pockets in his sleeping furs.

Did this have something to do with that man Nuliaq had put her legs around? Had Red Fox finally heard some gossip about Inuk?

Red Fox lay on his side, his dark eyes watching Elik as she searched the furs for her hair tie. Playful again, he walked his fingers along the line of her spine.

Her skin tingled. Elik turned toward him, moving to show that she would come to him again if he wanted. She was ready still.

He lifted his hands to her breasts, cupped them and pressed them till they overflowed his palms. She let him; she didn't move. He hadn't said a word yet, but she thought she saw the beginning of a smile.

She closed her eyes and sighed, wanting him to know that whatever he wanted, that was what she wanted also.

What he did, though, was to pull away.

Elik opened her eyes in surprise and found him studying her. There was no hint of a smile. He glanced aside to watch as Ivalu noisily tossed his toys up in the air, then climbed up on Nuliaq's lap and pulled on a breast. When Red Fox turned back around he said, "It would be good if you had a child soon."

Instantly, Elik tensed. She turned, started searching again for her missing hair tie, pulling the blankets up to hide her stomach as she did.

"It would be a child who was *piarqusiaq*, one who is born after others have died," Red Fox said. His voice was soft, not angry, not blaming. "Isn't that the best kind? Proof that Those Who Bring Death didn't follow you here, to the Seal People's place?

"Nuliaq, tell her—isn't it true how parents love a child even more after they know what death is?"

Nuliaq agreed. "I've heard it myself," she said. "Children like that are protected. They're loved even more than others."

Elik didn't answer. She looked at the back of Ivalu's dark hair, his mouth pressed to his mother's breast.

The next moment, it was Malluar's hands she saw, holding something that was also round, and dark, and small. Malluar's hands, rushing to hide the dead-born sons.

Without saying more, Red Fox rose and crossed naked to the urine pot. He pissed a strong morning stream, then, leaning back against the bench, he pulled on a boot.

"What's this?" he said, and with a sudden look of disgust, slid his foot back out.

Elik shook away the memory and watched with a growing fear as Red Fox peered inside the boot. Nuliaq sent Ivalu from her lap. She sent a narrow glance to Elik.

Something was there, inside. Red Fox lifted the boot but he couldn't see what.

Cautiously, he stuck in his hand, angled the boot to reach deeper. Something was there. He puzzled over it a moment, probing, feeling. Then he pulled it out.

"What is it?" Nuliaq asked.

"It's fur," he said, and his voice turned to ice. "Dog."

"In your boot—?" Nuliaq shook her head in disbelief. "Who would insult you?"

"Skinner." Red Fox's voice was flat.

"No," Nuliaq said protectively. "Little-Creek's dog is still outside, alive. I fed it already."

"What does it mean?" Elik asked. "A scrap of dog fur?"

"Not just fur. It's a dead dog." Red Fox pushed it out for Elik to see. Fur, not softened or scraped for use, but whole. Newly dead. Bits of fur, meat, and clotted blood clung to the skin. Sawed-off bones protruded.

"You were awake?" Red Fox glared at Nuliaq. She motioned, and Ivalu buried his head in his blankets, disappeared. "Someone came in here? You must have heard?" Red Fox demanded. "Surely you heard?"

"No!" Nuliaq's voice was shaking. "No one was here. I swear it. No one came in."

"Then how . . . ?"

"I don't know. I heard nothing." *Hush,* Nuliaq sent a hand signal to Elik. *Don't say anything. Don't speak.*

Elik slid across the bedding till the wall was at her back.

"Ivalu?" Nuliaq called, and the boy popped back out. "Why don't you go play with Little Eyes. Go on. Go see if that ball his mother was stitching is finished yet, yes?"

The house held silent while Nuliaq helped Ivalu pull on his one-piece boots and leggings. She handed him a stick of dried fish and he clamored outside.

Red Fox stood in the center of the floor, his hands opening and closing on empty air. He waited till Ivalu was gone, then silently he crossed the floor. He searched the door flap, the fire pit, anything for a human sign of melted snow. A boot track. Blood.

Nothing. He moved to the center of the house, stood for the longest while looking toward the gut window, searching for a crack, an opening where something—maybe not human?—might have slipped in?

Finally, he turned to Nuliaq. "Who else but Skinner? Who else would cross me this way?"

"I don't know," Nuliaq answered. "I did hear men outside. Earlier. This morning. Your cousin Bird's Mouth and Owl. Or maybe Samik. I heard them talking about a hunt."

"What?" Red Fox's eyes widened. "Are you saying I should have been awake and gone hunting? Are you calling me lazy?"

"No!" Nuliaq lifted her hands. "I meant nothing. Only that they hoped the weather would hold."

"Bird's Mouth isn't a partner with Owl. Why would

he hunt with him?" Red Fox tapped his hands against his sides. He looked to his boots, and then to the wall beside the entry where his harpoon shafts and coiled lines were kept.

"Where is Skinner?"

"I don't know," Nuliaq said.

"Probably in the *qasgi*," Red Fox decided. "Listen. If he comes here, invite him to eat. Tell him I hold no grudges. Tell him Little-Creek was a good wife to me, but three women in one house is too many. I give her back to him, gladly."

Red Fox gathered up a coil of ropes, an ice-testing stick with a barbed point. Another harpoon with a toggling head. "Tell him I'm going hunting, and this seal I'll bring home we'll all share in a feast. Can you do that?"

Nuliaq nodded as Red Fox found a parka and an old pair of boots. He hesitated before he pulled them on, and then grew angry at the sight of his fear. He grabbed the ties, then tugged so hard, they tore from the casing. The sound of ruined stitches followed him out the door.

With Red Fox gone, the women turned to each other. "What will he do?" Elik asked.

"Hunt. Talk to the wind. Let's pray he catches a seal. I've never seen him this frightened before."

Elik climbed from the bench, watching as Nuliaq took two sticks and, without touching the dog, dropped the square of its back-piece into the fire pit. A cloud of ashes lifted, then floated away.

"Did you really hear hunters?" Elik asked.

"Yes." Nuliaq leaned low, blew till the coals changed from white to red. "Owl, for sure. And maybe Samik.

Now that I think about it, it wasn't Bird's Mouth—his voice is deeper. This wasn't Skinner's doing."

"Then who?"

Nuliaq straightened, rested her hands on her knees. "If you haven't seen it for yourself, you need to know. There are more than a few people fear our husband enough, they would do this. Other things as well."

Elik nodded, but she didn't ask names. "Should we cleanse the house?"

"Let Red Fox decide. He brought it on us. Maybe he should be afraid. His luck is changing." Nuliaq prodded the skin into the rising flames. The fur sizzled and sent up a stink.

"I want to see Little-Creek," Elik said. "Red Fox might go there."

"After he hunts, he might. But she'll be fine," Nuliaq said. "I'll ask around the other women. Maybe someone overheard her husband's talk."

Elik lowered her head into the wind and hurried the few steps to Higjik's house.

The air outside was colder than she had guessed. The brittle sky stretched in shades of grey; the sun was too far below the horizon to brighten the sky, but clouds were visible. Thin streaks rushed quickly out of the north, blown by a cold wind—a male wind, the elders would say.

Old Sheshalik and Bird's Mouth and any other men not hunting would be sitting inside the *qasgi*. They would be talking about the ice and which way the open leads might move and whether more seals would come.

And if the seals didn't come, if they kept hidden,

stayed among their own kind, the men would slowly ask why. They would look around to see where the fault might lie. If someone among them was suddenly rich, if he came home with a bearded seal when others caught none, they would wonder about that. Or if someone took sick, or died, they would look to see what spirits were angry.

And if Red Fox was inside the *qasgi* while they talked, then the answers might be one thing. If he wasn't and Nuliaq was right about his luck changing, then Samik might listen a little more closely than he used to when Ice Stick talked. He might sidle up against his older brother, No Bird, and repeat what Ice Stick said. And Ice Stick and No Bird, who had seldom sat down together, would begin to whisper between them. Of all the men in the village, Bird's Mouth had the most to lose if Red Fox lost his honor. On the other hand, he also had the most to gain.

Outside Higjik's house Elik called a greeting, then entered without waiting for an answer; something that only a short while ago she would have considered too impolite.

Little-Creek sat in the same part of the sleeping bench as yesterday, swaddled in furs, except this time she was awake. Her face was still flushed but she seemed stronger, busy rolling sinew along her cheek.

Higjik sat nearby, using her teeth to pull a stitch through a torn boot. Spider was there, with two new bead and shell necklaces this time, and Nanogak again. And Skinner, the only man. He sat on the floor, legs extended. A flint core nestled in a pad on his lap. Hammerstone and flaking tools waited on the floor beside him.

"It's my sister-wife," Little-Creek sang out brightly.

Elik searched the wall pegs for a sign of Skinner's parka. If it hung near the fire, that would mean he had just come in. He might have spent the night elsewhere.

"Come and eat," Skinner called. "I have a house full of women, but instead of crawling to my bed, they praise your name all night."

"All night?" she asked. "Where were you?"

He scratched his stomach. "Here. Where else should I be?"

"Alone? Hunting? Red Fox is looking for you."

"I know where I'm safe," Skinner joked.

Elik looked to Higjik. "Is he telling the truth? Was he here?"

"I would have gladly sent away his snoring, but Little-Creek liked the sound. Why? What's wrong?"

Elik found a place to sit, not on the bench with the other women, but on the floor where it was easier to watch Skinner. He examined one of his flints, feeling for a platform to strike. "Did you hear the dogs howl last night?" she asked.

Uncomfortable now, Skinner shook his head. "Higjik told you, I was here all night. I heard nothing."

Spider didn't answer, but Nanogak agreed. "I heard no dog," she said, and then she turned. The door flap lifted and Ivalu peered inside. He wiped the mat of frost from his ruff.

While Higjik rose to fuss with the boy, Elik kept her eye on Skinner. "Red Fox found a dog's hide covered in blood."

Skinner snorted through his nose. "Why tell me?"

"Someone left it purposefully, for him to find."

"Not this man."

"If not you, who?"

Skinner looked up as Little-Creek lowered the sinew to her lap. "I did nothing," he promised her. Then to Elik: "Red Fox has his own enemies. He doesn't need me."

"If not you," Elik pressed, "then who?"

"I heard a story," Little-Creek said. "It was about a shaman, long ago. He had lost his only son, his favorite child. The village was starving because of his grief. He was so bitter, he sent all the game away. Seals and caribou. Even fish."

Nanogak shook her head. "But Red Fox didn't lose a son."

Spider sent her a cross look. "Come here," she called to Ivalu. "Tell me, where is my own boy playing?"

"In Mitik's house," Ivalu sang as he ran across the floor. He lifted his hands for Spider to pick him up, but then stopped, remembering something. He wiggled back down and ran instead to Elik. "This is for you," he said, and he held out a bowl.

Elik set it on the floor and turned back to Skinner. "If not you, then who?" she asked again.

"Even if I knew the name, I wouldn't speak it. I'd be dead almost before it was out of my mouth."

"What name?" Elik asked. Her jaw was tight, her voice strained.

The women were growing uncomfortable. Spider lifted Ivalu to the sleeping bench, then edged protectively closer to Little-Creek. Higjik, with quick, nervous motions, started cutting a frozen salmon into slabs, the slabs to smaller strips.

It was Little-Creek who broke the tension. She sat upright, brightened her voice. "I nearly forgot," she called to Elik. "There is something I meant to give you."

From the jumble of furs heaped against the wall, Little-Creek pulled out a basket. Skinner set aside his tools and rose, obviously glad for anything else to talk about.

He sent Elik a crooked smile and passed her Little-Creek's basket.

"It's for you," Little-Creek announced. "There isn't much, but you should have something. In payment—"

"Oh, but I did so little—" Elik protested, but then she stopped, took a second look at the basket. It was hers. Again. One of the many Skinner had stolen when he ran away.

"Take it, as a gift," Little-Creek insisted, and she took a loud breath, showing Elik how the cough was gone from her voice.

Elik kept her mouth shut tight as she took the basket and looked to the tangle inside. Something black shone at the top—the loon head amulet Malluar had given her the day she and Allanaq left. Carefully, she lifted it. The feathers were mussed and the head more naked then she remembered.

Higjik leaned forward. "What is it?" she asked.

"A loon amulet," Elik whispered. "That's all."

"There was a story about a loon," Little-Creek called. "There was a shaman who lived on a river near Uivvaq. He had swallowed a ball of fire and gone into a trance. There was blood coming out of holes all over his body. But a loon was attracted to him because of the light. It sat inside his chest till he returned to life, four days later. Afterward, the Loon was his helping spirit and it taught him to use a loon's head for an amulet so that whenever he tranced, the loon's power would come into him. Everything the loon saw, he could see."

Elik nodded, but she didn't speak. She opened the tinder-pouch she wore around her neck, set the skull inside on the bed of wild cotton, then slipped it back around her neck. She didn't feel angry at Skinner anymore.

Little-Creek didn't know the basket had been hers. Skinner wouldn't have told. He would have let her believe she was giving away a gift that could rightfully have been hers, wealth her husband should have brought home years ago.

She glanced to Skinner, but he was carefully assembling his flints, mumbling about the quality of the stone.

"Take as you wish," Little-Creek said. "It gives me pride, having enough to share."

Elik nodded and quietly set the basket on the floor. Then, catching the smell of Higjik's fish soup, she reached for the food bowl Ivalu brought her.

Higjik served Skinner first, then the women in order of age. Little-Creek then Nanogak then Spider. Elik lifted the bowl, waited for her portion of the soup. Till the moment Higjik reached across to take it.

The fire's light changed; a shadow flicked across Elik's hand. The bowl's oval rim was painted in a band of black. On the bottom, two caribou were painted, the male with his penis erect, the female dancing backward toward him, genitals to genitals, for luck.

She pulled the bowl back. What was this? Another of Skinner's tricks? It was her bowl, another one that had disappeared with all her other belongings.

"Ivalu," she turned to the boy first, hoping to catch Skinner in a lie. "Who gave you this?"

Ivalu looked at her with his large eyes. He didn't answer; he stood and jumped around the sleeping bench, behind Little-Creek, past Spider, who grabbed him a little firmer than was necessary and told him to hush.

Elik chuckled at the boy's game, but she was still annoyed with Skinner. "If you wanted payment," she whispered, "why not ask Red Fox?"

"For what?" Skinner spoke with his mouth full of fish. "That bowl? The boy brought it, didn't you see?"

"I saw him bring it from outside, where you left it."

"It's your manners that were left outside," Skinner said. "They're as loud as ever. If you don't want the bowl, I'll be glad to take it."

Elik lowered her voice before she called more attention to herself. She felt the smooth grain of the bottom, the black rim. The painted caribou on the inside weren't as dark as when the bowl was new. But that shouldn't surprise her. It was a long time now since Allanaq had made it. That had been . . .

Elik paused. She set the bowl down and took away her hand. Her mouth went dry. She looked to Skinner, then the bowl, then back again. "It wasn't you, was it? It's Allanaq."

"He's dead." Skinner said, not even caring who heard. "It's true, and you have to start knowing it."

"Who's Allanaq" Nanogak asked, but Little-Creek quickly hushed her. Spider sat with her hands clamped in her lap.

Elik shifted uncomfortably. "Do you know that?" she

asked tightly. "Did you go back? Did you look for him?"

"I didn't have to. He never came, did he?"

Awkwardly, Elik rose—everyone in the house was watching her. She stepped toward Ivalu, then changed her mind. The boy was playing in the heap of blankets behind Little-Creek. He was too young to help. "Nuliaq . . ." she mumbled toward Higjik. "I forgot. She asked me to bring her firewood. I have to go."

No one tried to stop her as she hurried into the twilight morning. She glanced to the roof first: no one was there. Not on top of the raised food cache; it was too empty for anyone to flatten himself there. And not behind the kayak stored on its rack.

She walked quickly along the hard-packed snow, trying to remember the names of all the paths, and what they called the houses. There was Floods in Spring, the name for Higjik's house, behind Nuliaq's, and Women's Path, which separated the two.

There was Stinkweed Grows, the name of the house that Samik and Pintail shared with Bird's Mouth and his wife Mitik. And Shore Side, the path connecting that house to the *qasgi*.

Red Fox's relatives. Red Fox's houses.

But where would Allanaq hide if he was alive? Ivalu had mentioned Mitik's house, but that didn't make sense. Didn't Allanaq hate Bird's Mouth because he was Red Fox's cousin? Or what if Allanaq had found Ivalu outside, and then gone back to wait. Where would he choose?

Not his old house; if he tried to build a fire against the cold, even the smallest thread of smoke would soon be noticed.

In her Long Coast village Elik would have known every name of every cousin, every first and second and third wife of anyone, and who was a namesake to whom, and who hunted for an elderly mother-in-law.

Not here. Here she still thought too much like a stranger. She had to think more like a relative. A relative who might be hiding Allanaq.

She turned, ignoring the wind. She forced herself to think clearly. He wasn't in Higjik's house, hiding under the bench. And she didn't think in Nanogak and Grayling's, though that would have possible, except that Nanogak could never keep a secret.

And not in the *qasgi*, and not in any of Red Fox's relatives' houses. But there was Spider's, and Ice Stick's, that was possible. As was Old Sheshalik and Inuk—but that would be too dangerous for Nuliaq. Or else with One Pot. She lived alone. Wasn't she related on Anguta's side?

She looked toward the snow-covered mound that was Spider's house, trying to remember what she knew. Spider was a cousin of Allanaq's through an aunt's husband's blood. What aunt? She didn't remember. But there were those new necklaces Spider had been wearing. One yesterday. Today, just now, two. And the nervous glances Ice Stick threw her in the *qasgi*—did he know?

Elik turned to where a few small children played on a caribou hide on a drift of snow. A man was sitting on the *qasgi* roof, his eyes watching toward the sky. She didn't think he noticed as she ducked inside Spider's house. She lowered her head through the outer entry, then pushed open the inner door flap.

The house was unlit, the skyhole covered with a

plank of wood. She felt light-headed suddenly, dizzy. She cleared her throat. "Hello?" Her voice cracked.

No answer.

Feeling with her foot, she measured out the few steps to the fire pit. She stepped up, reached overhead to open the skyhole.

A cone of grey light drew its path across her face, along her arms, and onto one thing more: the shadowed figure of a man pressed close against the wall.

"Allanaq?" she whispered.

A grass mat rustled and a man stepped forward. The same shadowed light that cut Elik's face drew a line across his. Allanaq's face. The swirl of tattoos on his temples, cheeks, and chin. The labret holes—she remembered suddenly, the way her uncle had pleaded with him to cut the holes beneath his chin. Help him to look more like Real People, not Seal People anymore.

"You came," he said.

"Of course." Elik groped behind her for the sleeping bench, for something to hold on to. She couldn't take her eyes off him. Whole and well. Alive.

"You saw the bowl I sent?"

"It was a good messenger."

"The boy—"

"Ivalu?"

"He wasn't born when I was here."

"He's Nuliaq's son. He's a sweet child. He—" Abruptly, Elik stopped, realizing what she said. The child's father wasn't known—Nuliaq had clearly—proudly—told her. But did that make the child Allanaq's part-brother, or his enemy? Elik looked closer.

His parka was worn and thin. Not the one she had made him, but a different one. Older. His face was drawn and tired, under the eyes, the corners of his mouth. How long had he been traveling? Three moons? More than that?

Awkwardly, Elik searched for something to say. "How did you get here? When?"

"Three days ago. You didn't know, did you? No one told?"

"Skinner said you were dead."

"Skinner," Allanaq snorted. "He's a weak man. He wouldn't know." But then, in a different tone, he added: "What else could I have done? No one knew Red Fox would be so close."

Elik winced. "You heard about that?"

"Ice Stick told me."

"He said his name was Kaviaq," Elik searched for a way to apologize, explain. "I didn't know," she said.

"Of course not," Allanaq said mildly.

Elik stole a look at his face. He hadn't understood. He thought she was speaking of Red Fox's house, not his bed. Or if he knew she shared his bed, he didn't realize she meant as a wife. And even if Ice Stick had told him she was his wife, he didn't understand it meant beloved wife.

She stepped back. Carefully, she took her thoughts and hid them till later, when she could decide how to tell. She didn't want him smelling Red Fox on her skin. It would have been one thing if Red Fox raped her. But he hadn't. She had called him husband. She had wanted him, as much as she and Allanaq had once wanted each other. The way Red Fox still wanted her.

"Ice Stick was surprised when Skinner showed up,

almost the same day I came back. We thought he was dead, that Red Fox had killed him to get you. Then when Skinner arrived, we guessed that you were traded, or left to worry about yourself while Skinner ran."

Elik nodded her head, answering nothing. "Ice Stick found you?"

"I found him." Allanaq smiled. "But wait—I forget myself—of course you couldn't know the story. I've been talking so much with Ice Stick and Spider, I don't remember who knows what. "

"Spider knows you're here?"

"And Old Sheshalik, and Grayling, but he kept it from Nanogak."

Allanaq paused, then more quietly he said, "It's more different than I'd guessed, coming home this way, hiding. Sheshalik's wife was still alive. And One Pot's legs were stronger; she used to be in and out of everyone's house, all day visiting and bringing gossip. I remember Higjik's food racks were so full, she had to dig a second storage pit in the ground. That was the year before we were hungry." Allanaq stopped. He shook his head as if he was confused. "I must have thought somehow that nothing would have changed."

Elik turned her face away. The sadness was inside him still, she could hear it in his voice, the way he talked. She lifted her glance, stared a moment at the clumped strands of his black hair hanging around his face. She remembered the way he liked to have her wash it after a sweat bath. She'd have sat with him when he came home, combing his hair, picking out lice and crushing them with her stone.

In the winter, he would have washed the oils out with the urine they'd saved in the tub, then washed again with snow. Clean shards of snow. Which he shook, and sprayed at her. And she would laugh and throw back her head, and he would be there suddenly, cold and fiery at the same time, nuzzling at the curve of her shoulder and neck, her head thrown back in laughter. She pushed away the thought. "Tell me about the boat," she asked.

"It's safe. The frame will last for my nephews to inherit. The skins will keep another year, certainly for two. Skinner was right about the coast route, if nothing else. The weather held and I would have been back sooner, but I found relatives at summer camps along the way. If it hadn't been for that fog, when I first drifted south with my father, I might have found them. He might have lived." Allanaq hesitated, following his memory till Elik had to ask again.

"They welcomed me at every camp. And they urged me to stay and visit till other cousins came back from hunting trips, so that more of the men could hear my story. The idea sounded good, and I waited. They pressed food on me. They welcomed my carvings. I thought they were saying they would come with me. By the time I realized all they were offering was a place to hide when I needed it, freeze-up was near. I had to store the boat and wait for the ice to harden so I could follow the coast again."

"You would have passed the raft Red Fox brought us on."

"Under snow? I don't know. When I finally arrived, I tried to go home to my own house first. I had to wait till dark, but then I found it. Ruined. I was furious. I thought Red Fox had done it, destroyed my house along with everything—"

"Didn't he?" Elik asked.

"No, Ice Stick told me the story. It was more as if the spirits wanted it for themselves. The first winter it stood empty, there were heavy winds and storms. The ice packed in too close to shore. It heaved and walked up on the land. My father's house was nearest. The ice climbed the roof; its weight brought down the beams."

"If you had been there," Elik said, "you would have been dead."

"I would have been," Allanaq agreed. "Which is why the house was abandoned. No one would live there after that. The luck was too bad.

"I couldn't make myself sleep inside. I walked back out on the ice and waited, hoping I would see someone, a relative I could trust. I built a small cave on the pressure ridge—it wasn't hard, except that I worried about bears. By dawn, I saw a man walking out to hunt. It was Ice Stick."

"Ice Stick," Elik repeated. "And he told you I was here?"

"I tried to send word," Allanaq said. "But it was harder than I guessed."

"The dead dog?" Elik realized. "That was you? How did you get it in the house?"

"I waited," Allanaq said, and the corners of his mouth turned up in a smile. "I didn't kill it until I was sure he was inside. I was on the roof when the light was put out. And then . . ." Allanaq shrugged. "I waited again. I've done a lot of that, it seems. Waiting. And then I went in."

During the night? Elik pictured him standing against the wall, a thing of shadows and eyes, all hidden while

Red Fox climbed on top of Nuliaq. And she had lain on her own side of the bed, listening.

What had he seen? Red Fox in Nuliaq's arms? Not in hers, she prayed.

Allanaq wheeled suddenly about. He gestured and Elik froze. "Did you hear that?" he whispered. "Someone's followed. Be quiet." He motioned her to hold still while he slid back against the shadowed wall.

It was unmistakable now, the paced sound of a cautious step. Someone listening, waiting outside the entry.

The door flap lifted; Allanaq leapt and caught hold of someone's hand. A man's. He grabbed him by the arm, and then the shoulder, then dragged him the rest of the way inside. It took less than a moment to see who it was: Skinner.

Elik stared in surprise. "You followed me?"

"Of course," Skinner pulled from Allanaq's grasp. Indignantly, he smoothed his parka. "Did you think people don't have eyes? The way you left the house. Spider mumbled—nonsense, but not all of it. I was worried for you."

Elik followed Skinner's gaze as he looked about the house. It was cold, she hadn't noticed that before. Spider must have been spending even more time with Higjik and Little-Creek than she had realized. But if Skinner was searching for more of Allanaq's belongings, they were too well hidden to find. Allanaq needed to do no more than slip behind the grass mats hanging against the wall, and he would disappear. No one could find him.

"So. Now we're together," Skinner said in a louder voice. "We have to make plans."

"Hiding doesn't work," Allanaq agreed. He crossed to the entry, waited till he was satisfied that no one else had come. "How near can you get to Red Fox?" he asked.

"Oh, close," Skinner said. "He trusts me more now because of Elik. I can get close."

Elik looked from Allanaq to Skinner to Allanaq again. They were talking as if nothing had changed, as if no time had passed from that day they divided the whale shares on the beach until now.

"We have to go carefully," she heard herself say. "Not everything is the same as you remember."

Allanaq looked at her in surprise. "Red Fox remains alive. My father's death unavenged. What else matters?"

"That, of course," Elik said, and then quickly: "We don't want to be caught."

"What we want," Allanaq said firmly, "is Red Fox dead."

"Yes, but . . . he could easily kill you first. He's powerful."

"We know that," Skinner scoffed.

Elik grew flustered. "I mean his relatives. There's Samik and Bird's Mouth. The four brothers."

"They were there," Allanaq voice tightened. "They raided my house, pointed their knives at my father's throat."

"We know that too," Skinner said. "But that was yesterday. We have to talk about now. And now, you haven't made this easy, taking so long to return. Red Fox is afraid of something, but he doesn't know what. He's watchful. That dog only made him more so.

"We have to find out who is with us, and who would bury a knife in our backs just to find out what would happen. Red Fox isn't the only man worried. You might not see it, hiding safely inside. You don't have to hunt. You don't have to go out on the ice."

"Safely inside?" Allanaq repeated.

Skinner looked to the fire pit. The one pot resting against the stones was empty. There was nothing cooked, nothing to offer a guest. "Where is Ice Stick?" he asked suddenly. "Hasn't anyone told you? People are hungry. The seals don't want to come. There's nothing but fish to eat. And here I am. I should be hunting, but my wife is ill and there's no one coddling or hiding me."

"Are you saying I am lazy?"

"Would I say that?" Skinner laughed at his own joke.

"And why," Allanaq asked tightly, "does a hungry man dream of food?"

"Hungry indeed," Skinner went on, enjoying the chance to complain. "And here I am with the one wife I have ever known, and she is ill, and must be cared for. How can you understand? You had a wife, but now her needs are another man's concern."

"What do you mean *had* a wife? Elik stands here. Alive."

Elik tried to step between them. "We should talk about plans?"

Skinner stepped aside, ignoring her. "Have you forgotten how you depended on me to care for your wife? That I hunted for her, while you went on your way? Slowed my own journey, so she could keep up? Have you been hiding so well, you haven't heard how Red Fox almost killed me because of the route I took for her sake?"

Allanaq listened stiffly. "I heard. From other people.

But what I also hear is you talking too much, and yet saying nothing."

Skinner went on, mischievous and careless. "Is it all a story someone told? The way Skinner happened on a lone tent. The way he wasn't expecting Red Fox, but there the shaman was, singing his drum songs. Following his visions of caribou and spirits—and women."

Allanaq scoffed, but Elik caught the way his hands pulled into fists.

"A shaman might not dream of women, but a man does. And Red Fox is also a man. All alone. No people in sight. Did Ice Stick tell you how he stole her from me? How I fought and bargained, but he took everything, weapons. Skins. Trade goods."

"He did not," Elik protested, but then she stopped, seeing the trap Skinner had set.

"I've heard something of this," Allanaq said, and now a sadness seemed to stretch over him. "The way a shaman uses thought to control people. Some people even say my father did that."

"My own wife told me how they sounded together, at night, the two of them. Elik moaning, and he pushing her on. My poor Little-Creek, she was worried he would use the same kind of thought-control on her. And yet . . ." Skinner paused, turned a calculating eye on Allanaq. "We are still exchange partners, yes? Cousins. What we have, we should share."

Allanaq nodded stiffly. "It's true. Even with Red Fox dead, I could be forced to leave the village again. I would need a place to stay, and food. We could go back where we cached the beluga meat. I've heard of feuds that last for generations before a family forgets . . ."

Skinner's eyes widened, but only for an instant. He smoothed his face, looked away.

Too late. Allanaq caught the look. "What is it?" he asked. "What's wrong."

"Nothing. Only the snow. I was remembering how difficult the journey was."

"No. That's not it. What are you hiding?"

"Nothing. No. But now that you asked—the whale meat. It's gone. That's all. I was going to tell you."

"What do you mean gone? We cached that meat. We planned on saving it."

"And I did, for as long as I could. But after Red Fox wanted your wife, I had to go somewhere if I was to find you again. Surely, you can see that? And I didn't tell. You have to know that. I never gave your name. She would be dead if I had. You have to remember that."

"Be quiet," Allanaq's voice rose louder.

"You wouldn't have the whale anyway, if I hadn't happened along the beach."

Allanaq had heard enough. He lunged for Skinner, sprang from the ground at the same time as he reached for Skinner's neck. He missed and slammed instead against his shoulders, knocked the smaller man to the floor.

Elik jumped out of the way as Skinner grabbed for one of the fire rocks. Too heavy—he let it go, reached for something, anything to grab, but Allanaq rolled him again, over toward the other side. He straddled his hips, took hold of his shoulders, and slammed his head back hard against the floor.

Skinner groaned, and their noise masked the sound of the door flap opening as Ice Stick stepped inside.

Instantly, he dropped the slab of fish he'd brought and reached for the knife handle tucked in his belt.

"No," Elik called. "It's nothing, they'll stop."

Allanaq lifted Skinner by the shoulders, slammed him again on the floor.

Skinner's moan was thick and ugly. Allanaq glanced over his shoulder to Ice Stick, then back to Skinner lying beneath him. With a look of disgust he climbed off Skinner's chest, left him lying there.

With an appraising glance, Ice Stick lowered his knife. "Be quiet," he warned, as if he were talking to children. "I could hear you. Anyone could have heard you."

"You're alone?" Elik asked. Ice Stick nodded.

Skinner rose dizzily. He rubbed the back of his head. "Doesn't a man's work entitle him to a share?" he asked. "Didn't I help butcher the meat?"

"Did you?" Ice Stick scoffed.

It took Skinner a moment to stand. He smoothed his parka. "I'm leaving," he said, and he stepped wide around Ice Stick. "I'm going seal hunting. And when you see the size of the bearded seal that comes to me, then you'll find out just where I'll share the meat. You'll see," he said again, then he stepped outside.

Allanaq sighed in relief. He brushed his hands off on his leggings.

Ice Stick shook his head. "You are looked for," he said to Elik. "I hurried to find you before anyone started to search."

"Who wants me?"

"Red Fox."

"Why?" Allanaq set his jaw. "What does he want?"

"I should go." Elik hesitated, then slowly, she reached out and touched his arm.

"Why? Because he says so?" Allanaq asked, but his voice had already softened. "Don't go," he asked. "Whatever he wants, don't do it."

Ice Stick disagreed. "We talked about this," he said, and he stepped up closer, between them. "Until we're ready, everything must go on the same as before. Red Fox mustn't suspect."

"He's right," Elik hid her relief, stepped out of Ice Stick's way. "If he found you, you wouldn't have a chance. I want you alive," she said. "Not dead."

And then to herself: *I don't want anyone dead.*

The house felt different when Elik returned. An odor lingered from the burnt dog hair. And the fire had been put out, though the stones held warmth; Elik touched the inside face to check.

It was warm still, though Nuliaq wasn't home, nor Ivalu. Nor Little-Creek, of course. Though, now that she thought about it, Elik knew Little-Creek would never bring her belongings here again.

Even if Red Fox hadn't put her out, with Skinner returned Little-Creek would only want to be with him.

She was going to miss her, though they would still visit, always. That was one of the kindnesses of being a woman—the same here as it had been among Real People—while the men went alone to hunt seals at the breathing holes, women stayed in the village visiting together as they worked, sharing food, company, caring for their children.

Elik pulled off her parka and straightened the

tinder-pouch that hung around her neck. She pushed the basket Little-Creek had given her back as far as the wall under the sleeping bench allowed. Then she stood and looked about the house.

There was so much to consider. She needed her thoughts to settle. Needed to understand why, now that Allanaq was back, she felt little of the joy she had looked for. She felt only anxious and confused.

She dredged a dipper through the tray of cold stew, searching for a leftover bite, but then she stopped. There were voices outside, nearby. She set the dipper back and listened toward the skyhole. The voices were guarded and low but she recognized Red Fox and another man. No, two men. She stepped onto one of the rocks, tried to catch their words, but the talk changed. They were done. The sound of footsteps crunching on snow moved nearer to the house.

Her stomach lurched. Elik had time only to jump to the sleeping bench and grab the gut strips she'd been sewing for Red Fox's parka. She tore through her sewing kit for a needle, then lifted a sleeve just as Red Fox straightened into the house.

Take a stitch, she warned her hands. *Thread a needle. Take a stitch.*

Even before Red Fox lowered his hood or dried the frost from his face, he looked to the sleeping bench to see if she was there. He didn't say anything; he lay his harpoon down on the fire pit rocks, unloaded his lines and his pouches and points beside it.

If a seal had come to him, there was no sign of it anywhere. No blood, no flippers. No word about butchering or taking proper care.

"Would my husband like to eat?" She asked as calmly as she was able.

She set down her stitchwork and stepped to the floor. *Boots*, she noticed. She'd forgotten to take off her boots. Clods of melting snow glistened on the toes, dripped as she crossed to the fire pit.

It doesn't mean anything, she warned herself. She was free to come and go, wasn't she? She was too nervous, knowing Allanaq was here. Anticipating Red Fox's anger. That was all.

"I ate," Red Fox said, and he reached for the same dipper Elik had just set down, raked it through the tray. He found a pinch of something solid and dropped it into the ashes. "For your hunger, spirits," he whispered. "What is given grows larger on the other side." He glanced up, caught Elik watching his hands.

She reached for a water bladder. "Are you thirsty? Will you drink?" She didn't ask about any seals.

"No," Red Fox said, then changed his mind. "Yes, I will drink. But not water." He squatted on the grass mat, opposite Elik. "I have a different thirst: a question which needs an answer. Tell me," he started, then he waited, watched as a line of water dripped from Elik's boots. "People are saying that a great thing happened in the village. That you healed Little-Creek. They say you pulled your eyes into the darkness, and found her soul wandering outside her body."

"Who said that?"

"People. Does it matter? They say that a terrible noise of spirits filled Higjik's house. I wasn't there myself, of course."

"I was visiting, that's all. And Little-Creek asked—"

Red Fox interrupted. "Little-Creek and her relatives.

Higjik, and hers. Why do you never sit with the wives of my cousins? Mitik asked about you, just now. I stopped there to talk with Bird's Mouth. Pintail was there also. Mitik's boy had a fever, just today. And she was wondering if, since you were so helpful with Little-Creek, you might not come there as well. Help her boy the same way?"

Nervously, Elik climbed back to the bench, looked over the strips of gut and sinew, the fishskin welting she worked in between each strip.

She tried paying attention to the work, but her gaze kept wandering to Red Fox. Each time she looked at him, he seemed to change. Red Fox had stepped inside the house. Now he was Kaviaq again, staring sadly at the floor. Red Fox feeding the spirits. Kaviaq biting his lip.

All her life she had been taught how the animals could lift up their outer faces and there, in the fur beneath their neck, their spirit-soul would be revealed. Is that what Kaviaq and Allanaq were doing—transforming themselves, so she would be confused? Kaviaq to Red Fox. Allanaq to Qajak. Then back again. Kaviaq. Allanaq. Red Fox. Qajak.

The pieced gut crinkled under her touch. The sound drew Red Fox's gaze to the parka. "That dog," he asked. "What did you do with it?"

Elik made her hands keep moving. "Nuliaq burnt it."

"So. That's the smell? It's too bad. I do have some power, no matter what people say. I could have tranced and searched inside; I'd have learned who killed the dog."

"There are still ashes?"

Red Fox watched while Elik pulled out a stitch she

had spoiled. "Strange, isn't it?" he asked. "The way it happened, that while I followed my vision to the river camp, the caribou turned away from their crossing place.

"And then there is my parka with a seam slashed open, so a piece could be used against me. And the seals refuse to come when I hunt, though other men go out on the ice, and they have luck. Not much, but more than mine.

"The women worry over their food racks. And I—I am the one they look to. And now, here is Little-Creek's illness, which you were kind enough to cure, with no need for my guidance. And this dead dog, an insult thrown in my face, but secretly. There are so many secrets. Like my enemy's boots—isn't it strange that they would shake from the roof of my tent, but not again, not once since I came home? And I was trying to remember—you never told me, did you, who your first husband was, before you came to Skinner?"

"Oh, but I did," Elik reminded him. "He was a young man from my village. I told you, Allanaq was his name."

"Ah. I remember now. Allanaq. That isn't a Seal People name. What does it mean, the word?"

"A stranger. It means A Stranger Who Becomes a Friend."

"Not even one of your own Real People? Why would they give you to a stranger?"

"He wasn't."

"But you didn't know him before you married?"

"No, I mean yes. He was my uncle's son. Another Allanaq's namesake."

"Of course, yes." Red Fox watched her closely. "The

breath-soul is born again through the name. But did you tell me where your people lived? I don't remember?"

"There is the Bent Point village," Elik said as calmly as she could. "Where the land points out to the sea. Then by kayak, two days following the shore and there is another place. The Long Coast village."

"Do you ever think about going back?"

Elik punched a series of holes with her awl. She took her time, muttering about how crooked the row turned. "It's very far," she said.

"Can you draw a map? Was it near where we met?"

"By the river camp? No." She lifted the parka to her mouth, stole a glance at Red Fox's face as she chewed a fold. "It was Skinner who chose that route."

"But first you lived along the coast?" Red Fox pressed her. "A point of land where a boat—an umiak, if it was lost—might be carried on a current?"

Elik didn't answer.

"Tell me then—this first husband, would he make a good hunting partner?"

"Oh, no," Elik said, hoping that was an answer he wanted. "He was a very jealous man."

Red Fox laughed. "Some people say the same of me. Still, it wouldn't be the first time two men fought over a woman and afterward, one crept into her bed, the other crept under the earth. But if we were to journey to your village—you and I—would he be willing to share you?"

"Why would we want to do that?"

"It doesn't matter. Just tell me—would he share?"

"A wife?"

"A wife. Food. Weapons. Whatever he has. Songs,

perhaps—magical songs? A husband might share those with a wife."

"He shared no songs. We were married only a while."

Red Fox narrowed his eyes. "But he might have had songs, this first husband? He might have been a shaman?"

"No," Elik said firmly. "No. All I learned was from Malluar. I told you."

"Were you never married with another shaman? Swear it."

"I swear it, except . . . once. I arranged a trial marriage to a shaman named Seal Talker. It was a long time ago. I was too young to be any use. Is that what you want to know?"

"A man can hide a name. He doesn't tell them all. This Seal Talker, he might have had another name you never heard. A Seal People name? A Seal People shaman, perhaps?"

"No. He was Malluar's cousin. Older than you. He died."

"When? Two winters? Three? Maybe you only thought he was a cousin? People lie. Old men like to talk; they talk to their wives—tell them secrets. Maybe this shaman taught you some of his songs? Powerful songs. What are you hiding? I trusted you and there's something you aren't telling."

"No. I have no secrets. Everything I know, you taught me."

"I didn't teach you to pull a caribou robe over your head and journey to the bottom of the sea. Or win a Loon for a spirit helper, when I never could. And this—" He stepped closer, grabbed the tinder pouch that hung between her breasts. "What do you carry? Another scrap of my clothes? My hair?"

"No! I wouldn't." Elik lifted her hands, but before she could stop him, he grabbed the cord and pulled. One snap and the pouch tore loose.

He forced it open, dug inside till he pulled out the small remnants of a loon's head. The dark feathers surprised him. Eye hollows. Missing beak. "Where is this from?" he asked.

"Malluar gave it to me."

"Why the Loon? When it refuses to be my helping spirit?"

"I didn't choose it. Any more than I chose the Wolverine, or the Squirrel. They came to me. They—"

"Came to you? What pride is this? Are you so great a shaman that the Loon who I called for so long, whose sight I longed for, prayed for, searched for so many years, should come to you instead?"

Red Fox's hand closed around the amulet. For one moment he stared at it, the hint of feathers showing through his fingers, the bulge of its head opening his hand. Then angrily, he threw it, hurled it across the house. His hand came back, all in the same motion, and he grabbed Elik by the shoulders, yanked her from the bench, and held her in front of him, his fingers digging into her skin.

"What have you done to me? Have I breathed so much of your air my mind grew weak? I can't hunt. The seals turn away—"

"Nothing," Elik cried. "I did nothing to hurt you. I wouldn't. I couldn't. I want only . . ."

"You're lying," Red Fox said. "Someone is lying," and he pushed her, sent her stumbling back against the bench. Her hands went out, caught the edge, and she righted herself. Tears gathered in her eyes but she ignored them and stood to face him.

"Is it a song you have? An amulet? Why would the Loon come to you, and from me it hides? Everything hides."

"I don't know. I can't control the spirits. No one fully can—" Elik lifted her arms protectively, thinking he might strike, but Red Fox only stepped away.

His foot struck his harpoon lying on the floor and it went clattering, rolling away. He stared after it a moment, then looked to Elik, then back to the harpoon.

He picked it up, checked that the retrieving line was firmly knotted, and then he pushed it at her. "If your shaman sight is so strong, show me how you call the seals," he said. "They will not come for me."

Elik stood with her hands at her sides.

Red Fox pulled back the harpoon. "Are you in your bleeding time?"

"No," Elik shook her head. "Please. What do you want? I haven't bled since my children died."

"When?" Red Fox demanded. "How long ago?"

"The season before the Shortest Ice Moon. I told you. "

"A full year?" He looked to the life lines etched in the harpoon head, studied it as if asking permission. "It's enough," he said. "You're released from all restrictions. There is no death on you. No need to carry charms or amulets."

He pushed her toward her parka, prodded her to put it on. She tried to move slowly, to keep him talking, but it didn't seem to help. His jaw was clenched and his eyes so tight, she didn't want to anger him more.

"Someone is trying to steal my soul," he said. "Now prove to me it isn't you."

He pushed the harpoon toward her, and this time Elik grasped it. It felt strange, solid but too long, as if she were a child trying to wear an adult's oversized boots. He handed her the coiled line and she slipped her arm through it, fixed it high on her shoulder. He took nothing else. No extra points, no clawed seal-scratching stick. No food and no water bladder to warm against her skin.

There was no choice but to follow him outside, out of the house and into the cold, grey sky.

It was windier than she remembered, but oddly warmer also. Not the bitter cold of a clear day, but as if the wind came dragging the weather behind it. As if there were spirits watching what they did.

The dog saw them leaving, and whined and danced for a chance to follow. It threw its weight against the tether, but Red Fox wasn't moved. He ignored it and walked away with a tense gait, as if he trusted nothing. Suspiciously, he glanced at the other houses, along the paths that led inland and then out to the ice, but no one was about.

He waited until they reached the piled ice that rimmed the shore, then he stepped aside and motioned to Elik that he wanted her to lead.

It took her a moment to get over the surprise, but then she kept on, tapping the unfamiliar ice-testing point through snow to check for softer ice. Red Fox, she noticed, carried his own bow and arrow case strapped lengthwise behind his back, but that was all.

He made no move to help, to say whether she did anything wrong, or wasted time or was slow.

The sky above them was more dark than light, no matter that it was daytime. A small arm of the sun's rays reached from below the horizon. Nearest the shore, the ice piled itself in shattered, uneven blocks that made the walking slow, but not dangerous.

Even so, it felt strange for her to be the one walking first, choosing the path. A woman often went out a short distance to help her husband drag home his seal, but Red Fox had caught so few, and she had hardly been beyond the houses since she arrived. Even at home among her Real People, it was the men who knew the ice. Women went ice fishing, but never far from shore. They trapped ptarmigan and other small game, but inland. Not on the frozen sea.

She tried not to be afraid. There weren't any open leads, and Red Fox had said nothing about walking as far as the moving ice pack.

The ice this close in was thick and safely grounded against the shore. She knew enough to keep her step wide, spreading her weight the way a boy was taught. She stopped once to ask about the path, but Red Fox's eyes were burning. He wouldn't let her talk. "If we find a seal," he said, "I'll force you to kill it, the way any hunter would."

The one time he did stop was at the height of the first pressure ridge. He called her to wait while he studied the sky. He scanned in three directions, watching the clouds for a sign of open leads, whether the storm had moved the ice pack, which way the weather might turn.

She rested on a brick of snow and watched him. In

an odd way, she felt safe. He wasn't going to kill her, she knew that. He hadn't beat her, and even if he did, it wasn't his fist she feared.

If she had any of the power he seemed so convinced she had, she would have used it on him, not on the seals.

She would transform him back to Kaviaq. That was all she wanted. To take this strange, half-angry, half-frightened man and change him back into what he once had been. Him, and that other husband of hers with his eyes that never rested. She rose, and Red Fox motioned her on.

They hadn't walked far beyond the pressure ridge when she saw the seal. It was basking on the ice, asleep. A shape of black with wet fur glistening.

It was nothing so large as a bearded seal, she gave thanks for that. She wouldn't want to cause Red Fox more grief.

She turned back around to see if he'd noticed. He had, of course. He came up beside her, nodded, pointed to her line.

Slowly, she unwound a few lengths of coil, untangled the loop at the end. "What do you want me to do?"

"Kill it," he said in a flat voice.

"I don't know how."

"In the First Times, men had only to lick their fingers, and they made a light to hunt by. You could try that."

"What if it dives back in its hole? How can I know when to strike? Or where to hit, or—"

"Hush. You'll frighten it away. Isn't this what you wanted?"

"No—"

"Teach me to be a shaman, you said."

"I didn't mean—"

"Share your songs, your amulets, you said. Now—this time—you show me. Call the seal."

"But I'll miss. How can I not?"

"Miss, and I'll force you to try again. This seal came to you. As will another. Then another, until finally you don't miss."

"That doesn't make sense."

Red Fox's clenched his hands inside his mittens. "Aim," he ordered. "If you're loud and the seal dives, I'll know you're hiding something. If you kill it, I'll know you stole my strength."

Elik lowered her gaze. She could think of no plea or explanation, no promise she could offer.

She glanced to the seal. It was still there but the wind had changed. It burned her cheeks, stung her eyes. She had brought no goggles, the way a man would have, to protect his sight from the glare.

What difference did it make? She would miss, and he would push her to another site, farther and farther on the ice. Maybe she was wrong, and he would kill her. Maybe they would hunt till they died.

Elik turned, studied the ice formations. They had come down the far side of the pressure ridge and walked only a little way more. If she kept in a straight line, the seal would see her moving. It would surely dive.

On her right side though, there was a broken ridge where the ice had once heaved up. She ran for it, then instantly crouched to hide. The wall was no higher than her waist, but the seal hadn't seen. Red Fox followed more slowly from behind. She crawled on, checking, then crawling, hiding and dragging the harpoon.

Finally the wall broke. She was too near the seal to run for another blind. She hefted the harpoon, tested its weight. She found the balancing point, moved her grip up and down the middle, trying to grow accustomed to its feel.

She felt clumsy; not annoyed, but humbled. Surely, her meager attempt would seem an insult to the seal.

The men often hunted with blinds they'd made from polar bear hides, or building snow-walls when the season was right and the warm sun coaxed the seals into a restful sleep. But how was she supposed to know how to hold a harpoon? How to lift and thrust and aim when she had never before tried?

She shielded her mouth with her hands, whispered to Red Fox. "Is there anything I should say? Or sing?"

He only stood firm, stone-faced, refusing to answer.

"My brother had a hunting song," she said, and this time she caught a flicker of interest. Red Fox leaned closer, but Elik changed her mind. She would not sing her brother's hunting song, she decided. She would compose her own. She would offer it as a gift, from inside her breath, to the seal's ear. Something so it would forgive her.

She closed her eyes. *Let it be sweet*, she prayed as the song came, as if out of a spirit's mouth into hers:

> *I have walked on the ice of the sea.*
> *Searching for the seals at their blowholes.*
> *Wondering, I heard the Song of the Sea,*
> *And the great sighing of the current below.*

Are your houses empty? I called.
Be strong. Are your houses so empty?
Be strong.

Slowly, she opened her eyes. A calm filled her, replaced the fear, the uncertainty. With steps as quiet as a man who'd hunted all his life, she stepped out from the blind.

The seal lifted its head. She waited for it to dive, but it didn't. Gliding more than walking, she took another step. Another.

The seal watched with a quiet ease. It lifted its head back, let the thought of warmer sun stroke its neck.

Her aim was open and, except for the greater distance the harpoon needed to travel, surely this wasn't so difficult as trying for a spruce hen or a rabbit in a tangle of brush. If the seal allowed her to come closer, her chances were even better. She had no true sense how strong her arm was, how far her throw could reach.

She looked back. Red Fox gave the slightest encouraging nod.

Be calm, she told herself. *This isn't a bear. It won't attack. It doesn't care that I'm a woman. As long as there's no smell of blood—*

She lifted the harpoon to a point just above her shoulder. She settled her hand behind her ear. Aimed. There were no words inside her now, no thoughts. Only the seal and her eye, the harpoon's firm weight lifted in her hand.

The seal watched as she bent a knee to the ice, fixed her balance. But she was careful. Each motion as smooth as another seal, as a bird feeding on a fish. She waited for the wind to slack, then readjusted the harpoon.

Except this time the seal turned. It leveled its head. Paused. It was listening to something, away in the other direction.

Elik turned and she saw it also. The tall shadow of a man. Skinner? Was that who it was? Skinner with something dark behind him, dragging along on the ground.

She looked back to find the seal had moved, slipped nearer the dark ice behind it. No—not ice. Open water. The seal had climbed from an open pool, and it was going to dive. Elik braced her feet, lifted her arm.

This time Skinner saw her. He stopped and waved brightly, carelessly. He pointed to the large seal he dragged by a line. Pointed to its neck, miming where his spear had struck.

Elik wasn't the only one to see his foolish pride. The seal caught his brash motion and panicked, slid hurriedly for its hole.

With all her strength, before the seal was gone, Elik sent the harpoon hurtling, driving toward the seal.

Red Fox's shout cut angrily from behind. "Skinner!" He cried, and he ran from the blind, arms lifted, his face raging with frustration.

Elik ran also, not toward the men but toward the ice where the seal had already disappeared.

Skinner stood in openmouthed surprise. He watched as Elik raced in one direction and Red Fox lunged crazily toward him. In a sudden panic, Skinner bolted toward the shore. Whatever was wrong, he didn't need to wait and hear. He raced, dragging the seal.

At the base of the pressure ridge he looked back. Without the weight of a seal to slow him, Red Fox was nearly on him. Skinner dropped the drag handle, flung down his harpoon and left it, left it all as he started scrambling, hand over hand, racing up the jagged ice.

Elik stood over the small circle of open water. The seal was gone and Red Fox's harpoon with it. Drops of bright blood splattered the snow, marked the short trail where her point must have stuck and wounded the animal. She wondered where she'd hit. In the neck? On its side? A rim of sea water already turning to ice glistened where the seal dove and the water splashed up.

She didn't think it was dead, but the point must have stuck, angled into the height of its back, or the shaft would have broken when it dove. She knelt but there was no print, no sign she could find. A mix of pride and fear filled her thoughts as she lay on her belly, drawn to the edge of the hole.

It was a foolish risk to take, she knew that, or she would have if she thought about it. She would have warned herself not to stand so close to where the edge might be thin. At least to plant a spear, hold tight to the shaft in case she slipped. She would have worried about polar bears and the silent steps they take as they stalk their prey.

Instead, she thought only of what might be down there, below the ice and the water to where the Seal and Walrus People, the Beluga People and all the animals of the sea lived in villages among their own kind.

She longed to see their houses and their *qasgis*. To see their villages where the wood that washed up on her people's shores was still living, growing taller than a man.

But she couldn't. The ice around the edge held a milky color, bluish as a woman's breast milk. The water was darker, reflecting the darker sky. There was a slight motion to it, the current's endless pull.

The world below the ice. The hole like a star, in her sky.

She pushed her hood away from her ear, trying to listen. What did they want, she wondered? Why were the seals hiding their faces?

And then she started singing, the same verse she had offered before. *"I have walked on the ice,"* she began, then repeating:

> *I have walked on the ice of the sea.*
> *Searching for the seals at their blowholes.*
> *Wondering, I heard the Song of the Sea,*
> *And the great sighing of the currents below.*
> *Are your houses empty? I called.*
> *Be strong. Are your houses so empty?*
> *Strength of soul brings health*
> *To the place of feasting.*

The words faded. In one ear she heard the wind. In her ear near the water the sound was dull, an echo moving through the depths. Maybe they were all inside their *qasgi*? Maybe they had left their villages because there was no food for them to eat?

But no, somehow she was certain this wasn't about food. There was another reason the seal had fled, and it nearly hurt, this feeling that she was supposed to know why. That time in the trance when the spirits helped her heal Little-Creek, they had told something else. And that other time also, when Red Fox said she could visit the house in the moon and the Loon had come. She remembered the Loon, and she remembered the souls of her sons. But there had been more. Why couldn't she remember?

She sat back up and felt the cold of the ice grabbing hold of her fingertips, stinging inside her mittens. She stood and drew her hood over her forehead. And then she thought of Red Fox. And Skinner.

A sour fear gripped her stomach. She rose, then turned in time to catch the last sight of Skinner fleeing over the crest of the ridge, along a pass where the jumbled blocks of ice shaped themselves like cairns, like giant men guarding the way.

She started walking, then running, then running harder as all the angry words she'd ever heard, from Red Fox to Skinner, Skinner to Allanaq, pounded in her thoughts.

By the time she reached the height of the ice ridge and started down the other side, it was already too late.

A small group of men were walking from the village path down to where the ice began. In a straight line, not far from where they walked, one man was lying on the ice. Another man stood over him.

With all the speed she could gather, Elik started running. One of the men was shouting, not from the shore—those people were only curious, hurrying to see what this was. The one who was standing held his bow in his hand, drawn back to the tightest curve.

Skinner was the one on the ground. She slowed her pace—she could hear better that way. And she could see: Red Fox had already sent his arrow. Skinner was hit. An arrow wavered stiffly from his shoulder. Red

Fox had another, already fitted and pulled tightly against the cord.

Skinner clutched the arrow's base. Blood dripped down his sleeve, red on white, it pitted the snow, disappeared in tiny holes. "Don't kill me," he begged. He didn't see Elik come up from behind. "I'm nothing. No one to bring you harm."

"You are loud," Red Fox answered. His face was mottled with anger.

"Think of my wife," Skinner's voice cracked with pain. "She gave you no harm. I meant only to hunt for her."

Red Fox's lips curled. "I want nothing of yours. You who steal and beg and live off women. You need to be dead."

"My wife . . . ?" Skinner repeated, then with a hope: "I'll tell you something. A trade? My life for your other wife."

Red Fox lowered his bow. "What are you saying?"

Elik tensed as Skinner looked her way. "I'll tell you who she is," he moaned. "If you promise . . ."

"Speak." Red Fox aimed his arrow at Skinner's throat.

"When we found you, I had just gotten her."

"From who?" Red Fox threatened. "Don't lie, or I'll kill you now."

"She never ate. She was like a woman married to the night."

"To Anguta?" Red Fox demanded. "Is that it? Was it him all along?"

"No." Skinner eased himself onto one elbow. "The son. I did nothing wrong. Ask her. Make her tell."

"The son?" Confused, Red Fox lowered the bow.

"Qajak? She was married to Qajak?" Red Fox turned to Elik with a grief so strong, she stepped back, covered her mouth with her hands. "All this time?" he murmured. "When the boots walked? When the visions came? The son was alive?"

"Don't hurt him," Elik whispered. "He only wanted to come home. I swear. He knows nothing."

"Who? Skinner? I don't care about Skinner. I care about Anguta's power. The son taught you—that's it, all along? The father taught Qajak his songs before he died. And he taught you? That's why the seal came?"

"No—" Elik stepped nearer. "The song was mine. The spirits gave it to me. Just now. No other time. Allanaq knows nothing. He—"

Red Fox grabbed for her sleeve, then her shoulder. He threw down his bow, shook her with both his hands. "How can I believe you? What have you stolen?" his face darkened with rage. "There's more, isn't there? What else?"

"Ask what she took from my Little-Creek," Skinner whined. "Ask that."

"Be quiet."

"I didn't steal—"

"In front of them—" Skinner lifted his good arm, pointed so Red Fox would see the crowd that had gathered. Bird's Mouth, Ice Stick, Old Sheshalik—all of them standing close enough to hear. The lies poured from Skinner's mouth, begging, pleading.

Red Fox's eyes widened as he realized he was watched. Shamed by his anger, he backed away from Elik. His jealousy, his fear—they had all been watching.

"She stole from my food cache," Skinner went on. "She stole my amulets—"

"Be quiet." Red Fox clenched his jaw.

"Ask anyone. She's strange. She—"

"Enough!" Red Fox cried, and suddenly his hand swooped to his boot top. A knife appeared and he lifted it as he kicked Skinner's leg, once then again.

Skinner whimpered and curled himself into a ball. He covered his neck just as Red Fox brought the knife down, plunged it into his side. Hard and deep. Between the ribs. Skinner screamed, then twisted. His body jerked.

Red Fox released the handle. He held his hands out as if to wipe away the touch, then stepped away. Skinner's scream faded to a moan, and then to air.

One last time, Red Fox turned toward Elik, but the anger, the rage she thought to find, wasn't there. It was fear that filled his eyes, and a sadness terrible and deep.

Without a look back to the dead, Red Fox walked between the men, pushed past them, up on the frozen shore to the houses again.

10

All fires were put out, all work immediately stopped.

In the *qasgi*, where the dead man's relatives slept, Ice Stick spread the word among the men. His wife Spider whispered the news in the houses, among the women: Skinner was dead. If proper care was not taken, his ghost might linger.

Until they were certain his soul had taken the path to the Land of the Dead, no woman could sew or cook, no man was permitted to hammer on stone. Red Fox passed the word among the elders: in every house no bowls or waterskins should be left open. No chance must be given for any evil *tunraqs* to follow the ghost and slip back inside, find the living, bring disease.

In Mitik and Pintail's house, where Red Fox ordered Elik to wait out the four days of mourning, there was little she was permitted to do. Sister and White Smoke, Red Fox's other relatives, joined them each day, and they would sit and nod and share a few small stories. But what they mostly did was to snatch quick glances at Elik whenever they thought she was asleep, whisper about the way they'd missed guessing who she was.

When she first moved in to share Nuliaq's hearth, her name had meant nothing more than the new wife

Red Fox brought home. Now it meant Qajak's wife. Anguta's daughter. And shaman.

The first few times they had brought their sewing and sat together, they had been curious and friendly. They had leaned forward, giggling to see her three short chin tattoos, the stitchwork on her parka, the way she tied her hair.

This time, with death so near, the women were distant and more cautious. They whispered and sat with their hands idle. They weren't permitted to eat, not on the first day, when they cinched their belts and listened at the skyhole while the men carried Skinner's wrapped body along the path to the burials.

On the second day they still watched her. The four women followed Red Fox's instructions, never leaving her in the house alone. Elik slept to pass the time, and little by little they began to grow bored with the watching. Pintail was a shy, quiet women. She nursed her baby and played with his toes. White Smoke was the careful one, watching that her talk stayed only on the little things that filled a woman's day, reminding Sister which of the rules were weak, and which were important to keep the dead away.

It was Sister whose prattling filled the house. She was a sweet girl with a wide mouth and small nose, but silly, hardly more than a child herself. She fell in and out of her fears as quickly as she thought of them. One moment she worried about who else besides Little-Creek was ill, the next moment she was jealous because Spider's new necklace had more smooth shells than hers.

Mitik was the eldest, the only one Elik worried about what Red Fox might have told her. Certainly, he trusted her. But Elik guessed that he also would have reminded Mitik that it was her husband Bird's Mouth who, as eldest of the four brothers, was the one most likely to inherit whatever Red Fox owned.

He would have nodded toward the meat dwindling on her food racks, and maybe mentioned that her son was old enough now, he might do well to have stronger amulets for his hunting.

On the third day, thankfully, visitors arrived. None of Nuliaq's friends, or Skinner's closest relatives who would still be in mourning, but women from Red Fox's side.

They came bringing food, frozen tomcod they had caught under the ice, which Elik ate as loudly as any of them. And they laughed again and brought gossip, mostly the good news that no sickness had reached any house, and that Little-Creek was sitting up and safely eating, now that Skinner's soul had walked away from the village.

Talk of the weather and the men's hunting grew more free. Both Bird's Mouth and Samik had caught one seal, though no other men had luck. And Red Fox said that once the mourning was over, they would go on with the midwinter Bladder Feast, whether more were caught or not.

It wasn't till the four required days of mourning were over and the fifth day turned uneventfully into night that White Smoke and Sister and their babies returned to their own house.

Mitik and Pintail's husbands still slept in the *qasgi*, and with no man to rustle the blankets and keep the women awake, the house quieted early. The coals in the fire pit were covered with ashes, the skyhole closed. Pintail fell asleep with her little boy's mouth pulling on her breast.

Elik waited on the mat that had been laid out for her at the base of the willow-covered gravel that formed their sleeping bench. Her boots and parka were set carefully within reach. She had slipped under the caribou robes with her outside trousers on, and memorized the steps to the entry, and which way the bear hide flap opened, and where the fire rocks sat, so she wouldn't trip in the dark. "Mitik? Are you awake?" she whispered.

"I'm here. I thought you were asleep."

Elik swallowed her disappointment. She'd been hoping Mitik was already asleep. Five days. It felt dangerously long. She had to get out, learn if Allanaq was still in Ice Stick's house, or whether he'd decided it was safer to leave the village.

If he was hiding, then she didn't dare mention his name. But if he wasn't, or if Ice Stick had accidentally told and word had gotten around . . . What if Allanaq thought he was safe, but Red Fox found out he was here? If only she could get outside, find him, or someone she could ask.

"I was thinking—" she whispered, but Mitik interrupted with a laugh.

"So it seems. You do that a lot—thinking."

Elik peered toward the darkened sleeping bench, trying to see if Mitik joked.

"Pintail is asleep," Mitik said.

"She is?"

"You were clever to wait. She didn't see your parka near the door. She won't wake up."

Elik sat up. She was more than a little surprised.

Mitik had guessed she was trying to sneak out, yet there was no hint of accusation in her voice, no anger. "I haven't heard from Nuliaq?" she asked cautiously.

"You haven't been allowed to. Red Fox can't seem to decide which of his wives he trusts less."

"He said that?"

"He said many things. Sometimes, I think he talks in the hope that sooner or later something he says will be true."

Elik waited. She wasn't certain what was happening. She had spent five days inside this house with Mitik, but they had never exchanged more than a few words alone. Red Fox had accused her of shying away from his relatives, visiting more with Nuliaq's. But he also said he liked keeping Elik for himself, that he didn't want to share her with anyone.

How much was going on that she'd been missing? How much didn't he want her to learn?

"It was a good thing, what you did for Little-Creek."

"It was a small thing," Elik said in the dark. "She was already nearly well."

"Ah, but if she died, that would not have been small."

"You aren't afraid of Red Fox?"

"I used to be. When I was young and his power seemed huge. Now what I fear isn't the man I see every day. It's what he brings behind him, the invisible world that he cannot always control."

"He isn't evil," Elik said, then she stopped, surprised at her own words. She meant them. She had known evil before, people whose hearts were closed to others. Red Fox wasn't like that.

"But what he did, killing Little-Creek's husband, that

could have brought evil. Still . . ." Mitik sat up and Elik heard the rustle of caribou furs shifting around her legs. "You may be right. But if Red Fox is so good, why are the seals hiding from his harpoon? Why do the men worry about the weather? You understand what I mean?"

"I think so," Elik said. "But I'm not certain what you expect me to do—" She stopped. Pintail's little boy had dropped his toy. Noisily, it rolled to the floor, and the boy would have crawled after it but Pintail woke and pulled him back beneath her robes.

"Do?" Mitik repeated, and this time her voice sounded higher and less serious, as if she could not safely say more. "What should you do? In the morning there are ptarmigan nets to check. And we need fresh snow for meltwater. And maybe I'll jig through the ice for more of those fish. For now, I'm going to sleep. In the morning I'll tell my cousin that I saw you safely in your bed. No one is out in the graveyard."

There was no more talk after that. Elik waited in the dark until Mitik's breathing fell to a slower hush and Pintail and the boy quieted in their places.

A strand of moonlight crept in through the gut window. In its light, Elik gathered her clothes to her chest, but she didn't put them on until she was safely outside. Then quickly, with the snow already burning her bare feet, she stepped into her boots, slipped the parka over her shoulders, and wondered where to search first.

She had planned on going back to Spider's house, where Allanaq had been before, but the dark and the cold and the sneaking out of houses reminded her of another night, long ago.

It had been back in the Long Coast village. She had

stood outside Grey Owl's house, her young heart pounding, hoping to find Allanaq. And she had. She followed him in the moonlight, all the way to the Long Coast graveyard, where his father lay buried beneath a pile of stones.

The burials? Why had Mitik said that just now—that no one was out in the graveyard? She knew that. Pintail knew that. No one willingly walked among graves at night, unless they wanted to rob the dead. Or—unless they were hiding themselves.

He was at the Seal People's burial place—she was as certain as if a cord was cinched tight between them. Allanaq would have gone to the one place no other person would dare, not this soon after a death, not in the dark.

Overhead, silver clouds blew across a moon so round, she wondered how it stayed anchored without rolling, crashing to the earth below. At Mitik's house behind her, a dog lifted its muzzle and barked. And on a toppled planking nearby, the wind lifted a scrap of an old boatskin. It took hold of a corner, sent it flapping as loudly as a summer tent. Elik bent her head and turned away from the lowering sounds.

The beach path leading to the burials was trampled and hard-packed by the wind. It followed the shore-line just above the ice, curving with the village toward the north. Elik had never followed the path this far before and the walk was longer than she expected. On each side the wind had crusted the snowdrifts and it seemed as if the path led her through waves frozen on the sea.

But it wasn't until the clouds passed away from the moon and the shadows changed that she stopped abruptly. The Seal People's burials spread out in front of her, more, far more than she had ever imagined possible.

They stretched in rows just inward from the ice, humped mounds covered by drifting snow. Shadows catching on pocked depressions. Burials below ground. Upright driftwood corner posts. Scaffoldings made of whale jawbones leaning to each side.

She had known. Allanaq had told her. Red Fox had told her, but she hadn't realized . . . so many dead. More than she could have ever imagined together in one place. So many people who had lived and died and been buried and then were born again. Like the great herds of caribou racing across the tundra, like seals in the water, they returned. Never ending.

And so much wealth: everywhere she looked she saw traces of gifts, bits of food. Tools, so their souls could go hunting. Points. Harpoon heads. Bowls and dippers to eat and drink from. Amulets to strengthen their luck.

She passed a scaffolding of driftwood poles where the snow surrounding the base was marked and flattened. Its floor, which stood above her head, was lashed together like a raft, with something in the center wrapped in skins. She could just make out the hump, the full length of a human body.

It was Skinner, of course. He couldn't be buried yet, the ground was frozen too hard to dig. He'd been laid out as with the other burials, not flexed as if he was a newborn child but straight, a full-grown man with his feet toward the sunrise.

There were grave goods also, laid alongside him on the scaffolding, hanging from poles: a long ivory swivel chain, animal-headed carvings, a small harpoon, baskets, probably full of arrow points, but not many. Skinner was no wealthy man. He had few relatives, few besides Little-Creek who would offer food and burial gifts another year from now.

And there, framed beneath the jawbones of a stranded, long-dead whale, she saw him. Allanaq.

He stood in the moon's shadow with his hood pulled forward, beaklike. He looked almost like a bird himself, a loon all black and shadowed. But what was he doing? Walking in a circle?

She approached quietly, watching as he paced off tiny, child-sized steps, in one direction first and then back again in the other.

Finally, he heard her. He stiffened and glanced toward the village to see if she'd come alone, but he didn't seem surprised, more as if he had been waiting, expecting her to come.

"Listen," he said without a greeting. "Do you hear that? That high-pitched sound, not the wind, but that other one? I think it's my father, whistling. A ghost can do that when it isn't trying to hurt you. That's how it lets you know it's near."

Politely, Elik dipped her head. She didn't want to hear any whistling. "A ghost can do many things," she said. "Not all are bad." And then, wanting to sound hopeful, she added, "Perhaps your father's content? Perhaps your coming back here will suffice, and there's no more need for revenge?"

"Content?" Allanaq winced and pulled back. "Of course he's not content. Look around you. Do you see anything resembling that thin pile of rocks your Real People called a burial? My father was too strong a shaman to be content with so little. But wait, I've been wanting to show you what I brought."

He squatted and stretched his parka into a table between his knees. A pouch appeared, something soft and well tanned, not small.

Watching him, Elik found a different look to his face than when they first had left the Long Coast shore, or later in Spider's house with Skinner. He seemed older than she remembered. Without the constant worry he'd had in the boat, blaming the world, and her, for everything that was wrong.

Allanaq shook the pouch and out tumbled ivory and antler carvings. A bone sucking tube, the kind a shaman used for curing sickness. A swivel chain with a walrus head carved at one end. Open-work ivory chains. Grotesquely carved death heads, hollow and small enough to wear on a man's finger. He turned them over, held one up.

"These," he said, "Ice Stick gave me. And these," he laid out three finely chipped harpoon points, "from Bird's Mouth."

Elik looked back to the houses, then to Allanaq again. "Bird's Mouth knows you're here? He gave you that, without telling Red Fox? Did Mitik know?"

Allanaq smiled. "I don't know about the women, but if there's any man left besides Red Fox who doesn't know I'm here, I'd be surprised. Bird's Mouth is no different than most. He helped Red Fox push me and my father into that boat, but that was four winters ago. Now, he's still young. He likes to live. His son Hawk killed a ptarmigan for the first time just a few days ago, with a rock. His wife Mitik is a good woman, she makes him proud. And he didn't turn down the gifts I brought. None of the men did. They have different questions this time: Where are the seals gone? Where were the caribou?"

"But what will you do?"

"Only what we planned from the first. What my father requires. I will kill Red Fox."

Overhead, in a line that curved and twisted across the sky, a band of northern lights began to glow, green and red, pale and quiet. They shuddered and stretched, not following the wind along the ground, but moving to another dance.

Elik pulled her hood tighter. Somewhere above the sky, a crowd of boys were playing ball with walrus skulls, stirring up the night, the lights. They weren't going to hurt her, they wouldn't fall on her head, or reach down and try to steal her. But even so, she didn't want them watching, listening to what she said.

Allanaq returned the burial amulets to his pouch.

"How will you do it?" Elik asked. "When?"

"First, I take care of my father. That way I can call on his spirit to help."

"You mean bury those gifts? But you can't bury them. You can't dig. Maybe you should wait for spring."

"No. I won't wait another season. I have one gift left to make. A box. Not large. I have these to put inside—" Allanaq reached behind his neck and pulled out a rawhide tie. Another pouch appeared, a smaller one. He smoothed his parka between his knees, more carefully than before. He tipped the pouch and a few small, narrow bones piled out.

"I brought him home, you see." Allanaq tapped the pouch again. Two more bones fell, the same size as the others. Carefully, not to let them fall, he separated them into piles, then rows. Four rows, and then a fifth. The bones were narrow, fitted so the capped ends of one widened to match the cup of the next.

The sight of them made Elik feel cold suddenly, cursed and frightened and foolish all at once.

Allanaq felt inside the pouch for more. "It's my father's hand. Before we left, I paid Drummer to care for the rest, to make sure he was never touched. But these I planned on bringing from the start."

With a worried expression, Allanaq looked to the ground. "I think one fell. I was searching for it when you came. Don't move," Allanaq patted the hard-packed snow between their feet. "You'll bury it."

Elik stared past the top of his lowered head. There wasn't any use searching. He wasn't going to find the missing bone because she had already stolen it. She had hidden it in her pouch, with her other amulets. The pouch had been in her carry-pack, along with her other belongings. Which Skinner had stolen. Everything.

And now, there was Skinner, cinched tight in a wrapping of sealskins. Dead. With no lips to tell what he'd done with her pouch, with the dead shaman's bone.

Allanaq slid the pouch with the rest of the bones back around his neck, but he didn't give up. He kept stepping and turning so the moonlight could brighten the snow, help him search.

"Maybe you counted wrong?" Elik suggested. "Maybe you forgot how many you brought?"

"No. I laid them out before we left. I made certain."

Elik looked back toward Skinner's burial. She could

just make out the straight line of a harpoon shaft leaning against the upright driftwood poles

What if more of her pouches were up there with him? She had no idea how much these people required in the Land of the Dead. Little-Creek would be a widow. Perhaps she needed some of his belongings for herself.

And how much of her things and Allanaq's had Skinner brought home, how much had been traded? She had seen needle cases and one of her combs. And the amulet from Malluar—but she wasn't surprised to find that one returned. Skinner was no great trader. No one but a fool would willingly exchange seal oil and meat for an amulet whose story they didn't know.

"Why not make your burial box?" she suggested. "Let your father's spirit decide for itself what it needs for peace."

Allanaq straightened from his search. "And how would I do that? How would I know unless he came and spoke to me in a vision? And even if he did, I'm not a shaman. What if I didn't understand the signs? My father cursed Red Fox before he died. *'Victory!'* That's what he sang. *'You will not see me safely dead. You who are living—will you recognize me when I return?'*"

"You've told me that before. But what does it mean?"

"I don't know. Perhaps he never expected to return alive?"

"It's more than that."

"Yes, but what? And while I may not understand my father's song, I can still try to bury him with all the rituals he deserved. And I can still kill Red Fox. Even if it was only me he'd put in that boat, and not my father. Even if my father hadn't died, I would still want Red

Fox dead. Sometimes I wonder if he didn't curse me also. But Elik, at least I can try to give my father peace."

"You can. You should. But you could also wait."

"Wait?" Allanaq looked at her. His eyebrows and eyelashes were covered in a hedge of frost. He squinted, blinked to clear them. "Haven't I already waited? If I do nothing, then it may as well have been my hand, my knife that did the killing. No. I want him buried and at peace."

"Your father was a powerful man," Elik agreed. "But what if he already reached the Land of the Dead, and you didn't know?"

"I would know. The dead depend on the living."

"The elders say the soul awakens again soon after it dies. It follows the trail to the Land of the Dead."

"If it dies at home, where it knows the proper path."

"Malluar once told me of a cousin who was murdered. His sons buried him with a knife. If you do that, she said, the dead are able to take their own revenge."

"Perhaps. But, Elik—I also need revenge. I can't hide from Red Fox and still call myself alive. If fear keeps a man inside a house, he can't hunt. If he can't hunt—"

"If he can't hunt," Elik interrupted, "he can still eat. If he eats, he is alive. If he is alive—" Elik stopped.

Allanaq had stepped back and he was watching her now, not listening. His face had changed. The hard line of his mouth softened, the anger faded from his eyes. He reached toward her, lifted his hands to her shoulders.

She nearly pulled away; it was a moment before she remembered how that had used to feel. His touch, the way his hands fit when he pulled her close. Her head against his shoulder. It had been so long since he'd held her that way.

A shudder passed through her. Seasons and winds and loneliness—she pushed them all away. She moved against him, lifted into his embrace.

They held each other, neither speaking, both remembering. Till finally, Allanaq let her go. "What do you want me to do?" he asked.

"Reason," Elik said gently. "Go slowly. Three things may happen. First, if you kill Red Fox, one of his relatives will surely kill you in turn. Perhaps when you're asleep, with a knife in your back. A bit of poison in your food. Samik would do it, no matter which of your gifts he accepted yesterday. And then Ice Stick, because he is your relative, is forced to kill Samik. Villages have emptied because of blood feuds. Whole families have died."

"But what if Bird's Mouth also wants Red Fox dead? If he can convince Samik and his other brothers how much better off they'd be if Red Fox was gone. Then we wouldn't need to fear?"

"Except, when have you ever known fear to end with killing? What if you succeed in killing Red Fox and at first no one blames you. But slowly, because he is a shaman and walks in two worlds, his ghost refuses to leave. No matter that you sever the tendons in his ankles the way you would an enemy, or burn his bones, or hide them far away—as he tried.

"After a while, someone grows sick in one of the houses. Children die in another. A fear begins to grow, crippling, deceiving—it dogs your steps, robs you of sleep.

"All you need do is look at Red Fox and see how it's

true. That's what people say is happening to him. That his fear of your father's return eats away at his mind. That his spirit helpers, tasting his fear, no longer come when he calls. No seal trusts his hunting songs. He grows more afraid."

"And what is the third thing that might happen?"

"Third," Elik said, "is that you let me help."

"You?" Allanaq hadn't expected that. "How?"

"I'm not sure yet. I ask only that you give me a chance."

Allanaq's mouth drew back to its tighter line. "I thought we agreed? Malluar warned you, you were not to trance, not to practice as a shaman. What have you done? There are stories I've been hearing—"

Elik lowered her eyes to hide her dismay. She had known he would say that, as if nothing had happened, nothing changed since that day they paddled from the Long Coast shore. But she didn't want to argue about that, not now.

Other women walked a careful path between two husbands; there were always stories. Sometimes there were too many men and not enough women. Sometimes one of the husbands was too old to hunt, and so they needed another. But two husbands such as these? How could she explain she wanted them both alive?

She took a breath, calmed her voice so it wouldn't shake. "Malluar was wrong to bind my shaman-sight," she answered. "She was wrong to tell me not to call on spirit helpers. She left me helpless. And now, alone."

"Alone? Is this a riddle?" Allanaq asked. "What are you saying?"

"I am saying that Malluar is gone. I dreamt I saw her soul feasting in the moon."

"In a dream?" Allanaq repeated. "Or were you trancing? What if it was a *tunraq,* trying to trick you?"

"I know what I saw. It was a dream," she answered, thankful that she could tell the truth. She lowered her gaze, but she felt his eyes on her, so close she wondered if he saw her thoughts, racing then retreating like a fox darting through the brush. She heard him take a breath; when she looked up, his gaze had softened.

"Tell me what you want," he said. "And I will try to figure what is best."

"I ask only that you wait. Malluar's soul is content, and I think I can show you that your father's is also. But," Elik said, and her boldness surprised her. "You must give me time."

"How much?"

Elik wasn't sure. "You said you had that box still to finish. What else?"

"The death mask he was never given."

"Death mask? What is that?"

Allanaq shook his head in surprise. "I keep forgetting, you're not Seal People. You don't understand, even now, how carelessly your Real People treat the dead. You follow few rituals, as if either you had no respect, or you were still a child, too young to know fear.

"When my father died he should have been buried with the openings of his face all covered. For the protection of the living, so his ghost isn't able to look back through the eyes, and for his own soul as well. His human eyes that no longer saw should have been replaced with eyes of ivory, to give him the clear-sighted vision of the loon."

"The loon?"

Allanaq didn't notice her surprise. "Ivory eyes, with pupils of jet," he continued. "I need to trade with someone for a loon's skull to bury with the rest of his bones. I need to carve two pairs of ivory eyes, one for the loon and one for him."

Elik looked to the sky. The band of northern lights had disappeared. In their place, a new layer of clouds had blown in. They moved quickly across the moonlit sky, changing, threatening.

"Give me until your carvings are finished," she said. "But let it be after the Bladder Feast. After everyone has come together in the *qasgi*."

Allanaq nodded. "Very well. But you have to know. I will wait with a hunter's weapon. If your first arrow misses, the second will be mine."

But for the pitch of wind, the village was quiet when Elik returned. Dogs slept. Skyholes showed no signs of morning fires. Overhead, through a clearing in the clouds, the three stars of the Great Stretchers showed where a woman in the Sky World tightened her rawhide lines.

Elik wondered if that woman had husbands, as she did. And if she did, were the two husbands jealous of each other? In most of the formal partnerships she knew, the husbands lived in different villages and slept with their exchange wives when they visited. Sometimes there were two husbands and two wives. Sometimes only one wife, and she visited between them, flensing seals and sewing winter clothes first for one, then the other.

That made sense, though she wasn't sure the husbands would choose it that way. Unless there weren't enough women to go around. It could also explain why she only saw the empty row of pegs in the sky, and never the line going round them. Because the woman who used the stretcher-pegs was always going back and forth between her two husbands' houses.

Would she be able to do that, Elik wondered? Stop her two husbands from killing each other by living with one of them at a time? Convincing them to live in separate villages? Which one would leave, and how was she going to make them agree? One shaman. One hunter. How was she going to keep them both alive?

Elik stopped outside Higjik's house. She hadn't been followed, she was certain of that. Even if someone did stop her, there were any number of simple lies she could tell. It was the truth that worried her: two husbands she needed to keep apart. And she had no real plan yet. Only one idea that had come to her while Allanaq searched for his father's bone.

She pushed aside the door flap, felt her way through the darkness of the narrow entry. Inside the house, no fires were lit. She straightened, then stood quietly, listening to the heavy sounds of sleep.

Someone was on the sleeping bench to her left. A second person lower down, on the colder floor. That would be Little-Creek. Higjik would be on top, in the warmer bed since it was her house.

Elik wiped the frost that had crusted her eyelashes, then waited to grow accustomed to the dark. She made out the ridge of the sleeping platform, the fire pit, the blanket-smoothed shape of a woman, head facing toward the fire.

Quietly, she knelt beside Little-Creek's shoulder. "Can you wake?" she whispered near her ear. She shook the older woman softly, not to frighten her.

"I hear you," Little-Creek said. She lifted herself to one elbow, looked about. "Where am I?"

"Higjik's house. Everyone's sleeping."

"Is something wrong?"

"No. No, we're fine."

Little-Creek sat up. "It's all over then, the burial? And that One Who Was My Husband—?" Carefully, she avoided saying the name. "He's gone? It's over?"

"Yes," Elik assured her. "Four days' mourning. It's over."

"I made sure I never cried too loud. I didn't want his ghost turning back. He wasn't a bad man, whatever they told you. He must have realized he could never survive a winter alone. That's why he came back for me. He was foolish that way, but he wouldn't harm anyone. He never did."

"No. Of course not," Elik felt for Little-Creek's hand, held it.

"They said I could be dangerous. That his soul would be frightened to be alone, since he never was skilled as a hunter. My tears would have drawn him to me. They painted my face red—you didn't see? They made me look frightening, horrible as a *tunraq*, so I'd scare him away if he came. But he didn't. And I haven't been alone, even to go out in the snow and piss, someone always comes with me. I'm not allowed to leave. They won't let me come for the Bladder Feast."

Little-Creek leaned closer. "I was thinking about you these last days. The women are all worried about how little food there is. But you could bring game, the way a shaman does. I'll tell you how to do it. There was a story I heard once of a shaman who flew up to the moon. And he was going to go inside, but before he did he saw a hare, and he pushed the hare right down through the star-hole he had climbed in through. You could do that. The hare fell to earth, and from that one animal enough more were born so the people could eat. They didn't starve."

"I'll remember that," Elik said. "Maybe I'll try. But Little-Creek, there's something I need to ask."

"No," Little-Creek touched her hand to Elik's mouth, hushing her. "Don't ask. Take. Anything I have is yours. Take as you like." She picked up the first thing she could reach: a cooking stone, small and rounded. "Take this, sew it in your clothes. It comes from the earth and it's stronger than fire. Wear it and you'll live long."

"Thank you," Elik said. "But there is something else. Can you tell me . . . your husband's belongings?"

"Your husband too," Little-Creek reminded her.

"Yes, mine too. But did he leave anything else? A box perhaps, or a pouch? It might not have been large."

"There was so little," Little-Creek apologized. "Most was given away, or sent with the burial. Harpoon heads, knife points. He did so well, this last season trading. But—what use would I have with a man's tools?"

A shuffling came from the platform, then Higjik's voice, rising out of sleep. "Who is that?"

Little-Creek covered her mouth with her hands, but Higjik had already risen.

"Ah—I was right," she said. She pushed back the frame over the skyhole and a moment later she was beside them, wide awake and squatting on her heels. "Have you heard the talk?" she whispered. "Even the men are saying Red Fox was wrong to kill Little-Creek's husband. It was one thing to put a man out of the village. Something else entirely to kill him with a knife in his chest. He was never more than a small and simple man."

Little-Creek slowly nodded. Her face in the dim light was pocked with flaking red paint, grisly, exactly as she had said. But what Elik noticed more was how much stronger she looked in spite of the paint and the days of mourning and worry. There was weight to her face again, and the skin beneath her eyes was no longer hollow. She might not have eaten well, but she had slept, and if the cough was there, Elik hadn't heard it.

"There's that basket I gave you," Little-Creek offered. "Do you still have that?"

"Basket? What basket?" Elik tried to remember. Then: "I have that, yes. I'd forgotten. Could it be in there? All this time?"

"Could what be where?" Higjik leaned eagerly forward.

"She asked for something of my husband's."

"Why?"

"I don't know. Why?" Little-Creek followed Higjik's glance back to Elik.

"There was an amulet of mine," Elik said. "An old one. I didn't want it lost."

"You're wondering if Skinner had it?" Little-Creek asked.

Higjik leaned closer, nearly into Elik's face: "What kind of amulet?"

Elik took the cooking stone Little-Creek had given her and slipped it inside her belt pouch. Higjik watched her carefully.

By tomorrow, Elik was certain, whatever she said to Higjik and Little-Creek now would be known by every Seal woman in the village. The same way they had known as soon as she found Spider's sewing awl, and tranced over Little-Creek's cough. "Can you keep quiet?" she asked. "If I tell—"

"Yes," Higjik promised. Little-Creek cupped her hands and spit, then rubbed the water on her face.

Elik made her voice solemn. "There was a man, a shaman who you knew. I will not name him, but his son is here."

She paused as both women averted their eyes, exactly as she knew they would. "This shaman, his boots were seen swaying by another man, a younger shaman. And so he thought he was alive, his enemy. But he isn't. He died far away from here. His spirit went to the Land Below the Sea and it will never return. Never. But you mustn't tell, because some people think it's better to worry that his spirit might return, and bring in trouble. They want you to be afraid. Now promise you won't tell."

"I won't," Higjik whispered. "I wouldn't."

"Who would I tell?" Little-Creek asked. "I haven't seen a face outside these walls in days."

The sky was dark when Elik returned, the wind so strong she kept stopping, turning to see who followed her, who hid inside the swirling gusts of snow. But no. No one was about. The paths were empty, the house dark when she pushed through the frosted door and stepped inside.

She felt her way to the fire pit, and then to the stand where her oil lamp rested. She reached inside her parka for her tinder-pouch, but she stopped, and held still.

She'd heard a flurry of whispers—was it Nuliaq? Ivalu?—coming from the far side of the sleeping bench. She waited with hands poised in the air. But no, it was nothing. The sound didn't repeat. She opened the pouch, pulled out her fire rocks and a clump of wadded moss.

"Who is there?" a voice whispered.

"Nuliaq?" Elik jumped. "I'm sorry. Did I wake you?"

"It's Elik," Nuliaq repeated, then: "No. I mean, yes. You're alone? Wait, don't light the lamp yet. Ivalu's asleep. Wait. Why don't you move over, away from the entry?"

Elik shrugged in the dark, set down the rocks. She felt around for the pile she kept of old seal fat, for a chunk to add to the lamp. And then she stopped and held still. There was a sound of blankets rustling. More whispers. And then bare feet, someone climbing from the bench. But the noise was too heavy for Ivalu, too solid for Nuliaq.

She waited, listening, and then jumped as something bumped her shoulder. An instant later, another brush. This time softer. A parka sleeve? "What's that?" she called. "Nuliaq?"

"I'm waking. I'm coming," Nuliaq answered. And now there was a rush of cooler air, the sound of bare feet hurrying toward the door. A shushing noise followed: the door flap closing.

Elik lit her lamp, then turned without waiting for the wick's uneven light to spread.

Nuliaq stood barefoot and naked in the center of the floor. "Where is Red Fox?" she asked.

"In the *qasgi*."

Nuliaq nodded toward the door. "Where have you been?" she asked, and she crossed back to the sleeping bench, put on her short, inside trousers.

Elik took a longer look at Nuliaq as she settled beside her. Her hair was more tangled than Nuliaq usually allowed. Her skin glistened with a layer of sweat that brought a smile to Elik's face as she realized what she'd interrupted.

The corners of Nuliaq's eyes wrinkled with laughter and she answered Elik's smile with a nod. They might have joked, teased each other about exactly what long body part Elik had felt on her arm, but Ivalu sprang up from the heavy fur coverings. Quickly, Nuliaq lifted her finger to her lips, hushing them both as the boy lifted a sealskin ball in one hand, a stick in the other.

He held the stick out to show Elik. "This is my arrow," he said proudly. "And this," he swirled the ball in the air, "is a caribou."

"A great huge one," Elik said. She smiled, then rose and crossed to where a bowl of broth wedged itself safely inside the fire pit. "What is this?" she asked.

"Bone broth," Nuliaq said, but then her face grew longer. "Red Fox was here. Last night."

"And what did our husband want?"

"You. He said he would come back in the morning."

Elik sipped from the bowl, then set it down. Nuliaq's glance was lowered now. In place of the laughter, a scowl wrinkled her brow. "He looked for you in Mitik's house," Nuliaq said.

Elik glanced beneath the sleeping bench. The braided handles of her grass and sealskin baskets reached out from under the sleeping bench. "I was with Higjik," she said. "What did he want?"

"From you, I don't know. Me, he accused of changing the weather, of working against him so he couldn't hunt. He said he'd seen me out on the snow flats. That he followed me when I went to check my ptarmigan nets."

"What did you do?"

"Nothing. I swear—"

"But he said you did?"

Nuliaq glanced to see what Ivalu was doing, then lowered her voice to a whisper. "He said he saw me pull down my trousers to urinate, out in the open. That I stuck out my vagina so the Wind would see, and the Weather. He said I did it on purpose to offend them, because I wanted them to tell the animals that my husband stank, so they would remember his smell, and hide."

"Does he think you want to starve?"

"I don't know what he thinks. Except that . . . something is happening to him."

Elik didn't answer. She watched as Nuliaq's gaze hung on Ivalu, the way he played, the way he laughed when he caught the ball.

Quietly, Nuliaq said, "Red Fox is changed. He is frightened. I have never known that man to be afraid, and I don't understand. He came in here and

he cursed me, and he stared at Ivalu. He picked him
up and stared into his eyes—too deeply. As if he was
searching for his soul. Ivalu cried and I shouted at
Red Fox. I shouldn't have, but he frightened the
boy."

She looked to Elik. "If I can't know where his
thoughts are, how can I know if Ivalu is safe? I want
my son safe. Why else have I stayed married with him,
if not to keep my son alive?"

Nuliaq caught Ivalu by the hand and drew him to
her lap. She offered him a breast to nurse but he
slapped at it and wiggled loose and grabbed instead for
his toy.

Elik crossed to the sleeping bench. She knelt and
dragged out several baskets till she found the lidded
one Little-Creek had returned. She set it on the bench,
near her furs, in case someone walked in and she needed to hide it. If she hadn't told Allanaq what she'd
done, she wasn't going to tell anyone else.

She remembered when Little-Creek first gave her
the basket; she had taken the loon amulet from the
top, then looked no further. This time she found it all.
The pouch Skinner had knocked from her hand—she
had completely forgotten. She had taken out the bone
and tried using it to bring Allanaq back. But the
Wolverine had appeared, and after that she hadn't
thought any more about the bone. After all, it hadn't
worked.

But was that true? Here was Allanaq, alive. Skinner
had brought her to Red Fox. And Red Fox had brought
her to the Seal People village. Allanaq's journey had
taken longer than he'd guessed, and yet he was here.
And Anguta also was home.

Elik turned to make sure her shoulders blocked Nuliaq's view. She emptied the basket and stared as amulets, sewing awls, and sealskin thimbles tumbled out in a heap. She sorted through the tangle of sewing kits and amulets that she would never have packed together in one basket. Sinew. A flint from a woman's knife. A gull's foot. A seal's nose. And a bone. One small bone. A finger. She pushed it under a corner of the bedding.

Skinner must have gone through her things. He would have opened every basket, handled her ivory needle cases. He must have carelessly tossed her things together again. Allowing Little-Creek to give them to her would have been no loss for Skinner.

She turned back to Nuliaq. "Can you do something for me?" Nuliaq nodded. "I need Red Fox kept away, for as long as you're able. If you can't, if he pushes inside, make a noise. Shout to give me a warning. I need time, alone."

Gladly, Nuliaq nodded. "As much as I can provide. But please don't tell me why. Sometimes, that man only looks at me and he knows I'm hiding something. Ivalu—" she tickled the boy between his skinny shoulders. "Can you go and find Little Eyes to play with?"

Ivalu planted his feet. "I want to see Father. He's making me an arrow. He said so." Nuliaq leaned down and whispered something that made him smile, then jump quickly out the entry.

Elik waited while they dressed in their outside clothes, then left the house. She waited again, until she was certain she no longer heard their voices. Then she tugged off her parka, hung it neatly on a peg. She removed her boots, pulled the ties out of her hair, loosened the braids.

She would have no necklaces. No amulets. No beads of any kind.

For what she was about to do she wanted to be naked, not watched by hungry spirits. She wanted to be open. Not guided or misled or lied to.

She lit a handful of dry celery, set it in the hearth for the scent to clean the air. Then solemnly, she set the bone in the bottom of her bowl and turned it so it lay between the male and female caribou, connecting them in a line.

She set the bowl on its stand, then poured in fresh meltwater, enough to cover the bone.

Inside the fire pit, a few white coals were banked beneath the ash. She swept back the layer, fed dry grasses and tinder to the fire, then waited for the heat to grow.

When it did, when the coals were red and the cooking stones too hot to touch, she added the stones to the bowl. Once. Twice. Three times. A fourth stone, then a fifth. Using Nuliaq's forked sticks, she pulled the cooled stones from the pot, replaced them with hotter ones. Until the water steamed, then boiled, then kept on boiling, far longer than a meal ever needed to be cooked.

She added shaved wood to the fire, and heated rocks to the water, nothing else. No sea water for the taste of salt. No fat for thickening or seal blood for taste. Only the bone, so that Anguta's soul would flow into the water.

And from the water into her. Bones and skin and muscle and light, his shaman-light would enter into her, completing another part of her initiation. As Malluar had said, the elder shamans transferred their wisdom into the young.

Time passed. The walls of the house seemed to grow thicker and deep, as if the house was a burrow underground, and she was a lemming and the house her den. She kept reheating and changing the rocks, kept the bowl full, the water boiling, the bone softening.

The brief winter day turned from morning into dusk.

Twice she heard talking outside the house. Once a man's voice. Inuk's, she wondered? Another time a woman's. Both times, she heard Nuliaq's voice—not her words—only her gentle, muffled voice leading the others away.

Finally, it was done. She removed the last of the heated rocks from the water, blew over the broth to help it cool.

When she sipped it, it was nearly tasteless, a soup as thin as air. But like air, it carried the Wind. And like Wind, the broth held power.

She pulled out the bone and started chewing. It was a small thing, after all. Not even an entire finger. Only part. She chewed, and with every bite she felt him nearer. In the floor first, as if he was underneath her. Then not in the floor, but in the walls. Inside the house.

"*Halala—halalale halala—halalale,*" she sang.

The fire dimmed and she heard creaking sounds, as if someone was walking. The gut window flapped overhead. A vole scratched against a corner hole.

Elik closed her eyes and there, finally, she saw him. A dark outline against a darker wall.

Her heart drummed so loud, she feared the noise would chase him away. But no—the figure held. Two arms, two legs, the head and torso of a man, but so large, he overflowed the house. His shoulders and head bent to fit inside the ceiling, his legs flowed along the floor.

He was light and shadow, and Elik didn't know what more. His body was covered in pinpricks of light, stars in a night sky. Light. Nothing flesh.

The man drew nearer. He loomed over her. Strong he looked, not old. His chin was sharp, his tattooed face not round as her people's were but angular, longer. And his nose also, it was prominent but beautiful.

His searching eyes slowed when he found her—if they were eyes—there was nothing flesh about them. They were more like ivory moons floating in that body made of stars. Ivory moon-eyes, inset with pupils carved of blackest jet. Yes—that was it. She suddenly recognized them—not flesh at all, but carvings as like to the pair Allanaq was making for his father's burial as any two things could be. And not only were his eyes carved from ivory, but he wore nostril plugs also, an older, yellowed ivory shaped like a bird's head. A loon's?

His face had filled with a look of surprise, as if he hadn't expected to find her, or to stand once again inside the warmth of a human house.

"Can you speak?" she asked. There was so much she needed to know, but her voice was thin and she was more than a little afraid.

The man watched her, but he did not answer.

She pushed aside the trembling in her voice, lifted it, tried again. "I have taken you inside me," she said.

"Your bones into mine. What you were, I shall become. But tell me, please, what else must I do?"

She waited. The expression on Anguta's spirit face grew smooth and masklike. She had prayed he would speak, but that didn't appear likely. He seemed to be looking through her, hardly aware that she existed. And now a new sound interrupted from outside, the angry tone of a man's voice near enough to the house, she could hear it above the wind.

She heard Nuliaq's voice, and then another man's after that. Red Fox. And someone else? Bird's Mouth— yes. No other man would dare argue with the shaman that way.

Uneasily, she looked toward the entry. When she turned back, Anguta was gone. No sign remained. No shadow, no lights. No hint that he'd been there, but for the one thick taste of bone lingering on her tongue. *Where was he?*

She rubbed her face; the fire and smoking grass made her eyes feel as raspy as if she'd woken from a dream. *Had he fled?* The bowl was on the floor in front of her knees. Empty.

But not her. He was inside her now, she was certain. She had swallowed him in with the bone. The ghost and the dead man and the shaman.

She took a breath and roused herself, then hurriedly bent to the fire pit and brushed a pile of ashes over the coals just as Red Fox stepped inside. The chill air sent a shiver along her back and she felt him behind her, peering about the house.

"I came for a robe," Red Fox said.

Elik lifted her gaze no higher than his boot tops.

"It was cold in the *qasgi*, and I was hungry. I

thought, perhaps a wife might bring a man something to eat?"

Elik wrinkled her nose in surprise. She thought she'd heard arguing outside, but Red Fox's words were as gentle as they'd ever been. He sounded like a husband, tired and thankful for the food his wife prepared.

"I'll bring fish," Elik offered, and quietly, without a fuss—knowing he wouldn't eat from her woman's bowl—she took the chance to put the empty bowl away. And the basket she'd left on the bedding—she pushed that under the bench, far behind her others. She wiped at her mouth, praying that nothing showed, that the broth had left no odor.

She found a salmon Nuliaq had brought in for a morning meal. It was thawed now, and slippery. She set it on a tray, held the tail so it wouldn't slide.

"You are well?" Red Fox asked. "It's warm in here."

"The fire caught while I was asleep," she said. Her back was to him, but she listened as Red Fox pulled off his parka, hung it on a wall peg. She heard him pull off his boots, then slide a dry pair of grass socks over his feet.

She cut away at the fish's dorsal fin, pushed it to the edge of the tray. She angled her knife and felt for the backbone, half expecting her hands would shake. They didn't, and with a nod to herself that Red Fox couldn't see, she kept on cutting, separating the meat from the bones.

He was standing directly behind her now.

She flipped the fish, sliced inward again. He came closer, so near she could feel the heat rising off his legs. It gave her a shy feeling she hadn't expected. Her stomach fluttered and she tried to think of something to say. "Ice Stick brought home a seal," she said, but then, realizing he could take that the wrong way, she added, "Perhaps it means the storm Sheshalik warned about won't come?"

"Perhaps," Red Fox said. "But there were many who hunted, and that was the only one caught. If you and Nuliaq have fish put away, you won't have to worry."

"Fish? Yes," she offered eagerly. "I can take more out. Nuliaq will be home soon, and Ivalu."

Red Fox squatted close beside her. He leaned and his arm brushed hers. "Not so soon," he said.

"But Nuliaq said—?"

"She said something, but Ivalu begged Samik to take him shooting at snow targets. And Samik agreed, but only if Nuliaq would stay with Pintail. That woman never likes to be alone. She has bad dreams. And the boy . . ." Red Fox chuckled. "He was so excited, Nuliaq couldn't say no."

Elik scooped the pink meat from the tray into a smaller bowl.

Red Fox rocked back on his heels and Elik felt his eyes on her hands, watching the way she held her knife, the way her arm grazed her breast. "It will be good to eat your cooking," Red Fox said. "A man grows hungry for food made with care."

"Didn't Nuliaq bring you food, to the *qasgi*?" Elik leaned forward, pulled her hair from behind her ears so it hung loose, hiding her face.

"Yes, but you do things differently. You use sour-dock, you make it sharper, or saltier. Something . . ." Red Fox paused. "I grew used to your food, by the river."

Elik reached for the thin section of salmon. She sliced away the tail and the smaller fins. She cut the slab into slices, the slices into chunks.

"I grew used to our talk," Red Fox said. "The way we shared our thoughts. Do you remember? A man could live forever and never know what that is. How good it can be."

"I remember," Elik said, and she set the bowl in front of him. Then, stealing a glance, she caught the strong outline of his chin, his profile. The coal-black color of his hair. He was still a young man. She didn't know why she kept thinking he was old.

And why wasn't he saying anything about Allanaq? She had been so certain he would ask questions, or worse—accuse of her lying. This was the first time they'd been together since Skinner told. But he hadn't mentioned any of it yet. Not Skinner's death. Not Allanaq's name.

Which meant he still didn't know that Allanaq was here.

And he also didn't know about the bone. She had more than half believed he would find it, even after she'd swallowed it. That he would be able to smell it, or see it, or taste it inside of her. But he didn't. He had entered the house and sensed nothing. That was all. She needn't be afraid. She rose and went to the entry.

Red Fox was still seated in the same position beside the fire pit when Elik returned with a mound of frozen blueberries. She added it to his tray. He scooped two fingers through the mix, pushed it in his mouth.

"It's good," he said, and he belched to show he was content. "This seal Ice Stick caught, it was just last night. He came home in the dark, and no sooner had Spider butchered the seal than Nanogak came in the house. She slipped beneath the furs with him. When she goes home, she'll carry his luck inside her, and share it with his brother, Grayling. And just now, I heard, Mitik is going to do the same thing for Bird's Mouth, so his luck will grow better."

Elik moved Red Fox's empty bowl aside, then offered him a water bladder to drink. He lifted the spout to his mouth, and she found herself staring at his hands, at the band of tattoos circling his wrist.

His fingers also, they were long and well formed, his skin darker than hers. Something in the angle of his hand reminded her of the way he had lifted the tent flap one morning when they were still at the river camp. She had rolled over and there was the sunlight, sitting on those same tattoos. He had laughed when he saw the way she stared, then pulled her to lie on top of his chest.

Red Fox set down the water bladder. "It isn't only the husband's harpoon that draws the seals," he said, and gently, he touched her shoulder.

Elik's breath caught; her voice came in a whisper: "This is permitted?" she asked. "Now?"

"You mean because of the Bladder Feast?" Red Fox smoothed her long hair, pulled it all to one side. "This is the best time. Ice Stick spreads his luck among the women. The women take it home to their husbands. And the souls of the animals will all be watching. They'll look down from the house in the moon, and they'll see how good we are. Even you, you had luck with a seal. You can share it with me." He whispered in her ear, then leaned closer and ran his tongue behind the lobe, inside her ear.

"Remember how it used to be, at the river? The animals saw us couple, and they came. Because of what we did, they will be born again. You with me. Here."

Elik shivered and then found herself wanting this, now, here, with him. Her eyes closed as she leaned into his touch. Her legs felt weak, then warmer. The warmth slipped higher, to her thighs.

She wanted him to keep talking, to hear his voice so clear and sure—the way he used to talk when he was Kaviaq. Not Red Fox. Before there were worries about food and seals, and whether the sky was angry.

He pressed her to his chest and she opened her arms, then clutched him tightly as he reached for the furs on the sleeping bench and dragged them to the floor. He leaned over her, and she opened her mouth against his shoulder, wanting the taste of his sweat, his salt, the memory of how this used to feel.

They had slept; Elik had no idea how long. Her stomach was noisy with hunger. If she had eaten, it must have been a long time ago. She couldn't remember when.

"You are noisy in there," Red Fox teased. He tapped her stomach. "Haven't you eaten? Or did you let someone steal the food from your husband's pot?"

"There's more of the salmon I brought inside," Elik started up, but Red Fox held her back.

"Stay," he said. "I like this better." And he walked his fingers over the rise of her hips, "There is a story," he said. "Of when Raven flew inside the mouth of a bowhead whale and found a spirit living inside, a woman."

Elik laughed and swatted his fingers away. Red Fox

pushed her till she rolled, then he pillowed his head on her stomach. The gurgling noise began again. She started to laugh, but Red Fox was suddenly serious. He stopped her. He lay his ear to her middle, leaned his arm over her shoulder to keep her still. He listened again.

He moved his hand along the soft curve below her navel, and then above the bone of her hips. On both sides, pressing, then feeling. When he looked up, his face was tight and watchful. "What are you keeping from me?"

"What do you mean?" Elik tried to sit.

Red Fox made her wait. He pressed his hand flat on her stomach. "There," he said. "Something is moving."

"I'm hungry—"

"You're lying. Or—" he stopped as Elik sat up. She pulled in her knees, covered herself with her arms. "Is it possible you don't know? When did you last bleed?"

"A year. I told you. Not since my last pregnancy. A year. It was winter, but still early. There was light." Elik tried pulling her thoughts together. "It isn't possible."

Red Fox shook his head. "I'm not a grandmother, to know which way a woman's time moves, which way it doesn't. But there is a child in you, whether you knew it or not."

"I did nothing wrong."

"And yet it shows," Red Fox took hold of her chin, not angrily. He lifted her face toward his. "Your eyes have a shadowed look. And your breasts," he looked down. He was smiling now, pleased at the thought of a child. "They seem darker, the veins show. When will it be born, I wonder?"

Elik pulled away. She hadn't known. She had felt nothing.

"But if we don't know when, then—we don't know, do we, who started the child?" Red Fox's smile fled. "It could be Little-Creek's husband, from before the river camp."

Elik felt for the wall behind her. She leaned back. She felt dizzy. Her ears rang, a high-pitched buzzing that confused her, made it harder to think.

"You were married with Skinner from the Moon When Young Geese Fly?"

Elik shook her head. "No! Earlier." She couldn't guess which path his thoughts were walking.

"He left the Seal People's village . . ." Red Fox counted back. "The warm season When Birds Return. So it had to be after that. Which means he traded for you . . . when? Not long after he left here? So if he started the child—but no. You would be bigger by now."

"And you will have two good children," Elik rushed to add. "Ivalu, and this new one." She thought of Little-Creek, still in mourning. Out of respect for her, she wouldn't say what she remembered, how Skinner shot his semen every which way, too soon and sometimes not at all.

"But then—there was that other husband? Qajak."

"That was long ago—" she said, but loudly, with too much fear. *Please,* she prayed. *Let him believe. Let him not ask more.*

Red Fox paid her no attention. "And Qajak's father? He's dead, I'm certain. He *is* dead. But the son I'll find. If he's alive I'll have to kill him."

"Don't! Please . . ."

Red Fox cocked his head. His mouth shaped one word: "Why?"

"He has nothing you want. Nothing."

"But if he returned," Red Fox reasoned. "He would kill me. You can't say differently."

"If he returned?" Elik repeated, but then she stopped, caught herself before she said more. *He doesn't know that Allanaq's back. Go carefully,* she warned. *Carefully* . . . "He wouldn't need to kill you, if he did come back. Not if he knew his father's soul was at peace."

Red Fox stood. "A man like that," he said. "With his father a powerful shaman—he would think only of revenge. And you," he nodded toward her stomach, "you would admit that, if you knew who the father was. I understand your thoughts, even if you do not. You're trying to protect the child."

"It's yours. It has to be."

Red Fox didn't answer. He found his parka on the sleeping bench, put it on, and then remembered. "You have the gut parka for me? Will it be ready by the Bladder Feast?"

"It's ready now," Elik said, and she pulled a clothes sack out from under the sleeping bench.

Red Fox held up the stiff sealgut parka. He glanced admiringly at the well-decorated stitches, the rows of bright, triangular puffin beaks. The bottom of the sack held another lump. He reached inside again, pulled out more of Elik's stitchwork. "That's mine," Elik said as she reached to take it from him. "I forgot it was there."

But Red Fox wanted to see. He set his own new parka on the sleeping bench, then next to it he smoothed the separate front and back sections of what turned out to be a second, smaller parka. "Black duck-skin," he said, and he smoothed down the shining feathers. He fingered the separate, remaining roll of loose skins: more than two full hands' count. Maybe more. He looked up in surprise. "You didn't catch all these yourself? We came too late in the year."

"Nuliaq gave them," Elik said, and she wondered if she'd done something wrong. "She had already sucked the fat, chewed them clean. So there was little work left. And Little-Creek also gave some. Even Mitik—she traded with me for the marmot I caught at the river. She's generous, a good woman. I like her."

She glanced to Red Fox; his eyes had taken on a distant, almost saddened look. "Was that wrong, trading for the skins?"

"No. A wife of mine should only wear parkas so fine. Didn't I promise that you'd be well treated? And now my own eldest cousin's wife accepts you, not only as a relative, but as a shaman. You should be glad. Isn't this what you wanted? The skins, they're very fine. Will it be finished in time for the Bladder Feast?"

"I hope so, yes." Elik took back the pieces, set them in a different basket. Her thoughts turned to Red Fox's other parka, the one she had burned. If Red Fox worried about this now, he didn't say so.

He tucked the sack under his arm, but he lingered near the door. "What a story that would be, a son of my body born with the name-soul of my enemy? Perhaps a grandson would seek revenge, as much as a son?"

Elik shook her head no. "Allanaq—Qajak—he knows nothing. I swear."

"How strange, that so many people can know so

little? And what about you? Aren't there things you may not know? Qajak is young, and the young are rash. How do either of us know his father didn't pass something along to him—maybe even after he died? Maybe his ghost made itself heard? It might have sung his strongest songs—in a dream or in a vision. Qajak might have them all along. Why would he want his wife to know?

"I had watched him so closely, those last days before I sent them away. He knew nothing. I was absolutely sure." Red Fox pulled himself from the memory. "Do you know why I put them out?"

Elik shook her head. She had heard this story, more than once, but never from Red Fox.

"I had no wish to kill Anguta, only to have him gone before we killed each other, and the Seal People were left without any shaman. Were I to have set Anguta in that boat without his son, there would be no hope he'd survive, not even that first day. As to his son, all his life he had the gift of a flintknapper's hands, not a shaman's inner sight. When he was a boy Anguta used to ask him to help with the ropes, to tie his hands when he tranced. To pass him his drum. Qajak grew up beside him, watching—too often, I think now—the frenzy, the pain that comes over a shaman in his trance.

"He loved his father, but he was a child. He was frightened. He didn't want those things happening to him. He didn't want his soul traveling in the dark, or listening to the voices of spirits speaking through his mouth. Qajak refused the training his father offered and finally, Anguta gave up trying to teach. I think that was when he also stopped caring whether he taught or shared."

"Shared?" Elik didn't understand.

"When Anguta stepped in that boat, he left without sharing his shaman-knowledge. It was the way he had come to live, but it wasn't good. It wasn't right. Seal People are taught to share, food of course, ancestor stories and stories from the First Times. The elders sit in the *qasgi* and share with the boys what they know of the ice, and where the caribou like to cross. Women teach their daughters to flense skins, and how to sew a waterproof boat stitch. A hunter takes a partner; the meat, the skin, the ivory that comes to them is all shared. Nothing is hoarded.

"What Anguta forgot was that the secrets the spirits reveal must also be shared. A man should tell.

"When I first came here, I had been living at Uivvaq, another Seal People village north from here. I was young, but not so young I didn't know what I was. A shaman. One Who Hears Voices—it was true. I heard them, and I longed for them, more than for women or food. Nothing else mattered.

"Anguta watched me before he took me in, he made sure I was someone who had been called, someone who interested the spirits. It was a long while before he was willing to initiate me and become my teacher. He taught me to be wary, lest a spirit enter me when I slept. And to be careful how I ate. He gave me gifts of amulets. And he made promises—"

"The same as Malluar promised me."

"I think so, yes. And as with your Malluar, he taught me a few songs, small songs. But mostly what he did was allow me to bind his hands when he tranced, and pass his drum. Qajak had already been refusing him, you see. So it was me he asked to mix the paints he

used on his masks. To gather wild celery. For a year.
Two years. And then . . ." Red Fox paused, shifting
through memories. "Then, no more. Another year
passed and somehow, in spite of his guardedness, I
grew strong. He grew jealous. Spirits spoke to me. To
him they began giving lies. When I asked for more
learning, he refused. He claimed that talk was going
around, that I had misused the magical words he had
already given and that when he tried to use them, they
were weak. He dared not tell more.

"I would have shared," Red Fox said. "Were I in his
place. Rather than know that all my oldest, strongest
secrets would be lost when I was dead. Maybe when
Qajak was young, he showed none of a shaman's gifts.
But on that boat, who knows what happened? What if
Anguta taught the son, and the son taught the songs to
his shaman wife—to you?"

Elik's eyes widened. "No," she protested. "He taught
me nothing. I know nothing of Anguta's songs. It was
as you said. He was a flintknapper, a carver. If I was
lying, you would know."

Red Fox opened his mouth to say something, but
then he shook his head, deciding against it. He held
Elik's glance a moment, then turned and looked away.
"I believe you," he said. "Perhaps I shouldn't, but I do."

They spoke little after that. Elik followed Red Fox
outside; then, as he turned toward the *qasgi* and preparations for the Bladder Feast, she lowered her head into
the gusting wind and turned along the path behind the
village. She had set her ptarmigan snares in a clump of
willow, and more than enough time had gone by since
they'd been checked.

The walk was slower than she remembered. The

wind came at her from the ground, blowing snow upward toward her face. She pulled her hands inside her sleeves, tugged her hood lower and tried not to think.

In a while more, she came up along the frozen creek, then followed its path as far as the first run of willow. From the scurry of tracks and chips of bark, the spot had seemed promising when she baited her snare. Even so, the first one was empty, though something had stolen the fish she'd wrapped in the noose. She twisted more of the dried fish, smoothed the snow, and righted the trap.

Her second snare, a little farther along the same line of brush, held a white, round ptarmigan.

The bird must have struggled awhile. The snow was pocked with fluttering wing and claw marks, but the ptarmigan was cold already, dead for more than a day. She untangled it from the loop and stored the bird in her bag, then baited the snare again.

From a distance, she could see the third snare was empty, its loop stretched between the willow fence she'd built to lead a bird in. But as she stepped near to check the bait, a ptarmigan rose in fright. Elik jumped back at the blur of white, the heavy rushing air.

Angrily, the ptarmigan flapped its wings in quick alarm, set up a noise. Elik held still, and the bird darted, then flew directly into the snare. The grass ties tore free and the slipknot tightened. The bird screeched and fought in protest, tightening the noose as it thrashed. But then, a little while more, and the bird was dead.

Two birds were a good catch; in coldest weather when the flocks dispersed, she couldn't hope for more. There would be food for the house, enough for a full day, maybe two. She had been eating less, she and Nuliaq all too aware of their dwindling fish supply, the little bit of seal that came their way. What would happen now to the child, also needing food? If there wasn't enough—?

She felt the bird's chest. Wherever it had been eating, it seemed to be doing better than they were. She smoothed the wings, then slipped the bird inside, beside the other. And then she stopped in surprise.

There was a slight fluttering beneath her belt, inside her womb. Not hunger; this time she knew the difference. This was more like fingers, the tiny fingers on a hand, drumming inside her bones.

Whose child was in there, she wondered? Red Fox's? Or Allanaq's? Or Skinner's, though that wasn't likely, from what she remembered of his mostly failed attempts. But it wasn't whose face the child shared that mattered, whether the nose resembled hers, or its eyes were like Allanaq's, or Red Fox's. She would love this child and welcome it, no matter the father. But the soul, the soul inside—that was another matter altogether. There was the free soul, that part of the soul that left the body during dreams and trances, and there was the name soul that could be reborn. Inside a person's body, the name soul would take on breath and live again, legs that walked, arms that threw a harpoon. But who—which soul was inside her?

She loosened her belt so her parka hung free, then dropped to her knees and scooped up a handful of the hard-packed snow. She stood again, pulled off her mittens and let them fall to her feet. Then she pressed her hands together, warming the snow, hurrying it to melt.

Drink, you who are thirsty. Drink from this gift of fresh water.

She slid her hands up inside her parka; then, without a thought to the cold, rubbed the icy shards against her skin. Round and round till the cold snow turned to water, the water dripped. *Drink,* she said again. *Drink deeply.*

And slowly she began to name them, the dead who might be hovering invisibly nearby. Malluar. Skinner. Her own mother, Gull.

Which soul would come at the sound of its name?

Iluperaq, the brother she had lost. Alu, her grandmother. Chevak, her father who'd been so frightened in life, she doubted he would have the courage to come in death. One after the other and some repeated, she named them all aloud. But it wasn't until she whispered the name Anguta that the fluttering began. She felt it, for the first time truly felt it; the weight of a soul, inside.

Anguta? she whispered the name again.

The child moved. She quieted her hands, held them steady.

Was it growing in there? She hadn't paid attention. But it was possible. No. More than possible. It was true. Her middle felt round and fuller than before. Red Fox was right.

And her breasts, didn't they lie heavier against her ribs? Hadn't she complained about her coarse parka skins to Nuliaq? Her nipples had felt raw and she'd blamed it on the parka.

Some women never knew they carried children, almost till the end. They didn't understand until a mother or an aunt started questioning, noticing what they had failed to count. But she had been pregnant before. She'd always lived among sisters, mothers, grandmothers who watched for such signs.

How then was it possible, except that she hadn't been thinking? She was a woman who hadn't bled, not in two long winters.

She felt it again: a lifting on one side of her belly, below her ribs. It moved. A child had woken. Laughed at the sound of its proper name.

Anguta?

Is that why his boots had swayed that day in the river camp? Because they had felt something, sensed the moment when their owner's soul flew near and entered her womb? *Anguta?* Was it true?

But then . . . A different fear knotted her throat. This wasn't the first time she had been pregnant, far from it. Yet each child that had tried to grow inside of her had died.

She didn't want to be like Malluar, burying children with breast milk still moist on their lips. She wanted her child—this child—to live. She wanted it safe. And Nuliaq was right. Red Fox was right—the birth of a child was all the more reason to want its fathers kept alive. Both fathers.

And here was another thought: In the end, no matter all her promises, Malluar had failed to share her shaman-secrets with Elik. And if the few stories Red Fox told were true, then Anguta also had failed to share with him. And standing here today, it seemed that for all the promises Red Fox offered, the same could easily be true again.

Elik moved her hands beneath her parka, feeling along the soft round swell of her stomach. The fluttering was gone. The child was asleep. But here was her promise: if this child inside her now, or any child, was born to be a shaman, then she would teach it.

On the day this child walked up to her with questions, she would answer. She would share. She would teach him to open his eyes to the spirits. She would guide him through the pain of his first trance, and teach his ears to hear the voices of the *inuas*, his mouth to shape their names.

11

There was no sunlight on the first morning of the Bladder Feast, only the dark hard sky of winter and the hiss of wind rushing between houses, angrier each day since Skinner died. It shifted constantly, unreliably, blowing snow so hard it blinded a person's eyes, turned all hope of hunting into a foolish, wasted risk.

Taking small, measured steps, Nuliaq and Elik dragged their carefully hoarded seal poke of soured birds to the *qasgi*. The path was difficult to find, and with their backs to the wind, they marked the way by the upright food racks outside each house: from Mitik's to Old Sheshalik's, then to Spider's, and then, thankfully, out of the wind and into the entry, into the sudden moist heat of the *qasgi*.

There was murmuring inside. The shrill high pitch of wind gave way to the sounds of preparations. Elik wiped the snow from her face and lowered her hood to see, but the talking had suddenly ended. Like a wave moving through the *qasgi*, the silence started near the entry, rolled toward the women's bench.

Elik turned to see what had happened, but Nuliaq squeezed her arm, warning her to hold quiet, not to stare. They dragged the heavy sack the rest of the way to the floor where the women who'd arrived earlier had already set out their food.

This time it was Nuliaq who stopped. Her face grew longer as she looked at the pile—huge heaping trays of fish. Racks of caribou ribs saved from the meager hunt—far more than people could afford to give. Except that being stingy was no better than being wasteful. Only if they were generous and shared would their future hunts be rewarded.

"Don't stare," Elik whispered. "You look as if you're counting every bowl."

"Maybe not the bowls," Nuliaq answered. "But maybe the seal bladders hanging on the wall? That's where the worry begins." She took Elik's hand, led the way past knees and feet to the women's bench.

"Do as I do," Nuliaq whispered. "This first part of the Bladder Feast, before the day when the sun returns, is mostly like other feasts."

Elik removed her parka, then sat. But it wasn't until she pulled her feet in as Nuliaq had, then squinted against the burn of smoke in the air, that she realized the women were watching her. Mitik and Pintail, Spider, White Smoke, and Sister. All in one motion, like a wave, they leaned forward along the bench, checked to see which way she sat, and then leaned back the instant she looked their way.

Had Red Fox told about the child? Is that what this was about?

She blushed to feel the weight of so many eyes on her, but they weren't done. Mitik leaned forward again, offered a half smile, and signaled—something with her hand, but Elik couldn't follow. One Pot coughed, then wiped her mouth, and White Smoke shifted uncomfortably. Pintail hid her gaze behind her baby, playing with his hands, dancing his tiny feet inside her lap, then leaning toward Mitik. "Did she see?" she whispered, louder than she realized.

Mitik shook her head, then signaled for Elik again, this time more definite.

See what? Elik frowned, and she followed Mitik's hand toward the men's row.

The eldest of them were seated in the warmest seats, near the fire pit where they always sat, in the center of the *qasgi's* open floor. The younger boys also kept to the rear, closer to their mothers. The rest of the men sat in rows, like arms from the head of the fire; but this time, Elik saw, they all were watching toward one side. She grew aware of Nuliaq's hand squeezing hers. Her skin prickled, but by then it didn't matter. She had already found the man they were watching. Allanaq.

She couldn't keep from staring. He sat on the outside of the main circle, shoulder to shoulder with Bird's Mouth on one side, Ice Stick on the other, like guardians.

But he wasn't supposed to be here. Hadn't they both agreed? He had promised to finish his father's burial box first. She thought he had understood, promised her a chance to prove that his father was content.

He sat in the same position as any of the other men, legs folded under, a white band on his forehead holding back his hair. All else was naked, except for his paint.

From his shoulders to his arms, from his neck to his waist and down his legs, everything but his face and penis was painted red with white spots.

Her anger fell away as she remembered another time

he had painted himself exactly that way. She grew dizzy with the memory, hot and cold and frightened and lonely, all at the same time. The first day she met Allanaq he had stood just behind Grey Owl in the *qasgi* in her village. It was at a Messenger Feast, when Real People from the Fish River and the Long Coast and the Bent Point villages had all come together. He alone had been a stranger. And she had watched, entranced, as he rubbed one side of his face with black but left the other side human. All through the day he waited, until finally it was his turn.

She remembered how he had swayed with the beat of his dance. And the way he lifted his arms to show his boat—he had reminded her of a creature, a crab who walked out of the sea onto dry land.

The paint was the same, but something was different. The size of the circles on his chest? Or the way they were placed?

That day, their eyes had met across the open floor. He had seemed shy, and younger—she remembered that now. As if his father's ghost stood behind his shoulder, whispering, frightened to find they were lost.

This time, Allanaq held his gaze steady. Nor did he seem anymore like that worried side-stepping crab. No. He sat proud—there was the difference—like a man who had come home. Not a stranger. A man among relatives.

And something else was different, not in Allanaq, but in the *qasgi*. She looked again to the circle of men surrounding him, and this time she saw it—they had seated themselves in different places than usual. That wasn't Bird's Mouth's seat, so close to Ice Stick. Every other time she had been in the *qasgi*, the men had separated themselves by family, the division as thick as ice on a winter lake. Yet here they were today, seated by age alone.

Old Sheshalik then Owl, Bird's Mouth then Ice Stick, Samik then Inuk. The eldest men were nearer the fire pit, the youngest in the rear.

But where was Red Fox?

Elik studied the *qasgi* more closely. The roof planks had been painted to show the stars and daylight. A row of spirit masks hung along the heavier beams. Wolf faces with their eyeholes slit open, so the spirits could see out. Human faces with twisted shaman mouths. There were charms suspended from the roof behind them, the beams all newly washed in urine. Overhead, from the height of the roof, was a large puppet-man in a skin boat, smaller ones behind that. There was an eagle with black feathers attached to wood. A loon with a beak longer than her arm.

And beneath the masks, the seal's dry bladders hung in small batches, tied by their cinched necks to spears that were stuck in the wall. They would be inflated in a few days more, at the end of the feast, when they were tucked alongside the skulls on the mound. For now, the painted black and red ownership marks dipped in and out of the crumpled folds, making it impossible to tell which man was honored with the largest catch, and who had caught but few.

Except that with a season so poor as this, no one here could forget.

Lower down, beneath the bladders, she noticed something else she had missed before. Someone had hung a grass curtain, separating off a corner of the *qasgi*. As she listened a noise began, a rushing sound of wings not unlike the ptarmigan that had thrashed inside her snare.

The sound grew louder, then faint, and then strong again.

All around her, the talking quieted. People turned to the corner. The woven curtain buckled and a moment later Red Fox appeared, drumming and dancing his way toward the center of the *qasgi*. He was wearing the parka she'd made him, panels of gut the color of smoke. Orange puffin beaks and a loon-skull necklace she didn't remember ever seeing before. There were sun and moon circles on his shoulder that made him look wild, beautiful and strong enough to chase any evil away. But what about a man?

Go back, she wanted to warn him. *Behind the curtain. Hide.* She hadn't meant for Allanaq to come. He had promised to wait.

Red Fox's feet lifted and stomped to the double beat of his drum. A sheen of sweat glistened on his forehead and all his attention seemed riveted, drawn to the other world.

There wasn't a whisper, not a sound as he settled himself to his seat. His usual seat, just in front of the fire pit. He shifted the drum over his lap, lifted the beater to start again, but then he stopped. She could see his breath catch, his mouth fall open. He had found him.

Allanaq sat directly opposite Red Fox. His hands were on his knees, his eyes forward, chin lifted to an angle. He had the look of a man who had given up on food, on talk, on every promise but the one he intended to keep with the man in front of him.

Allanaq waited only until he was certain Red Fox

had recognized him. Then he reached deliberately for the food tray in the center of the floor and plucked out the first bit of meat he touched. Purposefully, he rolled the meat between his fingers, then pressed it down through a slit in the floorboards, a taste of food so his dead father could eat.

Elik felt Nuliaq tighten beside her, but Red Fox had already caught himself, smoothed his face. He didn't allow himself a single glance toward Elik, didn't lift his eyes or acknowledge Allanaq's presence.

No one else dared to speak. Bird's Mouth and Ice Stick and most of the other men turned from Red Fox to Allanaq, then back to Red Fox again. The younger boys, who by now should have been hurrying outside to drop their bundles of wild celery down through the skyhole, waited uncertainly for instructions.

Suddenly Red Fox's entire body arched. He threw back his head, balanced his weight on his wrists behind him, and with a frozen, twisted expression, stared toward the roof beams.

At the same moment, a shrill sound began. Not from Red Fox—Elik was sure it wasn't him—but overhead. A voice like nothing she had ever heard. Thin and distant, it came directly out of the mouth of the wooden puppet. "There is but one shaman powerful enough to walk on the bottom of the sea. Great enough to visit the moon," it said, and it moved. Its hands groped the air. Knees jerked, then straightened, jerked again.

Elik turned a questioning glance toward Red Fox, but his body was rigid, more like the puppet than a living man. Only the veins that roped his neck pulsed tightly. His elbows bent at an unnatural angle. He was listening, that was the one thing she was sure of, that he was listening and watching the same as everyone else.

The voice moved. It jumped from one puppet man to the next, to a smaller one in an open, toy-sized skin boat. "Unless anyone here dares to name the dead?"

No one answered, and the voice jumped again.

This time it spoke from Red Fox's mouth, though it wasn't him. His lips never moved. "Unless anyone here knows a song?" The voice crooned and Elik shuddered. "A Song of Power?"

The voice must have weakened Red Fox, because now as Elik watched, his elbows gave out and he collapsed. He fell to the floor, then rolled over. He tried to sit. She almost ran to him—no one else seemed to care.

In a mocking, defiant motion, Allanaq folded his arms over his chest. Bird's Mouth stared at the floor. Ice Stick drew his mouth into a thin, straight line.

"Don't speak," Nuliaq warned, and she put her arm protectively around Elik.

"But what was it? What happened to Red Fox?"

"Nothing. He does that," Nuliaq whispered calmly. "Disguises his voice. That's all."

"No . . . ?" Elik looked to the puppet-boat. Its swaying continued, as if it rode an invisible wave. "It's something else."

"He has tricks—you need to know that. He used to make me help him, but I hate it. He pulls a hidden string, but most often it's when his spirit helpers won't speak. His trance doesn't pull him deep enough."

"Not deep enough?" Elik didn't understand. It was true that Red Fox worried more than he used to. He was preoccupied. Confused about his hunting. But to say he used tricks when his spirit helpers didn't come? "He never showed me tricks."

"Maybe. Maybe you didn't know. Maybe with you he had better luck?"

"Did Anguta also use *tricks*?"

"I don't know," Nuliaq said, but then she dropped her arm from Elik's shoulder, stiffened as she pulled away. "I was his wife. Not his pupil. Now hush—people will hear." Nuliaq glanced past Elik's shoulder to where Mitik leaned forward, clearly trying to listen. Nuliaq stared at the floor. "I only meant that the masks were tricks, the way he moves their mouths. And the carved boat."

Red Fox was talking now, not in that puppet-voice, but his own. He straightened, dusted his hands as if to show that the spirit who had borrowed his mouth was gone now. He was a man again.

With a wry smile, he nodded toward Allanaq. "So. You are alive?" he asked. His voice was dry and taunting. "Or how do we know, with all those spots, you aren't really dead, a ghost who rolled in dog shit to make sure the living could see you? Is that what your paint dots are? Dog shit?"

Allanaq held his peace, waited till he had the attention of every man and woman. He opened his mouth and pushed a lump of meat that had been hidden behind his tongue out to his teeth, where it showed. Then he curled back his lips and spit the grey mass into his hand, then pushed it after the earlier piece, down between the floorboards. "I am alive," Allanaq said.

"Alive, but your mind is asleep. You feed a ghost who is too dead to care."

Allanaq leaned forward and this time he spit on the floorboards: a drink of water to travel with the meat. "Perhaps," he said, goading Red Fox. "Perhaps not."

Red Fox bristled, then calmed himself. "You know nothing," he said. "You come too late to help your father. You are weak and his soul too dead to help. You don't even own his songs . . . or do you?"

Red Fox's fingers started tapping on his knee as he tried to measure Allanaq's reaction. "Do you? I'll spare your life, if you have any. You can't use them yourself, or you would have. But if you shared them, I could use them. They might summon the seals for all of us. I could trance with such a song, visit the seals at the bottom of the sea and beg them to turn this wind."

A sneering voice called from among the men, "The only wind is the one that follows you!"

"Who said that?" Red Fox snapped. He glared at the men behind his seat, and then along his sides, noticing what everyone else had long since seen. Cousins, nephews, Red Fox's relatives. None of them were seated along divided, family lines. They were one village. One group of men ranked by age alone. Samik mixed himself with Ice Stick. Inuk, with his eyes carefully guarded, leaned against Bird's Mouth's shoulder. Mink and Grayling. No Bird and Owl.

Were they challenging him? His own cousins? With his icy stare drawn in now, Red Fox picked up his drum and rose.

The jeering kept on: "Maybe it's Little-Creek's husband, looking for who to blame?"

Old Sheshalik shook his head, silencing the talk. "Enough," he called. "It's better to begin the feast. Let the shaman start his dance."

But Red Fox misunderstood. Angrily, he shook his drum toward Old Sheshalik. "I am the one who says when to begin." He began to drum, but again he misheard the men. Thinking Ice Stick had called another taunt, he spun about and lashed out with a kick, but he was slow.

Ice Stick easily jumped aside and Allanaq, assuming the kick was meant for him, started from the floor. Ice Stick grabbed for his arm to hold him back, but it wasn't any use. Allanaq wrenched free and jumped to face Red Fox.

The shaman stood his ground as if, finally, here was what he'd expected all along. Without saying a word, he passed his drum to Bird's Mouth, knotted his hands into fists, bent his knees.

Allanaq matched his stance. Both men lifted their fists, stepped to one side, then the other.

The floor cleared, men and boys clamoring out of the way. The fire flickered and glared. Elik rose unsteadily from the bench. On shaking legs, she wove her way between the men's shoulders, stepped over their feet.

No one moved to stop the fight.

Allanaq locked his hands on Red Fox's shoulders. Red Fox reached for Allanaq's chest, his heavier weight forcing Allanaq back. But Allanaq was taller, he bore down, stepping sideways around the fire pit rocks. He shifted his balance. Red Fox's knees bent—too far. He lost his footing and Allanaq jumped free, then leaped, quicker than Red Fox could follow.

He seized Red Fox under both arms, tried lifting him, throwing him backward, but Red Fox twisted and broke away. Allanaq's foot caught again on the fire pit;

he flung up his arms for balance, then ducked and leapt for Red Fox.

On the planked ceiling near the skyhole, a stray spark caught Elik's eye. She followed it, glancing to the rafters where the row of spirit masks hung.

The wrestling continued, but she wasn't watching now. The mask's open eye slits were staring directly at her. Their mouths twisted, turned up, then down, then changed their shape.

She couldn't have moved if she wanted to. She stood with her face lifted, her ear turned to hear. Voices. They were talking. Speaking to her.

The clamor of fighting faded in the background. It wasn't words—the sounds were more like wind. Wind, speaking through the open mouths of the spirit masks. Was that her name they called? What were they trying to say?

She looked to where the seal bladders hung from the spears.

She looked to Red Fox's puffed face; his arms squeezed tight around Allanaq's chest as he lifted the younger man's feet from the floor.

Then to the seal bladders again. Something had changed. They had moved. They *were* moving, even as she watched. They swayed as if a wind were lifting them—but there was no wind, only the bladders with the souls of the seals inside. Swaying.

She stood that way a while longer, watching, listening to the wind-sound, wondering if that was their voice. They saw her. They were speaking to her. But why now? Because Anguta's shaman-light had come into her, making her visible? Was that it?

She stood that way a while longer, watching, listening

to the wind-sound. Then she lifted her hand, pointed. And then she spoke. But the voice that came from her mouth was so high and thin, she almost thought it was a child's, except that it was hers: "The seal bladders," she said. "They are awake."

Nuliaq was the first to turn. And then One Pot, then Mitik, and then others, following where Elik pointed. One by one, the women saw her pointing. They grew silent. Spider tapped Ice Stick on the shoulder. Mitik motioned to Bird's Mouth to watch. The men turned from the fighting to watch.

"What's happening?" one of the women asked.

"Is it the wind?"

"Not inside." A man voice answered. "What if it's a *tunraq*?"

"What if it's Skinner? What if he's angry?"

"Where's Little-Creek?"

"Not here. It wasn't safe yet for her to come."

The pitched tension rose. The whispers cut through to Red Fox and Allanaq. They separated, and then stepped back to find the women huddled, the men all staring toward the hanging bladders.

Allanaq looked about, trying to understand, but Red Fox was quicker. He let out a single piercing scream and leaped toward the wall, arms flung out. He landed below the deflated bladders with his knees bent, his feet spread wide.

"It is not Skinner," he called, and he danced back and forth as if he'd known all along this would happen, as if it was exactly as he planned. "That man is safely gone to the Land Below the Sea."

"Who then?" One of the men called.

"The seals are anxious," Red Fox announced in his

sing-song voice. "They want the Feast to continue so they can go home. They wait to be feasted."

"Feasted?" Higjik snorted. "Or starved?"

Controlling his anger, Red Fox cocked his ear as if to show that he alone listened to a message that no one else could hear. "The *inuas* are angry," he said. "They promise that if I trance, they will speak through me. They will say what we should do."

Someone snickered among the men. "The way you told us there were caribou?"

Red Fox turned toward the men. In the press of faces and bare chests, he couldn't find who'd spoken. He moved his gaze to the women, picked Mitik out from the crowd. "You have been frightened," he said in a soothing voice. "There is no need. I will find the cause."

Mitik didn't answer. She squinted into the dim light, exchanged a glance with Bird's Mouth.

"The way you healed Little-Creek's illness?" a woman's voice called out.

Red Fox reeled, studied the women again.

Nuliaq had heard enough. She stepped forward, made her way to Elik's side. She put her hands on Elik's shoulders, faced the largest group of men. "It was Elik who helped Little-Creek. Elik who the spirits speak through—" She paused, waited for the nods of assent. *"Don't be afraid,"* she whispered in Elik's ear. *"You are ready. You are stronger than you know."*

Elik's eyes widened in surprise, but Nuliaq gripped her shoulders tighter. She turned to meet the women's glances. Loudly, she said, "Many of us have already seen the way the spirits speak through Elik. They share their secrets. She is one who sees light where others find only shadow. I say, let her be the one to ask why the Wind is angry."

A murmur of agreement rose through the *qasgi*. Then Allanaq's voice, challenging Red Fox. "Yes," he called. "Let it be her."

Elik lifted her hand to stop them before more fighting erupted, but Nuliaq held her back. *"Let it be,"* she said to Elik. *"Let it play itself out."*

"I don't want him to hate me."

"He won't. He'll respect you. They both will."

Red Fox dipped his head toward Allanaq. "Your words seem fair," he reasoned. "But this woman is only a new shaman. Are you willing to take the risk that her soul might never return from a trance? Let me be the one who questions the spirits. She'll be spared. I won't be hurt."

Ice Stick stepped forward. "I was there when she found the cause of Little-Creek's illness. The spirits spoke. They didn't hurt her."

Owl agreed. "I was there," he said. "If the spirits want to speak through her, they'll do it whether we approve or not. Let her call. If there's a reason for this poor season, we need to know."

Red Fox looked to Bird's Mouth, expecting his cousin to speak in his behalf. But instead of joining Red Fox, he lowered his gaze. Discreetly, he slid back behind the other men.

Red Fox hid his dismay. "I am old," he tried again. "It's true I am only a small shaman. But isn't it better that an old man tries and fails than you permit a pregnant woman to fight with spirits?"

"Pregnant?" Allanaq shook his head, denying it, then turning to Elik to see if it was true.

Red Fox saw his advantage. "I have seen it," he cried, loud enough to demand everyone's attention. He leaned far back, not toward the bladders this time, but the skyhole. And then he leapt, and his entire body seemed to swim through air.

"I feel them. My spirit helpers come near. *Eiee!* They are close by. *Eyaya-eya!* They are here. They speak. Can you feel them? They are here."

Nuliaq kept a tight hold on Elik as Red Fox sprang again. This time when he landed, he let his shoulders slump. His arms hung forward and he started swallowing in noisy, gulping draughts. He flung his head from side to side, stealing glances wherever he was able—to Elik, to Allanaq, to Bird's Mouth—until, finally, he was done.

Exhausted, he shook his chest. "A contest then," he agreed. "The Bladder Feast must wait another day. My spirit helpers are not afraid of her pregnancy. They say better a pregnancy than blood between her legs. They promise that if I visit them in their house, they will reveal the reason the seals hide from our sight. But they will only tell the truth to me."

Nuliaq urged Elik back toward the safety of the women's bench, but before they reached it, Red Fox was at their side. He was overheated from the wrestling. Sweat dripped from his forehead, giving him a wild, darker look. He sent a piercing glance to Nuliaq. She couldn't meet it. He took Elik's hand, motioned toward the bench. "It's all right," Elik said. "I have no reason to be afraid."

Red Fox looked to the entry, wondering whether to leave. But the noise and talk only grew louder as more people saw them standing there. They could say whatever they liked. No one would hear. "So—" he started, but then he hesitated. His face tightened and changed, as if it were at war with itself. "This is what you want?"

"I didn't plan this," Elik said, and she prayed he would believe her. "How could I have?"

"How?" he asked, turning the question around, then lifting his chin toward Allanaq. "I see now there is so much I never asked myself, or you. And when I think back to all those times you swore you wanted to learn—"

"I did. I do. We are the same, you and I. We are not rivals. I want no contest, only to share what we have. Didn't we always say how much alike we are—?"

"Is that true?" Red Fox stopped her. "I don't know. But what if you are wrong, and you are Red Fox to my Anguta?" He shook his head, then chuckled almost bitterly as he realized what he'd said. "Will you put me in the boat because I will not share? Which one of us lies, I wonder? Or is it only that you are young?"

"Please. I know I hid Allanaq's name from you, but only because I was afraid. Anything else, everything, I've told you."

"And yet you think you can best me?" He cocked his head, watching her. "Or did I miss something, and you refused Nuliaq just now?"

Elik's gaze fell. *He was right. And she was hiding more, even now. But why hadn't she resisted?*

Red Fox laughed sharply. "So. It's true. You think the spirits find you more pleasing. Or stronger, worthier than I?"

"No," Elik protested. "Your name was Kaviaq. I didn't plan all this. I didn't know who you were."

"At the beginning, maybe. But then, there must have come a time when you realized. And you thought to yourself, you could have it all? Malluar's wisdom. Anguta's songs. Red Fox's spirit helpers?"

"No," Elik said, and her voice cracked. Her eyes filled with tears. "It didn't happen that way. I found out who you were, and I was afraid, yes. That you would kill me. But also, because of how I felt. I loved you. But if you found out who I was, you would trade me away. Or kill me—how could I know what you would do?"

"How?" Red Fox shook his head. "Think back. Did I show you the path to the moon? Did I not give you a word in the shaman's secret language, and tell you about the pools you would see there?"

"You did. You showed me," Elik said, but she couldn't meet his eyes.

"Then that should be your answer. But enough. We are being watched. My cousins—and yours—they are waiting to see which of their shamans to trust. You choose. Do you want to trance first, or shall I?"

"You," Elik said. "But afterward, when we have time, I'll explain. I begged Allanaq not to come today. He wasn't going to hurt you. I planned it so that all three of us were—"

"Wait." Red Fox shook his head in disbelief. "He told you he wouldn't come, and you believed him?"

Elik's throat closed. She couldn't speak. There were too many things she needed to explain, and not enough time.

She joined Nuliaq on the women's bench. The mothers with the youngest children had hurried to leave and the *qasgi* was less crowded than before. The men settled themselves on the floor and against the walls. The food trays waited where they were, untouched. The dance drums that should have begun the feast were pushed out of the way.

Red Fox stood alone in the center of the floor. He ran his fingers through the ashes in the hearth, then rubbed them into his hair.

To keep this world of the living safe, separate from the invisible, Elik thought. She nodded. She would have done the same.

He called for a clean mat to sit on, so nothing could crawl up inside him while his arms were tied. He picked Bird's Mouth out from among the men, pretended not to notice how his cousin avoided his eyes. "Drum for me," Red Fox asked. "When the lights are out, and my soul leaves my body. Keep a way open for me to return."

Bird's Mouth agreed but he moved slowly, almost reluctantly. He took the drum, but the seat he chose was as far from Red Fox's accidental touch as he could reach. By then, the fire had been dampened, the *qasgi* made dark.

Elik listened to the shuffling sound of Samik binding Red Fox's thongs, then returning to his seat. Another man coughed. Bird's Mouth spit on the drum, then began the same slow double beat Red Fox had taught her at the river: loud enough to hammer a person's blood, repetitive enough to lull them to sleep.

She wished the dark weren't so thick; there was a part of her that would have preferred to see. She remembered when she was a child, and the shaman Seal Talker warned people never to watch while he entered a trance. He told of the way a person's soul would be stolen if they did. They would go blind. They might die, or worse.

But sometimes it would be summer when he tranced. Their caribou hide tents couldn't be fully darkened, and her mother would show her how to cover her face with her hands, so she wouldn't see. But Elik did see. She wanted to. She opened her hands and stared between her fingers, and tried not to scream as Seal Talker fought and thrashed and heaved himself against the floor.

Did it hurt him? She asked her mother later. But her father heard her questions—he always heard. And his arm darted out and cuffed her ears. *Stay away from shamans*, he warned her soundly. *Don't let them look inside your soul.*

The smoke burned and Elik's eyes grew heavier. She locked her arms around her legs, cradled her head on her knees. The only sound was the double beat of the drum, quick and loud, endlessly pounding.

Until slowly, slowly, something began to change. The drumming slowed. Higher up near the skyhole, a different sound emerged. Elik stiffened with anticipation. It was a sound like wind rushing through willows, but muffled, as if she were inside the tent again in the river valley.

She sat up straighter, pulled in her legs. If Red Fox's helping spirits had entered the *qasgi* she didn't want them finding her. She didn't want them hovering nearer to her than anyone else.

But then, out of the dark, someone screamed. It was long and shrill and Nuliaq's hands flew up to cover her ears. Bird's Mouth's drumming faltered, then lost the beat.

"It is enough," Red Fox cried. "Be done."

Somewhere near the bladders, she heard the sounds of a struggle. Two people fighting, maybe more? They grappled and fought as Red Fox begged his spirit helpers to speak, reveal the truth.

The fighting went on. The sound of feet slamming, and then claws scratching on the floorboards. She heard a wolf's howl and then the sound of wings, heavy and near. More scratching, and then human voices, so many that she didn't know what she heard, or how much time had passed, or what had happened.

Until suddenly, the quiet returned. There was a heavier shuffling and footsteps and finally, coals being blown to life. Someone fed shavings into the fire—Inuk, it turned out to be. Bird's Mouth opened the sky-hole. A thin stream of light revealed Red Fox lying on the floor. His hands and feet were free—the thongs lay strewn about the floor.

Bird's Mouth and Inuk, then Ice Stick and a few other men rose and waited to see if he was all right. Elik leaned to the side to see past them. Red Fox sat up but he seemed weakened by the ordeal. His eyes were darkly rimmed, his face mottled and shining with sweat. And now she saw a streak of blood at both his wrists and around his ankles.

Inuk walked a circle behind Red Fox, searching along the floor. What was he looking for? A knife? *Tricks*, Nuliaq had whispered. *Is that what Inuk was trying to find?* Red Fox sat without moving, unaware of the man's presence.

Bird's Mouth squatted down beside Red Fox. "What did you learn?"

"Tell us."

"Will the sky clear?"

Red Fox rubbed his arms. "Wild they are," he whispered, and his voice came out grainy and hoarse. "Different from us."

"Who is different? What did you see?"

"Harmony must be restored. Someone has transgressed. I see a house," Red Fox leaned to the side and pointed, as if everyone could see it on the floor, exactly as he had. "The house was the same as the houses of the Seal People, with a roof and a skyhole and a polar bear hide covering a door—except the door was tiny. There was a tunnel entry, with a fire burning in the room at its end. I crawled in," Red Fox said. He paused and lifted his glance, let it linger on the face of a man here, a few of the women there, gripping their attention, holding it with fear.

Elik listened closely. The vision was familiar enough, the house and light reminded her of her own vision, one she'd had when she first met Red Fox. She looked for Allanaq, found him carefully shielded behind Grayling and Owl. His head was bowed, but he was listening.

Red Fox's voice grew louder. "The walls shone with ice, and I nearly stopped. Gladly, I would have run, except that I heard a voice call. '*Qamma*,' it said to me. 'You are wanted.' And so I followed—why else had I come? The tunnel led to a room with a planked flooring, walls of upright poles. A sleeping bench was built along three sides—no different than a human house—except that on the bench four people were sitting. A Seal-woman with spotted brown hair and a round, dark nose."

Elik's stomach knotted. *A man who was part beluga, part wolf . . .*

"The next man had the tail of a whale, and the legs of a wolf," Red Fox continued, exactly as if she'd whispered in his ear.

"Next sat a Loon, and then a Wolverine, not animals, but spirits wearing their human faces. The Wolverine-man asked for a drink."

Elik listened in disbelief. That was her vision. She had told him that story. It was she they had called *Qamma* for. Why was he lying? Why didn't he tell what he saw?

"That's a good sign," Sister called, but Mitik hushed her.

"The sign will be outside," she said; then while others nodded and agreed, she turned a tight glance to Red Fox. "Tell us what they said."

"'We are thirsty,' they said. 'We have been treated poorly. Someone has eaten an animal of the sea together with an animal of the land. Why,' they asked me, 'when we never moved together in life, must we lie together in death?' They asked that I return and bring them water."

"Did they take back the storm?" One Pot called.

Red Fox accepted a dipper of water from Bird's Mouth. He lifted it, then watched Elik over the rim as he drank. She lowered her gaze. "They asked that first, I return with their water and bring the confession of whoever committed this wrong."

One Pot rose unsteadily from the bench. Nuliaq took her arm, helped her stand, then shuffle two steps forward. "Go," One Pot directed the men. "Tell us what you see outside."

Inuk and Ice Stick moved quickest. Samik pulled on his boots and parka, not wanting to be left behind. Within moments, most of the men were gone. Allanaq kept his seat against the wall. He sat with a quiet dignity, watching, but not staring at Red Fox. The *qasgi* filled with women's voices. A few more people stepped outside, and finally the waiting grew too hard. Elik reached for her parka, followed the others outside.

Except that as soon as she pushed aside the outside door, it was nearly impossible to see. There was no day, only white and wind and the prick of snow pelting her face. The cold burned inside her chest when she breathed, and she grabbed for her hood and lifted it, then shielded her eyes with her arm. She searched for the path, but couldn't see it, nor the houses nor the food caches. Nothing in any direction but wind and swirling snow.

And then, out of the storm, she heard men's voices. Bird's Mouth first—he appeared suddenly, almost in front of her face. His eyes and hair and forehead were caked with snow. His mouth held a look almost of fear.

Behind him, she heard the other men: *No change. No break in the wind.* They saw her, then lowered their glances and quieted when they realized who she was. They ducked their heads, made their way back inside.

No one had to tell Red Fox there was no change in the weather. By the time Elik followed in behind the others, he had already moved to sit between Old Sheshalik and Bird's Mouth. The center floor sat open again; his drum and thongs had all been cleared.

She lowered her hood and caught Red Fox's voice, explaining: "You see?" he said. "It is exactly as they warned. They promised nothing before I returned. Not for anyone. The Seal-woman, and the Wolverine-man were covered in the richest furs. They said—"

Red Fox stopped as he realized no one was listening. Every set of eyes, from the youngest to the oldest, had turned to watch Elik enter. He lifted a hand, pointed toward the bladders. But no one saw. His shoulders slumped at the insult. Didn't it matter to them that he was the one who had promised to find what was wrong? He would trance again, and next time—he prayed—something would happen. Elik would find nothing, and the people would look to him again. After she tranced, and they saw the wind remained. They would look to him.

Elik crossed the few steps from the entry to the caribou hide that had been laid out on the floor. Mitik came up behind her, took her parka even before she asked. Elik thanked her with a small nod, then closed her eyes and let the fire warm one side of her breast, the length of her side.

Why had Red Fox told them one of her visions instead of his own? Was this a test of some kind he was putting her to? But what if she succeeded in changing the weather after he had failed? Wouldn't that only justify his anger? Unless he was trying to see if she was worthy of his respect? Which was exactly what she had planned—for him to respect her power, enough so he saw the sense in sharing. He would turn away from Allanaq's fight. But he was proud; she would have to go carefully.

She opened her eyes. "Mitik," she said. "You and Spider go outside and tramp on the snow around the *qasgi* so nothing comes inside. Ice Stick and you, No Bird," she picked out men from both Allanaq's and Red

Fox's relations. "I need you to go on the roof and call loudly for the spirits to come cut holes in the sky, let the clear weather enter."

No Bird rose, but he hesitated. He looked toward Red Fox, expecting to be told to stay, keep his place. But Red Fox only sat. His hands were folded on his knees, his face masked and controlled.

Bird's Mouth motioned to No Bird, hurrying his younger brother outside. "Do as she says. There's no harm in trying."

"No harm?" No Bird asked. "We are already being punished. If this storm comes because we've done something wrong, it's Red Fox who should trance again."

"It was Red Fox who agreed—let her try."

No Bird rubbed indecisively at his mouth. He looked to Red Fox, but the shaman's eyes were lowered. He looked to his wife, Sister, then seemed surprised to see her motioning, hurrying him toward the entry. No Bird murmured something, an apology, an excuse—Elik couldn't' hear which—but he turned and followed outside, behind Ice Stick and the women.

Masking her relief, Elik took up a bundle of dry grass and started shaking it, pointing it in each of the world's directions. No sooner was she done than Bird's Mouth stepped up to her. She tensed until she realized the cold judgmental eyes she had feared weren't there. He stood respectfully in front of her, holding out the braided thongs Red Fox had used to bind his hands.

Elik lifted her hand to take them, but then stopped. She was a woman with a child inside. Surely the spirits wouldn't require her to writhe and flail on the floor? She looked for Allanaq, found him in the same place as before. But this time his head was lowered, hidden behind his hands. She remembered the pained look in his eyes when he spoke about her trancing. That time, among the graves, neither of them had known about the child. How much harder would it be if he also had to watch her on the floor that way?

Behind her, No Bird and Mitik and Ice Stick climbed back inside the *qasgi*. Their shoulders were riddled with snow, and with the way they dried their faces on their sleeves, no one needed to ask if the storm had calmed.

No. She would do this differently and the spirits would come or not. It would be their will, not hers.

She looked to Bird's Mouth. "No, thank you," she said modestly. "I need to see. In the land where I will visit, a woman must walk with care."

The *qasgi* filled with an expectant silence. One more time, she glanced about. Bird's Mouth stood beneath the skyhole, waiting for her word to close it. With his gaze lifted again, Allanaq watched from behind Ice Stick's shoulder. Red Fox stared at the wall. Only Nuliaq smiled her encouragement. She dipped her head, mouthed the words: *It's time.*

Elik nodded. "The way is made ready for me," she said.

"Let it be so," the ritual answer followed.

She took a breath, closed her eyes. Anguta was inside her—no one else knew that. He would be with her in this trance, and she would be powerful in a way she never had been. She would close her eyes on the world around her, and the *inuas* would see her strength. They would help her. She would beg them, and whatever they asked of her she would do. The storm would clear and the seals would come again.

In the dark, Elik grew keenly aware of the smoke burning her eyes, of an ache in the small of her back, a heaviness in her breasts—she pushed it away. Pushed away the discomfort of her dry mouth and the sound of blood pressing in her ears. She pushed away everything, and in its place held one thought, the one lesson Malluar had long ago taught: to seek the inner calm of *qarrtsiluni*, the place of vision and light where all the hidden spirits of the air, the earth, and the sea would be revealed.

Qarrtsiluni. She gave herself to it, let it fill her. Let it be as if the earth was falling away beneath her and she were being pulled down, far down, into a place where a song appeared in her thoughts, a prayer to the seals, telling of their need to hunt. *"We stretch forth our hands,"* she heard herself sing . . .

> *We stretch forth our hands*
> *To lift thee up from the sea.*
> *We are without food,*
> *Without fruits of our hunting.*
> *Come up then from below,*
> *From the hollow place*
> *Force a way through.*
> *We are without food,*
> *And here we lie down.*
> *We lie down.*
> *We are without food.*

Elik woke in a thick layer of darkness. She was lying on a planked floor, a hard mat beneath her. Vaguely, she remembered she was in the *qasgi*. Someone was talking—a strange voice, loud and thick.

But her thirst! Her mouth was dry beyond tolerance. She tried to call, to say something, but the rasping grew louder and closer. And the words, they were coming from her mouth, she could hear them now: "I see a seal," the words said.

But whose voice was that? Not hers. What did it want?

"A dead seal on the near shore ice—"

She couldn't stop the words, her lips moving, forming sounds against her will. She grabbed for empty air. She felt someone stop her, grab hold of her arms. But the flood of words—it kept coming.

"A carcass . . . abandoned! Raven gnaws its flesh. Owl watches from above. A hawk picks its eyes. And the seal cries for its thirst. It cries to return home, back to its house beneath the sea.

"Who promises water, then lies?

"Confess.

"Who abandons my soul on dry land, cut off from its homeward path? Confess, and the wind will cease . . ."

She started to choke, and then to cough. She doubled over, grabbed for her neck, her chest, until finally the gagging passed. Her eyes opened and she looked up to find Nuliaq's troubled face peering down at hers.

One last shudder wracked her body. "I am bones," she said, and though the words were strange, the voice was hers again, a hoarse and frightened whisper. "I am bones. Bleached bones. All flesh disappears—"

Nuliaq's frown deepened. She glanced behind her shoulder to see if anyone heard. "Where did you learn those words? Who told you to say that. No—don't answer. Just sit here. Be still."

She muscled Elik around to her lap, steadied her while she lifted a water bladder to her mouth. Elik drank while Nuliaq smoothed her hair and smiled and nodded toward Mitik and a few of the men, showing how she had come back, she was well again.

Elik's shaking calmed and she sat up on her own, but she felt cold now, chilled in every part of her body. "What happened?" she asked.

Nuliaq patted her shoulder. "Nothing. You lay quiet so long, the men already checked outside. There's no change in the weather. I'm sorry."

"No change?" Elik tried to remember what that meant.

"A little, maybe. Old Sheshalik said it wasn't enough yet to hunt without getting lost. He did say there were signs of moisture in the air."

"That's all? I lay quiet?"

Nuliaq stared at Elik's rumpled hair, considering. "You remember nothing?"

"Nothing," Elik said, then more urgently: "What did I do?"

"You slumped to the floor, the same as Red Fox in a trance. You lay quiet. And then there were noises, as if there were seals dragging across an ice floe. We don't know, we couldn't see. But then you started singing. You prayed for the seals to come. And then it was quiet, for such a long while, Bird's Mouth finally opened the skyhole, and when the light struck your eyes you started to choke. You were babbling. Talking strange words. Elik, I'm sorry."

Elik touched Nuliaq's hand. The weather had not cleared, but in an odd way she felt grateful, almost relieved. It hadn't been her wish to surpass Red Fox in a contest, or celebrate while he lost face in front of the village. That wasn't the way she had planned.

And yet, she was also troubled. Something more was needed to turn the storm. She hadn't expected that. She had thought that with Anguta inside her, the spirits would have been content. They would have consented to help.

Instead, it seemed now that though his spirit was inside her, it was asleep, the same as her unborn child was asleep inside her womb. It hadn't opened its eyes yet and till it did, it could not see. It knew no words, and so it could not speak.

Something more was still needed before the seals would answer her request. She didn't know what.

A shadow crossed the floor and Elik looked up to find Bird's Mouth standing behind Nuliaq. He stepped closer, then squatted on his heels beside her. "What seal were you speaking of?" he asked gently. "No one knows of any seal."

Ice Stick came and sat beside Bird's Mouth. Reluctantly, he agreed. "We counted every seal that was taken, every skull brought home and added to the mound."

Elik turned from Bird's Mouth to Ice Stick, to the seal bladders on the wall, trying to remember. She looked for Red Fox, and then for Allanaq; out of everyone in the *qasgi* only those two refused to look at her. She turned back to the two men in front of her, and then she smiled. Never, from the time she first came here, had she seen them willing to sit down together. Did they even notice it themselves?

She looked at them again. Bird's Mouth, the heavier, round-faced man. Ice Stick with his long legs and skinny frame. As unlike as any two men in the village. She had seldom seen them together.

Except once, she remembered suddenly. The tall frame beside the wider one—they had been standing side by side. It had been on the ice, before the storm began. They had been among the men when Red Fox shot Skinner. "No. There is one more seal," she said. "Skinner's seal."

Sadly, Bird's Mouth disagreed. "We were there when he died," he said. "He had no seal."

"But he did," Elik glanced up in time to find Red Fox's eyes widening as he too remembered. "He was dragging it home when Red Fox and I saw him, out on the ice beyond the pressure ridge. He'd been out hunting—"

Bird's Mouth stopped her. "What were you doing on the ice?"

Elik hesitated, long enough for Red Fox to jump to his feet and answer for her. "Nothing," he called. "I brought her along to help drag the seal home. Nothing more."

Elik frowned, then decided it was better to ignore the lie. "Red Fox had taken me out to hunt. We found a seal, but Skinner had already killed one farther out. It will be there still, at the base of the pressure ridge where he left it. Probably under a drift of snow—unless it was found by a polar bear and dragged away."

Old Sheshalik pulled himself up from the floor. "I've heard of stories like this," he announced. "A seal like that could easily bring bad weather. If it was allowed to lie there, forgotten. Wasted."

"This is true," Bird's Mouth agreed, and he looked

to Red Fox. "If it's left out there, what more could happen?"

Red Fox rose, stepped toward the fire pit to speak. "Nothing will happen," he answered, as if it was all so plain. "If the seal's spirit came looking for the man and the man was dead, the seal would go away. It will not search for something that isn't there to find."

Most of the men seemed to agree. Heads nodded. The women murmured among themselves. Red Fox let go the breath he'd been holding. He nearly smiled until, from his seat in the darker corner, Allanaq began to laugh.

Red Fox's eyes narrowed in again. He lifted his hands in a derisive gesture, but Allanaq pretended not to see. Instead, he turned, and tried to reason.

"Isn't it also true," he said calmly, "that since the man who caught the seal is dead, the seal's anger remains, like a sour taste in its mouth? It can as easily turn from the dead man's harpoon to the closest place it finds . . . the man's village? This village, that neglected it?"

"What neglect?" Red Fox answered, and his voice grew louder as he saw the men's faces grow longer, more puzzled. "Will you listen to a woman, worried because she carries a child . . . my child," he added, and he brushed Elik's shoulder in a concerned, protective gesture. "She has spoken about the years of hunger her people often faced. She is worried, and what new mother would not be, fearing there might be no food for the winter? Starvation in the spring when her child is born?"

And then, with a sudden high-pitched shout, Red Fox lifted his arms and jumped, then came down, snatching one of the large willow-hooped spirit masks from the wall.

Without taking the time to tie it properly, he held the mask in front his face, bent his knees, and started to dance. The mask was no human face but something twisted, one eye high and one where a cheek would have been. Through the hole of its hungry mouth, Red Fox made his voice solemn and loud. "The Bladder Feast must continue," he called. "The men must carry the bladders to the seal skull mound. But only those men who were honored with a catch. All others must stand back. The women must lift their bowls to the moon and pray that something drops down.

"Let the man who has no catch lend his wife for a night to a man who has. So the strength of that man's hunt will fill her, and she may bring it home. Let the man with no catch . . ."

Elik stopped listening. Red Fox's insults had driven Allanaq to his feet. His hands were clenched, his voice smoldering. "Enough! I will not be insulted," Allanaq said. "Not when I have traveled so far to come home. Have your feast, but don't look to see another day after. Not alive." Then he turned, climbed down the entry-well without looking back.

Red Fox spat another insult, laughing when it brought no answer. He started repeating his instructions for the feast, praising the men who had caught seals. Upbraiding the one man who had none. Until out of the corner of his eye he caught sight of Elik reaching for her parka. Perplexed, he lowered the mask. "Where are you going?"

Elik stopped where she was, then turned, searched for a way to answer. "Wait for us, please," she said. "I'll come back. I'll bring Allanaq. We have to . . . We need to . . . We need to all be here." Then she turned again, climbed over the women's feet, hurried as the men moved to open a path for her to leave.

"No. Stay—" Red Fox protested. "There's more you have to learn. I'll teach you. The women's dance. You have to learn."

He followed as far as the entry. "Tomorrow—we have to trance again tomorrow," he called, but she was already gone.

The instant she was outside, the wind rose and circled her feet. It was ground snow, *aganik*—gritty and hard. No softer *kanik* flakes that would fall from the sky when the storms had passed.

Elik lifted her hand against the freezing gusts and searched for a shape, a hint of which way Allanaq had gone. But there was nothing. No sign. No sound except for the wind.

She bent down to examine the path, but the loose swirl of snow made it too difficult to tell which tracks were new, which belonged to the men who'd gone out earlier. With a knot in her stomach, she listened to the plea in Red Fox's voice. She felt torn. Part of her wanted to go back, tell Red Fox not to worry. She would find the seal, and its spirit would lift the wind. Red Fox could hunt. Allanaq could hunt. Their house would fill with meat, not jealousy. Whatever gift the spirits gave her, she would share.

But first, she had to find Allanaq. Red Fox might be following, and they weren't ready to do anything yet but fight. But which way had Allanaq gone? To Ice Stick's house? That was likely. Though he might as easily have chosen his abandoned house, or gone to Little-Creek. Or even back to his ice cave, if he was angry enough.

She chose a path, it didn't matter which, so long as

there was a chance of finding him. Slowly first, then hurrying. The houses were barely visible, more like hills in a distant fog. She turned several times, stopping, taking her bearings, then turning again. And then somehow, thankfully, she saw him, the back of his parka the one dark shape against the dusk and grey of pelting snow.

This time she did call, loudly, praying he would hear. And he did; he looked back over his shoulder as if he'd been expecting she would follow, then waited for her to reach him. They stood with the ruffs of their hoods touching, a look almost of embarrassment between them. But then quickly, before he asked about the pregnancy, or the trance, or any of the questions she knew were there, she spoke first. "Where are you going?"

"I don't know, but I won't let that man shame me. Not again."

"No, he won't. I promise——" she added a lie: "He said so. If you brought the seal, he would understand. I know where to find it. You can bring it to the Bladder Feast."

Allanaq stood stiffly where he was.

"With a seal, he can't deny you anything. He said so. His catch would be no prouder than yours."

"One seal? Skinner's seal. What pride is that? It takes three bearded seals to fill a poke with oil. A family needs more if it doesn't want to starve. A hand's count. Twice that."

"In another season, perhaps," Elik tried to reason. "But this year? No one is boasting. We are all afraid."

"The seal isn't mine," Allanaq said, but though the words were firm, the sound was more a question.

"It belonged to your hunting partner, therefore to

you." Elik said, and she prayed he wouldn't remember how sorely she'd begged him not to become partners with Skinner.

"Why do you care? Why do you want me to have it?"

"I don't want you angry."

"I am angry."

"So the Sky sees. The Wind hears."

"As does my father."

Elik winced, but she wouldn't stop. Tentatively, she reached for his hand. "I know. I understand. But what pride do you offer your father, if you haven't proved to Bird's Mouth and his brothers and the rest of the village that his son is a worthy man? Bring home your hunting partner's seal. Feast its bladder alongside the others. And if it turns out that that was the seal who brought the wind, then you would be helping all of us. The seal, your father, Skinner, your people."

Elik waited. Allanaq had stepped away and she couldn't read his face. His shoulders seemed tense, his thoughts all knotted. He turned to the *qasgi*, then hesitated. He turned toward the ice, the houses, the ice again.

His silence made it difficult to wait. She opened her mouth to say more, to plead, even lie if she had to, but he turned before she could speak.

"I have it," he said, and one side of his mouth lifted. "We'll take the dog."

Was that a smile? Elik wasn't certain. "What dog?" she asked, but then she had to hurry, lower her head into the wind as Allanaq strode quickly along the path. She followed behind him—to Ice Stick's house, for a weapon, she thought—until he stopped at the tall food cache outside Nuliaq's house.

And now she saw what dog he meant: the large,

long-haired black and white male that often woke her at night. "Little-Creek's dog? What do you want from Little-Creek's dog? She told Red Fox to keep it."

"I know this animal," Allanaq said as he bent to untie its line from the post. "I used to catch it tearing rabbit skins off their stretching boards, more than once. It was Skinner's. That's why it was here with Little-Creek. It's a good tracker."

"A tracker? You mean on the ice?"

"Yes. And on the path. It'll follow Skinner's scent." Allanaq knelt in the snow while the dog pressed its snout into his hands, his crotch. Its tail beat eagerly as Allanaq held it by the long-haired scruff of its neck.

Elik took the dog next, while Allanaq gathered lines and an ice-testing harpoon. By the time they were ready, the dog was pulling excitedly from her grip. He jumped forward, unconcerned with the wind, as Elik led the way down from the houses and onto the piled ice that rimmed the shore, and then out.

The village was quiet when they returned with the seal. Allanaq stopped to change his grip on the drag handle. Elik knelt beside the dog, whispering in its ear to keep it calm and quiet.

Behind them the boat racks stood empty, waiting for another year. The houses too were closed, skyholes shuttered, saving wood. Even the *qasgi* showed no sign of life. Elik glanced to the seal mound where fresh snow blanketed the skulls on the top layers. White on white, they were buried now, nearly invisible. No sign of the gaping eyeholes showed. No voices, except for the high, shrill pitch of the wind—which was just as well. She didn't want to hear their words just now. Her own were confusing enough. She remembered them now, the words she had spoken in her trance. *The seal cries to return home, back to its house beneath the sea.* Those were the words. *Confess, and the wind will cease.*

But the wind had not ceased. Overhead, a narrow hazy band circled the moon—another sign the storm would stay.

She searched around the corner where she remembered finding the fallen skull. If it was there, it was too deeply buried under the snow to find. She would have picked it up. If she was able, she would even have climbed the driftwood legs and returned it to the others.

Why hadn't the spirits called back the wind? That was what she wanted to know. What else did they want from her? How could she prove to them she was worthy?

She turned, hurried after Allanaq.

No one was inside the house, though there were fresh footprints in the snow outside the entry, small ones that must have belonged to Nuliaq. Elik's oil lamp had been lit, though it was sputtering now, the wick too short for the shallow pool.

While Allanaq tied the dog outside and tossed it a bit of frozen fish, Elik dragged the seal to the middle of the floor. She took down her wick bag, refilled the lamp from a belly-sack of fish oil, then waited the few moments it took for the moss to catch and the light to spread.

The house was warm enough to take off her parka. She beat the snow from the arms and shoulders, then wiped her damp hair, her face and eyes. She was tired, past exhaustion, but there was too much work even to consider sleep.

She pushed the seal onto an old scrap of caribou, then dragged it nearer the lamp. It wasn't till she pulled out her *ulu* that she realized Allanaq had entered. He stood stiffly inside the door flap, taking in the row of Red Fox's harpoon shafts along the wall, the cooking pot, the rich piles of furs on the sleeping bench, and Elik.

Elik lowered her gaze, ordered her thoughts to stay on the seal, only on the work in front of her. She rolled the frozen body to its back, then quickly dug her knife in for the first slice through the skin. Then again, deepening the cut. A single line from the throat to the anus. Another around the head, above the flippers. The work would have gone more quickly if the muscle wasn't frozen so hard, but there was no time to wait for the seal to thaw. She peeled back the skin. Later, she would ask Old Pot which way the Seal People shared out their meat, whether the skin should go to one of Allanaq's relatives, since this might be considered his First Catch, or if Little-Creek should name the shares.

Tomorrow, after she'd slept, she would find a way to show Allanaq there was no more need to fight. The part of his father's soul that carried his spirit was inside her now. Anguta had come home, through his name. He would be born again.

For now she concentrated on opening the abdomen, exposing the intestines. A few more cuts and finally, the entrails were free, piled up beside her on the floor.

She stretched her shoulders, wiped her hands and knife on the mat, then turned to find Allanaq still standing by the door. Politely, as if she were the newest of wives, she lowered her gaze. "Do you want to do this part?" she asked. "For the bladder?"

Allanaq opened and closed his mouth as if he were

at war with himself. "In Red Fox's house, you think I can honor the seals?" he asked.

"It's only a house," Elik tried to sound reasonable. "Nuliaq said it was built by her cousin Owl before he married Higjik, and—"

"This is Red Fox's house, Red Fox's harpoons. And if I touch that seal, it will bring nothing but hate."

"I will do it then." Elik shrugged, trying to show it didn't matter. "All you need do is mix the paint to add your ownership marks, for tomorrow."

Allanaq stood absolutely still, his tension smoldering. "How can you work so easily?" he asked. "Pretending it doesn't matter whose house this is. Or whose bed—" he stopped, turned to listen as the dog barked sharply outside. He lifted the door flap, held it open the smallest crack. "Someone is coming," he said.

"Red Fox!" Elik scrambled to grab Allanaq's sleeve, pull him from the entry. "Get back," she whispered urgently. "You have to hide." She looked to the furs, the grass mat lining the wall above the sleeping bench. The skyhole . . . "Climb out," she pulled him toward the middle of the floor, but Allanaq resisted.

"What are you doing," he shook off her hold on his arm. "I'm not a coward . . ."

Elik stopped. Allanaq's face as he jumped back to the door was frozen and hard. He held a knife; one in his hand, a second tucked inside his boot.

The shuffling moved inside the cold-trap. It grew louder, the sound of something being dragged, a weight set down.

"If you won't run, then wait behind a mat. Please." She tried again to pull from the door. "Find out what he has to say," she begged. "Don't kill him."

"Why?" Allanaq flattened himself against the wall beside the entry. "Stand over there—" he pointed. "Move away. Why do you care so much whether he lives?"

"Bird's Mouth will kill you—by sunrise I'd be mourning. Red Fox could already have you killed by now. Easily. He didn't try. Maybe your father saved that seal for you. Maybe he wanted . . ."

The door flap lifted. A mittened hand reached inside and Allanaq leaped. He grabbed hold of a furred sleeve and yanked at the same time as he lifted his knife, brought it slashing down, cutting toward the sleeve, the arm. Except somehow, he'd forgotten about the bear hide door. His knife caught on the thick edge and slowed. He cut through hide first, then through the thick fur of a parka sleeve—too fast to stop himself as Nuliaq screamed.

"What—?" She stumbled forward, fighting for balance. Her gaze flew up to find Elik first; then reeling about, she turned on Allanaq. He had already loosed his grip and stepped back, as surprised as she was.

Nuliaq clutched her arm. The sleeve was cut. Blood wicked through, darkening the furs. "Bring something!" she called to Elik, then: "It doesn't feel deep." With a measured glance she looked from Elik to Allanaq to the seal. She sat herself down beside the fire pit, opposite the partially butchered remains.

"He thought you were Red Fox," Elik apologized, as she passed across strips of her softest calfskin.

"So I guessed," Nuliaq said dryly.

With Elik's help, they pulled off the parka, examined the cut. "It isn't bad," Nuliaq said. "Maybe you could bring some of that seal fat? I'll wrap it together."

Elik hurriedly sliced off a thin chunk of yellow fat.

"Draw a circle with it," she suggested as she squatted next to Nuliaq. "That helps stop anything from getting in."

Nuliaq lifted her brows.

"Malluar taught me that," Elik quietly added. "The shaman from my home."

"She might better have taught you about pregnancy."

Abashed, Elik lowered her gaze. "I'm sorry," she whispered. "I didn't know."

"And you?" Nuliaq glanced pointedly at Allanaq. "You're a husband. Did no one ever tell you that a pregnant woman must be careful? Always careful?"

Allanaq said something, too quiet for Nuliaq to hear. She choose to ignore it, fussed instead with wrapping the bandage around her arm. "So, Qajak?" she said when she was done. "You meant to kill Red Fox? Come, sit here by your wife's lamp."

Quietly, shamefaced, Allanaq sat where Nuliaq pointed.

"Share this story with me——" she said, and she used the same voice she might have with Ivalu. "Tell me what you've planned."

Allanaq rubbed his hands down the length of his legs. "He needs to be dead."

"Ah. I see. And do you remember who I am?"

"Of course I remember." Allanaq said tightly. "His wife."

"His wife, yes. And before that—your father's wife. Yes?" She waited for Allanaq's reluctant nod. "Which makes me your mother. And Ivalu's mother, don't forget that. So what I have here——" she lifted her hand toward Elik— "is a daughter-in-law who doesn't know enough to protect her unborn child while she trances. And a son who attacks his mother and plans to murder her husband."

Allanaq stared coldly toward the floor. "Tell me. Who is Ivalu's father?"

"Not Skinner," Nuliaq said.

"Don't play with me!"

"I'm not. Any more than Elik plays. The boy might be your brother—is that what you want to hear? It's true then, he might. But he also might be your enemy, if you try to kill Red Fox and someday, when he's grown, he takes it on himself to claim revenge."

"You don't want him dead, that's all. You've both been protecting Red Fox. Why?"

Curious, Elik turned to hear how Nuliaq answered.

"Everyone's been telling you, but you don't hear. Kill him and none of us win, not anything. Do you think you'll suddenly have more seal pokes filled with oil? You won't. More wives to stitch your clothes, or butcher your meat? No. Kill Red Fox and you might as well turn your knife around and kill Elik and her child. When Bird's Mouth or Samik or one of the other brothers starts a blood feud with you, there'll be no one in this village willing to adopt the child or take Elik in. Or me."

"She doesn't know who the father is."

"Nor will it matter. Red Fox would care for it. Even if Elik died. Will you say the same . . . ?"

"No," Elik interrupted. "Wait. It's the soul that enters the child that matters. The namesake-soul. Those who are alive will recognize it—"

Allanaq leaned forward. "What did you say? Wait. Those were his words. What my father said, before he died: *You who are alive. You will not see me dead now.* Did he mean we would see his namesake alive?"

Elik quickly nodded. "Yes. Your father died of his own choosing, without regret."

Nuliaq agreed. "Perhaps your father believed you would return. Not quickly, but he may have guessed—it's an easy enough thought—you would bring a wife. The wife would have a child. He would be born again, through his namesake."

"Just as the seal willingly dies, knowing its soul will return home—" Elik stopped suddenly; an image of the seal skull mound came to her mind. The heap of dry eye sockets, staring toward the sea. The words from her vision: *Who abandons my soul on dry land, cut off from its homeward path?*

But didn't the Bladder Feast return the souls to the skulls on the mound? Just as Anguta's soul would be reborn through his namesake, the seals would be reborn after the bladders returned to their skulls.

How were they cut off from their homeward path?

She lowered her gaze, looked to her hands. And then her fingers. The skin felt tight, the way it often did in winter, dry and glovelike. Almost as if she could slip it off, and only the bones would remain. Inside.

The bones?

Enik remembered now, as if a voice whispered in her ear, another part of the words that had come to her inside the trance. *I am bones,* the vision whispered. *All flesh disappears . . .*

"Disappears?" Elik repeated, but then she looked up. Nuliaq was staring at her wide-mouthed with the same expression Elik had found when Nuliaq held her in the *qasgi*—until she realized Elik had seen.

Quickly, Nuliaq turned aside. She hesitated a moment, then started talking quickly, nervously. "He could kill you," she said to Allanaq. "It wouldn't be difficult. Some bit of poison in your food. A sliver of bone you didn't know was stuck inside a bit of meat in your food tray."

"You swallow it. Your stomach starts to bleed. No one will reach a hand down your throat to make you vomit; people are too afraid. Or Red Fox could kill you the way he killed Skinner, with an arrow on the ice. Or he'll steal an amulet from a grave. Make it crawl inside your body. Like a worm, slip around your liver. Red Fox could do that. Don't think he can't."

Elik kept her eye on Nuliaq. Something had happened just now, she didn't know what.

"I know that," Allanaq said. "Which is another reason he needs to die."

"What of your own father," she kept on. "Everything you say of Red Fox was also true of him. Both are human. Both made mistakes."

"Everything my father treasured Red Fox stole."

"Not everything," Nuliaq said, and she started fussing with the bandage, picking at the knot.

"What else?" Elik asked. "What didn't Red Fox steal?"

Allanaq pursed his lips, watching them both, but instead of answering, Nuliaq yawned loudly and rubbed her face. "Ivalu," she said. "I should bring him home. It's late. He went to sleep hungry. I'll go get him."

She started to rise but Elik touched her arm. "No. Stay awhile. The boy's asleep. You don't need to wake him. But Allanaq, you're tired and perhaps sleeping here isn't best."

Allanaq nodded. "No. You're right. We are all exhausted." He nodded toward the seal. "I'll take the bladder. I'll go to Ice Stick's house."

Elik waited quietly while Allanaq gathered the seal parts into a scrap of hide, one moment more till his footsteps faded beyond the entry. She turned on Nuliaq. "Tell me . . . You know something? I can see it. What are you hiding?"

"What would I hide?" Nuliaq shrugged, but she turned stiffly toward the fire pit, stirred the ashes.

"No. There's something here. Tell me—I don't know where to guess. Not for my sake, but for Ivalu's. For the child inside me. If you can help, speak. Unless you want to starve?" Elik leaned forward to see the frozen expression in Nuliaq's eyes.

Nuliaq shifted again, but this time she also whispered, "Tell me—when you were inside the house, when you asked my help with Red Fox, what were you doing?"

"All right. I'll tell you. I ate one of the finger bones from Anguta's hand. Allanaq brought it back."

Nuliaq's eyes widened. She leaned over the fire, trying to hide her thoughts.

"You told me I was ready," Elik said. "'You are stronger than you know.' Those were your words. Now trust me. Tell me what you're keeping. I wouldn't—"

"Hush," Nuliaq said. "Don't speak—I have to say this quickly, or not at all. You told me Red Fox feared Anguta may have taught his shaman-songs to Allanaq? That Allanaq was waiting to use them now, against him." Nuliaq didn't wait for Elik's answer. "He didn't. Red Fox could pluck any thought he wanted right out of Allanaq's mouth. Anguta knew that."

"Then there are songs? It's true?"

Nuliaq slowly nodded. "It's true. Red Fox was right, but he searched in the wrong direction."

"You mean Allanaq knew, but Anguta taught him to keep them secret?"

"No. I mean he taught them to me."

"His shaman-songs?"

Nuliaq glanced to the skyhole to make sure it was covered. She touched Elik's arm. "It was toward the end of their rivalry, the months before Red Fox finally won. Long after Anguta had initiated Red Fox as a shaman, he began to fear he'd made a mistake. Red Fox, he believed, had grown too ambitious. For his own part, Red Fox believed that Anguta had turned into one of those old men who become bitter when they find himself growing older, weaker. Red Fox began to feel as if he had spent his youth serving Anguta for nothing, that the older shaman would never teach him more. And he was right. Anguta did keep secrets. He feared that if the day ever came when Red Fox learned his last song, that would be the day he died.

"During that last summer, when Anguta understood he was going to lose, before he prepared himself to die, he began to practice his most powerful songs. Alone. Always making certain first that Red Fox was gone for the day, hunting or fishing. He would ask me to stay and help, bind the knots when he tranced, guard him. And I did.

"I brought water. Left off food. Brought his drum. I bound his hands and knees so his body would be safe while his soul was gone."

"You heard his songs?"

Nuliaq nodded. "More than once."

"And you remember?"

"The last one, especially."

"All this time? You could have sold them. You could have been wealthy."

"For what? I have everything I need. And don't forget—I am not a shaman. In my mouth his songs are merely words, not power. And besides, how could I know if they would work for anyone besides him? I had no one to trade with that I could trust."

Elik held her hands together, trying to stay calm. "Which song?" she asked. "Which is it?"

"Anguta said it is the song that is the final part of a shaman's initiation, the song the shaman offers to his spirit helpers to show them he has moved beyond life and death, that he is able to see himself as a skeleton. He sings this song for his spirit helpers, Those Who Exist To Be Questioned, and they speak. That's all I know.

"Now, here. This is the song. Repeat it, then put it away. You'll know what to do with it better than I ever would."

"But you did know," Elik said, and she smiled. "You gave it to me."

"Perhaps. But I suppose I do have a reason, and I'm no different than anyone."

"What do you mean?"

"Anguta was good to me. He cared for me after my first husband died. And with Red Fox also, I never went hungry while others ate. I have never lacked for skins to sew. I owe both men my thanks. And . . ." She paused, took a breath. "I have another secret. Perhaps it's part of why I'm leaving the song behind. I am leaving with Inuk after the Bladder Feast. We have decided to take Ivalu and live with my brothers. I don't want those words to die with me. They were meant to be shared, not hidden. Here is the song:

Earth, earth,
Great earth,
Round about on earth
There are bones, bones, bones,
Which are bleached by the great wind
By the weather, the sun, the air,
So that all the flesh disappears,
Spirit, spirit, spirit,
And the day, the day,
Goes to my limbs
Without drying them up,
Without turning them to bones.

Nuliaq listened as Elik repeated the song. She leaned forward, eyes and mouth, arms and hands all rapt in the sound of her voice. It took a while after the words had safely faded before she could speak. "Yes," Nuliaq whispered. "That way. Yes. He is returned."

But Elik wasn't listening. She was thinking only of the words, still echoing in her ear. Anguta's words. Anguta's song, as much a part of her now as his light, his namesake inside.

She felt whole suddenly, as if for the longest while she had been a knife handle without a blade, unable to cut, a mouth without lips, unable to speak. Until now. She was changed.

She would be light and air. She would be bones bleached by the wind, a spirit whose flesh disappeared. It was the song the spirits had been waiting for her to acquire, to prove she was ready. When they spoke, she would hear them now. She would understand.

12

~

It was morning, though the sky was still filled with the thick dark of winter, when Elik straightened her mittens, then gripped the upright corner pole of the seal skull mound.

The wood was cold and slippery, pitted with shards of ice. But it had never been worked smooth the way an arrow shaft or the bow piece on an umiak would have been. There were angles to it and crooks where limbs had once grown, and finding a handhold and then a notch to wedge her foot turned out easier than she had dared to hope.

With her cheek pressed against the pole, she reached for the level edge of planking. She lifted a hand, and then a foot, and then somehow, suddenly, she pulled herself up and struggled onto the platform, higher above the ground than she had ever stood before.

There was an open ledge wide enough for her feet, but only around the rim, and the flooring wasn't flat. With her toes wedged under the jaw of one seal and her heels pressed against another, the layer of skulls reached partway up her shins. Elik let go of the corner pole and dropped to a firmer seat.

The skulls slid and spun and a few of them fell to the ground as she crawled to the center of the pile. She pushed back her hood and cupped her ear with her hand. The wind stung and her eyes began to tear, but it was better that way, easier to hear.

"My flesh disappears," she promised them, as she sang Anguta's song. *"And the day goes to my limbs, without drying them up."*

Carefully, afraid to have any more fall, she began arranging the skulls, laying them side by side and turned so that their hollow eye sockets all looked toward the sea. She tried to be gentle with them, as careful as if they were children, until she realized how long it was taking. Then faster, almost in a frenzy, she kept on rearranging, balancing, bracing each skull so their eyes could look to the sea. The same as the doors of the Seal People's houses faced the sea. The same as the human dead were buried with ivory eyes to help them see, out from the village and up to the moon, then down again, back to life.

Qamma, they had been calling her, all her life, and now she was here.

Elik pushed herself from her knees. She felt dizzy, standing there in the center of the mound. One side of the outer ring was finished, the seals lined out like people in a dance, but the pile behind her remained a jumbled heap. Her fingers were numb and her legs felt bruised from the sliding and crawling. She pulled her hand up inside her sleeves, only for a moment, to warm her fingers in her armpits.

She looked toward the sky—could it be brighter? Was that pale line along the horizon the sun? And the clouds—were they thinner?

It was the day called When the Sun Lifts Its Head. Old Sheshalik would wake soon. He would climb up the snow to his roof and sit and watch for the first sign of light. When he found it—if he found it—he would call a greeting and Red Fox would begin the feast that brought the end of winter. Daylight would return, a painted line rising above the horizon. People would come together in the *qasgi* and host the bladders, and sing and drum for them, and a new year would follow after the old.

A year of plenty. If the seal's request was honored. And that was up to her. She needed to finish, before someone came along and she was stopped, misunderstood. She stepped toward the edge of the circle; her back ached and the crawling made her dizzy. The pile behind her was higher where she'd pushed the skulls from the finished ring. White heads glistened and spun out of her way. She stepped again, but her foot caught. The smooth bottom of her boot slid along ice.

Her hand went out to break her fall, but it wasn't the shock of falling, or the pain as the back of her head hit, that caught her by surprise. It was the *qasgi* that appeared in front of her, and the Loon, speaking in a voice as sharp as bone.

"We see you," the Loon said.

Elik climbed through the tunnel entry, then waited to be invited further. Next to the Loon, the Seal pushed back her hood so Elik could see the human face inside, and then smiled. "We heard your song," the Seal said.

And then the others spoke, the Wolverine and the Squirrel who had become her helping spirit, the Worm and the Beluga—all in their human shapes. "We know you," they said.

"You are transparent."

"You are light, and you are strong."

"You must help us," the Seal said. "And we in turn will help you."

"Ask. Anything you need," Elik promised, "I will try with all my strength to do."

"While we are alive, we are drawn by your songs," the Seal said. "We haul up on the land to listen. We offer ourselves for the taste of fresh water your women generously bring. But afterward, we would come home again."

"But can't you?"

"Our way is blocked."

"What should I do?"

"Come closer, and we will tell you."

Elik stepped across the planked flooring.

"Return our souls to the sea," the Seal whispered, and reached out her hand.

Elik stepped through a puddle of water to reach her. "How?" she asked, but the Seal's gloves when she touched them were wet and slick as flippers. And her fingers, her hands—Elik stared at her hand, but nothing was there. No skin. No fingernails, and no blood. Only bones held together by air. The Seal's hand waited for hers, but Elik reeled back. Falling now. She couldn't reach. She was falling, backward . . .

No. Not falling. Swimming. As if her hands were paddling through water, feet pushing on ice.

Elik reached for a hand, and this time caught it, but it wasn't the seal, it was her hand, flesh again. She could feel it, bone and proper skin. And human voices, high-pitched and worried. Women's voices first: "I can't reach her."

"Here, I'll push you up. Is she dead?"

No, the seals are dead. Not me.

"She does this. I've seen it before."

"She is a shaman; maybe her soul is lost."

I am a shaman . . . not lost.

"Somebody run, bring her husband."

"Which husband? Who?"

Both, Elik tried to call, but the words wouldn't come. She tensed her shoulders, flexed her toes, and tried to wake more fully. She blinked, then looked up to find Mitik's narrow eyes staring worriedly into hers.

Mitik straightened Elik's hood around her face. "What happened?" she asked.

"My husbands." Elik grabbed for Mitik's arm. "Bring them both. I have to tell Red Fox."

"I'm here," a man's voice called from below her. "Get down. I'll carry her."

The ground felt as if it was shaking and swaying under her. There was a groaning noise, wood swaying beneath her legs. Elik let her eyelids close. The next time she opened them, Mitik was gone. Her eyelashes were rimmed with frost but she could see the sky, no longer black with night, but with a haze of clear, dusk light. Daylight had returned.

And there was Allanaq, outlined in shadows. Holding her. And farther away, the louder footsteps of more men. Rushing and stamping underneath her as if they were a herd of caribou. "Don't speak," Allanaq said softly. "You'll be fine."

"No," she tried to sit up. "I have to tell . . ."

But Allanaq didn't hear. He pulled her through the mound, half dragging, half lifting her feet. The neat circle of skulls broke and rolled into disarray. Skulls top-

pled and fell and the whole world swayed as he
reached for the edge of the platform.

And finally, there was another voice below them:
Red Fox, out of breath and indignant at the same time
as he sounded worried. "Where is she? What is this?"

Elik tugged at Allanaq's sleeve. "Through the ice,"
she tried to make him understand. "Tell him."

"What ice?" Allanaq spoke soothingly as he climbed
partway down, then pulled her the rest of the way after
him. On the ground, with her legs stretched out and
her shoulders against his chest, he took her fingers, lifted them to his cheek to feel if any warmth remained.

Someone was arguing with Red Fox. Elik leaned
around Allanaq to see him pull from the other man's
grip. But then Red Fox stood where he was, shoulders
pressed in between two other men. His eyes flared,
dark and angry.

"Home," Elik tugged at Allanaq. "Under the sea. Tell
him."

"Hush, you're all right now," Allanaq smoothed her
hair. "You aren't going to fall. We're going inside the
qasgi, not home yet. Can you stand?" He looked to
where the women pressed in close, trying to hear.
"Nuliaq?" he called. "Come help her stand."

Nuliaq broke from the women's line, and with Mitik
taking Allanaq's place, and Spider and Nanogak, White
Smoke and most all the women crowding in to help,
they made their way to the qasgi. By the time they
reached the tunnel, Elik had revived enough to crawl
in on her own.

Inside, the walls of the qasgi were gold and brown, lit
up by the fire's light. The air was warm, sticky and pungent at the same time. Elik followed behind Nuliaq to

the women's bench, and though she insisted she could stand, they wouldn't allow her to do anything by herself. Mitik pulled off her parka and smoothed it for Elik to sit on. Nuliaq took Elik's hand and pressed it against her stomach to keep it warm. Spider passed along a water bladder and One Pot held it for her to drink.

It wasn't until she drank her fill and wiped her mouth that they sat back and allowed her room. She lifted her eyes in surprise to find the walls and roof were washed clean and hung with newly carved masks that hadn't been there the day before. Sometime earlier, the bladders had been taken down and placed in the center of the floor.

The pile was small. Not enough seals for the village to survive the winter, if the weather didn't turn. Not enough meat.

Sheshalik was the first of the men to stand. Bracing himself on his nephew Inuk's shoulder, he made his way to the center of the floor, claimed the few seal bladders he had caught, then sat back down. The other married men followed in age order, one after the other, claiming the wrinkled, deflated bladders whose charcoal lines marked their name, then carrying them back to their seats.

Owl and Grayling and Red Fox. Bird's Mouth and Ice Stick and others. As Allanaq claimed Skinner's bladder, it was impossible not to notice how they tallied the number of the seals.

Someone had to be at fault. No Bird leaned toward Owl, Owl toward Grayling. People whispered, pointed, accused.

Finally, the men had all sat back. The bladders were left to soak, to soften the folded skin so it could be inflated again. For a while, there was drumming and songs, but only till the bladders were ready.

Someone gave a sign—Red Fox? Old Sheshalik?— Elik didn't see who. But all at once, the men lifted the crisp bladders to their mouths and started blowing, filling them with air, then tying them off at their necks with a lashing of braided sinew, then tying them again to the spears.

When the spears were returned to the wall again, Nuliaq leaned toward Elik. "The men are too quiet this year," she whispered.

"This is different?"

"Something is. Different, or wrong. Or maybe right. I don't know. There should have been dancing all through the day. And wrestling matches, games of strength, and feasting. Instead, Inuk told me the men are saying that Red Fox isn't himself anymore, that a spirit has moved inside his body and stolen his soul. It has to be so, they say, or else he would have convinced more seals to come."

Elik didn't have an answer. Whatever else Nuliaq said, one thing was true: a nervousness had moved into Red Fox. He danced, but his steps were like air above a fire, shaking and unsettled. He drummed, but the beat was nearly forgotten as his glance lingered on Bird's Mouth, on Allanaq, and Inuk and Ice Stick.

What did he think he would find? Knives? Angry whispers? Why was he so afraid?

Nuliaq nudged her elbow. Allanaq had been waiting, trying to get her attention. His eye met hers. He nodded, then slowly, ceremoniously, brought a sealskin bundle out from behind his back. He brushed clean the floor in front of him.

Elik's dizziness returned as she watched him pull back the corners of the sealskin. The finished bent-wood oval of his father's burial box lay inside.

She turned to see if Red Fox was watching. He was, of course. His chin was pitted with tension and his chest, beneath the gut-skin parka, seemed shrunken, worse, far worse than the time when Anguta's boot first swayed, or when he found the dead dog skin inside his boot.

In marked contrast, Allanaq's eyes caught the fire's light and shone with a look near to triumph. Deliberately, he arranged each bone on the open hide, making sure the hand's placement was exact. Thumb beside longer fingers. Small gaps left where tendons would have flexed. Where a hand, clothed in flesh, would have grasped a shaman's drum, lifted and struck it, sent his curse out, searching for an enemy.

More than once, Red Fox started to rise, but he faltered and sat back down. Uncertainly, he watched as Allanaq laid more of his carvings along the floor.

There were miniature antler hunting points with their barbs carved backwards, in absurd directions. And swivels and linked ivory chains that had no ordinary use. There was a burial mask made of three long pieces to frame a face, more to cover the nose and mouth. Etched lines wavered through the ivory, circles with eye dots that placed the person at the center of the universe, the way the soul was at the center of the person. There were tiny heads with grotesque, bulging eyes—death heads with hollowed bottoms to fit over dead fingers, to teach the dead to hunt with weapons of the dead.

How long had he worked on these carvings, Elik wondered? How many days while she sewed or checked her rabbit snares, and trained her thoughts toward the spirits, had this husband of hers trained his eye toward his carvings?

It was a wonder to her that people could be this way, Red Fox the same as Allanaq. Neither of them satisfied with simply eating and sleeping, but planning, working toward a day they couldn't see. Even as they understood they were powerless against greater forces, they still worked to make things true.

As if human people, lacking Eagle's sight, Raven's cunning, Wolf's endurance, still could work to change the heart of a day.

As if life were a carving to be planned in the same way Allanaq looked along a length of ivory, planning. Waiting for the spirit inside the bone to speak to the knife that spoke to his hand saying, *Yes this is the way it should be. Now make it so.*

And wasn't she also planning—how to stop these two men from fighting? Convince them to shape their plans together? Nuliaq had helped her realize it, with her talk about running away with Inuk and Ivalu.

Either she would bring them to peace and they would share one house, or she would stay with one and visit with another. Nuliaq had mentioned the village where her brothers lived—one of them might go there. Or there was Big Island, where Nuliaq's first husband had come from. Or Kuvak, a village that was inland on a river. She'd heard that aspen grew there, not only willow, that in two days walk a person could find trees growing higher than her shoulders. They could go to these places, any of them.

She wasn't sure about Red Fox, but she didn't think

Allanaq would object. After all, hadn't he lived among her people?

Except, as she watched him now, she noticed things that had escaped her eye before. It was something in the way the men leaned closely to see what he'd brought. They weren't afraid of him. They were his cousins, she understood that now, friends he had played with as a boy, partners he had learned to hunt with.

It was no longer necessary for him to hide in Ice Stick's house or pass the day among the graves, hoping that none of Red Fox's relatives found him. He even resembled the men here, not only Ice Stick who was a closer relation, but Bird's Mouth and his brothers.

Where before, among her Real People, he had been made to cut labret holes in his chin in the hopes he would look more like other men. He'd cut his hair and hidden his height, and even wished he could wipe away his tattoos.

And here was another thought: While it was true she had felt lonely, and longed for her home, not once since the day she arrived had she been made to feel like a stranger. Certainly, not in the way Allanaq had among her people.

Perhaps then, when this day was finally over and both her husbands were at peace, she would tell them she wanted to stay. Good people lived here, and there was still so much she needed to learn. Red Fox would understand that. Allanaq would smile. It was true.

The next time she looked up, Allanaq had folded the sealskin back over his carvings and put them safely away. Red Fox had turned his attention to Bird's Mouth and Ice Stick, who were standing together near the food trays, one drum held between them as they talked about the feast.

Red Fox shifted his seat, trying to hear. There was danger in the way they stood, familiarly, shoulder to shoulder as if it was their place to talk and make decisions without him. It was one more insult flung against his power. Angrily, Red Fox rose. With his back drawn stiff, he walked up to the men. He wanted them to see his displeasure, to know their talk amounted to no more than the plans of boys. "Give me the drum," he said. "We need to sing."

Ice Stick scowled and pulled himself taller, but Bird's Mouth touched his hand in warning.

The gesture angered Red Fox more, as if these two had any right to speak. "I am shaman," he said loudly, wanting people to hear. "It is to me the spirits speak. To me they tell what is necessary and what is good."

He turned to face the men. "Why do you sit?" he asked, "when every other year we offer up songs and drum for the spirits. We are their hosts today. We are not children."

Sheepishly, the men did as he said. Samik and No Bird first, others following. Taking a path that kept him well away from Allanaq, Red Fox moved to the center of the *qasgi*. He lifted the large drum and beater stick, set his feet wide, and leaned to one side. The amulets on the gut-skin parka danced and swayed. The puffin beaks clacked against each other. The opaque strips caught the light and shone like the moon in a dark sky.

His dance went on for a long while until, finally, Red Fox paused and set down the drum. While the other men kept up a softer beat, Red Fox began tossing bits of food around the *qasgi*. Four times he did this, always moving in the same direction the sky moved, opening the way for the sun to return. For the seals to be born, out from death and into life again.

And though she had known all along it was coming, Elik caught her breath and felt her chest clamp shut when Red Fox spoke. "To the mound," he called loudly. "The souls of the seals ask to be joined back with their skulls. It is time, they say, to return home."

She gripped the edge of the bench. Now. She had to say it now. Before he danced again, or tranced, or began one of the older rituals.

The seals were dead and without her they would remain dead. It was the same fear that had driven Allanaq all the way here with his father's bones. Not to let them die forever, but to find a way to life again.

She searched for Allanaq, saw him stiffen and nearly rise from his seat near the opposite wall. Vaguely, she felt Nuliaq's hand on hers, trying to hold her back. She shook it off, stepped to the floor.

The women moved to let her through. The last strain of drumming hushed. She felt the air change as people pointed, whispered, motioned each other to hold quiet, to hear her speak.

Respectfully, she stopped in front of Red Fox and lowered her gaze. "Not to the mound," she said. "I have seen a different vision." And then she waited, and though she didn't look up to see his face, she could feel Red Fox listening. He would hear the truth inside her words. He would listen, and he would see it in her eyes, the same vision she had seen.

"The Loon has lent its vision to me. The spirits of the seals have spoken to me. They ask me to tell their story."

She allowed herself the smallest hint of a smile. There. She had said it. Now he would know, all the patience, the trust he had heaped on her had not been wasted.

"The spirits have spoken, and as with the Gift of Song the Eagle taught in the First Times, so the Seal promised to speak now of the Bladder Feast."

Elik turned as she spoke. She glanced from face to face, wanting them, all of them, to judge the sincerity of her words. But then, out of the corner of her eye, the fire flared and a motion caught her attention. It was Red Fox. He was standing behind her shoulder. She hadn't even heard him move.

"No," he said, and his voice was gentle, almost fatherly. He crossed to stand in front of her, pulling attention away from Elik, back on himself. "There is no call for another contest," he said. "Our people have always known of the seal's thirst. We already are careful of their needs. We have always been respectful."

Red Fox stood tall; he wanted to look convincing. But he couldn't resist stealing a glance toward Allanaq, to make sure he was still sitting. He was. But there was Bird's Mouth, pushing himself heavily from the floor. Red Fox opened his mouth to protest, then decided against it. He tried not to look surprised.

Bird's Mouth stopped partway between Red Fox and the women's bench. He seemed sure of himself, but not so proud that he didn't lower his eyes politely. "It isn't so," he said. "We must at least listen to what Elik says. Unless we want to starve, we have no choice. If the Seal-spirit spoke—"

Red Fox couldn't listen. "I have no more use for contests," he said. "There are consequences for what we do."

"It wouldn't be a contest," Elik looked to Red Fox, wanting him to understand. "The spirits of the seals cry for their souls. They say they have been abandoned, cut off from their homeward paths."

"And you are so certain of what you say?" Red Fox stared gravely at her. "You would cross me?"

"No!" Elik shook her head worriedly. She needed to explain more, better this time. "I have made the shaman's journey to the Land Below the Sea. A Seal-spirit spoke to me, and a Loon, and others. They sent me back with a message: The souls that kept inside the bladders during their life ask to be allowed to go home, back to the sea. They ask that we return the bladders, not to their skulls that we already honor, but under the ice. There, they will put on parkas of flesh again. As countless as the blades of grass, they will be born again. If only we help."

Elik swallowed hard. She looked to the huddled faces, women she had worked with, eaten with. And not only the women, but the men as well, they all leaned expectantly forward, wanting to hear. All except Red Fox. She searched for a hint of acceptance, but his face remained mute, dark and unreadable.

Till suddenly, with an abrupt, angry turn, he stepped past Bird's Mouth to the wall where the bladders hung. He grabbed one of the extra lances that leaned against the wall, lifted it, then danced back, jabbing and poking at the nearest bladders. He didn't hit them, only mimed the motion, till his spear struck a roof beam. The bladders swayed.

Bird's Mouth scowled. "What are you doing? The bladders will break, and there'll be no food. They don't want anger here."

"And *you* know what they want? For all the seasons since the First Times, the bladders have gone to the seal skull mound, as *they* request."

Red Fox struck his spear on the floor at Elik's feet. "And how is it you claim suddenly to have sight, clearer than another's? What sign did these spirits give you? Or was it something you hoped for, then dreamt of, on your own?"

"I'm sorry. Forgive me," Elik said, and then, more quickly: "It was only the song. I only just learned it. The shaman's song—'*There are bones, bleached by the great wind, by the sun, the air. So that all flesh disappears.*' I saw that—my skeleton. Every bone. I heard its secret name. They promised, '*Spirit, spirit, spirit. That the day would go to my limbs.*' And my bones never dry. And . . ."

"What? What did you say?"

"That the day would go to my limbs . . ."

"No. Not that."

"About the skeleton?"

"Yes. Where did you learn that?"

Elik stopped. She had said too much. Her eyes searched for Nuliaq, begging her forgiveness.

Nuliaq nodded calmly. She understood. She glanced to where Inuk watched from his place beside Grayling and Owl. If Red Fox guessed their plan, there would be fighting. She didn't want Inuk dead.

Elik tugged at Red Fox's sleeve, pulling his eyes back to her. "It's only a song. The same one you gave me. Spirit. Spirit. Spirit. You taught me to say that."

"No." Red Fox's face twisted. "I taught you the word *torngrarzuk*, not its meaning. I never knew that. But neither did you. You couldn't have found it on your own. Is that Anguta's Song?" He grabbed her arm and she stumbled. He yanked her to her feet, then shook her. "You can't know that. I waited too long . . ." He shook her again, and she shouted. Her foot slipped and he tried to grab her but he was holding the spear, and she twisted and fell back.

By the time she lifted herself from the floor, Allanaq had jumped past her. He moved so quickly, she almost didn't see his hand slide across his boot, lift out the short antler-handled knife.

"Leave her be!" Elik heard his shout, but she was confused—this wasn't supposed to happen. The qasgi erupted in noise, yelling. Men shouting even as others yelled louder to hold quiet.

Allanaq kicked and the spear flew from Red Fox's hand; a knife appeared in its place and Red Fox pointed and jabbed. Allanaq jumped back, then rushed in, slashing at Red Fox. At his neck, his side. His knife point caught on a whirling amulet; Red Fox's moon snapped from its braid and flew away. His parka tore, but nothing worse. He smiled at Allanaq's miss, then leaped for a closer reach.

Elik watched as Allanaq kicked, and Red Fox's legs gave out. His knees buckled, but somehow the next moment it was Allanaq who was down and they both were rolling, falling on top of each other, struggling so fast and close and tight, she couldn't make out which was who and what was what, except that all of this was wrong.

None of it was what she wanted: two households, one wife shared between. She rose to her feet, lifted her arms in protest. She reached for Allanaq first, then for Red Fox, but she was too slow, too small to stop them.

Their hands darted and flew, but Elik only looked at

the patterns of their tattooed cheeks, temples, chin—so much alike. How could they not understand what she had from the start? They were part of each other, hunter and shaman and wife. With her, they belonged together.

Vaguely she heard Allanaq's cry, Red Fox's warning. They stopped, finally. Both of them stared at her. Their mouths were shaped with one expression. They were talking, but their words—they were too quiet to hear. And when she tried to touch them, both in the same embrace, she felt sluggish, as if she were diving through water.

She tried to breathe but her chest caught, as if she needed to come up for air. She held her side, below her breasts. Her skin was warm, and too wet. Sticky with blood. Her blood? No. It was her child's, spilling out when it should have been born.

A wave of dizziness washed through her and she started to fall. And a thought, the strangest thought, that if she could only have returned the bladders to the sea, then her child and the seals would both have been born—out from the *qasgi* and into the world. One into air, one to the sea.

She opened her mouth to breathe, to drink. She wanted to swim. To feel water against her sleek skin . . .

"Elik!"

Slowly—her human hands were almost too heavy to move—she pulled her fingers together. Like flippers. That was better. Swimming through water . . .

"Get away. She doesn't need you . . ."

"And you can heal her? Let go. I'll do it . . ."

That one was the Loon. The deep voice.

"She's bleeding . . ."

And that the Seal.

"Let go of her . . . What are you doing—release me! . . . Let me go! Bird's Mouth—you? And you, Samik? You dare . . . ? Let me go!"

Elik closed her ears. Deeper. She wanted to dive deeper. Someplace where their loud, human noises wouldn't thunder in her ears. Where the fighting would go away.

". . . Elik. Come back. You're all right. Open your eyes . . ."

No. She wanted to swim, to visit the qasgi again. But it wasn't there. If they didn't call Qamma, she couldn't get in . . .

The harsh ripple of noise and arguing was too loud. The glare from the fire burned too brightly. She tried to turn, to escape the brightness, but a different pain flared, deep in her side.

The child—had she lost another child?

Her breath caught as she looked down, already knowing what she would find. There was blood on her hands, and she tensed as she raised her fingers toward her face, waiting for the smell she remembered from those other times. The smell of fluids and blood and death that should have been life.

She sniffed, but it wasn't there. She opened her eyes. The blood on her fingers was bright and red and clean. No smell. Whose blood . . . ?

She struggled to lift herself, but there were arms again. And Allanaq's familiar eyes above hers.

"Try not to move. The bleeding's stopped."

Stopped? Elik felt along her side, gently, till the pain flared in a single, biting point. "The child . . . ?"

"No," Allanaq tried to calm her. "You took a knife

wound below your ribs. You jumped into the middle of our fight."

Elik gripped his arm, lifted herself higher. His face was drawn, his eyes filled with concern. "I'm sorry," she said.

"Don't talk," he said. "Rest. I'm the one who is sorry."

"But I have to speak . . . Return them to the sea . . ." She searched the *qasgi* till she found Red Fox, standing against a corner post, his eyes intent with concern. He looked disheveled and out of breath, worse than Allanaq. But she didn't realize why, until she caught the way Bird's Mouth and Samik—his own cousins—stood on either side, not supporting him, but tightly pinioning his arms. Red Fox's hands were bound.

There had been more fighting. She must have fainted, as Allanaq said. Bird's Mouth was also cut—not deeply, but more than a scratch, from the center of his chest toward his shoulder. Long, ruined strips dangled from Red Fox's gut-skin parka.

Red Fox tensed when he saw her notice; he jerked his shoulders, tried to get free, but it wasn't possible. There were four arms to his two, and his hands were tied. Behind his cousins stood other men, watching and more than willing to take their place. Humiliated, Red Fox gave it up.

"He might have killed you," Allanaq said.

"No. He was trying to help."

"Bird's Mouth dragged him off you. You didn't see. He could have killed you as easily as me."

"It isn't so," Elik tried to make him understand. "He lost face. He was ashamed, that's all." Elik grit her teeth, pushed herself up to stand.

Allanaq reached to hold her back, but then let go. A shuffling sound at the entry caught his attention. A moment later and Ice Stick climbed up through the entry-well, into the *qasgi*. He pushed back his hood, immediately looking for Elik and then Red Fox. "The wind has quieted," he said, and there was a note in his voice, almost of awe. "The clouds open. The sun shows its light above the horizon."

"It's true," Elik called, as loudly as she was able. "The seals heard my promise. They spoke to quiet the wind. The bladders must be returned to the sea."

Most of the women and all the men were standing now, pressed into a knot. She searched past shoulders and heads, watched as Bird's Mouth and Samik eased their grip on Red Fox and stepped forward, trying to hear. Red Fox must have been waiting. He drew his strength into his arms, pulled free.

Bird's Mouth reeled, expecting to find a knife in his side, but Elik called his name. She pointed, a warning gesture toward the bladders. Bird's Mouth looked to Allanaq. There was no disagreement. With a look that was near relief, he freed Red Fox's hands. She motioned again, and Bird's Mouth led the men to start taking down the bladders and the spears.

Taking small, brittle steps, she made her way to Red Fox. "This will be good," she said, and she lifted her hand to touch him, but he held back, cold and distant.

"You'll see," she tried again. "We will trance together, or alone. Whatever you prefer. The spirits who spoke to me will teach you the same."

"The same?" he repeated, as if he were speaking to a child. "And how do you expect to make this happen?

Will you pull my soul out through my eyes, as I did for you, to make me safe?"

"No! I will teach you the song, the same as I learned. I'll share."

"Yes." Red Fox said. "There is that. But what I want to know is—did you have it all along? Did it come to you? In a vision you wouldn't tell?"

Elik couldn't meet his eyes, and this time it was Red Fox who stepped closer. "No?" He took hold of her chin, gently. Lifted her face to see if she lied. But then he glanced behind her to the qasgi. A few women followed Ice Stick back outside. The men had all taken their spears down from the wall. Allanaq stood beside Owl and Grayling, watching, but keeping back. And just behind them, Inuk's long, narrow frame rose taller than the other men. At his side, Nuliaq stood with Ivalu's hand in hers.

Red Fox stared. His face grew long. Elik didn't have to turn around to guess what he'd seen. "Nuliaq told me," she whispered, and Red Fox repeated the name.

"Nuliaq? Not even Anguta, reaching from the dead. It wasn't enough for Bird's Mouth to betray me. Nuliaq. She's known it all along?" Red Fox gave a laugh. "And who next? Who else will come and betray me?"

"No, don't blame her. I made her tell. I did this for you."

"For me? And how is that?"

"The seals gave a vision to me. But the vision will be shared. It doesn't matter which of us learned it first. It's to be shared."

"You believe this?"

"Yes." Elik promised. "I do."

"Perhaps you are right, then," he said, and he lifted

his gaze, not to the people this time, but to the walls, the painted masks, the skyhole.

Something in his expression reminded her of herself the day she and Allanaq left the Long Coast shore. The way she couldn't get her fill of looking around her house, committing to memory exactly how the stones shaped a square for the fire pit, and how the damp smell of spring touched everything, the bedding, the food, Allanaq's hair.

Mitik came up behind her, and Elik lifted her arms while she and Nuliaq helped tie a belt around her side. The men had finished their walk around the *qasgi*, and now, from the eldest first to the youngest married man, they pushed their bladders out the skyhole, onto the roof.

Only a few moments later they were all outside, faces lifted toward the stars. A few were visible now, pale and flickering against the grey sky. No one would have argued that Ice Stick was wrong. The sting of cold and the freezing wind were gone.

The signs of better weather were all there: dogs barking toward the changing wind, a heaviness in the air, almost of moisture. The bladders danced and bobbed from the spear heads as the men started toward the ice. Allanaq walked ahead of Elik, among his cousins. Red Fox walked apart.

In all her dreams, each time she had prayed this day would come, she had seen herself standing between both men. That wasn't possible yet. She saw that now. There were still things that needed to be said, alone with Red Fox. With the three of them together. Tonight, or tomorrow at the latest. Red Fox would be calmer; they would have the chance to speak.

They walked a circular route beyond the village,

glances deliberately avoiding the seal skull mound as they turned toward the landfast ice. No Bird and Inuk and a few of the younger men hurried ahead, searching for a sign of either a seal's breathing hole or a lead of water that might have come open during the storm.

Elik kept among the women, walking slowly but managing not to fall behind. Nuliaq walked near her side, but with Ivalu. She spoke intently to the boy, naming each of the men he might one day call on for help, girls who would be eligible for wives.

Elik picked up her pace, walking with an off-sided gait till she came up alongside Red Fox. He had taken off the torn gut-skin parka, exchanged it for a plainer winter suit. Three inflated seal bladders swung from the end of his spear, but he carried it carelessly over his shoulder, not lifted and not proud.

Red Fox turned to make sure it was Elik, then started talking, quickly, as if they had never left the *qasgi*. "I believed her," he said, "Nuliaq. I asked, and I accused her. But the truth is, I believed her each time she claimed she didn't know."

"She meant no harm," Elik offered.

"Of course not," Red Fox said, and this time Elik noticed an odd, flat sound to his voice. She glanced to his face, but from the side she couldn't see his eyes.

"Even now," he said. "She isn't my enemy. It's Anguta, as it's always been. The difference is that now, he's won."

"That isn't so—" Elik protested, but Red Fox wasn't listening.

"It was his last threat," he went on. "*You who are living, will you recognize me when I return?* And I didn't. Not in Ivalu, who surely is his. And not in you."

"But the child is yours." She wanted him to believe that.

"Is it? But what of the soul, inside? I tried to stop him from returning. Yet here is he, surrounding me. He lives on. I shall die."

Elik couldn't answer. The wind blew steadily, with none of the force of a storm. The ice was smooth here, no longer rough the way it had been nearer the shore, and safe. The walking wasn't difficult. They kept on in silence for what seemed a long while until, from farther up ahead, one of the men lifted his arms to signal open water.

It was a narrow crack in the ice, a lead that rafted and closed again, not far from where they found it. By the time Elik and Red Fox and the last of the women reached it, the men were already taking their bladders from the spears.

There were scratch marks and smooth, glassy ice, a slick trail showing where a ringed seal had hauled out. Perhaps it had slept before diving back in. Perhaps it had come up to see the sun return.

The water was dark, a thin line narrow enough for even a small child to jump across. It followed the ice, as if drawn between two worlds. Air above. Water below.

"Here," she said. "Where the crack is new. The bladders must be deflated. Then pushed under the ice, to find their way home." Her voice wasn't strong, but the men heard and she stepped back, allowing them room.

Sheshalik and Grayling and Owl, Ice Stick and Samik and No Bird, one after the other the men took turns kneeling to the ice, using their spears to help push the bladders down.

Behind them, Elik let her eyes close, only for a moment, to let them rest. She would have preferred to sit down, except she didn't think she could stay awake. She wasn't dizzy enough to faint, but she felt weak, and the cold had seeped deep inside.

She listened to the brittle crinkle of gut as the men collapsed the bladders, the harder noise of spear shafts tapping the ice. There were voices, and the wind. But then, cutting through those, a new sound began. Something different, a sound as if it was summer and the ice had gone out. As if waves were breaking against a gravel shore.

Elik opened her eyes, rubbed her face. Nuliaq had stepped in beside her, and Inuk had just risen from the water—the last man to watch his string of bladders sink and disappear. But the sound wasn't coming from him. It was Red Fox.

He had jumped across the narrow gap and was standing opposite Inuk, but so close to the edge, his boot tips curled over the ice. The wave sound that had woken her surrounded him, but there was another rumbling sound now, louder than the first. As if rocks were crashing, breaking from a mountainside. The noises faded, then grew louder as Red Fox leaned over the water, quieter when he pulled himself back.

It went on that way, as if an avalanche was following the bladders, battering and trying to block them. It only stopped when Red Fox jumped back from the ice edge and started dancing, leaping, and then scowling where a fog rose over the distant end.

Nuliaq's grip on Elik's arm tightened each time Red Fox neared the edge. She looked to Inuk, signaled him to keep quiet and near the men.

Red Fox crossed back, but he paid no attention to Inuk. Instead, as if there were spirits inside of him that no one else could see, he started mumbling over a rolled-up sealskin that one of the men must have carried over. Elik was sure she hadn't noticed it before.

The roll was large, with one skin inside another. He unrolled the outer one, then stretched it to lay it flat. He stood over it, with his hand cupped to his ear, listening. When the wave-sounds didn't return, he seemed upset again, as if something was wrong.

He pushed back his hood and with a great show of difficulty, tugged one of his mittens from his hand.

There was a moment, Elik wasn't certain, but she thought he glanced her way, checking to make sure she watched him. Their eyes met and instantly he turned, flung the mitten into the open water, the same place the bladders had disappeared. When the mitten bobbed to the surface he grabbed a spear from Ice Stick, jabbed and pushed it down again.

When it hung there, just below the surface, he untied his belt—his amulet belt with its pouches and ivory carvings—and threw that in after it. He leaned out, not even checking that the ice was safe, goading the belt to follow where the mitten and the water-sounds had gone.

They sank after that, the mitten and the belt. Red Fox tossed the spear behind him and as Elik turned to watch it slide, she was surprised to find the women had all backed themselves away, safe beyond Red Fox's reach.

Nuliaq stood with Ivalu gathered into her arms. She whispered something in his ear, shushing him, trying not to draw attention. Even Allanaq had moved to the end of the men's row, placing himself nearer to Elik. She wasn't certain it was necessary.

Red Fox looked exhausted. He had made his way to the sealskin, sat heavily down. He waited to catch his breath, then calmly, he lifted his arms, calling for attention. "I have heard the moaning of the dead," he said, and his voice came out raspy, but recognizable. "There are huge dogs blocking the paths. Giant stones threaten to crush the souls. The seals speak. They ask me to follow, to help them reach their *qasgi*. This is their message."

Red Fox let his arms fall, but if he expected encouragement, or even a show of fear, it didn't come. He seemed troubled for a moment and he paused, but then he picked out Bird's Mouth. "Cousin," he called. "You must bind my hands and wait for me as you have it the past. While my body lies in a trance and my spirit travels."

He paused, this time longer. Elik wasn't certain what was wrong. His gaze was hidden, she could not guess where his thoughts had gone. Behind her, the women started shuffling. "He wants his audience back," someone whispered. "It's too late for that," came a reply.

Elik turned, but she couldn't tell who'd spoken. White Smoke and Pintail stood with their shoulders pressed together. Spider held her older boy's hand tightly in hers, then stepped toward Higjik. The whispers could have come from any of them.

Bird's Mouth stepped forward from the men's row, but then he waited. Red Fox unrolled the second sealskin, but instead of laying it on the ground, he wrapped it over his shoulders, fit it over his head so the fur that had once covered the seal's head now covered his, the nose angled toward his mouth. He turned, looked directly at Elik, and motioned her to come.

Elik's stomach caught. Behind her, she heard Allanaq's voice, and then Nuliaq's. Calmer. Something was wrong, but she didn't know what. Elik rubbed her face. She was exhausted, she realized. Stiff, and in pain, and tired. More than anything, she was tired. She kept hearing only part of what people were saying.

She wasn't even certain what she was supposed to do until Nuliaq stepped forward, touched her arm. "You have to go," Nuliaq said. "But be careful."

"What can he do? He isn't going to hurt me."

Nuliaq had been carrying Ivalu. She shifted him to her hips, but he stiffened, then wiggled from her arms. They both watched as he danced away, singing his newest lesson: "Nanogak's sister was named Ivalu, so Nanogak calls me sister. And Mitik's grandfather was Ivalu, and so I am his namesake too."

Nuliaq turned back to Elik. "He won't hurt you," she said. "There's too many people here. Go on. But be careful. Later, we'll talk."

With her arms pressed tightly around her side, Elik crossed the few steps to the sealskin. She sat and stiffly drew in her legs; then, before she realized what he was doing, he lifted the sealskin and pulled it like a roof over both their heads.

Elik startled and nearly pushed it aside, but Red Fox began talking, more earnestly, plainer than he had in days.

"You have to listen," he said. "And remember. There are things you need to know. First, in the house. Pry up the floorboard that rims the entry-well; the one on the shore side is small. It's loose. You'll only need your fingers, not a digging stick. You want to be careful. There's an amulet there, a necklace strung with loon skulls. It belonged to Anguta. I tried to use it, but it brought me no visions. I never heard it speak."

"You're giving it to me?" she asked in surprise. She tried to see his eyes, whether he was lying or testing her, but he'd pulled the sealskin close and his face was hidden. "Why should the amulet work for me, if it was dead for you?"

Red Fox had no answer. "Give it to your child, when it's born. But don't tell him, don't—with all your questions and your wondering—ever say that I was one who refused to share. I am not hoarding. Nothing I have remains hidden. But listen. There is one thing more."

"What?" Elik pulled back, then wished she hadn't. The move seemed suspicious and afraid, but Red Fox only sighed. He let the skins slip back.

"Who can say?" he whispered. "We know so little, we who are human, without strength. The song came to me when I was young, I never understood how. But when I sang it, the animals came, their spirits spoke to me. Use it or not, as you wish, but I'll say it only once: *Aya iya, aya wa-iya, My body is all eyes. Look at it! Be not afraid. I see in all directions. My face is turned from the dark of night. Aya iya, aya wa-iya.* Now you."

She didn't dare hesitate. "*My body is all eyes,*" she repeated "*Be not afraid. Aya iya, aya wa-iya.*" Then, anxiously, "What does it mean?"

Red Fox was calm when he answered, not accusing. His eyes took her in; his voice was tender. "It means you have what you wanted. And I am content."

Then, before Elik could stop him, he let the sealskin fall, rose heavily to his feet. He picked out Bird's Mouth, motioned with his hands.

Bird's Mouth must have been waiting. He stepped forward and pulled a length of rawhide from his belt. It was all so quick, it must have been planned ahead of time. Nuliaq had been right, Elik decided. Red Fox had known he would trance. Bird's Mouth must have carried the rolled-up skins all the way from the *qasgi*. She would have noticed, if it weren't for the pain in her side. She wasn't paying as much attention as she should.

"I will guide the bladders," Red Fox called loudly. "I will plead with the spirits who block their path, and help them reach their destination. Come," he yelled, and he lifted his arms toward Bird's Mouth.

With a practiced hand, Bird's Mouth began wrapping the tie around Red Fox's hands. Another man stepped out of the clustered line to join him; it was Inuk.

Instantly, voices began murmuring behind her. Elik shifted her glance, searched for Nuliaq, and almost didn't find her. She had pulled herself back to stand, half-hidden between Mitik and One Pot. Her hood was tugged forward; Elik couldn't see her face.

Without saying a word, and with his gaze carefully lowered, Inuk took one end of the tie from Bird's Mouth, passed it back around the shaman's wrists, and pulled hard.

Red Fox stiffened and stared straight ahead. Wherever his thoughts had gone, he didn't tell.

Bird's Mouth tied the knot off at his wrists, passed it again toward Inuk. The two men waited while Red Fox stepped closer to the open water, then lowered himself to his knees.

Elik followed Red Fox's eyes: the current moved, but was slow, quieter than she would have guessed. Somewhere below, helping spirits waited at the bottom of the sea. The water was black now, too dark to see, but there had been lights when she went down there in her trance. Like stars, they had strung themselves along the path. Red Fox would find the way.

A child's voice rose above the silence. It was Ivalu. "Why do we have to go back?" he asked, and Elik turned to find Nuliaq leading him away by the hand. Mitik walked at her side, leading her own son Hawk, and Pintail also, with her youngest inside her parka.

"Tighter," Red Fox called, and he lowered himself again so that now he was lying with his face and side pressed to the ice, his knees drawn toward his chest. His voice was muffled. "Already, I see far ahead. . . . There is light . . ."

Inuk stood behind Red Fox's shoulder. He passed the length of rawhide to Bird's Mouth, who stepped around, blocking Elik's line of sight. Resolutely they finished the ties, cinched Red Fox's wrists against his ankles, tugged his chin against his chest.

Elik's eyes had nearly closed when his splash broke the quiet. Water pooled over the ice, touched the edge of the sealskin. The moon's light caught on the small tipped waves, then closed again into darkness. That was all. She stared as the spooled length of extra line slipped away, following behind Red Fox into the sea.

She sat there, remembering a story Malluar had once told, of a shaman whose two sons worked with him when he tranced. What they did was to go down the day before and arrange the thongs they would use to tie him.

The shaman tranced, and went below the sea, the same as Red Fox did now. But what the sons actually did was to pull their father down through one ice hole, and up through another that was hidden a short distance away. A coiled line had been arranged the day before, the way her father used to set his sealing nets between ice holes, using the current to carry the willow net under the ice, then hooking it, bringing it up another hole. For years, no one knew how the shaman had done that. Just when the people gave up on seeing him alive, there he would come walking into the *qasgi*, just like that.

Carefully, Elik leaned over the open edge, watched to see if there was a sign of any change yet, a ripple to mark Red Fox's return. She wanted to be the first to find him, the first to see his fingers break the surface, his face come lifting toward the air.

Except, she was so tired. Her head sagged and her eyes begged to close. If he took much longer, she would fall asleep. Her side stung where she'd taken the wound, worse than before. It wasn't the child though; she wasn't worried about that. There were no pains in the small of her back, or low down in the cradle of her bones. Only in her side, but the day had taken its toll. She couldn't sit any longer.

One more time she searched the fractured ice, then stood and turned, and stared in surprise. Everyone was walking away; she hadn't even heard. Not only Nuliaq with Ivalu, but Ice Stick was gone and Bird's Mouth and Inuk. Had Red Fox come up through another hole? Is that what happened?

She picked Samik out by the bright skins of his parka. Old Sheshalik from his slower step. And Grayling—his was the hood with the foxtail Nanogak had stitched for the Bladder Feast. Perhaps the men had decided they should hurry, come back with their harpoons and catch the good weather while it held?

Allanaq stood off to the side from the others; as soon as she saw him he motioned for her to come, hurry along. He waited till she caught up, then smiled, not wide—the night felt too burdened for that—but with a warmth that reached for her, pulled her to his side.

The path had been drifted when they first came out; it was trampled now, easier to follow. They walked along behind the others for a while, not hurrying and not talking, until Elik wondered about the hunting. "Who will come back?" she asked. "Do the men need to finish the Bladder Feast before they can hunt?"

"Hunt?" Allanaq shook his head. "They wouldn't do that, not with death so near."

"You mean the bladders? Not even to hunt, while the weather holds?"

Allanaq slowed his step. "But you were here, of course you were, when Skinner died? It was no different for your Real People. For four days no one was permitted to hunt. The women didn't sew. No one worked."

"I understand," Elik said, but she didn't, not really. "The seals must not be angered, or frightened from the shore. But won't Bird's Mouth and Inuk need help?"

"Help with what?"

"With Red Fox, when they pull him up?"

Abruptly, Allanaq stopped. He looked closely at her face. "You don't know?"

Elik's stomach twisted with unease. "Know what?"

"It's over," he said. "You need to be inside, and safe. Especially with a child."

"What . . ." Elik shook her head in denial. "What are you saying?"

Allanaq grew worried. "He isn't coming up. Didn't you know that?"

"That's not true. Nuliaq said—"

"Elik, he's dead. He knew what he was doing."

"He didn't say that. He said, '*My body is all eyes.*'"

Allanaq shook his head. "What else did he tell you?"

"He told me where to find . . ." She stopped, faltered, and then saw it suddenly, the weight of Red Fox's pain, her part in it. And this plan. His answer.

Allanaq sighed deeply. She stepped closer and he opened his arms, folded her inside. There was no need for him to ask what she now thought. Only to stand here, hold each other, and then go on. "The elder initiates the younger," he whispered in her ear. "It was a generous thing, a gift."

Elik looked up at him in surprise. "Yes," she said. "Generous." She stepped back. Her throat knotted and it was difficult to speak. She looked to the sky, and then through the wind, to the fields of rougher ice leading back to the village.

"He was a shaman," she whispered. "Like your father. His soul might be hurt, but it also lives on. Allanaq, he'll—" she stopped again.

Allanaq was staring at the ground, but he glanced up the moment she was quiet. "Come," he urged her. This isn't a safe place to be."

This time she nodded. It wasn't necessary just now to say more or explain. And he was right. There was death here. A shaman's soul lingering near its grave.

She felt the child kick inside as they started walking. He was right about that also—the need to be careful.

This child was going to live, and there was so much she was going to teach him someday, when he was older, ready to understand.

She would take him in an umiak and they would return to the Long Coast shores. She would teach him the names of his relatives, men who might be good hunting partners, girls who would be skilled and useful wives. And she would teach the Real People about the Bladder Feast, how the souls of the seals ask to be returned, into the sea. How the skulls of the seals should be saved, honored with great care.

Elik felt another kick, a lighter fluttering inside; she pressed her hand against it. She had heard stories of children like this one, the way they hungered to be born. The way they were willing to fight death for a chance to live. There was a word Red Fox had used. *Piarqusiaq*. One who is loved because his birth comes only after others have died. Red Fox was right. This child was one of those.

Author's Note

It was on the coast of Hudson Bay, Canada, during the Fifth Thule expeditions of 1921–1924 that Knud Rasmussen met and spoke with the Iglulik shaman Aua. And it was there, in the shelter of his snow hut, that Aua told Rasmussen the words which a novice desiring to be initiated must say to an elder shaman: "I have come to you because I desire to see."

If the shaman agrees to take on the student he—or she, since either a man or a woman might have such a calling—removes the pupil's soul through his eyes, brains, and entrails. As Aua explained, the novice shaman must then obtain his enlightenment. Nothing will be "hidden from him any longer; not only can he see things far, far away, but he can also discover souls, stolen souls, which are either kept concealed in far, strange lands or have been taken up or down to the land of the dead."

To my knowledge, no western ethnographer has ever actually witnessed the initiation of an Inuit shaman; those events were cloaked in secrecy, and often took place in isolation and enforced hardship. Even so, I began writing *Daughter of the Shaman* with the hope that, since it was my second novel in this genre, the background research would go quickly and smoothly.

My filing cabinets already overflowed with articles on paleo-Eskimo archaeology. And I had long since decided on the cultures my main characters would be modeled after: the Norton people who lived approximately two thousand years ago in the areas surrounding present day Nome, and the Ipiutak whose semi-subterranean houses were excavated further north along the Alaskan coast, on the beach ridges of Pt. Hope. From the archaeology, I knew that their daily lives were based on a subsistence cycle dependent on sealing, fishing, and caribou hunting, and that the Ipiutak had left behind intricate artifacts of ivory, stone, and antler, as well as remarkable burial ornaments.

I had also decided that the new book needed to finish Elik's story as she and her husband Allanaq journeyed back to his village. But as it turned out, writing a sequel presented different problems than a first book, and I soon realized that while Elik's coming-of-age story may have been appropriate for exploring her culture in *Summer Light*, I couldn't simply reintroduce the material with the same broad brushstroke and expect it to remain interesting and new.

Before I could think about plot, I needed to know what kind of person Elik had become, what yearnings and expectations would life hold for her? *Summer Light* had ended with Elik as a new shaman and a wife—a woman who heard the voices of spirits. But were there actually shamans in ancient Ipiutak, and if there were, what might their lives have been like? Asking such questions was easy; hoping for answers required a certain amount of faith in the research process.

As I had done before, I set up camp in the Alaska Room of the Noel Wien library here in Fairbanks and immersed myself in the literature in hopes that eventually the facts and details would come to life. What I found was that working back and forth between the needs of the fiction and the goals of an ethno-history where a culture is not only explored, but rendered into something comprehensible, was very much like solving a mystery.

One of the first things I learned was that while Elik may have begun a quest to become a shaman, her training was far from complete. From Rasmussen's report I found that "Many Iglulik bands did not consider a novice fully qualified to shamanize for five years after the vision quest. Helping spirits were acquired during the interim and seance techniques were practiced. The most important skill was the ability to journey out of the body as a free soul. . . . The last thing a shaman learns of all the knowledge he is obliged to acquire, is the recitation of magic prayers or the murmuring of magic songs, which can heal the sick, bring good weather or good hunting."

In his book *Shamanism* (1964), Mircea Eliade also refers to Aua's teachings: "The future shaman himself becomes able to draw his soul from his body and undertake long mystical journeys through space and the depths of the sea." The shaman must be able to see through his flesh, into the parts of his skeleton. He must survive the "inexplicable terror . . ." that comes "when one is attacked by a helping spirit."

With accounts such as these it soon became obvious that gathering information would not be a problem. As I continued learning, Elik would also learn the steps necessary for her initiation. The spirits would come, as they had for generations of shamans, in animal form, changing to human form, in dreams and trances, and whether she wished them to appear or not.

But I still didn't know whether there were shaman two thousand years ago. Would Elik have attempted the same trance Aua described, praying and drumming and singing to the spirits of the animals who lived in the moon or under the sea?

Returning to the library and with visits to the university museum, I searched for a connection between Aua's "shaman who must learn to pass through the air with his hands tied behind his back," and the ivory and stone artifacts uncovered at the Ipiutak site in 1939 by archaeologists Froelich Rainey and Helge Larsen. My first link came in the shape of a bird.

Summarizing Rainey and Larsen's work in *The Coming and Going of the Shaman* (1973), Jean Blodgett writes "Archaeological evidence indicates that a loon had special significance for the people of the Ipiutak culture—perhaps as a shaman's helping spirit. The artifacts from this culture include numerous carvings and representations of loons as well as an actual loon skull with artificial eyes. The loon's eyes, made of ivory with jet pupils, closely resemble the artificial eyes used to fill the eye sockets of human skulls."

Comparing their own discoveries with contemporary accounts, Larsen and Rainey write, "According to Jochelson (1926), loons were the most common guardian spirits of shamans among the Yakut of Siberia as well as among the Tungus of the Transbaikal. On the grave of a Tungus shaman who died around 1800 were four posts, each with a wood figure representing a loon. Among the Eskimo we also find that loons are related to shamanism. At Barrow, Alaska, a loon's bill is tied to the forehead of a dancer. Fillets made of a loon's head, neck, and back were worn as part of a dance costume at Kotzebue and Sledge Island."

Here then were a few of the puzzle pieces I'd been seeking, a link between the loon that was so reverently placed in Ipiutak graves two thousand years ago, and our era. Between the loon's ivory eyes, and the northern story, still told in many forms, of the loon who magically restores the sight of a blind boy. Other connections followed—the sound of wings in the darkened *qasgi*; the journey of the shaman who, birdlike, must fly and also dive—and I borrowed them, laying out the path Elik would travel.

In 1960, on the beaches of Cape Krusenstern, Alaska, archaeologist Douglas Anderson excavated a series of Ipiutak houses. Near one of them, he uncovered a large mound of seal skulls. "There, several thousand seal skulls, as well as a small number of polar bear lower jaw bones, had been heaped in a pile half a meter thick in places. . . . The remains of these three substantial posts, outlining a triangular area one and half meters to a side were located below the skulls. . . ."

Corroborating Anderson's work, I found a reference from the missionary Crantz, who noted in 1767 that "The heads of seals must not be fractured, nor must they be thrown into the sea, but be piled in a heap before the door, that the souls of the seals may not be enraged and scare their brethren from the coast."

Anne Fienup-Riordan, working with the oral traditions of the Yup'ik of western Alaska, explains in *Boundaries and Passages* (1994), that the head of the seal, "although severed from the body, still possessed the ability to observe human action and to recount its experiences to its fellows. By feeding and honoring the seal's head, and placing it to face in the proper direction, human hunters simultaneously celebrated the seal's successful passage into the human world and its special power to communicate with and return to its underwater home."

In fact, many of the incidents that occur in *Daughter of the Shaman* are not so much invented as adapted. From the traditional Eskimo belief in reincarnation for example, comes the fear of Allanaq's dead father. Elik's assumption that Red Fox would return from death was suggested by Joseph Campbell's mention in *The Masks of God* (1959) of the shaman Aggjartoq who was "lashed to a long pole and carried out onto a lake, a hole was cut in the ice, and the pole with its living burden thrust down through the hole. He was left in this position for five days and when at last they hauled him up again . . . he himself had become a great wizard, having overcome death."

With a goal of turning ethnographic material into plot and background, characters and story, I have of course taken many liberties. While in more technical writing this would be problematic, as a fiction writer, there seems sufficient justification in extrapolating as much as I do. Is it possible to understand or empathize with a culture as foreign as the Ipiutak? Perhaps not. On the other hand, my interest lies not in finding answers, but in exploring that very human attempt to wrest meaning from the capriciousness of weather and sickness, hunting and death.

For those who are interested in such things, the names used in *Daughter of the Shaman* come from a variety of sources. Some, such as Sheshalik, are Alaskan place names. Others are words, such as Nuliaq which means wife. Elik is a Copper Eskimo word for shaman, meaning *One who has eyes*—another reference tying supernatural vision to a shaman. In addition to authors and articles mentioned above, and the books

previously cited in *Summer Light*, I would like to direct
readers' attention to the following works:

Bodenhorn, Barbara, "I'm Not the Great Hunter, My
Wife Is, in *Etudes/Inuit/Studies*, 1990 14(1–2):55–74.

Burch, Ernest S. Jr., "The Eskimo Trading
Partnership in North Alaska," in *Anthropological Papers
of the University of Alaska*, Vol. 15, No. 1, 1970.

Fienup-Riordan, Ann, *Boundaries and Passages*,
University of Oklahoma Press, 1994.

Fitzhugh, William W., and Susan A. Kaplan, *Inua:
Spirit World of the Bering Sea Eskimo*, Smithsonian
Institution Press, 1982.

Lowenstein, Tom, *The Things That Were Said of Them*,
University of California Press, 1992.

Morrow, Phyllis, "It Is Time for Drumming: A
Summary of Recent Research on Yup'ik Ceremonialism,"
in *Etudes/Inuit/Studies*, 1984 8:113–40.

Spencer, Robert R., *The North Alaskan Eskimo*,
Bureau of American Ethnology, Bulletin 171, 1959.

Songs used in the book are, for the most part, from
Knud Rasmussen's *Across Arctic America*, 1927; *People of
the Polar North*, 1908; and *The Intellectual Culture of the
Iglulik Eskimo*, 1929. Esoteric sayings are also adapted.
For instance, the words Red Fox speaks upon arriving
home are from Ivan Veniaminov, *Notes on the Unalashka
District,* 1840. The sacred words Red Fox gives Elik in
the final chapter were recorded by William Thalbitzer
who worked with shamanism in East Greenland in the
1930s. Versions of the story of the grandmother who
turned herself into a man are widely known around the
north.